Praise for Elizabeth St. Michel

The Winds of Fate Reviews:

myBook.to/TheWindsofFate

The Winds of Fate "...captivating romance that takes us to the world of seventeenth-century London...Sexual tension and legal and familial intrigue ensue with the reader cheering on the lovely pair."

—Publishers Weekly

The Winds of Fate "has everything...full of passion, betrayal, mystery and all the good stuff readers love."

—ABNA Reviewer

"Original...strong-willed heroine...I love all of it...the unlikely premise of a female member of the aristocracy visiting a man who is condemned to die and asking him to marry her."

—ABNA Reviewer

Surrender the Wind Reviews:

http://hyperurl.co/qnu96k

Surrender the Wind "The lush descriptions of the southern countryside, the witty repartee between the characters, the factual descriptions of battles woven into the storylines, and the rich characters kept me glued to the pages."

—Alwyztrouble's Romance Reviews

Surrender the Wind received the "Crowned Heart" and National "RONE AWARD" finalist for excellence. "With twists and turns... and several related subplots woven in, no emotional stone is left unturned in this romance."

—InD'tale Magazine

Sweet Vengeance

DUKE OF RUTLAND SERIES BOOK 1

Elizabeth St. Michel

ISBN: 0997482427
ISBN: 9780997482423
Library of Congress Catalog Number: 2017909901
Elizabeth St. Michel

For my son,

Edward

Skill and confidence are an unconquerable army.

Chapter 1

England 1777

Captain Jacob Thorne forced his way past an army of servants, coming face to face with his father for the first time in his life. The shadow of his past that haunted him. Same cobalt eyes. Same build. Older version of himself. "You think arranging a title would purge your guilt of disposing my mother? I'm a bastard. You put your face on mine but that's all you gave me."

"Would that I could, I'd give you everything. Yet I do have the ability to sponsor you for a title. My estates are vast. Choose what you will," said the Duke of Banfield in the library of his ancestral home.

The bloodletting of Jacob's soul began. The rejection that drove him, fed him for years. "Get my cousin, Ethan Thorne out of Old Mill prison," he demanded.

The duke trembled on his cane. "I don't have such power. He is an enemy of the Crown."

Silence bounced between them, clogging Jacob's throat. "The only thing I have ever asked and you refuse. To think you would do me a favor?" He turned on his heel.

The duke clasped his arm. "Wait. What you are asking for is treason. I will need time."

Jacob glared at the duke's fingers where he dared to detain him. He had killed men for less. An American privateer with a price on his head, Jacob had taken a huge gamble to get Ethan out of British hands. Who was he fooling? The real reason was to see his father. "Time, I don't have. I'm very popular with every ship in the British Navy breathing down my neck."

"Please, remain. You may change your mind about staying," said his father who had cared not one whit of his existence.

Never. Jacob narrowed his eyes on the rich trappings of the library, everything he disdained about the aristocracy and representative of the father he had mourned as a boy. He itched to throw the shelves of leather-bound books to the floor, rip the rich paintings off the walls; tear up the Aubusson carpet beneath his feet.

"You are my eldest—" The duke's voice choked.

The doors snapped open and the equivalent of a sea walrus dressed in a ridiculous Neptune costume, trident and all, entered. "Eldest what?"

The duke dropped his hand. "I gave orders not to be disturbed. This is Humphrey, your half-bro—"

"I'm your cousin from the Colonies," Jacob said.

Humphrey brightened like a puppy, nose up, tail wagging. "A cousin from the Colonies? You never mentioned we had relatives there, father."

Jacob gave a sharp bark of laughter. A half-brother? Of course, the duke would need a legitimate heir. Didn't take him long to wed and bed to produce one, casting his mother aside, an insignificant house maid. Not the dissipating sting of a slap. More like a punch to his gut, driving the precious air from his body.

The duke's face paled, shoulders slumping, he hobbled toward Jacob, his free hand lifting, palm-up. "Go to the Rutland's costume ball and meet Humphrey's intended."

Jacob shrugged. Why not? To see what a title bought? Sometimes the hardest choices were to see which bridge to cross and which to burn.

Jacob's collar chafed. He was the last person in the world to wear vicar's clothing, but it was the best his father could produce at the last minute. Through a crush of satyrs and Satans, Persephones and Pandoras, he followed Humphrey. The Duke of Rutland had spared no expense for the masquerade ball. Indeed, the surroundings were beautiful, the music soft and lilting and the smiles and chatter of all the revelers predicting the evening to be every success London society had expected. How he'd like to turn his cannons on every one of them.

A feverish murmur swept through the ballroom. Jacob turned and followed their gazes to the balcony. Diana, goddess of the moon, both bewitching and captivating, her grace defying mere earthly mortals consented to descend from the heavens. He could barely get over her beauty. This was beyond perfection.

The rich, platinum blonde of her wig had been swept atop her in an elaborate swirl, anchored by tiny pearls. A gathering of curls had been allowed to escape, accenting her luminous eyes under a domino stylishly framed with diamond applique. Her slender figure was well served by a high-waisted gown, the bodice, plunging low to enhance the deep valley of her swelling breasts. The diaphanous silk swirled about her legs as she turned to accept a dance from a young man that devastated her stable of admirers. The sight of her ensnared him as it might any red-blooded man in the room.

Humphrey cleared his throat. "She is my intended, Lady Abigail Hansford Rutland."

A knot of jealousy churned in Jacob's stomach. So this is what a title bought.

From over her dancing partner's shoulder, Abigail's eyes drifted to the gentleman standing next to Humphrey. She misstepped and almost halted altogether. Then she did something she rarely did. She stared at a man. She even caught herself doing it and would have chided herself, except that she couldn't stop staring. How could she let this happen with a cleric, yet this man seized her curiosity like no one ever had.

He stood straight and tall. A pronounced aristocratic nose and a strong jaw held a wide full-lipped mouth. Not a handsome face really, but a distinctive one. The Duke of Banfield had begged a last-minute invitation. Humphrey's cousin? Vicar Banfield from America?

As a man of the cloth, he did not wear a domino—an encumbrance of his office? Dark, from the long black frock coat and pants to the black hair pulled back in a queue, his bronze skin contrasted with the white shirt tied at his neck. The severe dress did not detract and complimented his striking features. Abby frowned. He seemed a man suited more for the outdoors, not one who spent his time sermonizing biblical works. Why hadn't Humphrey ever acknowledged possessing relatives in the Colonies?

Across the ballroom, her father, the Duke of Rutland, nodded his approval with undisguised pride and encouraged her air of refinement in holding court over so many young swains. Despite his disproving nature and sometimes harsh words of late, Abby was never one to disappoint. But how she hated the pretext of her engagement. She had dallied too long. Her father had given an ultimatum and the threat of selecting the first suitor to his liking loomed real.

He had left her little choice. Her gaze swept to her intended and dearest friend, Lord Humphrey, the Marquess of Banfield, his cherub face animated in conversation. Growing up on neighboring estates, it seemed logical they would marry. Since they were good friends, she had convinced Lord Humphrey to fake a prolonged engagement that they would later end. The desperate ruse secured her more time until she decided what she wanted to do.

She begged pardon from her dancing partner, smoothed the white silk layers of her gown that swished about her legs and sidled to Humphrey. She threaded her hand through his arm; Humphrey smiled in return, made hasty introductions, and returned to the fever of fierce discussion.

"The rebel rascal should have his brains blown out and thrown overboard. Excuse me, Lady Abigail," said Captain Rowland Davenport, dressed in full naval regalia. "We chased that Colonial devil and gave him a broadside but the rogue disappears every time. I vow I will hunt him down."

Abby accepted a proffered glass of champagne and surreptitiously glanced at Vicar Banfield to see his reaction to Captain Davenport's bravado. The vicar regarded her with a pensive expression, his head cocked slightly to one side. It struck her how he resembled a younger version of the Duke of Banfield, Humphrey's father.

"Since the American, Captain Thorne makes his favorite cruising ground the coasts of Great Britain, he has created a laughing stock of the Royal Navy," said her Uncle Cornelius, her father's best friend and the powerful Duke of Westbrook.

"He appears a decent sort, treats his prisoners in a gentlemanly fashion," said Humphrey and his contention earned him a chorus of snorts.

The vicar grinned at her.

Did her knees wobble? Ridiculous.

"That's after the Yankee traitor relieves them of their property," Uncle Cornelius said. "The devil has a predilection for acquiring my ships. I've been nearly bankrupted, not to mention insurance rates are prohibitive and commerce almost annihilated."

Abby looked away from the Vicar. What was the matter with her? She was the daughter of one of the most powerful dukes in England. Bolstered by that confidence she raised her chin. "I don't understand why the colonists choose to pick a military resolution to their grievances rather than a political one."

The heat of several pairs of eyes scorched her. Uncle Cornelius's glass eye stared at her.

A violinist slipped his bow across the strings. The discord shuddered up her spine.

The vicar casually folded his arms in front of him. My God! Did his gaze wander over her body, or was it only her imagination?

Captain Davenport stroked his throat. "Females are too frail for talk of politics."

Abby bristled at his condescending tone and drew herself up ready to correct him when Humphrey patted her hand to assuage the gathering storm clouds. The champagne she sipped rolled over her tongue in a bitter aftertaste. Captain Davenport disgusted her. Rumors abounded that he had assaulted housemaids in his employ. The truth disclosed by her own frightened maid whom he had attempted to molest that very afternoon.

"She is agitated these days," Humphrey provided.

How dare he suggest she yielded to hysterics. Abby ground her heel on his toe.

In amplified crescendo, Humphrey squealed, "We are all agitated."

"They are pirates," Captain Davenport said. "They operate outside the law pretending to be under letters-of-marque, issued by a Colonial government not recognized in English courts and plundering any quarry ripe for their choosing. The undisciplined savage even had the superb audacity to post a proclamation at Lloyd's Coffee house in London."

With her maid's debasement fresh in her mind, Abby let go of Humphrey's arm and placed her hand over her heart. "Was it the proclamation that stated Jacob Thorne, Commander of the privateer armed Brig *Vengeance* shall sink, burn, destroy, and capture British merchant vessels?" she quoted directly from the *London Chronicle*. "It appears the American owns an unusual blend of confidence and brashness."

Captain Davenport waved a hand in dismissal. "I suppose the cloddish Colonial would present a romantic notion for your sex?"

Her fingers flexed on the stem of her glass before she released it on a tray. "He appears to enjoy naval combat, anticipating his foes' maneuvers and then running, feinting and striking, much like a lithe boxer. Did he not use his daring seamanship to escape from the British frigate, *Solebay?*" She dared to use Davenport's ship as an example and stood rewarded with his pinched expression, the captain's incompetence hinted by her ridicule.

Humphrey choked.

War had been declared.

As Humphrey gulped the rest of his champagne, she darted a glance at the vicar. Did his mouth quirk in a half smile? The man stood a mystery. She couldn't wait to get Humphrey aside and berate him for keeping such a secret.

Captain Davenport's eyes bulged. "I guarantee Captain Thorne and his crew will be caught. I will have the pleasure of hanging them."

"I do hope something is done," she demurred. "The colonial privateer has a penchant to raid the British coasts to show us how vulnerable we are in our own beds. Heavens, to think he could be right under our very noses."

How odd the vicar's interest in the linen covered tables behind them. Did he have a sudden passion for crystallized fruit and marzipan? No. He assessed the open French doors.

Then he looked directly at her, catching her staring at him. His lips curved into a dangerous smile as he lifted his champagne glass in the merest hint of a toast to her. He had the most amazing eyes, a striking cobalt blue and—predatory.

The jolt she received from those eyes made her conscious of his familiarity and she did everything in her power not to look away. Did her face turn as bright as the punch in Humphrey's glass? If only the floor would open up and swallow her. He was a man of God and she was acting like an infatuated eight-year-old.

Refusing to be cowed and to win support for her argument, Abby directed the conversation to him. "What do you say, vicar, about your countrymen?"

He considered her question, his expression neutral. "Many in America are loyal to the Crown. But Britain made a sad mistake believing that the colonies would never band together in common cause, and instead remain thirteen independent states, jealous of one another."

His voice, a deep rich baritone, possessed a firm no-nonsense edge and slipped over her like warm velvet. No wonder he was a man of God. He could woo all sinners across hot coals to a path of righteousness with that voice.

"Your pardon my lady," the Vicar held her gaze. "I concur with the captain. The rebels are unrepentant and pathologically unapologetic for their errors in judgment."

Abby glowered. Well, what did she expect, a ringing endorsement from the clergy? She was about to say more when her eldest brother, Nicolas, approached with the appearance of a bored, jaded aristocrat. He jerked his head toward the gardens. "A word." His strained tone belied a different mien.

Abby gritted her teeth. Begging apologies, she smiled to her guests to disguise the panic leaping into her throat and followed dutifully in her brother's wake. *He knew.*

He led her outside, down the steps and past a row of arborvitae before pivoting on her. "You think you could keep your disgraceful scheme from me? How could you use Humphrey in such a manner?"

Abigail winced under the heated gaze of her brother, Nicolas Rutland, heir to the Duke of Rutland. He was right of course. To induce Humphrey to fake a betrothal was shameful. "There's nothing to do for it. Father has commanded me to marry."

"No more can you hitch up your skirts to ride a horse, swim in your petticoat in the river or put goldfish in Lady Worth's soup. Father has to curb your hoyden ways before your reputation is ruined."

Abigail winced. So he had heard about those latest events too. "I admit it's unworthy but it is only a temporary arrangement. Father has been impossible since Mother died." Her voice trailed off. If only her mother were alive to gentle the severity of Father's rigid demands.

Nicolas used to be her ally. Blue-eyed and dark-haired, he grew unbendable like her father as he matured into the duke's role. "The fact of the matter is Abby, you don't know what you want. As a Rutland, there is an unyielding requirement of position and power. You are nineteen, time for you to grow up and become the lady you were destined to be."

Nicholas was right. She didn't know what she wanted. She did know she didn't want to marry, at least, not yet. "Why can't I have the same opportunities as you? Why do I have to choose from shallow fops whose nannies still wipe their noses, their only pursuit title, privilege and money?"

"Compose yourself, Abby. You caught yourself up in your own scheme. You will marry Humphrey. He's a fine match."

Abigail clamped her mouth shut and swiped at a tear. She would never marry Humphrey. He was adorable and that was where it stopped. Romantic inclinations remained nonexistent. Love had to be a powerful, soul-shattering affair.

Nicholas put his arm around her shoulder. She looked to where he stared, outside the gardens, as if he could see beyond the horizon. In companionable silence, they stood watching a crescent moon rise as they had done when they were children. The reality of adult life brought complications. The love she held for her brothers and father carried an incredible bond that would never be broken. Her chin quivered with the disappointment she would cause them.

"We all have responsibilities." He turned on his heel, strode up the steps two at a time and disappeared into the house. A slight drop to his shoulders spoke volumes. The mantle of his heritage he wore like a heavy yoke. They were polar opposites. Abby refused to accept what was dictated while her brother nobly accepted his fate.

To find solace, she sought refuge in her mother's garden, letting her hand graze across the tops of roses. Except for a new minuet drifting over the gardens, the silence paralyzed her. How she wanted to throw her arms around her brother and tell him how much she loved him. How much she wanted to tell her father the truth, the lie of her engagement and beg his forgiveness. A wind picked up and stripped the roses, scattering petals on the ground. To ward off a sudden chill she rubbed her hands up and down her arms. Abby wavered. Was she being watched? She whirled. The vicar moved off the bottom step.

"I suppose you heard everything," she accused.

"Enough to offer a sympathetic ear if you are so inclined." He sat on a stone bench and patted the space beside him. "You are confused. There is a fear of commitment and emotional vulnerability when one confronts a new situation."

To accept an invitation from a man who seemed more of a fox than a vicar took all the force of will Abby possessed not to squirm. But the need to pour out her personal feelings, to sort out what was inside of her, outweighed her fear. She glanced at him again. How angelic he appeared now. Wouldn't talking to a stranger be a balm for her soul? "You are a man of the cloth and bound to keep confidences?"

"Yes, my child. What is bothering you?"

He leaned forward, easy in his skin. Rested his elbows on his thighs and looked deep inside Abby, or so it seemed. His probing gaze made her uncomfortable, intrigued, and almost naked. If her emotions weren't so unbearable, she'd be less inclined. She took a deep breath. "To tell you the truth, I crave adventure. Instead I'm trapped."

"Adventure is just a romantic name for trouble. It sounds exciting when you think about it, but it is perdition when you meet it face to face in a dark and lonely place."

"Isn't the purpose of life to live it, to reach out without fear for newer and richer experiences? To explore the forests, climb the mountains, cross the seas."

The vicar shook his head. "To set your life on the cast of dice is hazardous. You are a young woman of circumstance conditioned to a life of security and conformity. A young woman who must be protected and yield to her husband."

Abby narrowed her eyes. Of course the vicar would support her father. "It's not fair. Men own all the possibilities. I want to discover things like my brother, Anthony, who has a scientific bent and discovers marvelous wonders. The lights are on in his lab," she pointed. Or like my brother in America."

"You have a brother in America?"

Oh, that voice of his, those resonant, powerful masculine tones most likely wooed the sheep in his flock to fling open their purses. "Joshua, my older brother told me many wonderful things about America. He's been in the wilderness," she looked wistfully away. His long absence worried her. Her mother's brother, Thomas Hansford, who had moved to America was an ardent patriot and lived in Boston. He wrote them letters when he received communication from her brother, but Joshua had been out of touch for a year. She warmed with the memory of how Joshua had secretly taught her to throw a knife with precise accuracy, a skill learned from trappers he had met in the wilderness. Wouldn't the Vicar be surprised that she could part his hair?

"So that's why you championed the American cause?"

With the toe of her slipper she drew an arch in the gravel. "Not exactly. I confess I dislike Captain Davenport. He desires to catch Captain Thorne to gain promotion to relieve him of the shadow of nepotism. I had to win the debate, so I played the Devil's advocate to provoke him. My pride was at stake. Can you forgive me for this sin?" Did she see his lips twitch?

"You are forgiven," he nodded. "Do you have other views on Americans?"

Warmed by his absolution, she plopped down beside him. Her hands itched to take off the domino, to tear off the massive wig, but it gave her an air of security where no one would recognize the real Abby. She darted a glance at him. Did he really want her opinion? An irritation lay fresh in her mind. He did not support her debate. To taunt him she would give him what he deserved. "Only what I've heard. The colonials are a lower species, rude and sleepy gentlemen, ill-natured, narrow-minded, and absent of refinement."

"All that." He stretched his long legs in front of him and a strong thigh dared to touch her gown. She pretended to be unaware of the muscular warmth emanating from her toes up to the roots of her hair. Her face throbbed with mortification. He was a Vicar, wasn't he?

She peeked up at him to see his unguarded mirth before he assumed a bland countenance. "Do you know anything about the notorious Colonial Captain, Jacob Thorne?" She was dying to know anything about the rebel privateer, the latest sensation that had all of England talking, and not one bit remorseful of gathering gossip to share with her maids.

Despite the Vicar's relaxed manner there existed nothing casual about his nature. Her skin prickled. Something wasn't right.

He narrowed his eyes. "What have you learned of him?"

Flustered at being thrown off track, she slanted her head. “According to my maids, he is an ogre with a single blinking eye, a belly as round as the width of his ship, and he walks with a limp.”

“A limp?” he choked.

Swallowing her laughter, she held her hand up. “He gobbles children whole, drinks ale from a turtle shell and picks his teeth with fence posts. They say he’s Satan himself and a brutal commander. If truth be known,” Abby giggled, “he’s probably a pussycat.”

“I hope you haven’t internalized your maids’ prejudices. A pussycat?” He feigned horror. This close she could not help but notice his fine chiseled features, the broadness of his shoulders nor the shock of thick dark hair that tumbled over his forehead. She yearned to smooth it back.

She gave herself a little shake. Why was she noticing these things?

His arm circled her shoulder. “Do you have any confidence in the ability of the Colonials to fight? You’ve heard of the rebel’s victory at Saratoga? You might like the Patriots.”

Abby jumped up, ill at ease with his bold mannerisms. Were American vicars less constrained with their solace? And was the vicar a Patriot? Why he didn’t seem loyal to England at all. She twirled to face him. “I can imagine myself in their shoes. Americans feel like exploited outsiders.” She suppressed a smile and tilted her head in further reflection. “I might like the Patriots. I also like pedants and nitpickers.” He threw back his head and broke out into a bark of laughter, and then, his eyes settled on her...cold and stony. Abby shivered, an inner voice warned this man was not to be trifled with.

Why had his demeanor changed?

"Why are you marrying Humphrey?" A vein pulsed at his temple.

Abby blinked. "I-I'm—" she stammered. "I'm sorry I began this conversation." Humphrey had not told his cousin the engagement was a sham. She shrugged her shoulders. To recover the former lightness yielded an exercise in futility.

"Is it part of the family code to keep status and power?" His scathing tone, sharp as a scythe through wheat, reverberated through the night.

Her mouth opened and closed with a plausible explanation. She stepped back until the back of her skirts hit the garden wall. Eventually she would have to acquiesce and marry an aristocrat. Someone she did not love. An odd, twittering little laugh escaped as she remembered how wretched her situation was. "My life is preordained. The subject is something you would not understand."

The vicar's face hardened. "I'm afraid I do," he answered. "You're willing to sell yourself, Lady Rutland. And the price is what the aristocracy dictates. It's a bad arrangement."

Abby turned her back to him. She could not look at the vicar, could not expose herself to the expression she'd surely catch on his face if she did. What did he know about duty?

"You are peddling yourself like a broodmare."

His assertion stung like a bitter dose of medicine. She didn't hear the vicar drawing near, and when his hand came to rest on her shoulder, she started, gave a little gasp. It wasn't so much surprise that had made her jump, but the unexpected, sultry charge the vicar's touch sent surging through her body.

"Turn around, Lady Rutland," he said. "Look at me." He was standing in front of her now, his eyes, searching her face, missing nothing, uncovering secrets she'd kept even from herself.

Or so it appeared.

Jacob Thorne fought against his anger, fought against the attraction he felt for her. Never in his wildest imagination did he believe he'd meet someone who fascinated him as much as Lady Abigail Rutland. To think she stood up to male chauvinism with that arrogant bastard, Davenport. *Pendants and nitpickers?* He was utterly captivated and wondered what she looked like beneath the mask and without the wig. She was an intoxicating combination of humor, of exhilarating intelligence and disarming vexation.

And she was Humphrey's fiancée.

Humphrey, that dewy-eyed puppy, likeable as he was, could never in a million years keep up with this temptress. Despite his resentment, Jacob did not want to see Humphrey hurt.

"I'm not one of your boot-licking fops to whom vague statements are satisfactory. I want to hear the entire explanation, and I want to hear it immediately. Is it, too, for status and power?"

"Humphrey and I are best friends," she whispered, managing a wan smile.

He raised her hand and brought it to his lips. Her eyes never left his. "My tolerance for elitism matches my tolerance for lying. Why are you getting married to a man you don't love?"

But she was untouchable. Because she was untouchable—he wanted her?

He was a bastard. How he hated aristocrats. She was as far from his reach as the ocean that divided them and how he hated that division.

Tears blurred Abby's vision—she tried to blink them away. "I have reasons." How could she tell him her motivations were selfish? She was the spoiled wealthy daughter of a duke forced to face her destiny, yearning for freedom. He'd only disdain her lie.

He dropped her hand and planted his hands against the wall, effectively trapping her between his arms. Abby swallowed. His eyes smoldering like the unblinking gaze of a hawk focused on prey.

"There's nothing to do about it," she whispered. The smell of earth, and oddly, salt and sea filled her nose, and invaded all her other senses, too, and made her dizzy. "You don't behave like a Vicar. Why has Humphrey never mentioned having a cousin in America? Release me—now."

Abby amended her initial opinion. He was beyond a holy man. By no means did he fit the saintly comportment of a vicar. His posture, awareness, and confidence belied a man who cut his teeth in battle. Without a doubt, he'd have Captain Davenport for his breakfast.

He didn't move. His voice was a rumble, low and rough, like thunder. "I'm going to tell Humphrey to end the engagement before it is announced."

Abby flinched, her hands pressed to his chest in self-defense. Her fingers burned. She dropped them immediately. "You cannot do that," she cried, aghast at the prospect. "It will ruin my plans."

He growled and grabbed her by the shoulders. "You don't love him."

Fear gnawed at her, eating away at the calm she fought to preserve. With the possibility of him carrying out his threat, Abby dredged up a drop of courage. "I think you are the enemy. You're as bad as that privateer they were talking about." To be a prisoner of such a man?

He leaned toward her and her heart hammered with the veiled threat. "The nearer you get to your enemy the easier you can strike." Abby didn't understand a word he said as his lips hovered above hers. "Like confronting a jackal in his own den." None of what he said made any sense at all.

"You can't stop me." Her lip quivered and her hand rose. His eyes narrowed and he wrenched her hand in a vise-like grip. She refused to cry out.

"Yes, I can," he ground out.

"How?" Abby challenged.

And that was when he did the unthinkable.

He kissed her, and not gently, not like the chaste kiss some fop had once bestowed on her. No, the Vicar kissed her hard, as a lover would, crushing his mouth down on hers—and instinctively, she parted her lips. She moaned with the taste of him, felt the kiss deepening in ways she'd only been able to imagine before that moment.

That terrible, magnificent, soul-shattering moment.

The Vicar drew back too soon, and Abby stood there trembling, as shaken as if he'd taken her, actually made her his own right there in the garden, both of them standing up and fully attired.

"I'll bet your intended never kissed you like that," the Vicar said. He let go of her shoulders and raked his hand through his hair. "I'm sailing out tonight."

Before she could say a word, the vicar pivoted and walked away, heading towards Humphrey's estate in long angry strides.

Abby stood paralyzed. She could not go back to the ball, could not sneak up into her room and hide beneath the covers. Her feet were rooted in mortar. She simply could not move.

Damn Humphrey's cousin. Damn him to the depths of Hades. Humphrey would never kiss her that way; never send pleasures of awful, dazzling desire quaking through her like splintering shards of lightning. She touched her fingers to her lips. No, never again would she feel what she had before, during and after the Vicar's mouth landed on hers. In some mysterious way, it was as though he'd staked a claim on her, conquered her so thoroughly and so completely that she could never belong to Humphrey, or any other man, as long as she lived.

The Vicar had stirred an uncontrollable desire within Abby by merely kissing her and at the same time, satisfying that desire. In that brief sojourn to the deepest, truest part of her nature lay the harshest reality. The Vicar cultivated a satisfaction that had exposed what a man's attentions—one certain man's attentions—could be like.

She pressed her fingers to her temples. He left her wanting. Desiring more of what she could never have—and for that, she hated him. Thank goodness, she'd never see him again.

A footman rushed down the stairs, his wigged hair askew. He nearly collided with her. "I've been searching for you for the last half hour, Lady Abigail." He handed her a note.

Abigail adjusted her domino and recovered enough to open the envelope. Her father wanted an impromptu meeting with her and her brothers about her fake engagement in the laboratory. *Now.* She felt the blood run from her face. *The lie she told.* Consequences sprouted like mushrooms. Of course, Nicolas had snitched. She hated him. She hated her father. He'd never bend. He would make her keep her commitment to Humphrey.

She tore her domino off, threw it on the ground, and stalked off toward the laboratory. She was late. Her father's ire escalated when kept waiting.

She walked stiffly, picking up speed along the hedgerow. Unexpected, alarming feelings intensified, cold and clammy as death. Beads of perspiration broke out on her lip. Was it a result of the lie she told? A premonition? The lights of the laboratory loomed ahead. Abby picked up her skirts and broke into a flat out run.

A bright flash blinded her. A massive explosion knocked her to the ground. Heat singed her dress and hair. Glass shattered and cut into her skin. Tongues of fire lunged at the firmament in a horrific blazing inferno.

"No!" her scream rent the air, but was lost among the firing and crackling of timbers. Black smoke billowed. Sulfur permeated the air, an acrid acid taste. She scrambled to her feet, the laboratory gone. Greasy arms suddenly surrounded her.

"Let me go!" She dug her nails into the interloper's flesh. His breath reeked with liquor and something else she couldn't describe.

A filthy rag was thrust over her nose and mouth. She gagged, a sickening sweet scent. Bile surged in her stomach. She choked. His arm reached about her neck. Her heels dug furrows in the lawn, her slippers lost. The last vestiges of the laboratory sailed into the air, and picked up by the wind, drifted to the trees and set them ablaze.

A thin reedy voice laughed in her ear. "Don't bother struggling, Lady Abigail. They are all dead." He cackled, an inhuman sound she would never forget. "Revenge against our hated enemy, the Duke of Rutland is a victory *we* will savor for a long time. Since you are the apple of your father's eye, we have planned a separate, slow death for you. To pay back your family for the humiliation we have received."

If she had not lied, her father and brothers would not have been lured to the laboratory.

Abby clawed and kicked her assailant. This couldn't be happening. Pain exploded behind her eyes as he dealt a stinging blow that snapped her head back, for such a solid-sounding crack that for a harrowing moment she feared he'd broken her neck. Her hairpins fell to the ground and her hair tumbled in disarray to her waist. Fear galvanized her past the pain to struggle to her feet.

She couldn't keep her eyes open. The sickening odor suffocated her. Her muscles slackened. Her thrashing weakened. Lights contorted in front of her eyes as she slowly sank into oblivion.

Chapter 2

Abby retched. Dark as pitch the world swirled and wavered like a dream. Her head pounded and in a feverish spasm, she strained to rise, arms flailing, her fingers dragged through cold slick dampness. Mold and the stench like that of a sewer made her eyes water. Nausea rolled again and looped the pit of her stomach. Her knees gave out and she crumpled forward racked with dry heaves.

"Easy girl." An arm shot around her shoulder. Someone tucked her head beneath his chin. The rocking did not stop. A huge dip followed and she lost her stomach once more. Abby collapsed against the only warmth she could secure.

Foul water dripped on her shoulder. She shivered uncontrollably, her mind failing to grasp what was real and what was not real and her throat burned from the effort to speak. A bottle was placed to her lips followed by a soft murmur that induced her to drink. She spat it out, the water like poison. "Where am I?"

"Welcome aboard the *Civis,* the belly of Satan's ship."

Abby attempted to digest that piece of information. She rubbed her wrists.

"I removed your bonds, lass. I feared the ropes too rough for your skin. I didn't know if you'd ever wake up, believing you had been over-drugged. We're two days out of Ireland."

Abby shook her head. *Ireland? A ship?* Memories clawed through a surreal fog, slashing her mind, escalating like rain pouring through a downspout. Images tore open, explosion, glass shattering, fire, pain, terror and death. Her hands shaking, she touched her neck, raw from where her assailant had choked her. She placed a knuckle in her mouth to stifle a sob, the awful grief, the reality of her father and brothers dead.

"My name's Simeon Smith, and I'm your traveling companion to some unfortunate destination. I was the cook for Lord Gratham. His wife, Lady Gratham kept the stable master as her stallion until he blackmailed her. To cover the extortion, she sold the family silver and said I stole it. I threatened to go to the Earl with the truth. The next thing I knew, I was bound, gagged and thrown onto this ship—a tidy way of getting rid of a problem. Did you offend some peer of the realm?"

To have incurred the wrath of an angry God wrought from her own wickedness. Her falsehood had reaped evil and she railed against the costs. Tears burned her cheeks, disaster placed at her feet.

A few gray streaks of light illuminated from above. Abby turned toward the man named Simeon, an older man with a wizened countenance, a long, hooked-nose and whiskers. She imagined him drawing on a clay pipe as he fished from a dinghy.

Could she trust him? Compassion lay palpable in his voice. Under dire circumstances and against their will, they had been thrown together as prisoners, cut-off from the world. He shrugged out of his coat and covered them both, offering his meager warmth. Her chest tightened. Even in the darkest of places she found a mercy. Yes. She could trust him.

"I am Lady Abigail Rutland, daughter of the Duke of Rutland." When Simeon moved away, she clutched his arm. "There will be no class differences. We are equals on this voyage." She resettled the coat around them.

A well-spring of terrible guilt rose, releasing a floodgate of tears. Abby cried out her transgressions and sins, soaking Simeon's shirt. How she had faked her engagement, her time in the garden with the vicar, the horrible man—never, she vowed, would she have romantic inclinations again. "They are still alive. I know they are alive. Fate could not be this cruel. I'll do anything to get them back. I'll take whatever punishment meted out. I'll do anything," she argued and pleaded, the bargaining, a failed and desperate act. "Without my family, there is nothing to live for."

"You rebelled against what wasn't right for you, a part of growing up to defy authority. You love your father and brothers. There is no doubt in that."

A dirty rag was produced and she blew her nose. She touched the left side of her head where it swelled, tender beneath her touch. She ripped off a wool cap. Where had it come from? Her fingers glided through sharp pokes of hair. Her breath hitched. "My hair has been shorn." Abby palmed the shirt beneath her heavy coat. Bindings had been bound around her breasts to flatten them. Her cheeks burned with her degradation. "Why?"

"Someone went to great pains to make you appear as a lad. I'm guessing to fool the Captain who might be superstitious about having females on board." Simeon slapped the back of his neck. "Sometimes the lice bite worse than the rats."

"Rats!" Abby cringed. A rustle of scratching drew up the floorboards.

Simeon banged his boot on the planking. "Speaking of rats, before we were heaved on this ship, I was bound and gagged in the room next to yours in a dockyard shed. The walls were thick but my hearing's keen. Two men argued, one had a cultured voice like a gentleman, the other had a high-pitched tone, rough like a crofter. I imagine your father, the Duke of Rutland has enemies. As a powerful duke, there is always someone who lurks in the corners with a score or two to settle. Can you think of anyone important enough to try to murder your father?"

"You said two men? The man who had captured her had said, '*we*'". Whoever had done this demonstrated tremendous hatred of her family. To take on the Duke of Rutland was madness. Abby frowned. She had been protected all her life to the point of never thinking about her safety. She had not seen her kidnapper. But never would she forget his awful voice.

Simeon stroked his beard. "Both men were angry. Something about the timing had gone wrong and they feared discovery. A message delivered was late. Does this make sense?"

"Just before the explosion, a servant said he had been looking for me for a half hour." Abby locked her hands to force their stillness. She had been in the garden with the vicar not in the ballroom which explained why he had difficulty finding her. "Knowing my father and brothers they would not wait. They would come looking for me." Hope burned like a vestal flame. Never in her entire life did the duke or her brothers wait for more than five minutes. Had their impatience determined their salvation? "They are not dead. They have to be alive."

"Hang onto that thread of hope, Lady Abigail. Live to bring justice to your family."

How could she ever thank this solid wonderful man who had given her a reason to survive? "If we ever escape, I promise to have my father use his power to exonerate you."

"Thank you, my lady," he hesitated. "They mentioned a Nicholas, sent on a ship to Brazil under an unsavory Portuguese sea captain to be enslaved in the cane fields. Do you know him?"

Abby caught her breath. "My brother." Her vision blurred to a faded but not forgotten remembrance, Nicholas holding her close as they watched the moon rise.

"I must warn you, Lady Abigail, the men who did this were pleased for they looked to end your life by the cruelest measures. That means you must watch out for Captain Benjamin Lee. He secured a tidy sum to take you and me aboard with no questions asked. It's a dirty business. Captain Benjamin is a former slaver; he's had plenty of experience to keep himself free of indictment. He will destroy any evidence."

Abby shuddered. Simeon was right. Strong rumors of slavers tossing dozens of heavily chained slaves overboard to avoid prosecution had been whispered in London parlors. She made a silent vow. If some miracle occurred, if somehow, she survived this journey, she would seek her revenge against her family's enemies.

"I hate to entertain what would happen if the crew or captain were to find out you were a female. Keep your hat pulled down and your voice lowered. If you must respond, say little, gibber as one of your father's tenants."

The hatch rasped opened on rusted hinges. A gruesome visage leered. Abby inhaled. Scar tissue covered the right side of his head, the absence of an ear, and grisly mutilation.

"Exercise time." The scarred man blinked. "Is the lad awake or dead?"

"One-Ear," Simeon whispered. "He's crazy. Stay close to me."

Abby buttoned her oversized coat and followed Simeon up the ladder, keeping her cap pulled over her ears, her head down. Her knees wobbled from the after-effects of the drug. At the last rung she was hauled into the air and thrown onto the deck in a teeth-shattering jolt. A chorus of laughter burst out. The crew scrutinized her. They were rabble and nothing compared to them in all Christendom. Brutal ghoulish vultures, scarred by pox, dressed in rags, stinking worse than below decks. The faces of beasts grinned with rotting teeth. Gnarled hands clenched from sodden, starved and lustful, stunted bodies. Abby scrambled to stand behind Simeon.

Simeon whispered to her. "Only the cruelest of Masters, Captain Lee can suppress them, ill-born, lowly, thieves and bastards. They can lift a sail or slit your throat with equal facility. Hold yer tongue. If they get a whiff you're gentry you'll be talking to St. Peter. Be brave."

A shadow passed over her and she turned. Captain Benjamin Lee, a fearsome creature with the appearance of a robust cadaver.

Beneath the dull blue seaman's uniform he wore, sinewy muscles bulged with obvious power, and the hair on the back of his hands was coarse and black. Was it possible the darkness of his eyes, the downturn of his thin lips flaunted more cruelty than his crew? Abby trembled. The glare of his inspection rattled tremors up her spine, her future, a vision of doom. She whispered to Simeon. "Can I be brave if I'm afraid?"

"That is the only time one can be brave," murmured Simeon.

Captain Lee's lip curled in disdain. "You will earn your keep aboard my ship. If there is any trouble, a taste of the cat will teach you a lesson."

One-Ear slapped his knee, cackling. He scuttled aside when the captain strode by him.

Someone thrust a bucket and scrub brush into her hands. She knelt on the deck and for the first time in her life, Lady Abigail Rutland performed physical labor.

The Civis, Abby translated from the Latin word that meant civilized. The ship and its crew represented anything but civilized. In the weeks of incarceration, Abby and Simeon's collective skins fell gray and lifeless as the pewter clouds hanging in the skies, their eyes sunken and lusterless even under the impetus of fresh air. Beauty and cleanliness and perfume were not for her. She hated the poverty, sordidness and cruelty from the daily beatings of crewmates to picking the weevils out of her daily share of bread. She worked before the sun rose and after it descended, too exhausted to care about the filthy hold where she and Simon slept. *Justice.* The thirst for it flooded her veins.

For over two months she endured being the object of abuse by the crew, encouraged by the captain who showed pleasure as the abuse heightened. To remain invisible grew impossible. Despair loomed, naked and cold and fatal as a knife's blade. Simeon maintained her optimism. They would jump ship at the nearest port and find transport home.

The Civis ploughed through the icy waters of the Atlantic. One-Ear crawled down from the crow's nest. "Captain, she's bearing down on us. Has the stinking odor of a privateer."

Simeon whispered, "I hope they outrun our pursuer. American privateers make Captain Lee and his crew look like babes in their nappies. The colonials seize, plunder and derive pleasure in cold-bloodedly dispatching their enemy. I fear for you if we fall into their hands."

"You thieving dogs of London's' sewers, raise the tops'l," Captain Lee ordered, his voice frightful as a serpent's hiss. "We'll be lambs to the slaughter if we don't outrun the Yank."

Underneath his bold words, the captain visibly quaked. What terrors caused a cruel captain like Lee to keep looking over his shoulder?

The harvested wind pressed the merchant ship forward. Over the stern, she watched their pursuer disappear. Simeon's words rang like the tolling of a bell. Abby grabbed the railing, uttered a soft acknowledgement to a higher power, relieved the merchant ship had outrun its predator.

She had read about the legalized pirates, men authorized by the rebel colonies in America. The men who manned the privateer vessels were the elite of adventurers—bold, daring, dangerous men who relished a fight and who had much to profit from the capture of British ships. Prize money was awarded to the crew who captured British vessels, whether merchant or warships and many men had earned their riches in this way.

The discussion at her engagement ball emerged like a hand, icily cold and clammy as death. The warnings of privateer ships that "haunted the seas," and how they outwitted the best of British Admiralty. Even Captain Davenport had been outfoxed. To Abby, the threat at that time was nonexistent. Now surveying the thick mist enveloping them, Abby shivered. How could the *Civis,* a mere merchantman, defend against an attack?

Adventure is just a romantic name for trouble. It sounds fantastic when you think about it, but its hell when you meet it face to face in a dark and lonely place. No doubt the vicar's wisdom had merit.

As the sun descended, heavy waves battered like thunder against the hull of the ship. A storm brewed and so did the tempers of the crew and captain. Her stomach gnawed with hunger. Simeon was under the weather and begged permission of the captain to go below. After finishing her chores, she crossed the deck to settle in for the night, not looking forward to picking through the salted meat, and praying it wasn't from a rancid cask. Wind whipped through the sails and she stared overhead, unable to see the top of the mast through the fog.

Someone tripped her and she slammed to the deck. Air wheezed out between her teeth. One-Ear and his friend, the navigator laughed. She attempted to rise then was kicked in the stomach. Abby clutched her side, rolled and scrambled to her feet. She dodged a fist aimed at her face then stomped on One-Ear's instep. His bones cracked beneath her heel. He keeled over, grabbed his foot and yowled like a cat in heat. Abby glared. How she hated One-Ear.

A knife flashed. If only she had not sent Simeon below. The navigator tossed a knife between his hands. Abby scuffled back until pressed against the pinrails. The sound of the ocean roared and the waves licked below. The navigator leered over her. She recoiled from the rank smell of rotting teeth. From her right, One-Ear loomed, limping forward with a sword. Her fingers moved over the shaft of a belaying pin and yanked it out. A huge wave smacked the ship. The floor heaved upward beneath her feet. She wound her wrist in the ratlines. The belaying pin dropped into the ocean. Water pitched over them. She shrieked her voice lost, sucked into the hungry sea. The merchantman bowed and righted, seawater slid off the decks. The navigator slithered down her body into a heap at her feet. A sword stuck in his back.

She gasped, her hands flew over her mouth. One-Ear, sprawled on the deck gave a short bark of laughter. The aberrant wave had caught him off balance and he had inadvertently skewered his friend. His lip curled. "You'll pay for this."

Simeon untangled her hand. "I ought never to have left you."

Captain Lee's roar over the Atlantic seemed to still the sea, the squall that they had caught the tail of, spent. "You spawn of rats and swine. My navigator is dead. Who is at the bottom of this?"

Abby shook. Without a navigator, they were lost on a desert of waters. The ship plunged and her foulest nightmare mounted.

One-Ear limped to the captain, pointed a finger, his nail like a yellowed corkscrew. "They waited in the shadows and attacked us."

"It's not true," Simeon protested. "They attacked the lad."

"You rotting progeny of whores. Am I to believe a thief? String them up!"

Hands rushed to do the Captain's bidding. Coarse ropes girded her wrists to the mast. Abby whimpered. Simeon's eyes bulged. Nine ugly tar coated cords knotted at the ends whistled through the air. A few lashes could slash a man's flesh to ribbons.

"The floggings will continue until morale improves," One-Ear chortled and hung lanterns so all could watch in the gathering darkness.

Abby reeled. Simeon moaned and Captain Lee laughed. "When I'm finished shredding your hide, you'll be food for the fishes." Captain Lee raised the cat.

Simeon broke out in full body tremors. Abby turned away. Nothing could save them.

For a month, Captain Jacob Thorne had shadowed the *Civis*, following her close then letting her have some distance and finally coming up fast upon her. His nose twitched like a hound picking up the spoor of a fox trapped in his hole. The sails of the *Vengeance* were let out. Darkness cloaked their swift motion through the water. Their progress took too long. Every muscle in his body strained.

Jacob raised his scope and smiled. The captain of the *Civis* was busy meting out punishment on two of his sailors. The distraction allowed the *Vengeance* to come up on their starboard undetected. He narrowed his eyes to the old man and boy tied to the mast and cursed the cruelty of the merchantmen's captain. None of his concern. *One...two...three.* He gestured with his fingers to signal his crew.

"Fire!" The sides of the *Vengeance* shook, her cannons blasting at the helpless quarry. The Civis's captain swiveled, his brutality forgotten and the look on his face laughable as he recognized his negligence.

Dear God! Abby swung violently from the cannon blast.

The whip halted mid-air. Sailors toppled to the deck.

"Privateers!"

Captain Lee's eyes, abnormally large, dilated with his fear. "When those privateers are done with you, you'll be wishing to be back under my whip."

She twisted her head and squinted through the fog and darkness. What could be worse?

Again, cannons blasted into the helpless merchantman. Billowing clouds of smoke to larboard blotted out everything. Abby choked. The acerbic odor caught in her throat and set her to gasping and coughing. The crew scrambled to get their weapons.

From the bowels of Hell, she emerged into another more horrifying layer of the netherworld. Confusion and clutter met her dazed eyes as men rushed about, daggers in hand, positioning weighty guns and dragging kegs of powder into place. One-Ear brandished a sword, his scar paler; all were sweating, and their eyes held a mixture of terror and grim resignation. Her head swam and she leaned dizzily against the mast.

Captain Lee stood on his foredeck screaming orders. Another cannon blast rent the air, proving the *Civis's* defensive efforts pointless. Lee's outrage transformed to shock, the miscalculation of an enemy and his impending doom.

Abby clawed at her bonds and swiveled to search the gloom. The gray mast of a ship loomed out of the heavy mist. It towered the merchantman and barreled alongside, furling tops and mainsail, stripping to mizzen and sprit. No way could the *Civis,* boasting only six guns and a limited supply of powder, maneuver away from the more agile, heavily weaponed ship that bore down on them.

Fire!" Lee ordered. A barrage of shot from the *Civis* whistled over the American's main deck, missing line and rigging, an errant shot knocked the breasts off the figurehead at the bow.

There was a quick intake of breath among the seamen, and then all at once, a deafening roar, and the merchantmen vibrated. The privateer swept up at such a speed the hulls rammed like a meteor crashed into the earth. Abby's bonds ripped free and she cried out, pounding the deck, half stunned as gun-rails collided, splintering and shattering.

Through the curling smoke, men sprawled on their bellies. Her heart hammered and her nails dug into her palms.

"Lady Abigail, free me."

Through the horror, Simeon roused her. She grabbed a sword and swung to free him. The clunk of metal, digging into wood, grappling hooks cast over the merchantmen's side exploded adrenaline like quicksilver through her veins.

Privateers! Dozens of them, swarmed onto the deck from the other ship. Men fell, spouting blood on the deck from great, black gashes, and screams of agony sounded chillingly amid the din of gunfire. Burning gunpowder and fresh blood drifted up and roiled her stomach. Abby grabbed Simeon's hand and vaulted over bodies, dodging swords and cutlasses, her ears ringing with the clangor of battle. Barely ten paces, One-Ear crumpled, his smile frozen, his eyes vacant, staring to the heavens. Captain Lee stood skewered and collapsed in a heap of tangled limbs, his face contorted in anguish as he writhed helplessly before her eyes.

Abby halted, welded to the deck, a helpless, terrified witness of a horrific spectacle, both fascinated and repelled by the awful violence. A hand tugged at her sleeve. Abby looked up at Simeon, his face pale beneath the grime.

Run. Now. Make your quicksand feet move before you're dead.

Abby dodged fallen bodies and sword thrusts with incredible agility. She stumbled behind a knot of barrels and collapsed. Simeon squeezed in beside her, concealing them with a tarp, a ridiculous gesture. There existed no haven for them. Her fingers trembled, the tumult of battle surrounded them, ebbing and flowing. Suspense pounded through her body, building an awful, almost unbearable tension. The battle raged—an endless, desperate struggle. *When would it end?* If only she had a hint to what was happening. She detected nothing beyond the thunder of guns and the cries of the wounded. The ship tilted. Would they sink? She peeked through a slit, darkness and smoke filled the distance. Simeon clasped her hand, white-knuckled she clung to him, gaining no comfort.

No longer could she bear the suspense. She jumped up. Simeon yanked her down. "Do not risk your life in that bloodlust. If we survive the battle, you must maintain your disguise."

Darkness and smoke filled the distance as she dared to peer through a slit. The night grew strangely quiet. She strained her ears for some sound. No gunfire, no screaming, nothing. A wind whistled eerily over the barrels. Waiting, she bit her lip, tasting the bitterness of smoke.

Boots pounded up from the companionway. "Captain Thorne! It's like you predicted. The *Civis* has a treasure in her hold, guns, powder, casks of hardware and wine."

Captain Thorne! The rebel, who incensed the Admiralty, enraged the King, terrified maids to cross themselves and hide beneath their beds. He was the terror of the seas and she was in his clutches. Dare she jump ship and become a feeding frenzy for sharks?

"Have you made a search for everyone on board?"

"Aye, Captain, best we could tell."

"Empty the *Civis* at once before she sinks. Chain the surviving sailors in our hold," a baritone voice demanded. Was it a trick of her mind the familiarity of that voice?

With trembling hands, Simeon wiped grease from the barrels on her cheeks and tugged her cap over her ears. "Let me do the talking. The Americans hate aristocracy a hundredfold."

The tarp ripped away and she and Simeon were hauled from their hiding place. A bright lantern glowed from the mizenmast. Abby blinked. The privateers gaped at them, their eyes bright and suspicious. They were a motley horde, dressed in grubby, bloodstained breeches and striped jerseys, with sweat gleaming on muscled arms and dark growths of beard on their wary faces.

And then, from out of the uncouth mob of feral beasts, strode a tall muscular man with cobalt eyes in a tanned face, eyes that blazed the light of dreadful determination.

The Vicar!

Abby's legs trembled. She locked her knees into place. The ship spun dizzily. Never would she faint. She was a Rutland. No, her mind had been tricked by an over-active, sleep-deprived, twisted imagination. The vicar emerged as Satan himself, brandishing a sword, and with a brace of pistols and razor-sharp knives tucked in his belt. Was it possible sulfur fumes rose from him?

The crew melted away. Abby barely noticed them, her eyes primed to the man who stepped past them and stood, legs apart, facing her. Gone was the severe black dress of the vicar. He seemed taller, more powerfully-built, wearing black satin breeches and a white silk shirt, open at the throat, exposing his sun-burnished skin. The shirt lay damp with sweat and clung to his body, revealing bulging muscles in his arms and shoulders. His hips were slim above thick, powerful thighs. His black hair was ruffled by the wind, and she observed the expressive sweep of his dark brows, the sensuous bow of his lips—lips she remembered only too well. Even now, she could remember their texture, taste and feel.

One hand poised solidly on his hip, and in his other hand, he held a sword...pointed directly at her. There was no humble cleric about him now, only the fusion of primitive predatory instinct, and indisputable command.

Simeon crossed himself, crumpling under the worst of their fears, the reality of the American privateer that struck terror in the hearts of so many.

He spoke to them most eloquently. "You will save yourselves pain and trouble if you willingly concede to surrender, suffering no losses to yourselves. Or—" he swept his arm in a broad gesture behind him to the dead "—you can fight and join your companions."

Words stuck in her throat. Simeon hyperventilated to the point of passing out, and she feared his age and taxed heart would be the death of him.

Captain Thorne swaggered to within inches of her, his sword resting on her throat. Abby swallowed. "Be aware, I ask politely only once. After that, I'll not let my charity stand in the way of exercising what is necessary." He jerked his head to his men. "You have many of my crew to verify my contention."

How dare he torment an old man? Something broke inside her, a bit of the terror seeped away, replaced by a hot, bursting fury that swelled through her like a powerful tsunami. Tired of the bullying and living in fear, she shoved the sword away, glared mutinously at him, then stepped forward, her two giant boots with the toes curled up, grazing his shiny black ones.

He raised an eyebrow. "It seems the lad wishes to do battle," he said to the men about him, his expression amused. A hearty burst of laughter followed. "I admire a lad with spirit. Do you have a name?"

She squirmed uneasily. On the *Civis* she had been crudely called, slave.

"You do have a name, don't you?" Captain Thorne inquired with a hint of sarcasm.

She nodded in the affirmative. "Uh—Ab-Abe, sir. She nodded her head more vigorously.

"What's your friend called?"

He referred to Simeon who was now plagued with hiccups. "Simeon." So much for Simeon doing the talking.

"You have an economy on words. Mind informing me why you two were tied to the mast before we attacked?"

Abby exhaled. How fortunate that their plight aboard the *Civis* had earned them an offer of sympathy. A better door could not have opened and she seized the opportunity with gusto. "We were both kidnapped and put on the *Civis,* used as slaves." Adopting the language of her father's worst crofter, Abby lowered her voice and told of Simeon's plight, colorfully adding her own details to demonstrate the brutality of England's aristocracy. She spat on the deck.

The captain rubbed a hand through his hair. "What is your story, boy?"

She didn't speak and turned away, her eyes brimmed with threatening tears. The image of her family's demise wavered in front of her as if it had happened the day before.

Jacob noted the lad's distress and pointed to Simeon to speak. He had seen the two of them lashed to the ship's mast that had hastened his taking the *Civis.* He wanted answers.

The old man worried his hat in his hands and quelled his hiccupping. "The lad is newly orphaned, his parents good folk murdered by vile miscreants. With no one to turn to, he ended up cold, starved and living on the streets, begging for food. To satisfy his gnawing hunger, he stole a mere loaf of bread from a duke's kitchen. For that offense alone, he was enslaved on Captain Lee's ship, beaten and the object of abuse by the crew. The boy defended himself against two of the crew members. In the scuffle, the navigator fell on his friend's sword. In Captain Lee's eyes, we were guilty. Our termination was decided."

Thorne eyed the lad who held his head down. Jacob guessed the old man had assumed the role of protector, weaving an excellent tale with parts true and the rest with the right dash of woe. There remained not one dry eye among his crew. Thorne sighed. He was not convinced.

The lad had spunk, dared to meet him toe to toe when any other man normally quivered. Thomas, his cousin had that same defiant impulsiveness.

Thorne wrinkled his nose. A bin of rotted fish smelled better. Dirt smudged face and tufts of dark greasy hair stuck out from beneath the lad's hat. He rested on a barrel and placed his sword tip into the deck, drumming his fingers on the hilt. "What skills do you both have?"

Simeon straightened and puffed out his chest. "I was a cook. An excellent one, sir."

A murmur spread favorably among the crew. Thorne nodded. "Good. You can replace our cook who died in the skirmish." Not having a decent cook was almost as bad as not having a navigator. And you, lad? What can you offer?"

The boy looked down at his oversized boots. "I can clean the ship."

"I have a proposal for you. You can be my cabin boy, keeping my room clean and running errands about the *Vengeance.* If you excel and work hard, you'll be taught the skills of seamanship and earn a coin or two."

"Cabin boy?" Abby's mouth dropped open. The captain perceived it to be overwhelming gratitude. To be in close confines was impossible. How could she avoid him?

"Well I ain't emptying no chamber-pot, the food better not be crawling with maggots, don't expect me to sing "Yankee Doodle," and I don't fancy shootin' anyone." She wiped her nose on the back of her dirty sleeve. How easy the crofter's speech came to her.

Then Captain Thorne did something that made her question his sanity. He threw back his head and roared with laughter. "I won't require you to shoot anyone. Anymore demands?"

"Beggin' your pardon, Captain Thorne," Simeon interrupted. "The boy's been through a lot. He's grown attached to me and will work well in the kitchen." Simeon moved a pace to speak low and confidingly, "The lad's simple, if you get my drift."

Simple! Her teeth grated as Simeon's inventiveness escalated. But in Thorne's lair? No way. "I'll scrub your deck until you can see your face in it, but I ain't going to be no cabin boy."

A long, lean finger thrust into her face, almost meeting the tip of her nose. "Now look, lad. You can bet I'll take some of the starch out of your breeches if I need to. I've saved you from Captain Lee, but I have no intention of playing nursemaid to any quick-tempered little ragamuffin. So have a care for your manners."

Abby folded her arms in front of her. "I can take care of meself."

Captain Thorne scoffed in disbelief. "By the looks of you, somebody needs to take you in hand. When did you last wash, when you were born?"

"You're the most meddling rebel I've ever met.'

"And how many have you met?"

Abby stared belligerently. "You're the first."

Thorne chuckled and rose, apparently impatient to get under way. He clapped her on the shoulder and she stumbled. "If nothing else, Abe, you should make for interesting company as my cabin boy," he emphasized, tolerating no refusal to his command.

She remained mute, pointedly ignoring him, then stared off into the distance behind him. Abby inhaled. Captain Lee raised his pistol. There was no time for warning. She ripped a knife from Thorne's belt and threw. The knife spiraled, end over end, flashing in the air. A gun exploded. A shower of wood-splinters fell from the rigging.

Air whooshed out of her lungs. The crew tackled her, pinning her to the deck. Her arms jerked behind her back, curses deafened her ears. The tangy scent of blood ousted the smoke wafting away on the breezes.

"Let go of the lad." Thorne's baritone thundered.

Abby scrambled to her feet, pulling down her hat. A knife protruded from Captain Lee's black heart, the gun in his hand smoked, the barrel pointing skyward. The shot intended for Thorne's back. Her stomach heaved to her throat.

Dear God! She had killed a man.

Thorne waved his crew off. "I owe you a great debt for saving my life. The lad has skill and will make a *fine* cabin boy." His crew murmured their agreement but his gaze probed hers. “You’ll protect my back as long as I don’t find a knife in it.”

And then Abby vomited on his boot.

Chapter 3

For three days aboard the *Vengeance,* and under Simeon's watchful eye, Abby learned the elements of cleaning the captain's quarters, dusting, polishing, and organizing the room's contents to the highest of standards. No way did she desire to incur Thorne's wrath. Didn't he measure up to his reputation during the takeover of the *Civis?* She winced. Would she ever accomplish the square corners on the bedding?

Having maids to do all her bidding, she had never paid attention to their labors and the difficulties they went through to make her life so easy. If she had a stain on her gown, it was cleaned or discarded and replaced. If she chose not to rise, breakfast was brought to her on a silver tray. When she fell ill, a doctor was summoned. If her stallion didn't please her, a new thoroughbred was pulled from the stable. Jewels, furs, silks, satins, every amusement, every luxury was provided before she even thought of it. Everything she had taken for granted.

She twisted the sheet in her hands. "Simeon, there were at least two men involved in the plot against my family. Do you think there are more?" Round and round she worked the puzzle in her head. How many times had she gone over the scenario with Simeon?

Thorne charged into the cabin, bringing the wind with him and tossing his tricorn where it skittered across the table. "Why is Simeon here?"

Abby released the sheet. To dive out the gallery windows presented a better option than meeting the wicked Captain Thorne face to face. Images of the carnage from the battle loomed and she lowered her chin, a conscious act, ensuring her overlarge boots, and tattered coat buttoned to the neck hid her femininity. From habit, she pulled her hat down. Now she would earn a cuffing for she was incapable of making a bed. She gripped the sheet within her hands, bracing for a blow.

Simeon stepped between her and the captain. Her heart went out to him. "The boy's been ill-used, and simple," he pointed to his head, "needing me to instruct him how to do his job. He wants to please you, sir."

"Then tell him to quit cowering. Where's the spirit I saw three days ago?" Thorne waved Simeon aside. "You're dismissed."

Abby interpreted the directive to include her. She hitched her pants and shuffled to the door only to get yanked back by the collar. She choked. No way did she want to be alone in the cabin with Thorne. So far, she had cleaned his quarters when he was elsewhere on the ship, then bolted to stay under Simeon's protection in the galley—anywhere Thorne was not.

"Not you," he spoke to Abby. "Finish the cabin. Simeon, my stomach's rumbling. Tell me what victuals you plan for dinner?"

In the doorway, Simeon straightened like a peacock preening his feathers. "Braised beef with dried mushrooms and onions slowly roasted in a cabernet wine sauce with herbed potatoes. Do you wish your coffee served with your meal or with your apple flan dessert?"

Thorne slid into a seat and groaned. "Do whatever you wish. You warm my heart on this foul-weathered day. My crew and I will be fat as elephants."

Simeon glanced to Abby. "I best bake the bread so it will be served warm with the meal."

Abby rolled her eyes and snapped the sheets in place. Simeon's rapture with Thorne's praises galled her. Men and their stomachs. That's all they thought of. One more week of platitudes, Simeon's head would swell the size of a barrel. But to censor him equaled betrayal. Nobility parceled compliments, considering the act beneath them. Servants served and earned ridicule for their efforts. She was suddenly ashamed of her class.

"Abe, you can come and help peel apples when you are done with your duties," said Simeon, offering her an excuse before he departed.

The cabin closed in on her. The sheets refused to line up. She bumped into a table and books upended, clattering to the floor. She muttered apologies and skittered out of Thorne's range in case he decided to strike her. Yet he remained unaware of her presence, engrossed in calculating his charts, making markings and writing in his log. She tucked the soft blankets under the mattress and studied him. On the tip of her tongue remained many questions. Thorne's relationship with the Banfield's, peers of the crown whose loyalty exhibited the highest integrity. And he had been invited to her ball as a vicar. The pieces didn't fit. Humphrey, a bit of a whey-face, was the most easygoing soul who would think twice before stepping on an insect, opposed to his so-called pirate cousin who wielded guns, swords and knives without the slightest provocation.

Americans were a coarse, unruly breed, but this man exhibited sophistication. His cultured voice rivaled any English aristocrat, and his intelligence was obvious. No doubt stubbornness lay stamped in that unshaven jaw. To her estimation, he was a score and ten years. She pictured him the lord of a fine estate. She fluffed the feather tick, smoothing out the bumps until they lay flat. How did a man like that come to command a privateer ship when his manner spoke of wealth and refinement?

Her thoughts drifted back to Humphrey and their childhood escapades. Their adventures directed from Abigail invariably spelled trouble. Humphrey always tried to take the blame. Abigail would not let him. She told the truth to her father…except for the deception of her engagement. Her heart clenched.

"Boy, come here."

He had caught her woolgathering. Abby dragged her feet to the end of his desk. Why did he wear such a heavy scowl? Had she done something wrong? Like she had with the captain of the *Civis*, she covered her head with her hands expectant of the coming blow.

"What are you doing?"

Abby peeked between her arms. "I'm waiting for you to hit me."

He let out a heavy sigh. "I do not abuse children. Can you read?"

Abby kept her head bowed studying his stained boot tapping beneath the desk. The same boot she threw-up on after she killed Captain Lee. Her teeth ground together. Simeon informed Thorne she was simple, the charade must be maintained. She shook her head.

Thorne rose and unlocked a chest at the end of his bed and threw it open. Abby had dusted the chest and craned her neck to see what was inside. Gowns. Gorgeous colorful gowns. If only to don a gown and twirl around.

Why did Thorne have ladies gowns? Contraband? Did he have a paramour? Didn't all pirates have dozens of women? To think he posed as a vicar. How he had fooled everyone at her ball and she the biggest fool of all, to fall into his arms, to become another of his conquests? Abby fumed. If only she could point a British-Man-O-War in his direction.

"Most of the contents are for my cousin in Boston." He muttered and beneath that shock of raven black hair, he rummaged to the bottom and pulled out a book. "We will begin your lessons." He sat at his desk and kicked a chair up next to him, opening a primer she had recited when she was a precocious child of three.

Abby gaped. "Lessons? I'm no good at learning." She pivoted to the door. Cleaning his room was one thing but knee to knee contact between teacher and pupil? He kicked up a chair next to him and hauled her into it. Abby gave him a disparaging look. Spine straight as a mast, she settled on the edge.

Jacob opened the book. "Nonsense. Every seaman needs to have proper learning. A," he said, pointing to the letter. "B…," he continued.

Jacob wondered why he was helping the boy. *Because he had stolen a loaf of bread from an aristocrat and was enslaved and whipped on a ship.* His fists tightened thinking of the Banfield estate, the lush gardens, the long drive leading up to a castle, the army of servants. So much wealth and this boy starved?

Wasn't that his true war? The war against the aristocracy of England, denouncing the old rules that paid homage to the entitled and privileged while the rest of the masses starved.

His gut kicked, his body reacting to memories of his family. His uncle and guardian, Hugh Thorne, lived larger than life to a young boy, who thirsted for a father. As he did with all his children, Hugh encouraged Jacob's education providing him the best of tutors. Involved in numerous business pursuits, Hugh stood a stalwart and principled man and cultivated Jacob's interest in shipbuilding, a demanding and growing enterprise in the New World. Under Hugh's stern eye, he nurtured Jacob's unusual aptitude and, typical of New Englanders, worked him hard to better understand the mechanisms of the world. In addition, he sent the boy sailing, to learn the sea and the many refined skills needed to prove the crafts he built. His intentions lay clear. Jacob would inherit fifty percent share of the shipyard.

Events rapidly changed when the British shut down Boston Harbor. The suppression of King George's representatives converted the taciturn Hugh Thorne into a staunch and ardent patriot. Jacob remained immune and moved out from under his uncle's roof more concerned with the leisurely pursuits of life. He could not sympathize with the rebellion and openly defied his uncle's declarations, seeing no good to come from it. After all, business in the shipyard was booming with repairs to British ships.

His uncle fell at Breed's Hill and after the battle, Jacob rushed to the field. His uncle died in his arms. Hugh extracted a promise from him that he'd care for the family. Instead Jacob drowned his sorrows in ale oblivious of the state of affairs surrounding him. His Aunt Esther died of the influenza, but more likely from a broken heart. Good or bad, everyone's life was made by choices. For Thorne, he had chosen rum to heal the wounds of his dead Uncle Hugh and Aunt Esther who were like a mother and father to him.

To think he'd derive pleasure from confronting his real father, The Duke of Banfield. How many times had he fantasied that meeting, striking his father to the ground? Had his father forced himself on his mother? How vulnerable she was, finding herself with child, forced to seek refuge in America with her sister and her brother-in-law. She died when he was ten summers.

He had asked his father to free his cousin Ethan Thorne, a privateer rotting in a hellhole of a British prison. Each day his death loomed, starvation and beatings, the daily fare. Ethan was like a brother to him. Jacob's real father had failed.

In the gloomy silence, Abe looked expectantly to him. "Why do I have to learn?"

Didn't Thomas fight everyone on everything? Thorne grunted. "I have read many books, gathering their beauty, their wit or wisdom against dark days. I have known belly-low hunger many times over, but I have known a worse hunger—the need to know and to learn."

"Dark days?"

The boy's question had a far-reaching sensitivity. "I had a cousin once. His name was Thomas. He was about your age."

"Had?" Abe's eyebrows disappeared under the loathsome cap.

The air grew thick with unspoken emotions. Abe was so like his young cousin, Thomas small of stature, slim, beardless and with all the sensitivity and discovery of the world awaiting him. The seductive temptation to break through the barriers of buried aches mocked Jacob. Wasn't it less damning to tell the tale to a boy, a simple one at that, who would not judge?

"In 1765, the British crown commanded unwieldy restrictions and unfair taxation. Soon Boston became the pulse of the Colonies rebellion. In answering volley, the King cracked down and surrounded the harbor with a siege. My family suffered under the Quartering Act, the forced imposition of housing His Majesty's soldiers. My eighteen-year-old cousin, a beauty, fell under the scrutiny of a British sergeant. One night, she had gone out into the barn to check on a mare that was foaling. She screamed for help, and then was struck unconscious by the British sergeant. He planned to have his way with her but Thomas surprised him. The British sergeant ran the boy through with his sword. That lying redcoat bastard, had me arrested for the murder." Under the British siege of Boston, Thorne's word against an officer of the realm carried no weight at all. After a hasty trial, the reality of a noose came clear. Transported from prison to the gallows, friends furious with the injustice, created a diversion and freed him. Thorne recruited several sailors. Under the cloak of night and right under the nose of the English occupiers, they threaded a needle among anchored British Man O' Wars, sailing free of Boston Harbor to take on the deadly trade of privateering.

"I was very close to Thomas. I should have been there…" If only he'd not laid waste to his drunken stupor and forsaken his cousins.

He had responsibilities, had disregarded his promise to his uncle. Through his contrition, Thorne had disclosed his sins to the lad. Why? Was the admission a way to seek absolution? Or was it the way the lad leaned in and listened attentively?

Abby blinked. Thorne's story and loyalty to his family touched her heart. She had to restrain herself from not touching his sleeve as she listened without judgment to his sad tale and the crimes he suffered. In England, she was far removed from the American conflict, leaving her indifferent and immune to their cause. Being this close gave her a unique perspective. She offered up a prayer to ease his anguish with the realization that the devastation he bore created revenge in him. She must remain guarded.

Thorne resumed the lessons, his voice squared patient and rhythmic. Abby repeated the letters and phonetic sounds as instructed, the tedious exercise boring her to tears. Her father had procured the best of tutors for her brothers and had insisted on her education. Extremely competitive, the Rutland siblings thrived on ruthless competition with their little sister. In fierce debates, she had triumphed over her older brothers, amazing her father and tutors. She smiled.

Wouldn't Captain Thorne be surprised to learn she had scholarly proficiency in Latin, French, and German, and could perform elementary calculus? Plus, she owned a firm grasp of the sciences and philosophy. To eradicate the whimsy flowing through her mind, Abby shook her head.

"Tell me to slow down when you don't understand," he said, in that deep smoothly accented voice that rolled up her spine. "Learning is difficult and takes time."

"Z," she repeated, and bestowed on him a proper idiot grin to maintain her disguise when he pointed to the letter. Why was this renowned privateer teaching an orphan to read? Here was a man who caused her maids to shiver with stories of goblins and monsters and demons. He was not a malformed creature, nor shaped like a centaur or griffin. No. He was a flesh and blood man, unquestionably attractive, sturdy, rugged, with a lean, hard muscled body, and those cobalt eyes, so clear and perceptive.

"C-a-t." He moved onto words and exaggerated the consonants and vowel for her.

"Cat," Abby followed. To think he'd enraged the King of England, crippled the economy of the greatest power in Europe, and outwitted the strongest naval fleet in the world.

Like confronting a jackal in its own den. The cryptic response he had given in the garden before he had kissed her made sense now. Of course, he moved close to his enemies, to learn their movements. How close she had been in guessing his identity. She gritted her teeth. And now, the tables were reversed. Was she not an orphan boy? Abby smirked. Her disguise the night of the ball with the heavy platinum wig and mask fooled Thorne.

Pleased with her progress, Thorne's fingers flexed over the edges of the book. Her mother had taught her a person's personality could be read in his hands. His were calloused hands from rough work with long tapered fingers, hands that indicated confidence and strength.

Abby fidgeted with the inkwell. He moved it from her, his finger grazing hers. She jerked her hands beneath the table and took in their appearance, broken nails, filthy and calloused fingers, nothing to remark any womanliness.

Thorne checked his pocket watch. "Enough lessons for today. Go help Simeon serve dinner." Abby shot to her feet, overturning her chair. Under Thorne's curse she righted it, and flew from the room.

As the ship's bell tolled five, dinner was served. The table was set with linens, gleaming silver, Staffordshire china edged with rose bouquets, and a tall candelabra, winking with beeswax candles. Like one of her father's footmen, Abe held up the wall, serving and removing dishes when required, and then poured confiscated wine from the *Civis* into crystal glasses. Most of the accompaniments, she surmised, pilfered from merchant ships.

She objected to thievery of any kind. Bred into her remained high moral principles and she examined the cost and benefits. For his efforts, Thorne stood to gain a rope about his neck.

With his ruddy cheeks, chafed by the wind and ever present smile, Benjamin Lewis, the gunner patted his rotund belly. "I don't think I've ever had a meal like this in my entire life, Captain."

Long-limbed, clean shaven, brown hair pulled back neatly in a queue, Joseph Lawton, Thorne's lieutenant raised his glass to Simeon who cut through puff-pastry, serving hefty portions of dessert. "To the best prize, we ever collected. You are worth your weight in gold, Simeon."

Abby's mouth watered. Truly, Simeon had outdone himself and deserved the praise. Thorne raised his glass with equal enthusiasm, his leg hooked over an arm of his chair; he leaned back and surveyed his men, indisputably the sovereign of his kingdom.

Her mind drifted, thinking of the man who kidnapped her. With only the memory of a thin reedy voice, how could she distinguish her unseen enemy? Certainly, he was not aboard the *Civis.* Who had kidnapped her? Who had set the fire? How many were there?

Enos, the ship's carpenter stabbed his beef. "A couple weeks 'til we reach Martinique?"

Abby tensed. Martinique? She recalled what little she had learned in geography and read in the papers. An island ruled by the French in the Caribbean, renowned for American rebels to disburse cargo. It made sense. The *Vengeance* was loaded to the hilt with the *Civis's* valuables and Thorne would need to unload at an allied port.

Her stomach was empty but her head was full of vengeance. If she could get back to England, she knew she could get help to find the men responsible. Round it swirled, memories of every painful offense, devising new and interesting ways of bringing her families' enemies to sudden, gagging, writhing, agonizing justice. Could she and Simeon escape once they landed in Martinique? Could they find passage home? She toyed with a button on her coat, tamped down the glee rising in her throat, unable to wait to inform Simeon.

"Boy. Come here and fill our glasses," ordered Thorne with a resounding chorus of agreement. "To the *Civis* and the profit she gave us and—" he raised his glass and the men followed with hearty laughter "—may all of England's aristocracy swim in a special place in hell."

Abby stiffened. If he was related to the Banfield's, why would he hate them? A strong fire was stoked in Thorne, enough to hold a booted foot on the neck of all aristocrats. Simeon's warnings flared. *Tread warily.*

To earn the rebel's trust grew paramount and as the evening lingered, she eagerly topped off their glasses of wine. By midnight, all four were deep in their cups. Abby's feet smarted from unbearable blisters spawned by shuffling around in her large boots. She stretched her limbs, stiff from standing so long.

By accident the lieutenant's posture and bearing resembled a British governor. He helped himself to an extra portion of apple flan. "What plans do you have for your birthday eve, Enos?"

Enos's cheek-bones stood up, and below them were deep hollows, like egg-cups. He pawed his short craggy beard and puffed his chest like a bantam rooster. "I have a girl named Sally to attend my needs."

Another woman present on the boat? Abby stood to attention. She had seen none.

Thorne dropped his chair to all fours. "I hear fair Sally is missing something of late."

"Aye sadly, that she is," Enos concurred, staring into his glass.

Thorne slapped Enos on his back, threw back his head and roared with laughter. Then he did something that verified his madness. He broke out in song, his deep rich baritone followed by his men, pounding the table, picking up a familiar nursery rhyme, and inventing their own ribald lyrics.

Sally lost her breasts and asked the mate if he could find them.

Leave them alone and they'll come home wagging their teats behind them.

Abby clapped her hands on her ears then yanked them down to her sides. Heat stole up her cheeks. Of course, the object of their passion was the certain anatomy of the *Vengeance's* figurehead, named Sally. The *Civis* had clipped her breasts with cannon fire.

"What's the matter, boy?" Thorne slurred his words. "You lived on the streets of London. I'm sure the doxies curled your ears."

She was about to correct him saying she had no familiarity with prostitutes. She stared at the ceiling instead. Thorne rose from his chair, an indication to his crew he was tired and that the festivities had concluded. The crew bid their adieus.

Abby yawned, thirty minutes more of hauling dishes to the kitchen.

Thorne waved a hand over the table. "Tomorrow boy. Now come here." He stumbled in the corner searching then rising unsteadily, he produced a small pair of boots. "Can't risk you falling overboard with those over-sized boots. The *Vengeance's* prior cook wore them. Since he was killed in a skirmish, he won't need them."

Abby's mouth dropped open. "I don't know what to say, Captain Thorne." To wear a dead man's boots! She closed her eyes to hide her horror, visualizing the rows and rows of boots and satin slippers lining her wardrobe room.

Thorne flopped on his bed pleased to see her overwhelmed with his gift. In seconds, he snored. Abby leaned against the bed post. Asleep, Thorne did not appear so monstrous. She wondered about his conflicting nature. He certainly gave an orphan boy a chance, teaching him to read, money for labors, and the gift of boots, even if they were from a departed soul. Her chest tightened with his thoughtfulness. Without covers, he'd catch cold. Abby pulled the blankets around him. With the boots under her arm, Abby grabbed up a plate of leftovers, snatched a book off the shelf and closed the door behind her.

Chapter 4

Abby awoke to the chime of bells, the churn of waves and murmur of masculine voices. She lay perfectly still, trying to pretend this was not real. She refused to open her eyes. So long as she kept them closed she could imagine she was back home, in her own bed of pressed linens and snuggled beneath her silk damask counterpane. In a few minutes, her maids would come in with tea and cream, sprinkling the exact amount of sugar required for her taste. During the next few moments, plans would be discussed for the day's events along with the gowns and accoutrements to accompany those activities.

But inevitably, the odor of tar and pitch, and the keel of the *Vengeance* cutting through waves, dashed away the fantasy. Enclosed from the rest of the ship, the bow had become her new bedroom, offering an oasis far above the atrocious conditions aboard the *Civis.* She stretched across her new mattress, a nest of damp rope coils, the hardness branded into her back. Beneath two worn blankets, she ducked her head and shivered. If only she could keep warm. Compared to life aboard the Civis, her life was easy. Captain Thorne was not the monster as reported. One thought blurred into another. Why had he used the ruse of a vicar? What drove him to be a privateer? His family had been treated badly but what really made him do what he did? Why his intense hatred toward aristocrats?

Resigned to rise and greet the day's onslaught of chores, she ripped off her blankets and groped in the half-light. The cold slapped her flesh as she bound her breasts. At some point, the night before, which she could not remember, she had peeled off the bindings to collapse into exhaustion. Her fingers worked clumsily over the buttons of her coat, but she managed to do herself up. For her personal needs, a chamber-pot had mysteriously appeared and she smiled, courtesy of her knight in shining armor, Simeon.

Abby grimaced, and examined the boots from the dead man her proud benefactor had bequeathed. After bandaging her feet, she closed her eyes and slipped on the well-worn boots. Rewarded with the comfort and perfect fit, she uttered a brief prayer of gratitude for the dead cook. With one last look, she tossed her blankets over Rousseau's, *Reveries of a Solitary Walker,* concealing the book she borrowed from Captain Thorne, and seized her empty plate.

In the galley, Simeon raised an eyebrow, a silent reprimand to her late awakening. "Captain Thorne is still at rest."

She translated her boon. *Good.* Far be it from her to point out the captain's excesses and wished him a healthy headache. She didn't care if he rose from his bed the entire day.

Simeon plunked down a plate of muffins. She took a bite and closed her eyes, reveling in the warm cinnamon sweetness. What a loss for the earl, his former employer to lose such a genius in his kitchen. No chef for the Rutland's dared to compete with his skills. How did Simeon pull off his culinary miracle every day? Of course, the capture of the *Civis* provided a wealth of excellent fare. In terms of food, Abby relaxed her morals, bearing no objection to Thorne's thievery. It was certainly an improvement over the rancid, rotted meals presented by Captain Lee. Under Simeon's supervision, extra rations were furnished and her pallor and strength improved.

Bored, Abby finished helping Simeon in the galley, then climbed topside. Shouting from above jerked her attention skyward. High in the riggings sailors hailed one another. Through sheets of canvas she barely discerned them, growing dizzy and fascinated with their labors so high above the sea. She had forgotten to breathe for the span of several seconds. Never would she dare to attempt such a venture. Heights terrified her.

Curiously, John Dawson, a crew member, his face like a rosy withered apple and with deep set eyes and the look of a scatter-brained philosopher, crooked his finger, motioning her to the forecastle. He was the buffoon of the ship. She forced her gaze downward, keeping her pace slow. A lump grew in her throat. A sailor brushed past her and climbed to the foredeck, leading other sailors with him. She observed the men pairing up to lower barrels in the hold, the last of *Civis's* confiscation. She'd find out what John Dawson wanted then be on her way.

Images of One-Ear and the navigator loomed. Abby hesitated. Did she dare let her guard down? She squared her shoulders. The rebels were different than the sailors on the *Civis.*

Hearty laughter drew her attention to the forecastle where the ship's carpenter hefted two massive breasts. Abby stopped. Michelangelo would be rendered speechless. Artfully carved by his own hands, Enos gloried in the hail of whistles and cheers. Sailors fondled and kissed Sally's enhancement. Enos pumped his fist into the sky. Abby's toes curled in her boots as Enos was lowered on scaffolding over the bow to repair the maimed figurehead.

The oppressive presence of rebels reared everywhere. She had not ventured out that much since her capture, staying in the bow or in the galley with Simeon and now alien to the bustle of the sun-brightened day. Sailors hoisted more sails. The ship moved at full tack. Sweat flowed freely as the men strained to lower the cargo into the hold. A vulgar curse made her jump aside. She stared while the largest black man she had ever laid eyes on heaved a barrel on his shoulder past her. John Dawson waved impatiently.

She stopped five feet from him and debated to get Simeon. No. She had to fight her own battles. Elmer hooked his thumbs in his belt. He towered over her and her palms sweated.

"What you doing, boy" he called boldly. "Are you an English spy?"

"No, sir," she stammered, her voice dropping in key on the last word. The other sailors stopped. Did they seek some diversion from their boredom? The hairs on her neck rose.

"Hey!" The sailor grinned over his shoulder. "This redcoat's got a relative around here. There, boy!" he pointed to the chicken pens. "Do you suppose one o' them is your mother?"

"I have to clean the Captain's cabin." She yanked her hat lower and bristled under the uproarious laughter of the crew. She pivoted refusing to be the target of their humor.

In the next instant, her hat was snatched from her head, baring the mop of shaggily cropped blonde hair. She threw her hands over her head to hide the uneven thatch, at the same time opening her mouth to vent her outrage. She clamped her mouth shut and grabbed for her hat, only to see it sail high in the air.

"Tarnation seize me!" John Elmer hooted. "That's a fine hat!"

Another caught the hat and inspected it. "I think it'd make a fine hat for our chicken."

As Abby reached him, the hat sailed off again. She curled her fingers into fists. "You beetle-browed bastardly colonial!" she shrieked, "Give me back my hat!"

Elmer caught it and, with loud guffaws, tossed it on a chicken pen and set his foot on it. A well-directed boot found his bony shin, and his laughter exploded into shouts of pained fury. He hopped around on one leg. She grabbed her hat and jammed it over her head.

With a roar, John Dawson seized Abby and lassoed a rope beneath her arms. "You'll pay, you little redcoat brat!" he snarled. She kicked and bit her assailant.

The rope grew taut and her feet and arms flailed. Hoisted high into the air, the rope swung with the pitch of the ship. Out over the sea, the hungry waves called her name. Enos gawked from his scaffolding. Back through the shrouds, she clawed to get a handhold. Like a pendulum she sailed, dizzy and helpless, her heart hammering in her ears. Black spots formed in her vision. Sweat streamed down her back. Below, sailors gathered like seeking ants around a tasty carcass. Was that her screaming?

"Put him down, now!" Thorne commanded.

Abby dropped fast. The deck menaced. She crashed face down. Had she broken every bone in her body? In deep hiccupping breaths, the world swirled. She crawled into a ball, praying the spinning would stop. She heard a wind snap at the sails, and in the wake of its shattering, the silence was ominous.

Two boots, one of them stained, appeared in her line of view. “You men!” Thorne barked. “Lieutenant Lawton will find more worthy chores for your attention than abusing a child. You will report to him immediately! John Dawson, plan on doing dogwatch.”

She lifted her head. Dawson and his cronies scrambled sheepishly toward the poop deck. Thorne hauled her to her feet, his face carved of granite. If only she could stop trembling.

Gradually the captain’s stern visage softened as he stared at her. “I’m sorry, boy. My men are a long way from home. I fear their manners and judgment need improvement. Quit shaking.”

Though the words were softly spoken, his tone carried an unequivocal authority. She fidgeted beneath his close inspection to see if any injury occurred. Slowly she brought her breathing under control and darted a glance at the sails above her. “I fell from a tree and broke my arm.”

“I see but how will you make a good sailor unless you conquer your fears?”

Abby flinched then narrowed her eyes. “No way am I going up there.”

Thorne responded with a low chuckle of amusement. “Ornery little orphan,” Thorne muttered and gestured officiously. “Come and be quick about it.”

In dumb surprise, Abby stared after him. “I’m telling you, I ain’t going to do it!” She had survived swinging out over ocean and a near death plummet to the deck. Blood whizzed through her veins like a tsunami.

Thorne had gone only a few paces when he sharpened his voice and, without a glance in her direction barked, "Hop to it, boy! Don't stand there gawking."

Abby ran into the back of his boots. He turned abruptly, grabbed her waist beneath her coat and lifted her onto the ratlines. Abby squelched a scream and hung frozen, her hands clenched around the ropes. "Get me down, you cloddish colonial!"

His arms stretched over her head. His feet anchored beneath hers. The captain's amused chuckle reverberated through her back. "The best way to swim is to be thrown in the water."

His breath tickled her ear. Intimately his body lay against hers and they both swayed in unison. Abby gasped. The ship plummeted, sea-spray washed against her cheeks, then the ship bowed upward. Her stomach flip-flopped. "We ain't swimming. We are flying! It ain't natural."

The Yank roared with laughter in her ear. "Keep moving, boy. I'm right behind you."

"I see nothing funny. Must be rebel humor, you dim-witted barnacle. You could talk the legs off a donkey," she muttered then followed the line of the mast that disappeared into the canvas. The climb was formidably long enough to take her into the next world. "And where do you think we are going?"

"Keep going," Thorne ordered.

"You thatch-gallows rogue. Are you sure a cannon ball didn't smack your head?"

"That's enough besmirching my character, boy. I'm not an abuser of children, but if you tempt me enough, I may change my ways."

A broad hand pushed up her buttocks, the warmth of his palm on her nether parts burned through the wool of her clothing, heat unfurled in its wake. Abby yelped and ignored the unprecedented thump of her heart and focused.

"If I didn't know better," Thorne offered an off-hand remark, "I would have guessed you had an easy life up until now, Abe, you're as soft as a woman."

Abby about died. She managed to draw enough breath to hurl another insult. "Your mother should have thrown you away and kept the stork."

"Careful," Thorne warned. "Or I'll take down your breeches and blister your backside."

She crouched like a wild animal. "You lay a finger on me, rebel and I'll—" Abby squeaked as he pushed at her again. She clutched the rope lines, hauling upward, the wiry hemp abrading her fingers. If only she did not fall. The wind whipped, thrusting the sails, and in answering volley, the *Vengeance* shuddered and creaked. Was she climbing the mast of a ship far above the surface of the earth and in the middle of the ocean? Since the night of her ball, everything that had befallen her was unbelievable. Was this any different?

The ship dipped unexpectedly and she slid downward, her boot bumping violently against Thorne's head. He cursed. She decided she would rather read about adventures than have them. In a book, adventures had a happy ending.

Except there was something wonderful about striking out like this, off into the clouds, and the freedom it allowed. Despite being scratched, sweating and terrified, each time she took a rung, each time she put one foot above the other, she felt a sense of heady accomplishment that rivaled any exhilaration she had ever experienced.

When she climbed up to a platform she practically shouted her victory. And what she saw there placed her in complete awe.

It was beautiful. Beyond beautiful. A sense of wonder broke over her. She found herself standing atop a blue world. From her vantage point she could almost reach out and touch the horizon where the infinite hues of blue sea merged with the sky. Sunlight danced off the water, white caps rolled endlessly, wrapping her in an aura of magnificence so enthralling that her heart caught at the sight of it.

Thorne heaved his bulk up beside her. "What do you think, lad?"

Think? She had never felt this way before. The pervasive enchantment seeped through her bones, the sight of the water, the sky, the colors, the sounds of the wind all drugged her with their seductiveness.

He stood in a slant of sunlight from the east, grinning at her. Behind him the mainsail strained with the awesome power of the wind as if the majesty of nature bowed to him. His white shirt, deeply V-necked, billowed and was girded low on his hips with a black belt. His black pants fit snugly and he had shed his boots and hat. The breeze toyed with his hair. Abby had the same strange sensation looking at him as she had looking at the majestic seascape. Like the sea, he was not threatening, but impressive. And seductively wild.

Abby laughed aloud and Thorne laughed with her. Was his reward, Abe's exultation? She leaned back and reveled in the heat of the sun on her face and the wind to cool her skin. In companionable silence, they each enjoyed the other's company.

But it was Abe looking at him not Abby. Thorne wanted to see the world through an orphan boy's eyes. She had the distinct feeling he needed Abe's joy. So Abe emerged to fill the void in Thorne. He had saved her demise from the *Civis's* captain and for that she was extremely grateful. To give him a friendship for the remaining time yielded an act of mercy. Her mother taught her whenever one was in need there was an opportunity to make a difference. An act of kindness could change the world, like throwing a stone in a pond to ripple out and create a wave. In two weeks' time, she'd be free and on her way to England. Smiling, she glanced surreptitiously. There in the depths of the captain's cobalt blue eyes a sorrow lurked. The grief and bitterness revealed itself for just a moment before shuttered. Thomas's death had broken a part of her Patriot.

Thorne slapped Abby on the back. "Amidst all that squalling, you got over your fears."

Abby nodded. "You were not offended by my insults?"

"Camouflage is a game we undertake, but our secrets are surely revealed by what we want to seem to be as what we want to conceal. You were scared, that's all. I'm sure there is more to your story. In time when you feel you can trust me, you can tell the rest."

A wind blew up from the east and Thorne looked west. Abby followed his line of sight where collective mare's tails glided across the sky. "Fair weather. Hide behind your insults all you want, but make sure they are not done in front of the crew. There will be consequences."

Reality whooshed on her like a savage zephyr. If he knew her for who she was the end would not be so pretty. Thorne's blood would curdle. To see joy through a hated aristocrat's eyes? The American War of Independence spoke freedom, standing against the old rules of landed gentry. Her roots damned her, and if her genuine identity lay revealed, her life would hang grimmer than aboard the *Civis*. Abby's conquest of heights died a bitter pall.

Do not get too comfortable.

"Time to climb down, lad. Get your pallet and bed down in my cabin. It will spare you of the pranks put on by the crew."

Abby choked and coughed to clear her throat. "I ain't goin' to bed down with any Patriot, that's for sure."

Chapter 5

"You test my patience, lad, but you will observe my tolerance as a virtue," ordered Thorne.

With her back to him, Abby knelt on the floor of the Captain's cabin, smoothing her rude pallet of rough linen tick stuffed with rags. "You have all the virtues I dislike and none of the vices I admire."

"What did you say?" He bellowed like a bull.

"I hope you don't snore." No amount of begging, pleading or protestation against her sleeping in his cabin changed his command. Simeon had interjected and received a blistering that would have withered the rock of Gibraltar. Abby slapped the blankets on her bed.

"What's the problem now?"

"You remind me of a farmer who could not get his mule to plow so he took a plank and smacked the animal on the side of the head."

Thorne sank in his chair and rocked with laughter. "If nothing else boy, you are pure amusement. Do you think comparing me to a mule will change my mind? Didn't your mother teach you manners?" He turned with an air of dismissal back to his paperwork, leaving Abby speechless and her cheeks flaming with indignation.

She hitched her britches. “My mother is rolling in her grave me beddin’ down with a rebel. You best get yourself some extra cannon ‘cause you’re going to need it come time the redcoats capture you.”

“I’ll be worrying about that when the time comes, if it ever does,” the captain replied. “I can imagine you’ll be ready to fire the first salvo.”

“I’m going to sleep now, rebel. Can’t say it’s been nice talking to you.” She flopped on her pallet. “Don’t stay up too late. You needing your beauty sleep and all because I’m sure you love nature in spite of what it did to you.”

Thorne rubbed the back of his neck. “You can think of me as your elder brother.”

Utterly impossible. Abby, shook her head in frustration. No harm would come to *Abe,* she was certain. At the same time, he was so dangerous to *her.* She touched her fingers to her lips, remembering his kiss in the garden. He made her feel too much, assaulting her body with sensations and filling her heart with inexplicable yearnings.

Dissatisfaction rose with his response to her taunts. She gazed restlessly around the room she had learned to keep meticulously clean. It was a fairly large, wood-paneled cabin, adequately lit by an oil lamp that rested on his sturdy walnut desk across from the bed. In the corner, near a tall oak chest topped by a washbasin, sat a wooden table and high-backed chairs where he and his officers dined. Bordering the top of the room lined a shelf of books. The bed bore a feather tick and blue coverlet with several plump pillows. It was a comfortable arrangement, much nicer than the bow and certainly better than the freezing damp hold of the *Civis.*

Abby fidgeted with the lack of privacy. The bindings around her breasts chafed and she scratched at the wool of her greatcoat not daring to remove it. Comfort did not belong to her. No doubt, it proved safer to maintain a barrage of insults. *How long before he discovered she was a female?*

From beneath her blankets she watched Thorne in repose, the dreaded American Privateer who struck terror in the hearts of her countrymen and befuddled the King of England. Eight bells, she counted. Midnight. When would he retire for the night? She didn't have long to wonder. After a few minutes of shuffling through his papers and making brief notations with a tall quill pen, anchored at the top of his desk, Thorne shoved the chair back and moved away from the desk. He glanced in her direction. Abby feigned sleep.

He began unbuttoning his white silk shirt, revealing a jagged scar near his heart. Heat expanded in her cheeks. *Turn away.* She lay frozen and mesmerized.

She had never seen a naked man. Despite growing up in an all-male household, her father and brothers remained the souls of circumspection. The male anatomy touted untoward for a lady. Certainly through the rough talk of sailors, she had learned things that set her ears to burning. But this was Thorne, the man who kissed her so insensibly and for his sin, she ignored the strictures of proper conduct.

He sat on the bed, the mattress bowing beneath his weight and pulled off his boots and tucked them neatly beneath. He stood up, shirked off his shirt and unbuckled his belt. Long, strong fingers unbuttoned the top of his breeches. Anticipation thickened the air in her lungs. A thick, silky trail of dark hair began just above the navel and slid down into his open breeches. He crossed to his desk and made a quick note then dropped the quill. Retrieving a chart, he unrolled the parchment, making additional measurements. Abby licked her lips. He seemed so tall and immense as he stood menacingly near like a threatening dark avenger.

He sipped his wine and she imagined tasting that same sweet wine on his lips. In the lantern light, his lean and handsome profile, starkly etched, mushroomed an awareness of a strong, living healthy man that filled every pore of her being.

She resisted the instinct again of closing her eyes. While contemplating his map, he stirred; a slight ripple of muscle warned of his enormous strength then reached down to his breeches. Abby gulped. Distinctive warmth flooded the area between her legs. He turned down the lantern, casting them in darkness. Abby bit her lip. The chair shook from when he tossed his breeches on it. How long did she hold her breath before she dared to breathe?

Thorne settled beneath the thick feather tick, adjusting it to his comfort with the bed squeaking beneath his weight. Lying rigidly on her pallet, Abby became even more achingly aware of how hard it was to be in the same proximity of Jacob. For perhaps a half an hour she lay there, willing her heart to slow, and hearing the cabin grow quiet as the man in the bed stopped shifting, and his breathing grew even and regular.

The night bent over her like a new mother watching her child. She stared out the stern windows, one blurred star; faint glimmering like a bee flooded the loneliness in her soul like a tempest. Memories and emotions struck like a blow. The fate of her family gnawed at her confidence. The fear of not knowing what happened to them ate at her insides. She had to get back to England. *Now.*

Weary of navigating in Jacob's world, she grew more cognizant than ever that she was a duke's daughter and at great peril. Where was Nicolas? She imagined the horrid conditions he faced on a slaver bound for Brazil. Even if he survived the voyage, toiling in the hot tropical sun laid waste to a man in no time. Who might have wanted to hurt her family? She swallowed against the knot of emotion lodged in her throat.

Mentally she listed all the transgressions against her. A shriek of anguish tore itself from her lips before she could strangle it. She curled herself into a ball beneath musty blankets and sobbed uncontrollably.

Thorne awoke. Like a gnat circling his ear came a sniffle, a sob then full blown howling. "Good God, can't a man get sleep on his own ship?" He whipped off the covers, hitched on his breeches then lit the lantern. "Come here, boy."

This was not what he envisioned when he'd vowed to take the boy's fate into his own hands. Had he gotten himself into a bigger fix, ordering the lad to sleep in his cabin?

Something about the boy called to him, and to some degree, aroused paternal feelings. In a moment of reflection, he admired the lad's spirit. The way he stood up to him in the aftermath of battle and how he survived aboard the merchantman. It was widely known how England's aristocracy resolved their problems, settling on an unsavory sea captain for a mere pittance. The abducted were murdered at sea or sold into slavery, tidily sweeping away any scandals imminent for peers of the realm. Lee's reputation had even reached his ears.

Bold as hell, the boy leaned to twelve or thirteen summers, and somewhere beneath the grime, Thorne surmised, a face smooth as a peach. Abe's sarcastic propensity was a way to cover his fear. In Thorne's youth, he suffered Abe's impulsive nature, getting into fights and rebelling against authority. Years of maturity and experience shaped him. With the right hand guiding the youth, he was certain the boy would develop into a strong man, Thorne, the sculptor, Abe, the clay. He was Abe's protector now.

Jacob let out a loud breath. Huddled beneath his blankets, the lad cried. "I'll haul you by your drawers if you don't come over here."

He almost laughed with the boy's rapid flight off his pallet. Abe slapped his hat on his head and stood with his head down, so pitiable and pathetic it tugged Thorne's heart. He reached out and put his hand on the boy's shoulder. An acrid odor of rancid bacon grease and fish lingered. "You must brew the filth to match the stink. I should have you keelhauled to clean you up."

Abe stiffened and Thorne laughed. "I doubt it would do any good. Tell me lad, what troubles you?"

Blue eyes, bloodshot from crying, studied Thorne. Was the boy gauging his concern? A gamut of emotions played across his face from disbelief to curiosity. Abe swallowed hard.

"My mother died months ago. The doctor said she was too old to bear any more children. She died in childbirth. Then my father and brothers were murdered." Fresh tears left clean tracks through the soot on Abe's face.

"I was put on Captain Lee's ship." Between sobs Abe enumerated the atrocities he faced aboard the merchantman. "What's killing me is I have no idea who hated my family to do this. I want justice."

"You want justice?" Thorne shook his head, incredulous with the boy's bluster. "Noble but impossible. Whoever did this to your family had influence. You have no resources and would end up worse if you sought justice against someone powerful. I've had those experiences firsthand."

There was a war going on. He was fighting against the injustices of England's tyranny, the same injustices, Abe had suffered. Jacob's future was nebulous. He couldn't tear into England and seek vengeance for the boy. He'd do his damnedest to educate and care for him.

Abe burst out in a fresh torrent of sobs. His voice escalated a high soprano then hiccupped into a lower octave. Jacob produced a handkerchief and the boy blew his nose. "On top of everything, I killed a man."

Thorne's chest tightened. Like a madness, shades of guilt swung through the lad's brain. The boy's moral compass impressed him. Despite suffering inhumane treatment and the prospect of death from the *Civis's* captain, the lad endured guilt from killing him. Abe squeaked. Thorne had gripped his shoulder so hard he didn't realize it. He relaxed his fingers.

"You removed a piece of scum from the face of the earth. If you hadn't have done it, I would have dispatched the vermin. Most importantly, you saved my life."

Abe swiped his face with the back of his hand and nodded, mollified for the time being with Jacob's words. Talking out his troubles had been a catharsis for the boy.

Jacob combed his fingers through his hair. "Get some sleep."

Abe relaxed a bit, ambled to his pallet. The deep dark well of sorrow he must come to grips with on his own was a journey Jacob traveled every day. Why didn't he take off that inferno coat? Jacob frowned. He'd let him have his way. Tomorrow he'd insist on the boy taking a bath. By the time Thorne turned down the lantern, Abe was fast asleep. He took an extra blanket off his bed and covered the boy.

Jacob settled into his own bed with his hands folded behind his head. His cabin boy could be completely exasperating, yet there was something about him that was likeable. Jacob just had the usual difficulty of defining the later. Remarkable how similar their lives were. Both were orphans. Both lost their mothers from dire circumstances. Both had family that had been murdered. Both wanted justice.

Chapter 6

"My mother-in-law told me if she were my husband, she'd give me poison," said Enos Lee over his shoulder as he tacked a sail above Abby's head for shade. "I informed her if she was my wife, I'd drink it!"

Hilarious guffaws rumbled like thunder by more than a few sailors. With her back supported by the mainmast, Abby sat on a rope coil with yards and yards of canvas across her lap, implementing her embroidery skills to repair tears. The work was time consuming but she enjoyed the easy camaraderie of the crew who had genuinely warmed to the young lad she was impersonating. From Simeon, she had gleaned that Thorne had given the crew blistering remarks, resulting in remorse and apologies about the hazing incident. In fact, Ben Lewis and Enos Lee were deferential to the young cabin boy.

"I've seen his mother-in-law," said Benjamin Lewis, his cheeks ruddier in the wind. She has so many double chins she looks like she is staring at you over a pile of pancakes. Her ability to stuff beef hocks in her cheeks and whistle *Billy Boy* is legend. Even the devil gets a fright with her meanness. The only difference between her and a vulture is the vulture waits 'til your dead before it eats your heart out."

Enos slapped Edward Martin on the back. "She said she'd dance on my grave, so I'll be buried at sea if you please. But not too soon, I have that angel of my wife to get back too."

"Here, here. I have my own missus' sweet arms to get back to," said Abner Bosworth, a lanky man who spoke like a parson flourishing his sermon.

In a bout of silence the crew fed on each other's homesickness and their yearning for home in Boston. Abby looped a length of thread through a needle, knotted it and commenced to stitch, pining for her family, too. Opposed to the band of convicted felons aboard the *Civis*, the *Vengeance's* crew was tame. Farmers, shopkeepers, and fishermen turned sailors loyal to an upstart country, brave family men longing for their wives and children, their resolve ceded to a rebellion to make the world right. She admired them. They risked their lives, fortunes and sacred honor for the price of liberty and the contagion of their rebellion grew in her heart. They couldn't possibly win their war, not against the greatest empire and, certainly, not against the most powerful navy in the world.

But for now, she understood the fervor of her Uncle Thomas Hansford, her mother's brother, a patriot and successful businessman who lived there. She had met her uncle only three times when he visited her family in England. He had recanted many tales, painting an exciting picture of life in the burgeoning Colonies.

Lucky Pascale, the only black crewmember joined their circle. He was an enormously muscled man with a smooth round face, broad flat-nose and dark eyes that discerned everything. He never spoke. "Why do you call him Lucky Pascale?" Her voice dropped, proficiently rough-hewn. The language of a blacksmith? *How far had she come?* Her mother, if alive, would be mortified.

Elijah Brown sighed. Another yarn was to be shaped and she sat an eager audience, enchanted with their sea-ditties and outrageous stories.

"Now that is a very good tale and one I can attest firsthand. We picked him up near the Bahamas. He was adrift for several days, no sustenance, surely starved, lacking water, in the middle of a squall, a water spout bearing down and sharks surrounding him. He made a sorry sight so Captain Thorne ordered sails cut and we brought him aboard. No one aboard speaks Creole but what we can glean, he is an escaped slave. Our friend, Pascale is very lucky."

Abby laughed. During the past two weeks, the crew had become her family, regaling the captain's young cabin boy with more anecdotes than she could possibly dream. It occurred to her she was having an adventure. She had all the freedoms of a boy, climbing the masts, and enjoying the repartee of the sailors. Abby had never had an adventure unless you counted meeting the King on her eighteenth birthday.

"Why one time—" Freckled and sunburnt from wind and sun, Samuel Parks' eyes twinkled, not to be outdone. "We had not a breath of wind for a week, and one night a heavy fog came down. Nothing but danger surrounded us. What could we do? We could not see from one side of the ship to the other and shoals lay dangerously close. Then I got an idea. I climbed up the mast, cut-up the fog with a sword and stuffed it in a ditty bag. Cook served up portions of fog with gravy and in two days' time, we had eaten our way out to clear skies."

Abby smoothed a hand over her stitching. What would be their reaction if they learned she was a woman? Of nobility? She shook her head. No longer would they be open with their conversation.

She stretched then pulled the wool collar of her coat away from her skin to let in a cooling breeze. Beads of perspiration dripped down her neck and back. As they headed into equatorial waters, the weather warmed and in the broiling sun, she dreamed of shedding her coat. She closed her eyes temporarily, appreciating Enos's small gesture of comfort and the shade the canvas allowed.

"And then there was Captain Thorne." Enos waved his arm in a dramatic arc. "We were outgunned and outmanned, a Man-O'-War bearing down on us so fast and so close I could count the teeth in the grins of her sailors. We had only six guns opposed to seventeen. The captain ordered the men to saw spare masts to the length of guns, painted them black, mounted them on buckets and stuck them out portholes. He filled the rigging with men and so overwhelmed the enemy with the dummy guns, they surrendered immediately." Enos slapped his knee and chortled. "We helped ourselves to their guns and ammunition and sailed away rejoicing."

Abby privately scoffed at the exaggerated stories yet she carried a vivid memory of the damages of maritime forces of the Americans. Despite their diminutive strength, they could shake the formidable Royal Navy. They terrorized the English and Irish Channels, picking the bones of their prizes with disdain, her dear Uncle Cornelius nearly ruined.

Captain Thorne's exploits were the most notorious. His pursuits of glory, fame and money, gained, she grudgingly acknowledged through intelligence, self-confidence and probably some luck.

"Bold as brass he sailed the seas, actually flew the *Vengeance* over six Men-O'-War and captured ten merchantmen while they slept like babes in their berths." Enos snapped his fingers. "Like a magician, Captain Thorne and the ten merchantmen vanished like ghosts."

"More ghost stories, Enos?" Thorne paused momentarily, his hand clasped behind his back. "You'll have me riding the wings of dragons and changing raindrops into pearls." Beneath her lashes she watched him climb to the foredeck. Without a doubt, he was a reckless daredevil commanding a collection of half-disciplined human beings ready to obey every order he decreed, his exploits extolled by his crew with all the admiration and respect of a demigod.

"The captain is merciful. When he discovered he had captured a ship owned by a widow, and it being her only income, he restored all her profit back to her."

"What of the prisoners? What happens to them?" Abby blinked. *What would be her fate?*

"Like the ones we took from the *Civis* are chained below, fed well, and will be traded or bartered for money." Martin spat a fine stream of tobacco juice. "Far better treatment than the redcoats give, our men stuck in freezing dunghills or baked in airless barges to die."

A crick grew in Abby's neck and her legs fell asleep. She rose and moved to stretch the sleepiness from her limbs. The men sang a sea ditty, one so raucous it would curl the ears of a courtesan, her cheeks warming beyond the heat of the sun.

She climbed to the stern and stopped five feet from Lucky Pascale, who stood gazing out to sea, the most forlorn creature she had ever seen. She had never seen a black man before let alone converse with one. No one was near. She let her voice drift over the sea and spoke in perfect French. "It must be lonely not able to converse with anyone. Please know that I am your friend and you can talk with me. It will be our secret."

He never turned to her. While gazing out to sea, Pascale folded his broad strapping arms, gleaming ebony in the sun and bowed. If he were surprised with her fluency in his language, he did not show it. "I find it refreshing to speak in my tongue," he said in eloquent French, exotically accented. "I was a manservant for a cruel master. It thrilled him to torture me. He killed my wife and son in the most merciless way. Chained to a tree, I tore at my bonds unable to help them. Their screams still fill my ears. I did not care if I lived or died, but here on this ship," he glanced to the men over his shoulder, "I have the will to live."

Abby pressed a hand to her throat. "I am sorry for your loss. I know what it is to lose loved ones."

Pascale smiled and tilted his head knowingly, his wise eyes focused keenly on her. A nervous tremor rattled up her spine. *Did he suspect?*

"A boy brings the needle to the thread. He does not put the thread through the needle."

Abby gripped the taffrail. "I don't understand."

"Mademoiselle." He hesitated while Abby's mouth worked up and down like a beached grouper. He smiled and bowed again. "Please know, Mademoiselle, I am your friend and that *your* secret is safe with me."

Chapter 7

Simeon frowned and grabbed a cinnamon shaker from the shelf. "*Mademoiselle?* Are you sure Pascale won't say a word? We don't need any more trouble."

"I hope so." Abby drummed her fingers on the table, not sure of anything.

Simeon stacked bowls of soup on a tray with warm bread from the oven. "Take this tray to the gunroom. Enos and Samuel have taken ill. There is a tonic I made armed with a sedative." He caught her arm. "I cannot caution you enough to remain vigilant and remember who you are."

Abby picked up the tray and moved to the gunroom which doubled as a barracks. Cannons were locked into place, the portholes shuttered. She sidestepped around the munitions and found Enos and Samuel swinging in their hammocks. After laying her tray down she offered Enos a bowl of soup. He refused. She raised clasped hands to her chest. What could she do to help?

Remembering her nursemaids, she placed her palm upon his forehead. Indeed, he lay warm, his face a ghostly pallor. A day ago he'd charmed her with humorous anecdotes. Now he faded, helplessly ill, and she felt sorry for him. So far away from the comforts of home.

"You must drink." she said, adopting the same firmness her nursemaid used. She helped him to a sitting position and encouraged him to drink the broth. Weak as a kitten, he collapsed onto his pillow. Abby patted the broth that dribbled down his chin then helped him rise again to drink the concoction Simeon had prepared.

"Are you trying to poison me?" His wrinkled face sucked hard like a balled-up prune.

Abby apologized, listened while he blew off steam then tucked his blanket around him.

"You'll be up and feeling your sunny self in no time." She cooed other words of comfort then repeated the process with the less stubborn, Samuel.

She took a fresh linen, dipped it into cool water, wrung it out and placed it on his head. He basked in the attention she gave him.

How natural it felt to care for them. "I'll return with tea, so rest."

Samuel stopped her. "She is perhaps, the most beautiful in the world. The Captain finds her irresistible."

"Irresistible?" Did the medicine make Samuel incoherent? She cleared her throat. "A lady friend of Captain Thorne?"

"The *Vengeance,* the most beautiful vessel in the world, has carried terror and alarm through the West Indies and out of her wantonness; she's chased the enemy's far superior force."

Abby rolled her eyes and sniffed Simeon's tonic. The medicine talked.

She opened the portholes to allow fresh air to circulate, and then picked up the tray, thinking of her former life. Her every need was considered a bastion of fashion, privilege and disregard for those with less. Unconcerned with annoying daily errands and problems, her days were filled with parties, balls, riding horses and other pleasurable pursuits. If anyone knew of her current deeds, they would be scandalized.

And she couldn't be happier.

To be useful was a new experience. Abby spent the rest of the day busy with chores, attempting to compensate the void with Enos and Samuel unable to do their duties. Repeatedly, she returned below decks and encouraged them to drink and sip more medicine, aware of her patients' needs.

With her hands on her hips, she surveyed the spotlessness of the barracks. Thorne did a good job. The physical health and well-being of his crew came first. The crew had clean clothes, were fed and provided with a work environment as scrubbed and secure as possible.

The dissimilar failings of the *Civis's* captain created terrible discomforts for her crew. The decks leaked from above, drenching the men who slept in hammocks, immersing them in cold and darkness. The stench compounded the reeking water in the bilge, accumulating rotting refuse and the decaying carcasses of drowned rats. It was a wonder the sailors of the *Civis* survived.

Reluctantly she owed the success of the *Vengeance* to Thorne. As commander, he upheld an exceptional example for his men, infusing discipline, a concern for his men's safety, and a sense of fairness and cleanliness.

The next time she checked, Samuel was much better and her heart skipped a beat with the success of her ministrations. She laid her hand upon Enos's brow. Her body tensed. His condition worsened. Shipboard sicknesses rose fatal. Something different had to be done. To heal and get uninterrupted rest, Enos needed to be isolated from the crew.

Abby darted to the quarterdeck and commenced organizing a storeroom, pilfering blankets from Captain Thorne to make a comfortable pallet. When everything was done to her satisfaction, she recruited Pascale to carry Enos to his new accommodations. In a laborious ritual, she ladled care and concern for the aging privateer forcing down liquids, applying cooling cloths and poultices.

Nothing else mattered. The captain would have to wait for his cabin to be cleaned. She would bear his wrath later. She refused to eat or sleep. Enos's fever spiked. He gibbered through bouts of confusion. Sweat beaded his brow. Coughing spasms racked his body. He shook uncontrollably. Abby rinsed and reapplied cool cloths countless times. She begged Simeon to brew more concoctions and refused to leave Enos's side. Simeon shook his head, a silent assent. *Enos die?* Tears filled her eyes. Abby prayed.

Thorne had seen occasional glimpses of his cabin boy scurrying from the quarter deck to the galley. The boy had cared for his crew. He puzzled over the boy conversing with Pascale. No one had been able to communicate with the escaped slave beyond hand gestures. Clearly the enormous black understood everything the boy commanded. In Pascale's arms, he had seen Enos, his shipwright transported to the quarterdeck.

Simeon held up the lantern. Thorne surveyed the scene. His cabin boy lay asleep, his head pillowed on his arms next to Enos. Short shafts of blonde hair curled from beneath Abe's cap. Supplies were stacked neatly against the far wall, providing enough room for a pallet. His missing blankets covered Enos. He wrinkled his nose. A tray with bitter smelling substances lay at his feet.

"Medicines and poultices," Simeon explained.

"The lad has a good heart," Enos whispered hoarsely and Jacob stared incredulously. "Wore himself out taking care of me night and day. Wouldn't have made it without him."

"Glad to see you back in the land of the living." Thorne gave the old salt a drink of water, and then lifted the cabin boy in his arms. The lad was light of weight, his face gaunt. He'd order more rations for the boy. Abe moaned and nestled to get comfortable in his arms, spreading his fingers against his chest. Jacob's skin tingled. He ducked through the doorway, so conflicted by the gesture he hurried away to his cabin.

Watching them leave, Enos said, "Has a woman's touch, don't you think, Simeon?"

Chapter 8

Abby woke to the bright light of day streaming through the gallery windows. Why had no one wakened her? How was she in Thorne's cabin? She threw off the covers. Enos. Had he died and no one told her?

She flew from her bed and dashed to the quarterdeck where she found Enos, gobbling a bowl of chicken soup and warm bread, appearing a picture of health, his recovery miraculous.

"Simeon made this special just for me." He scooped down spoonfuls. "Pardon my manners but I'm starved."

"I'm happy to see you well." She wanted to whirl, her arms stretched out, instead she clasped her hands together, and the first time in a long time, she had a bone-deep sense of satisfaction infuse her.

"You are a saint. I'd be visiting Davy Jones locker if not for you. I'll never forget."

Abby grew misty-eyed and turned away. She muttered something about chores. As she ducked into the passageway, warmth radiated through her, along with a strange euphoria. Her thoughts scattered. Suddenly, she couldn't think straight. She headed to the bow, her private retreat where she wouldn't be disturbed and...

charged full bore into Captain Thorne. She hit him with such a force it knocked her cap off and sent him sprawling on the hard plank floor with a thud.

Dazed, Abby scrambled on hands and knees to pick up her cap, stuffing her hair into it a second before he recovered with a loud expletive. With a growl, Jacob came to his feet. Swearing an oath, the captain flung out a hand to catch her by the collar then yanked her up until she was eye to eye, her toes pitched above the floor. She started to slip from her coat. Her nostrils flared. He'd see her breasts bound beneath her thin shirt. There was no way she could explain it away. In his tight grip, her arms ached locked over her head, and his manhandling was the last straw.

"Get your hands off me," she shrieked. "You got no right to lay a hand on me!" She kicked, her feet flailing air.

Like a lump of clay, she was dropped, her coat torn off and her shirt trailing out over her pants. She snatched her coat and moved into a deeper shadow.

"I'm sorry." He began to dust himself off, chagrined at his own quick temper. "I'm sure it was an accident and—" He looked at her sharply, "It was an accident, wasn't it?"

"Yes," Abby relented a bit. "I didn't see you in the dark."

"What were you running away from?" Then he chuckled. "I'll bet you were afraid I'd come to fetch you for a bath."

She gulped at his words, terror struck in her chest. She turned so he didn't see her expression as she thrust her arms and head back into her coat. Like a turtle, she emerged and entertained a well-placed boot in his rear...until she saw him clenching a bloody rag to his arm. "What happened?"

"I want you to stitch my wound."

She shook her head. "I've no experience with flesh wounds. You need a doctor."

His jaw tightened from the audacity of refusing his command. "Physicians are in short supply in the middle of the Atlantic. I have no other recourse. You stitched sails, you will do it."

Abby paled and squeezed her eyes shut, praying the ocean would suck them down a whirlpool. Panic rattled up her spine. Sinking a needle into flesh? She stepped back. "I-I can't."

Jacob prodded her toward his cabin. "You can. It's an order." He chuckled, a deep baritone. "Why so squeamish? You're not turning into a milk-fed, girlish maid are you?"

Abby's heart gave a frantic leap and lodged in her throat. To refuse would arouse suspicion.

"I need a cabin boy with back bone." He taunted.

Abby scowled then slipped into the easy banter of a fishmonger. "I guess I can do it as long as you don't start screaming and blubbering all over me. I'd hate to have the crew know you're really a peacock concerned about soiling his lace cuffs and pink satin waistcoat."

The captain gave her a shove from behind.

"Pink? I hope you think I have better taste than that." In the captain's cabin, he eased into a chair and angled his head to the needle and thread on the table, then shrugged, a graceful movement, peeling off his shirt. "Help me."

Abby swallowed. Outside of a chaste peck or hug from her father, she had never touched a man. Her eyes roved to his lips. Heat flooded to her face, the crush of his mouth, a lingering memory.

Her finger itched to caress the smooth line of his lower lip and the firm curve of his jaw. The Captain possessed a face destined to make a woman lust.

Gingerly she helped withdraw his shirt and retreated to her shy and reticent self. His skin felt warm and he smelled of earth and sea. *What was she supposed to do now?*

"You have to thread the needle."

His patronizing put enough starch in her knees to jerk her out of her musings. Her older brother, Nicholas had a wound like Thorne's. Misjudging the height of a hedge, he fell from his horse, his leg impaled on a stick. Lacking turpentine and myrrh, her scientist brother, Anthony, poured whiskey over the wound, explaining the need to clean the injury. He further enlightened her on the use of cultured maggots to debride the wound of impurities. She wrinkled her nose. Like physicians, cultured maggots were in short supply. She opened a bottle of rum and poured a generous amount on clean linen.

Thorne found it amusing. "Haven't you had a taste of rum?"

"Can't say it's been a part of my learning." She pulled the blood soaked cloth away then stepped back and grimaced. It was an awful gash about six inches long. Her stomach fluttered. She dabbed his wound to clean off the dirt.

"What did you do, get into a fight with a chicken?" she said, her insult an attempt to ease her own panic. Aware of Thorne watching her every move, she dipped the thread and needle in the amber liquid, threading the needle the way Pascale suggested.

She stopped and stared. "What? Do you need a bite stick?"

Sinking her top teeth into her lower lip, she pushed the needle through his flesh. The two sides pulled together. She closed her eyes and swallowed down bile.

He cleared his throat. "I'd like you to finish before I'm a gray-haired old man."

Her eyes flew open with his goading and she set to stitching. "Be lucky if I don't sew those lips of yours shut." She muttered beneath her breath.

He gave her a warning look then stared straight ahead, a silent affirmation to finish the task. After a few strokes, she gained her embroidery rhythm. She entertained sewing puppies or perhaps a bouquet of flowers on his bicep. How would the Captain fancy that? "I'll have you sewed up nice and pretty so you can boast to all your lady friends how you got injured in battle. I promise not to tell anyone you got clumsy with the capstan. You do have lady friends, don't you?"

Guessing by his insulted expression, he took her comment as a slur on his manhood.

"I have plenty of lady friends," he said, his words laced with venom.

"Not that it's any of my business but where do you keep these ladies?" Abby prodded.

"There was a girl in England I met," he paused, his eyes suddenly seemed faraway and…dreamy.

"Was she one of those fancy ladies?"

"She had a pedigree a mile long. Rich, Spoiled. Beautiful. But I'd rather boil in oil than pick up with the enemy."

Rather boil in oil?

"Ouch! Take it easy. Do you know how exasperating you are?" He glared at her, and then after a long stretched out moment, his lean cheeks flexed. "A thought has crossed my mind."

Abby froze mid-stroke. "That thought must have been a long and lonely journey."

"I think you've had experience at this."

Abby shrugged indifferently. So he would rather boil in oil! Piqued she thought of a million other tortures. "If you count the time I watched a donkey's rear being sewed up when a mare took a chunk out of him."

Thorne bellowed out his laughter from her pluck. "I hope you are not comparing me to a donkey's rear. It has the same refined ring as your statement on my attire."

If she wasn't so nervous, she might have admired the fascinating play of muscles that rippled along his ribs and arms. "Quit moving. I can't stitch someone who's so intent on braying. If you must know, I have complete respect for you, Captain. I would never compare you to a donkey's rear," she said, finding it interesting that he hadn't forgotten her slur about the pink satin waistcoat. "It's always the badly dressed that are the most interesting."

She'd never admit otherwise. To do so would fan his vanity. His clothing was perfectly tailored and his bearing well-bred; and somehow, in spite of this polished veneer, he managed very well to resemble a complete and utter pirate.

"I appreciate your benevolence."

He sounded like a vicar now, albeit a sarcastic one. "Your pink lace won't help you win the war, so you might as well play dead.

My advice is to play dead with the ladies, too. You could sit in an oat bin and the mules would even step back." She suppressed a smile.

A vein throbbed at his temple. "If you're finished," he said, his words clipped. Sharp.

She finished stitching and surveyed her work. She wound bandages around his arm, then darting a glance at Thorne, she saw him studying her beneath his dark lashes. She turned away, busied herself with picking up the dirty linen and dishes, neglected from her days caring for Samuel. "This room is a mess. It's a wonder the rats aren't taking bets on who gets the bed."

"Any more compliments, Abe—" he opined, "—and you'll have me blissfully embracing ignorance by stringing you up the yardarm." He struggled to shrug into his shirt.

Abby sighed, then dropped everything to assist him. "You're going to make a mess of those stitches." She retrieved her tray and paused at the door, victory insufficient until she seized the last word. "If your ignorance is bliss, you must be the happiest person alive."

"Where do you think you're going?" Before she could answer, he rudely hauled her back into the room and sat her in a chair. The plates and bowls on the tray clattered and she shielded the cups before they toppled to the floor. The scrape of his chair brought up to hers. "Lessons. You've avoided them the past couple of days."

She plunked the tray on the table with a loud clunk. "I played nursemaid to your crew if you'd noticed."

"I noticed. I'm also grateful. My cabin boy needs a decent education."

Abby snorted. "And you have decided my education?" She didn't want to spend any more time than necessary with the captain. He'd been scrutinizing too much.

"You'll eventually work in my shipyard. You'll need basic reading and ciphering skills."

"Shipyard! Since when do you have a shipyard? I thought you're too busy being a thief." Thorne looked like he was ready to throttle her.

"I do hold an honest occupation. You could be a little more grateful," he warned.

"What do you do in a shipyard?" She was all ears.

"Build ships." He stalked across the room, grabbed a parchment, slapped it on the table and unrolled it.

Abby studied the fine architectural drawing, the skeletal framing of a ship and the finished product. She ran her finger along the drawn hulls, masts and bowsprits. Mindboggling were the numerous details, every peg and screw, right down to the type of wood used for every joint. Thorne's name signed at the bottom with a flourish. Was this his design?

Suddenly shadows of the past haunted her. Memories emerged. As a young girl, she had played hide and seek with Humphrey at the Banfield estate. She had hidden beneath the desk in his father's library and to conceal herself further, had draped charts from the top over her. She had been sure the footsteps drawing near were Humphrey's. Instead the Duke of Banfield, Humphrey's father had discovered her. He pulled the charts away and crooked his finger for her to come out. He never reprimanded her despite the escapades she had involved Humphrey. Abby smiled. The Duke had a soft spot for her. What came to mind was the way he rescued his charts and held them to his heart. Abby had seen what she knew of now as architectural drawings of a ship and Boston printed at the bottom. Was there a connection?

"She'll be the fastest schooner to sail the high seas." He said as proudly as if he'd given birth. Abby nodded, impressed with the magnitude of such a creation and admired the captain's genius as he explained why it was bred to run faster. His excitement was infectious and the deep timbre of his voice grew seductive to a point where Abby leaned into him. She jerked back, a prisoner to her charade.

What was she doing? Her coat chafed at her neck and sweat dribbled down her back. She longed to strip the boyish garb and sink in a long luxurious bath, to rid the bindings cloying her breasts that held her hostage. The refinements of a lady she yearned for, so far away. A little moan escaped and Thorne took it as approval. She swallowed. Lines were blurred and confused. Where did Abe begin and Abby end?

She looked down at the sorry condition of her clothes suddenly ashamed of her wretched appearance. She stank and was filthy, a circumstance she had never had to bear. In the past few months her hair grew stringy and greasy and itched at her neck. To keep her disguise, cutting her hair again was a necessity. Discovering a knife in Thorne's top drawer, she had dragged her feet with the task and practically wept. Alone, she had brought a knife up to her curls but dropped the blade, abhorring the removal of the last vestiges of her former self. Instead she tied her hair back with a leather thong in a queue, adopting the fashion of Thorne and other members of his crew.

Despite her vanishing femininity, the freedoms of a boy allowed her to navigate in a man's world, standing on the deck, enjoying the magic of the night with zillions of stars scintillating in a velvet sky...and Thorne patiently teaching the constellations. Certainly she enjoyed clamoring about the ship, being part of male camaraderie, working and being useful. The status quo of the male world that remained prohibited to females.

Yet those freedoms yielded the chains of a lie. She resented the lad and his unnatural status. Fears escalated. To secure her survival, she forced her mind over her heart to maintain control. Clearly vulnerable, bitterness grew from the insane ruse, her feminine charms stowed beneath the veneer of a cabin boy. She grew wistful, to wear a dress, to whirl on a ballroom floor. How easy to turn her head and receive the rapture of a kiss.

Jacob stood abruptly, retrieving the primer for his student. She followed him with her eyes. Her shoulders dropped. The realization of any kind of relationship with Thorne was impossible. There existed a war between their countries and a social chasm a world apart. If her father were alive, he would never accept him. Thorne settled far beneath her station and was a criminal.

Her hands shook with a future that loomed shadowy and treacherous, the enemy unknown. Questions hammered without resolve. What would she find when she arrived in England? Who would she turn to? Who could she trust?

"Would you like to learn navigation?" he asked her for the second time.

Remaining silent, Abby nodded. Obviously energized by his pupil's attention, Jacob unrolled the charts. Why did he spend so much time on an insignificant orphan boy? He spanned her hand across the map to indicate the expanse of the Atlantic and the distance they had conquered. A connection roared to life within her soul, deeper than before. She jerked her hand away.

Jacob showed no response to her silence, making measurements on the maps. They neared Martinique. She was glad to know they would be landed. Not knowing where they sailed and the uncertainties of the sea and storms, and attack by other ships, preyed on her mind. Hanging over her head was the potential brutality of Thorne if he ever discovered who she was. The retribution to the British Empire placed on her head.

"Pay attention, Abe. I don't think you are as simple as Simeon has claimed."

Hands large and calloused, fingers long and confident stretched over major points of the charts. She struggled to focus on his navigational measurements, adjusting to the lines of latitude and longitude, the measurements he had made of the stars and sun with a sextant, then implementing a new invention, a chronometer that gave accurate time. He used the number of knots recorded when they threw the rope behind the ship to garner their speed. Thorne smiled his lazy pirate smile and her heart fluttered. She frowned and looked at the map, the identifiable land masses sketched in the Caribbean. Some of the details were elusive others tattooed to her memory. A few additional days of instructions and she'd nail the basics.

"Two days' time," he predicted before they reached Martinique.

Chapter 9

Water sloshed over Abby as she struggled under the weight of the bucket she carried. Thorne had ordered a bath for himself. Several trips to his cabin to dump steaming hot water into his tub exhausted her. Never again would she take for granted the servants who carted the water for her bath to her dressing room. Placing the bucket on the floor outside his cabin, she paused with her hand closed on the door latch. Thorne moved about his cabin.

Be quick about it boy, before my water cools," he ordered.

Why didn't he stay on deck until she finished hauling the water? She backed into the room, averting her eyes and placed the bucket next to the tub. Thorne eased into the tub, water sloshing with displacement.

"Hand me the soap off the table." Abby threw him a bar then ducked to leave, too uncomfortable with his nudity…yet drawn to the breadth of his shoulders that surpassed the small tub, a body made perfect of lean hard muscle.

"Where you going boy?"

Abby fidgeted. "What do you need? I'm no nursemaid to scrub your back."

Thorne turned around, his frown as menacing as a dark thundercloud. She retreated to the corner and prayed he did not see the flush rising to her face.

"Abe, you surprise me. Under all that blunt and bluster, you are practically a macaroni. Scrub my back."

Her throat dried. Even if she wanted to speak, her tongue refused to move. Dropping down the belly of a volcano suddenly appealed to her.

"What is taking you so long?" He tossed a sodden sponge over his shoulder.

It soaked her. She measured the distance to the door but he'd have her before she could escape. She studied the planks on the floor, counting the pegs, and compelled her feet to move to the tub. Her arm went numb and for the life of her, she could not raise it. Distantly she heard the ship cut through the waves, the wood creaking, the wind filling the sails.

Conscious of her pulse thudding, she stared at the sponge in her hand. Against all forces, she raised her hand to move in small circles across his back. Muscles flexed beneath her touch powerful and dangerous. Abby drew back, aware of her instincts twitching, flickering in definite warning. Then her hand as if on its own volition, glided down and up his back, making her acutely aware of the heat that radiated from him.

Muddied thoughts imposed the battle with the *Civis* and with single blows Thorne had crushed the merchantmen. Now that menace lurked beneath her palm. It gave her a heady sense of power. The scent of bay soap lifted into the air and was countered by the tang of the sea. She sunk the sponge into the tub. He leaned back, her hand imprisoned by his smooth buttocks. Abby gasped, tugged free then dropped the sponge.

"Take the bucket and rinse my head." His response was curt carried in a cool distant tone.

Abby obliged. He shook his head, water spraying all over the cabin then rose to his full height, towering above her, manly and strong. *Zeus in his perfection. Damn him!* Her insides shook, warring between a world of fascination and her old world of what was chaste and proper. Wickedly mesmerized, she turned away to hide the embarrassment she could no longer mask.

His feet dropped to the floor. He pulled the linen from the bed to dry himself. He yanked on his pants. She stood aware of every movement. Abby darted to the door but a long arm reached out and snatched her collar. Her stomach lurched.

"You aren't leaving until you take a bath. I'm not going to tolerate one more day of your rank smell." The blast of his breath thumped her cheek.

"I ain't taking a bath. It's for peacocks."

The look he sent her should have withered iron, but she was adamant and gave not an inch. With a disgusted snarl, he jerked on his shirt and boots. "I'm going topside to finish measurements. You better be washed or I'll strip you myself and brush you clean to the bone."

He wouldn't dare!

The door slammed behind him and quaked in its hinges. Abby took a deep breath then slammed the bolt into place, pivoting toward the bath. The unexpected prospect of shedding her clothes and submerging in warm water rejuvenated her spirits beyond compare. She nearly ripped the buttons off her wool coat, next her shirt, bindings then shirked off her pants. She eased into the tub. Capturing the sponge in one hand and soap in the other, she scrubbed until her skin tingled fresh and pink eradicating the filth from her body. Her full breasts bobbed freely in the water, tender to the touch from the rude confinement. Someday she'd have the pleasure of burning those bindings. She washed her hair then ducked beneath to free her golden locks of grease and grime. As she settled back to soak, a sigh escaped her lips. How she longed to stay forever.

She spared a glance to the bolt on the door. No. It would not hold back a bellowing bull. With regret, she stepped from the tub and dried herself. She pinched her yellowed and stained shirt between her fingers. She refused to put it back on and let it fall to the floor. She retrieved the key to Thorne's chest, worked at the lock and she flipped it open. Abby's breath caught with the beautiful gowns that filled the trunk. She picked up a beautiful sapphire gown and fingered the satiny folds. Looking in a mirror, she dreamed of wearing the luxurious garment. Were they for really for Thorne's cousin or a paramour? Her throat constricted. Why would she think any different? Was he not a flesh and blood man?

She blew out a breath and reluctantly returned the beautiful gown to the chest. Thinking of the set of events that led her to the present, she stared down at her empty hands. Doubts killed her. Would her family estates still exist or would the state have seized it since no relatives remained? Uncle Cornelius, the Duke of Westbrook. He would use his power and help her.

She covered her face with her hands. Oh—to see her father and brothers again. Guilt rose. Anger and self-loathing lashed her insides. The lie she had fabricated, her father and brothers, her engagement to Humphrey. Self-censure became quicksand. Abby swallowed. To have her old life back, she'd marry Humphrey and please everyone.

Worse yet, emerged the most terrible privation of loneliness and the feeling of being unloved. The very air she breathed felt like long sharp needles. Giving it up, she rifled through Thorne's armoire.

Thorne pounded on the door, leaving her no peace.

"Why is the door locked? Open it now. Why are you so girlish, Abe?"

Abby ripped a shirt off the hanger and stretched her arms through the soft silk. She tripped, stepping into her pants then wrenched on her coat. She bent to unbolt the door then remembered her hat. After retrieving it off the table she plunked it on her head, stuffed the wet ends of her hair beneath. She slammed the chest shut, and then scurried to open the door.

"A woman could dress faster!" Thorne battered the door and Abby opened it, his hand caught mid-air. He glanced to the floor. "Get this mess cleaned up."

To comb his head with a three-legged stool.

Her bindings trailed near the tub. Automatically she pulled her jacket tighter and inched over to kick her discarded shirt over the bindings to hide them. A trial was evident—she was tried and tested and found herself of more common metal than she ever imagined. Thorne plopped on the bed while Abby picked up her things, and then disappeared from the room.

At the top of the stern she gazed out over endless sea. Her bindings were back in place and she had her ration of lemon juice. A wind from the north cooled her cheeks. The tropical sun bore down with its entire wrath. Most of the sailors had shed their shirts, and rolled up their pants, continuing with their chores whistling merry tunes knowing land was not far off. Abby suffered beneath the sweltering wool and watched the capricious waves roll and curl running into the other. The red and white striped flag, *"Don't Tread on Me"* flapped in the breeze, an emblem for the Americans defining magnanimity and courage.

"Land! Martinique!"

The crew shouted in adoration. An island with stiff high peaks of rich forests rippling in waves of lush green. Beaches of golden sand rose from crystal clear waters in bluish and light green shades, palms nodding lazily over it, a sanctuary, untamed and savage.

Like little children the crew whooped carefree and joyful, impatient with lowering sails and rigging as the *Vengeance* glided into sparkling amethyst waters of the harbor. Chains rattled followed by the spray of water as the anchor dropped from the ship. Several sailors dove overboard and swam to shore, their confinement ended.

Simeon had sprained his foot, badly foiling his escape. A cold knot formed in her at leaving her loyal protector but, to remain was unrealistic, and discovery of her sex imminent. Pascale declined to leave ship. To go about a French island and be recognized as an escaped slave invited a death wish. He'd stay behind and care for Simeon. Against their warnings, she ventured unaccompanied, reassuring them that in her present disguise she'd be safe. She smiled. How easy to find a ship to take her home.

Thorne, all dressed up for business, sat opposite her in the boat rowed to shore. How dashing he looked in his navy broad coat with gold trim and brass buttons glinting in the sunlight. She sat with her back to the bow, the oars squeaking in the oarlocks, a windward breeze whipping up and blowing against the back of her head. Seagulls coasted above them, rising-up in a hurtling curve, then diving down into a splash to feed on a school of fish. Abby met him with a grin and memorized every detail of his features.

He caught her staring. She quickly peered over the gunnels to make a study of the corals that branched wildly in the waters beneath. Beyond the reef, the sand shifted empty. To look anymore was meaningless. Her heart tugged. She would miss Thorne and his crew and her brief idyllic sojourn aboard the *Vengeance*.

Chapter 10

Martinique

On the shorefront overlooking the harbor, Abby stopped a man. "Monsieur, I have just arrived in Martinique and learned my father, a businessman from Paris had traveled to England and was taken ill, necessitating me to get to him as soon as possible," Abigail improvised, her fortunate fluidity in French provided a saving grace.

The French émigré shook his head. "Did you not hear of the treaty signed between the American Colonists and France, creating an alliance? England and France are at war! Of course, you have been at sea so would not have this knowledge." He lightly patted her shoulder. "Martinique is under French sovereignty. No ships will be traveling to England." Impatient to be on his way, he pointed to a large white columned building. "There's Governor House, perhaps you could get help from the Governor General."

War? Abby reeled from the state of affairs and bid the man adieu. She passed the enormous blocked walls of a sprawling Fort Royale. The cannons set on the parapets aimed to any invader approaching the harbor, a grim reminder of her vulnerability as a British subject, an enemy of France and the Colonies. How could she have been so naive? She scrambled to grasp the current political leanings that put her smack in the middle of a hornet's nest.

Under the shadow of Fort Royal, she wandered through the narrow streets, thankful Jacob had given her coin. She stopped at a fruit vender to purchase sweet bananas, a welcomed change in the usual fare aboard the ship. Brightly colored cottages yielded to an eclectic collection of larger homes. Some were two-story plantation houses with huge wrap around porches; others were fronted with Greek columns, and others were immense stone edifices with mansard roofs that mimicked traditional French Chateaus.

Enos and several of the crew members had dropped into many of the taverns near the docks. Uncomfortable with that aspect of male doings, Abby pressed forward ignoring their shouts and good cheer that was far from anything she felt now. The sun reached its zenith and she baked in her coat. Beneath the shade of a palm tree, Abby rested on a lava rock, her heart weighted down by her travails. How had things turned out so wretched? She had nowhere to go and no one to turn to.

On the slopes above the city, slaves hummed a somber tune while cutting tall grasses. She swatted at a buzzing dragonfly and inhaled the acrid scent of rotting coconuts scattered on the ground. Remotely she studied the abundance of brightly colored flowers and lush green landscape surrounded by a bright clear bay that held her prisoner. To escape was as impossible as holding the wind in her hat.

Weeping was not an option. She had to get back to England. But how?

She nudged a coconut with her toe and glanced up to see Thorne with his broad shoulders and tricorn hat move down a street of prominent homes, all purpose and business. She and Thorne were a lot alike, both adventurers seeking justice. Thorne's uncle and cousin had been killed by British soldiers, and his other cousin was held a prisoner—all by her country. She understood his hatred of an enemy. She also grasped how that hatred could be focused on her.

King George's malicious neglect of American prisoners of war resulted in starvation, disease and tortuously achieved the same results as hanging, his legacy rooted in cold-blooded suffering. She shivered. *Did she not face a quid pro quo?*

Why wasn't Thorne swilling rum with the rest of his companions? She fought a compulsion to let her mind go onto something new, shrugged, and then gave in to her inclination. She pushed from the rock and followed. One of his long strides equaled two of hers. To make-up the distance, she sprinted, careful to drop out of view when she drew too close. He climbed the steps of a stately yet modest home, knocked and disappeared.

Abby squatted under an array of crimson bougainvillea. *Did he have a paramour awaiting him?* She snatched a papery blossom and crushed it in her hand. Drumming up a series of Abe's insults did nothing to quench her thirst to know. Growing up as a girl in her family, she was shielded from delicate male conversation. She compensated this division with the refined art of eavesdropping, a terrible sin. If she had to pay a penance, it might as well be full-blown atonement.

She scrambled across the street and flanked a porch half-hidden by shrubbery. Briars scratched her wrists as she climbed a flowered trellis and peered through the open window. She considered the beautifully appointed room of wainscoting, paintings and

Queen Anne furniture, obviously owned by someone of wealth. Deep masculine voices in convivial greeting, thundered toward the room, Thorne among them. She swung out of view.

"Any news?" Thorne asked the American representative and businessman, William Bingham. He sat, took a glass of wine, sampled it and waited for Bingham to close the door. Spies were everywhere. The information shared between them was secret, not to be overheard by servants.

"Most of a sensitive nature," said William Bingham.

"As counsel serving the Continental Congress in Martinique, I've been busy gathering information and arranging smuggled shipment of weapons for our army. I enjoy a relationship with the Governor General, friendly with the American cause. The "Privateers of the Rebels," as we are known, are furnished with everything we want and with as much willingness and alacrity as if we were subjects of France. I have a letter from Rachel." William presented a missive.

"How long has it been since you've returned to Boston?" William asked.

"Two years." Thorne said, tearing the envelope open and scanning the contents.

"Much has happened in two years. From my last communication, dated six months ago, Boston Harbor, courtesy of George Washington, is in the hands of the rebels. You need not worry about the murder charges. Rachel has proved an ardent campaigner for your innocence, claiming the charges were falsely asserted by that vile British officer to cover his own wretchedness."

"I must return immediately," Jacob raked his hand through his hair. "I would appreciate your precipitous administration in unloading the cargo I captured. I plan on sailing immediately."

"Bad news?"

"My cousin, Ethan attempted to escape and is facing possible execution. There is hope for a prisoner exchange with a captured British Colonel in Boston. With the chaotic and inconsistent prisoner exchanges, Rachel recommended I manage the trade personally."

"I am sorry, but I caution you of the risks. Four out of five of our men die on the prison hulks the Brits have anchored in New York Harbor. You are our most valued captain and I'd hate to hear of you captured." William leaned forward. "Recent events would hearten you to hear our cause has improved. France has discreetly sent us a large quantity of war supplies. With the new alliance, I expect soldiers, supplies and their *Navy*. There is talk of an additional alliance with Spain."

Abby inhaled sharply, the heavy scent of jasmine from the vine tickled her nose. If two superpowers and the Colonies aligned against England, the results spelled disastrous consequences for her country. An uncontrollable sneeze burgeoned. Abby pinched her nose. She gasped. Her breath hitched. *Achoo!*

She jerked back. The trellis gave way. Her back slammed into the ground. Breath whacked from her lungs. She struggled to suck air. Dazed she pushed at the tangle of cloying flowers and thorns and scampered to her feet. Her hands kneaded her chest, willing the air to fill her lungs. She stumbled to get her hat and rammed it on her head.

William stared, but it was the fury etched in Thorne's face that set her feet into a flat out run. She glanced over her shoulder. Thorne catapulted from the open window.

"Abe!"

Where to hide? She zigzagged through a labyrinth of streets. Buildings whizzed in a blur of repetition. She pulled up in an alley and hid in the shadows. Thorne passed. One. Two. Three. She bolted in the opposite direction and knocked a woman to the ground. Amidst a barrage of curses, Abby pulled her up. With her cane, the old woman struck her. Thorne pivoted. Too late. Abby let go of her arm and the woman flailed like a windmill in an ocean of skirts.

Thorne's shadow covered hers, his breath hot on her ear. She dodged in front of a horse carriage and tripped. The horses reared. Hooves clawed the air. Frozen, Abby held her arm up, waiting to be crushed.

"You little fool!" Jacob grabbed the reins and yanked downward to control the beasts. Abby rolled away. The carriage owner uttered a stream of oaths then snatched his whip high to beat her. Thorne seized the whip and flung it. The enraged Frenchman pelted Thorne with curses.

Opportunity prevailed and she outdistanced Thorne. Darting up a street, she plunged into a tavern and peeked between the louvers of a shuttered window. Gulping in heaps of air, she waited until her breathing evened. She wiped the moisture from her brow with her sleeve and lamented her terrible curiosity and spying on Thorne. She massaged the stitch in her side, debating the lesser of two evils, imprisonment with the Governor General of Martinique or Captain Thorne?

A large hairy arm snaked around her waist. "Look what we have here, brothers," he hailed his comrades in French. "An urchin to entertain us. Yvette!" He barked. "Show us some sport and deflower the lad."

The patrons roared their approval. Rough hands plied Abby's coat. She scratched and bit her captors. If they discovered her sex, she'd be raped. Tossed onto a table, her legs and arms secured, she thrashed and ground out French expletives, heightening their hilarity. She yanked her foot, and escaping its bond, dispatched a well-aimed kick. The sailor crumpled. His companions guffawed. The hairy ape tossed a bag of coins to Yvette, a red painted woman; the most outrageous female Abby had ever laid eyes on.

Yvette slid from her chair and sashayed toward them, affecting an exaggerated roll of her hips. The men lolled mesmerized. She twirled a black lock of hair in her finger and pouted before the ape, thrusting her overabundant cleavage in his chest. Her black eyes flashed. "Who's to say I desire a lad when I can have a man like you?"

The ape colored fiercely. His companions slapped his back. Yvette turned and ran a finger down Abby's face. "Hm-m? I ravish a beardless boy. It will cost you more." She trilled her demand and weighted the bag in her hand. Coins threw through the air, landing on top of Abby. Someone scratched a bow across a violin and a lively tune began. Yvette danced around the table, plucking the coins from Abby and tucked them in the space between her massive breasts.

Like a Pied Piper she drew them, prolonging her performance. Abby pleaded with her eyes. The prostitute simply smiled, widening her circle, sinuously dancing between the sailors then out of their reach. The men frothed with her antics. Yvette whirled, her black hair a cloud around her shoulders. They pounded the table and stomped their feet, increasing the crescendo of shouting, deafening Abby.

Yvette snapped her fingers in the air. The sailors ceased. "Bring the boy to my chambers. He is a babe and will take coaxing. When he is a man—" She heaved her breasts with an inflated sigh. "We will return."

Several sailors lifted Abby high over their heads. The ape stopped the procession. Yvette lowered her hand to his manhood and halted his belligerence. "Later, my love."

A grinning fool, he stepped back and let the parade pass. Up the stairs and into a room they went, whereupon they hurled Abby onto a broad unmade bed lumped with dirty linens. The men vanished. She heard a key click, turning the lock from the outside. Yvette barred a plank to secure the door from the inside then peeled off her clothes, coins falling to the floor.

Abby held up her hand to ward off the unthinkable as Yvette scooped up her bounty. "You don't understand."

"I understand perfectly. A relationship with a woman? No. My motivations are mercenary. I have bartered a fortune and I'm going to retire for an early night."

"How-how did you know?" Abby leaped from the bed.

"I know many things. I know men are stupid." She opened her shutters to let in the fresh air. "In a few minutes, they will be deep in their rum. I will moan and jump on my bed. They will be amused." She threw Abby a coin. "You will need it English."

Abby's mouth dropped open. "You knew?"

"Your accent is good but not perfect." Yvette waved her to the balcony. "You can leave. The vine is sturdy and goes to a back alley. Adieu."

"Wait. I've been kidnapped and taken aboard an American privateer's ship, the *Vengeance.* I need your help. Is there any way you could get two letters to England...one to my father—" her breath caught, hoping against hope he was still alive, "—and one to a family friend," Abby pleaded, her eyes beseeching the woman. The French prostitute did not have to do her any favors.

Yvette sighed. "I am a sucker for hard luck cases. There are writing materials in my vanity. I will see what I can do."

Abby wrote the letters, sealed the envelope with wax and kissed the prostitute on the cheek. "Thank you."

She had found a grace in the darkest of places. The prostitute blushed. Abby sat on the balcony, flipped her legs over and planted a foot in the vine to test the strength. If only the ground was not so far.

But she could do this. The masts on the *Vengeance* were higher. She swung out. She stared at her handholds, inching down. From the bottom of the balcony there was an eight foot drop. Her feet dangled. She clung and hoped she did not injure an ankle. Abby closed her eyes, swaying like a dead leaf in a winter wind, terrified to let go. Her arms ached, her hands grew clammy. She had climbed the mast of a ship. Why did she fear this small leap? Abby gasped, losing her grip. She fell in a whoosh, caught in strong arms.

Abby opened her eyes and quailed.

"Captain Thorne!"

"Precisely."

Chapter 11

Abby remained stubbornly mute, visually recalling every inch of their journey to the *Vengeance,* terrified, then humiliated, the spectacle Thorne had made hauling her through the streets and down to the beach, catching the eye of every citizen of Martinique. No one had dared to cross the wrath of the American.

"I should blister your backside," Thorne said, staring her down. His neck muscles were corded so tight she thought he'd explode.

The sun had set and she chafed, listening to his constant upbraiding in tune with the scrape of oarlocks, his hands a death-grip on the oars, rowing her to the ship, his captive again. On deck, Pascale and Simeon darted worried glances to one another. One look at their Captain's menacing expression confirmed the hazard of voicing objection. No chance of support from either of them. Thorne grabbed her arm, prodded her down the companionway then thrust her into his cabin. Was it possible his scowl grew more ominous?

"I'm not listening to your lame excuses. The crew will be ordered to keep you locked up where I know you won't be tempted to spy. Your chicanery has cost me."

"You think I care about your treason and stupid war," she bit out, tired of Thorne's bullying. Beyond the transom windows, the coast dimmed a dark purple smear in the waning light. She plunked her hands in her coat pocket and gauged the distance to shore.

"Don't even try it," he read her mind. "The sharks will find you a tempting repast."

Her nostrils flared. "I wasn't spying." She rubbed her bruised arm and wished she could groan her misery in her own natural tones.

"I can't imagine why you were poking around the very house I had to do business. Tomorrow you will give full explanation." He jerked on his coat. "I'm going to finish my affairs then I'm going to seek some overdue pleasure."

Pleasure? Abby folded her arms across her flattened bosom. "I don't care a whit what beasts you visit or what pox you bring back. Don't keep me up all night with your scratching and wailing."

He took a step toward her and she shrank. "I should have listened to my earlier intuitions and had you tossed overboard. My charity, a penalty for picking up lost strays." He smoothed on bay oil for his night out.

Why did it rile her?

Angry as she was of his mistreatment, she regarded his face in the deep dusk and soft yellow glow of candlelight. It sometimes surprised her just how striking he was. She didn't like standing so close, not when he smelled so fresh and spicy, and she had the awful odor of rancid grease to her hair. Self-consciously she tugged down her hat. The contrast between them was excruciatingly painful when she allowed herself to forget that he was a traitor and remembered he was a man and she, a young woman. When he glanced at her unkempt appearance, she shrugged her shame.

"I suppose you must marinate in it to catch what you're trolling for." Her derisive gaze swept him from the toe of his polished boot to his handsome head.

His lips flattened into a snarl. "Tonight you will forego victuals and tomorrow there will be triple the chores…and that's just the beginning of your punishment. I'll be reminded in the future to resist the temptation to trust a snooping rat." He slammed the door. The lock rattled.

"It's the little ones that have the worst bite!" She pounded the door, her words wasted on his booted steps, stomping up the companionway. She kneaded the muscles in her neck, fixated on all the injustices she suffered. Her stomach rumbled and, like water down a drain, her confidence flowed away. *Failure.* Martinique proved to be a catastrophe. Now Jacob was convinced she was a spy. The cost of her prying drew her further away from England and attached to it, hopelessness grew. In a day or two she'd be on her way to Boston, embedded in the middle of enemy territory and plummeting deeper into a war that was none of her concern.

She collapsed on Thorne's bed. It would be a matter of time before her identity would be discovered. She covered her face with a pillow unable to banish the nightmare. Pascale knew. The perceptive, Yvette had picked up on her disguise. How long before the shrewd Captain Thorne realized his cabin boy was a woman? Abby flinched. Thorne shoved off from the side of the ship, to some harlot greedy for coin. Without a doubt, she conceded, Yvette was right. Men were stupid creatures.

Abby tossed the pillow aside and rose. Thorne's rowing to shore ebbed, leaving the evening laden with the desolate sound of waves lapping against the hull. A windward breeze cooled the cabin and she drew near the transom windows where light fell from the soft silvery radiance of the moon. Surrounded by a million stars, the somber moon was fated to be anything like it in the night sky. She was a prisoner, trapped by a rebel, and lonely, so miserably alone and forlorn, a sharp ache scored deep within her chest. Never had she known such confinement. The trilling brightness of a whore's laughter amusing Thorne made the walls close in on her, threading through her head and turning the room into a torture chamber.

There was a plus side to Thorne's departure. She was unrestricted for the night. She stripped off her hat, coat, shirt and bindings. Released from the bonds, she massaged her aching breasts. From a bucket of clean water, she bathed and washed her hair. Standing in front of a mirror, she stared back with misty eyes, combing her hair until it dried. She found no comfort in what she saw. The solitary figure in the silvery glass looked more like a young woman than her usual attire allowed. Her breasts were more rounded with maturity and better diet. The light shoulder length hair she had refused to cut and tied back in a queue was released from its leather thong and curled softly.

Abby's eyes roamed to the chest that held so many beautiful gowns. Gowns he had procured for his cousin in Boston. A strange yearning to dress in something pretty and ladylike, to be treated as a woman, beckoned her. Oh, to be able to smile and laugh with her own feminine joyfulness, instead of having to curb the softer looks and lower her voice to a deepness that made her throat ache.

The guise of stripling cabin boy commanded the charade she must play. Each day bred its own repugnance. To don those wretched clothes and assume the male persona grew more grueling. Little by little, the masquerade had stripped her of her womanhood.

With a cry, she moved to the chest and flung it open, revealing a rich array of gowns. She donned the splendid sapphire with the low-cut bosom, barely modest, and smoothed her fingers over the fine silk. Even without undergarments, the material sinfully molded to her.

In her mind she observed the tall, lean form of Captain Thorne swoop past, and on his arm, a woman elegantly dressed. His face was animated and attentive as he wooed the lady, and on bended knee he vowed his love. The woman's hand extended as if bequeathing knighthood upon the handsome head, and his lips marked the slim fingers and traced a path along the bare, white arm. The vision broadened and the full red lips he kissed became the countenance of a seedy whore.

The dream in which "Abe" could share no part vanished. Doubts beat a wild tattoo. The walls of her beliefs, like thistledown in the wind, blew away and disappeared. Boyish. Distasteful. Unappealing. She shook her fist to the heavens, then lowered her hand and stared at an empty palm. Nothing. Nothing dissuaded fate's lot.

Yawning, she stepped from the gown, folded it and returned the garment to the chest. She donned a clean shirt from Thorne's drawer, her unwitting benefactor. She sighed with the luxury of sleeping with the silk against her swollen breasts. With certainty, he would not return this evening lost in the arms of some licentious strumpet. Abby kicked her offending garments to the far corners of the room then wiped tears from her cheeks. Exhaustion from the nerves and disappointment of the day overcame her. She settled on her pallet, allowing a fitful sleep.

Did the watch bell ring? Abby lifted heavy eyelids. The night swathed in black velvet yielded to a waxing moon and showered the room bright as day. A muffled thump and a woman's chirruping laughter startled her into full awareness. Two people moved down the companionway. A crew member and his strumpet? The captain would have the sailor's gullet filleted for bringing a doxy on board. But who was she to interfere? Abby put her hands over her ears to lock out their amorous murmurings. The lock jiggled. The door flew open.

Thorne. Of course. He staggered into the cabin. Drunk. The whore kissed him then slipped off his coat. She tossed it on the desk. Charts fluttered to the floor.

"Wait while I lock the door," purred the whore, her French accent, promising erotic indulgences.

"Ah, Lucky Lucette, bring me to heaven," Thorne slurred, attempting to focus.

Abby's ears scorched. Huddled in darkness, she lay rooted to her pallet. Drat! Why did the randy fool have to come back to the *Vengeance?* There was no way to escape. Stupid. If only she had not scattered her clothes. Her bindings lay in a heap under Thorne's desk. Her pants peeked out from beneath the bed. Where was her coat?

"Lucky Lucette?" Reeking with rum, Thorne wobbled. He raised his hand by the bed, had difficulty completing the task then dropped it. His eyes lighted when Lucette plucked off her blouse, and took his hands to ply her massive breasts tipped with dark areoles and tight nipples.

Abby's breath quickened. She knew she should look away but froze, fascinated. Mesmerized she touched her own breasts beneath the silk shirt. Her nipples hardened.

Lucette danced away from him. The whore lifted a bottle of rum from the table and returned to Thorne. "Pleasure yourself with refreshment, Captain." She rubbed her rounded breasts up against him as she poured the liquid into his mouth. Thorne fell on his bed and pushed the bottle away. The strumpet leaped atop him and squealed her delight, her skirts hitched up over her hips, revealing the dark hairs of her mound.

Abby's skin flushed with the erotic display. Her nostrils flared, the two intruders unaware of a witness to their love-making. She must leave. Except strolling half-naked on deck was not an option.

"You're a big fellow, like a bull in his pen too long." She clenched her hand over his manhood and squeezed. He groaned as she wriggled off. With skill she removed his shirt. In two successive thuds, his boots hurled to the floor. She coaxed more rum down Thorne's throat.

Abby peered from beneath the covers.

Lucette unbuttoned his pants and tugged them off. "Captain! How you impress me! You are a banquet to be devoured." She ran her fingers up and down his chest.

Thorne snored.

Abby narrowed her eyes when the whore enticed him to drink again. Abby didn't know how much Thorne had downed but clearly, he was in his cups and would not wake for a long time. The whore pressed to his lips the near empty bottle, lifting his head and prodding him to drink. The liquid dribbled from his mouth.

Warning instincts clanged. Thorne could drown. Abby rose. She edged behind the harlot. Her fingers searched for the drawer with a knife hidden inside. The same knife she had contemplated cutting her hair with.

From eavesdropping on her older brothers, she had learned of a whore's trick to inebriate their customers, rob and sometimes kill them so they would not be identified. Despite her war with Thorne, he lay defenseless. He needed her protection. Her toe hit the bucket of water she used to bathe and she smothered a groan. Did the whore hear her?

Lucky Lucette slapped his face and laughed. "You mindless, captain. You will not know what hit you."

Abby watched while Lucette search through his coat, and then his trousers, stuffing coins and papers into a pilfered pillowcase. The whore put on her blouse and reached beneath her skirt.

"I always carve a farewell into my customers."

Abby's breath caught a flash of light. The whore raised her hand. A knife gleamed. Abby picked up the bucket.

Water drenched the whore. She came up sputtering and turned to her assailant with a snarl knotted on her lips. "You bitch! Where did you come from?"

"I watched your contemptible ruse," Abby growled. "You're a thief."

With her booty clutched to her chest, the whore swung her knife. Abby reared. The blade swiped an inch from her face. She crouched then rammed the table into the whore. Lucette fell back onto the bed next to Thorne. Not where Abby wanted her. The cabin yielded far too narrow. Abby took a tentative step back. She stretched her hand behind her. The whore landed on her feet. Abby opened the drawer and prayed Thorne had not removed the knife, her eyes trained on her opponent.

Lucette shoved the table aside and sneered. "I will carve your face before I plunge my blade into your heart."

Moisture beaded on Abby's lip. Her fingers trembled, rifling the contents of the drawer. She inhaled. Her hand seized upon the hilt. Lucette rushed her. Abby sidestepped and put out her foot. The whore tripped and slammed onto the floor. Her bag flew. Abby kicked the whore's prize where it clanged against a far wall. Lucky Lucette twisted, and with a ferocious roar, jumped to her feet, tossing her knife from hand to hand.

Abby revealed her knife. "Leave and we will forget this ever happened."

Lucky Lucette's eyes widened. "I'll not leave until I have what belongs to me."

Thorne groaned. Was he hurt? Abby glanced to him. The whore dove to pick-up her bag. With trained ease, Abby threw her knife. The blade pierced the whore's hand, pinning her to the floor. Lucette cried out. Her weapon clattered to the planks.

Abby kicked Lucette's knife under the bed. With a wary eye on her opponent, Abby pulled out the blade and unbolted the door and hissed, "Get out!"

Suddenly Pascale filled the doorway, his eyes as big as silver thalers, assessing the chaos in the cabin.

"Pascale, heave this thief from the ship!"

Lucette gripped her bloody appendage, pleading and begging to be rowed to shore.

Abby shoved the whore from Thorne's room, glad to be rid of the vermin. "Don't ever let me set eyes on you again, Lucky Lucette. Next time, my mark will be more lethal." Abby pointed her knife at Lucette. The whore scrambled up the ladder faster.

Grinning, Pascale gave her a full salute. "The captain still does not see you are a woman? What will happen when he discovers his cabin boy to be a femme fatale?"

Abby shrugged with Pascale's nonsensical opinion of her. The hem of Thorne's shirt grazed her knees. Heat rose fiercely to her face. Abby's hand flew to her mouth. She slammed the door.

Pascale chuckled from the other side. "Mademoiselle, you face death and you worry about inconveniences."

Abby leaned against the back of the door and frowned at Thorne. *Inconveniences!* She blew her hair out of her eyes, resisting the urge to throttle Thorne. Unconscious, the hounds of hell would not wake him. After surveying the mess in the room, she righted the table and lit a candle. She wiped Lucette's blood from the floor and, pinching the rum bottle between two fingers, she deposited the offending liquid outside the door. Gathering her bindings and pants she dropped them on her pallet.

Where was her coat? She scanned the room. The corners of the worn garment peeked out from beneath Thorne. She sighed. To retrieve her coat was another matter. Abby averted her eyes and tugged. Impossible. She lifted his legs onto the bed then rolled him to his side. The garment didn't budge. If only Thorne weren't so heavy. She pursed her lips. What to do? The plunk of oars in water indicated Pascale rowed Unlucky Lucette to shore. Simeon with his present infirmity could not negotiate the stairs let alone lift Thorne.

No. She could not do this. Handling Jacob was like handling a lightning bolt. Why had she been so stupid to throw her clothes around?

The candle sputtered and in the wavering luminescence, Thorne's bronze-hued skin showed dark against the linens. The long, muscular form was superbly proportioned, with broad shoulders tapering to narrow hips and lean thighs, and a furring of hair dwindling to a thin line that traced downward over his flat belly. Her face grew hot. Abby looked away. She could do this, couldn't she?

She climbed onto his bed, wedged her knee along his back. Abby closed her eyes, his skin warm and intimate against hers. A low moan passed his lips.

Abby's eyes flew open. Did he wake?

Jacob rolled to his back carrying her with him. His arm flopped out like a child, his eyes closed. Rum! He'd sleep well into the next day. Tomorrow he'd be roaring like a lion with a thorn in its paw, trumpeting the mother of all hangovers. Good for him!

A shaft of light streamed from the stern and illuminated his face. Did she dare touch him?

The captain was the kind of man who dealt with revenge.

Desire won over common sense. Helpless against the yearning woman side of Abby, she traced the fine line of his jaw, the stubble rough to her fingertips. She continued her exploration and ran a finger down his fine aquiline nose then outlined his lips, compelled by his classic beauty as a man, the chiseled appeal of some long lost Roman warrior. She smiled, intoxicated with the heady sense of touching him.

Did an immortal dare trifle with a God?

Awareness of him filled every pore of her being. Kneeling beside him, his bare, hot flesh next to hers, she dared to stroke both her palms down his throat where a pulse throbbed, and then across the broad expanse of his chest. A crackle of energy, hot, raw and carnal heated from the muscles that rippled with her caress. Power surged, gliding her hands down his sculpted abdomen as if saying the word, the seas would rise.

How often had she lain on the pallet, watching him dress when he thought *Abe* was asleep? To wash him in the tub, to run a wet sponge down his back as the dirty, filthy, ragged cabin boy…this was far different…Thorne's oblivion, and the anonymity of the night, giving her the wicked freedom to explore him.

With a flash, the specter of the whore intruded. Abby curled her fingers, her nails, pressing half-moons into her palms. Anger warred with the strange excitement that pulsed through her veins.

Distant memories flooded…the evening at her ancestral home. To be kissed by Jacob Thorne roused reckless and dizzy sensations.

Meandering in her mind like an onrushing stream was the delicious vision in the garden. He had leaned forward and, in one swift movement covered her mouth with his own. If only he had not kissed her so senseless. The taste of his mouth, silky and warm, lingered like a sunrise, extravagant and full of promise. She gave her head a little shake.

She tugged her coat, but the buttons caught on the other side of him. Damn. If only she could shout her frustration. Abby yanked with such force Thorne woke. With a growl he grabbed her shirt. Her mouth opened under the stare of narrowed cobalt eyes.

No! Abby pushed on his chest. All the slack from her shirt was pulled up in his fists. Cool air brushed her naked thighs. Taking a deep breath, she shoved and gave a mental curse at her stupidity for blundering with nothing on but a silk shirt.

Jacob frowned very much aware of the woman on top of him, though the lingering intoxicants clouded his brain. His mind slowed and listed like a ship with spent sails and could find no reason for why a woman persisted to struggle in his grasp. Was he in a brothel or was this a dream? Dumb as a sheep, he could not fathom where he was, or how he got there.

He narrowed his eyes. He dare not let her go. The enchantment would vanish as the foam on the sea. He gripped her tighter, the shirt in his hand ready to rip. He rather liked that idea.

"Who are you?" He chafed at the thickness of his tongue. "A sea nymph?" His mind worked as if a door were set ajar, into some unseen world. Was it magic that allowed him this lovely companion? Who was he to argue? After all, it had been some time since he had the pleasures of intimate companionship, and his body's most primal instinct kicked in with a vengeance. Surely no significant mental prowess on his part was necessary to fulfill his hunger. His wit, though numb, was rather logical and having discovered a reason, savored it with relish.

He feasted on her form and lovely face while his mind raced for answers. There yielded no recollection. He shook his head to clear the cobwebs, unable to get over a face so beautifully blinding. Certainly he would remember who she was? Her hair, a rich glowing gold, paler in the faltering candlelight and although short, curled softly about her shoulders. Her features were flawless, her nose straight and delicately boned. Beneath soft light brows, her eyes were a baffling blue. And he imagined, when between sunlight and starlight, held endless shades of azure, from periwinkle to the dazzling blues of a summer sky. Under his warming perusal, her creamy skin blushed.

To take things slow with this beauty would be a penance. His cock throbbed. The more she fought, the harder he got. She breathed hard and the movement gave a tantalizing glimpse of rounded breasts outlined by the soft silk she wore. He resisted the urge to bury his face between her breasts and suckle her nipples until they rose firm and taut.

"You are drunk. Let me go," she begged.

Her voice, a siren's song was vague and familiar. Jacob's mind gathered through a soft haze, like a mermaid's dream, floating over ships and sea. Let her go? Never. He smiled. "Never will I let you vanish." She stilled when he touched her lips with his finger. "You are tender as the flush of a rose petal and delicate as the light of a solitary star."

Abby rolled her eyes. He was reciting poetry to her. His words held no credibility. Of course, the rum talked. To escape was impossible, to brazen out the situation was the only possible solution. His confusion, apparent, Abby played upon it, her quick wit shaping a plan. Through the rough talk of sailors, she had learned things that set her ears to fire.

Her teasing laughter broke the silence of the cabin and she was thankful the shadows that hid her near state of undress. "Surely, I need to remove my garment before we can continue, Captain?" She mimicked the sweetly-smoothed purr of a French courtesan and he halted. The deception proved simple enough. Could she play this part as successful as that of a scruffy cabin boy?

Thorne eased his grip, and she guessed from his expression, he was attempting to comprehend, yet the strength of his fingers clasped her still, wary she would evaporate. "I could never forget or forgive myself if I let you go."

"En amour on pardonne mais on n'oublie jamais." In love, we forgive but we never forget. Abby whispered in perfect French, not that Thorne would understand a word of it. He did not know French.

"Hurry my beautiful nymph."

Beautiful? Of course, the rum again, his mind was sluggish. Abby's feet slipped to cold hard planking. She assessed the time to grab her bindings and pants and flee.

A traitorous shaft of golden light penetrated the silk she wore and laid bare her soft curves before his eyes. Thorne groaned. Lust flared through his eyes and he snatched her shirt in his fists and hauled her into bed. Two buttons ripped off as she knelt beside him. Her breasts exposed to his heated glare. "Do you think I'd let you disappear?" He was obviously rather pleased with his logic, betrayed by an irresistible boyish grin. Her heart dipped.

"Really, Captain," She rested a hand on his chest and pushed him back, conscious her bottom lay bare where he pulled the slack from her shirt. "You need your rest. There's a chill in the air, and you'll surely catch your death," she told him as he attempted to focus on her face. "I've an errand to run. I won't take long. I'll be back."

Abby grinned at her own cleverness. There was no errand, of course, but in his drunken state, he'd be happily dozing soon after she left him.

He reeled her in like a fish caught on a fly, clutching her shirt until she was an inch from his face, the idea clearly not to his liking. "It's been a long time since I've been with one so fair, and..." he could not finish the sentence.

Abby patted his shoulder. "You rest yourself a moment, Captain," Abby coaxed, trying to ply the folds of material from his fingers, anything to gain more material to cover her nakedness. "I must be about my duty."

Thorne cursed. Abby looked at him in surprise, not daring to speak. Her heart pounded. Her blundering knowledge of men flew in the face of ignorance. This was not a flirtatious parlor game.

"I demand a kiss," he countered huskily, "so as not to grow weary of the wait." He pulled her hard against his torso. Her breasts smashed against his chest. Her nipples hardened with the contact and his huge swollen arousal seared against her feminine center. "Give a poor sailor a sampling of your wares that I might better anticipate your return."

The seductive whisper stroked her like a soft, warm caress. Had it not been for the incessant pressure of his body sweeping away any feeling of confidence, Abby would have smiled in relief. Yet Thorne rose far too bold to tolerate even the slightest degree of security. He laid his hand on her bottom and pressed her to him and she became acutely aware of her inexperience. His body was on fire, desire pulsed through his swollen, rigid flesh. Her instincts reeled and like a bird caught in a cage, flight rose futile. A well-versed courtesan would not react in shock nor repulse a kiss. If only, she had a way out. Abby ventured an uncertain path.

She bent to meet his lips, his dark eyes a wicked gleam in the ghostly moonlight, his lean features starkly etched. An inexplicable feeling flickered within her breast, and she halted briefly with the rising excitement that thickened in her belly. With renewed courage, she drove it down. Of course, she could do the deed, and then go.

A light teasing kiss, just enough to satisfy his needs. He crushed his mouth to hers like he wanted to devour her, flaming her with a heat that seared along her spine and curled her toes. She closed her eyes, reveling in the strength of his embrace, the rum taste of his mouth, the hard pressure of his loins, yielding discernment that this was a strong, virile man, treating and desiring her like a woman. Would she faint?

Through a haze, she lifted her head. In the silence that passed between them, she breathed unsteadily. “You are tempting, Captain. I must go. I will return.”

He frowned like a child, his favorite toy taken away. Except he was no child. “No more?”

Abby swallowed. Her brain clouded with sensuality until recognition dawned. A tingling swept up the back of her neck and across her face. She managed to give him a tantalizing taste of her honey-smooth laughter. “In time, Captain…good things come in time.”

Jacob’s glare lessened. “Promise?” he murmured against her ear and brushed his lips against her throat.

Abby’s stomach lurched. She felt as if her body was as tight as a drumhead. What was happening to her? For the past weeks, he considered her nothing but a ragamuffin, seeing no trace of her womanhood. The fool! Well, she would give his besotted mind a taste of her contempt.

Every bit as raw and blatant as it was seductive she forced a demand from his lips. Her hands plunged into his hair, pulling his head closer. Thorne’s arms crushed her full against him, and his mouth turned across hers, invading, demanding, taking hers with a sensual, leisure thoroughness. His hand slipped up to cup her head while he greedily devoured her moist, lips. His hard chest pressed against the peaks of her breasts and sent pleasure so sharp it was almost painful. His fingers stroked the shortness of her hair and even in his befuddled state—she *knew* he ached for more.

Abby’s limbs trembled with the intoxicating potion of his hot-blooded kiss. His tongue passed slowly along her parted lips, then invaded to explore, leisurely, dreamily possess. Reality fled from her grasp. No need to struggle. His thirst would be quenched, she rationalized, and he could sleep the entire night in his bed. For this moment, she settled in those broad, wished-for arms, and allowed the woman in her to experience the embrace of a man. But not just any man.

Captain Thorne.

Thorne loosened his crushing embrace and Abby's arms trembled as she supported herself. His fingers brushed ardently down the side of her throat and suddenly inside the yoke of her shirt. He unfastened the last remaining buttons and feasted his eyes on her swollen breasts. Abby gasped. Cool air touched her and what she saw there paralyzed her. The eyes that met hers were not hooded but fully alert, and smoldering with heat. The pressure of his muscled thighs beneath her quickened her heart.

She struggled to move away from him. The threat loomed too real. "Captain Thorne, your eagerness astounds me. I'll be on my way and return in a short while." He caught her round the waist and rolled her beneath him.

A crooked grin crossed his face. "I know without a doubt that once I release a maiden of the sea, she will forever fade from my reaches, an illusion that is not real."

If love is nothing but an illusion, then what is real? "Si l'amour n'est qu'une illusion alors qu'est-ee que la re'alite'?" she said huskily, trying to distract him with assurances of more if he let her go. Abby pushed on his chest, the weight of his body covering her and her defenselessness to muscle and sinew that had been honed on drawing up heavy sails and lugging hefty cargo. She struggled and the full result of his intentions came clear. Her shirt open, and her bare thighs nudged apart, brushed with the scorching heat of his manhood.

Thorne laughed and his dark head swooped down and kissed her. No longer was he in a crippling stupor. His tongue thrust hard into her mouth.

Abby turned her head to the side. "Release me!" She shoved and wiggled to the edge from beneath him.

From her command, he raised on his forearms, Abby's body aware of his ardor pressed to her thighs. She rolled and came to her feet on the floor. She had every intention to keep right on going, but her breath was jerked from her abruptly as he halted her flight. The tail of her shirt firmly twisted in his grasp. The top cut into her shoulders. Desperately, Abby shrugged and yanked one arm free. The shirt coiled tightly about her other arm and held her captive. Adrenaline leaped through her veins. She crouched and braced her feet against his effort to haul her back. On his side, Thorne could not pivot to pull her nearer. With her free hand, Abby yanked at the twisted silk, while Thorne fought to disengage his arm in the tangled bedding.

"Please," Abby managed to purr silkily, concealing her panic. "Release me to administer my duties. I vow to return." Her arm slid from the fabric...almost free. She tasted victory. In warm seductive tones, she cajoled, "Your patience will be rewarded, my Captain, until then—"

The shirt slipped. She was free! But so was Thorne! His arm flew out, catching her elbow with a strength she had not imagined possible in one so inebriated. She pried at his fingers. He drew her toward him and any chance of escape vanished with the silk shirt that pooled to the floor. He drew her down upon him, and her body tensed, his manhood hard and thick pressed with urgency against her thighs. He rolled her beneath. His dark head lifted and buried his face in the valley between her breasts. Warm hands cupped her swollen breasts, freed from their bindings, weighing the mounds like treasured bags of gold. His thumbs scraped lightly over her rigid nipples and her breath caught in her throat. He drew one nipple at a time in his mouth lathing a hot torturous path with his tongue. A shuddering excitement passed through her, and the strength from her limbs melted away.

Raising his head, he stared down into her eyes. "You are the most beautiful creature I've ever laid eyes upon. I demand to have you, now."

Abby shook her head in denial. Fear mixed with the heady pleasure of a rock hard body pressing down on hers. Her eyes open, she whispered huskily into his ear. "I must go."

"I've paid the night and will see the transaction completed."

Abby licked her lips and seized the opportunity. "But Captain... therein lays the problem. You have not paid."

He frowned, though disappointed, refused to let go of his prey. Debate measured in those hard, flint-like eyes. He kept her pinned and reached over to his side drawer and produced a bag of gold. He showered the contents on her. The clink of cold coins gleamed on her skin then slid to the bed. "A hundred night's worth," he triumphed.

"Please, Captain, I beg you. I simply can't—"

"Jacob." His husky whisper commanded.

"Jacob." Her own whisper filled with dread. His eyes glittered down at her dangerously, and his mouth curved into a satanic smile. Abby turned her head aside and closed her eyes. His mouth grazed her cheek, and then his hand was beneath her chin, forcing her head around until his mouth covered hers, his tongue prying her trembling lips apart. A strange heat began to pulsate in her loins. His hands moved down her side, curved over her hips and squeezed her buttocks. He nudged his knee between her clamped knees. The burning heat of his staff touched her intimately, intruding the soft womanly folds of her flesh. Distinct warmth flooded the area between her legs.

"Oh! She moaned and frantically pushed at him. She heaved beneath him and he laughed, dipped his head and suckled her breast. His fingers slicked against one small, sensitive piece of flesh at the core of her, replaced with the unrelenting pressure of her tight, resisting flesh and she heaved beneath him, straining against the broad expanse of chest. "Jacob, listen to me—"

He lifted her hips and rammed his length into her. A burning violent pain exploded in her loins. "Stop!" Abby pressed her face against the base of his neck, biting her lip until she tasted blood, while tears trickled down her cheeks. His mouth all but consumed her and he kissed her so thoroughly and possessively that the pain of the intrusion began to lessen. Leisurely, languidly his lips gave her pleasure and with each passing moment, alien budding warmth grew within Abby, a feeling she could not deny. She responded to his wild, ardent kisses and her arms crept about him, holding him close, the ever-present, throbbing heat of him set her to fire. He began to move and groaned as her body arched, offering more.

With one hand he lifted and kneaded her breast then suckled in worshipful silence his eyes glazed as he watched her face. She writhed incapable of reason, attempting to put a name, a place, anything to grab the elusive, keening, cloying craving he demanded. She sobbed with shame at her growing wantonness as his hands stroked her body seemingly everywhere. His breath came in jagged bursts. Each thrust became more potent, harder, faster, echoing the pounding thunder of her heart, bringing her to a new plateau of pleasure, and each level was so filled with bliss she felt she would swoon to go any higher. Yet higher she climbed, her world tore itself free of restraint, her legs circled his waist as she matched him in rhythmic splendor, two beings blending together in a whirling eddy of passion. She strained against him and whimpered into his mouth. With an instinctive movement she surged to meet his next thrust. He sucked in his breath sharply, then tilted her hips to embed his staff into her completely, shuddered and went limp.

His big body sprawled across hers, and still merged, his flesh pulsated into hers. Overcome with wonder, Abby absently stroked the slickness of his back, touched to the depths of her soul. They existed—two spent embers rising on a zephyr and floating ever so slowly back to earth.

"Ma générosité est aussi illimitée que la mer, Mon amour est profond: plus je te donne." My bounty is as boundless as the sea. My love is deep, the more I give to thee. A bard's words echoed peacefully and came easily to her lips. Where had she heard it?

Abby's mind came back together from the ends of the world where it had flown. Aware, she could feel his heart beat and every breath he took along with the musky scent of him that clung to her skin. Her eyes felt heavy and she let them slide closed as she snuggled against his warmth. His arm was flung across her, and his breath tousled the wispy curls upon her brow.

Remotely she heard the ship's bell toll, signaling that the break of day had commenced and with it the dawning reality of what she had done. The intelligent, sophisticated Lady Abigail Marie Hansford Rutland, daughter of the Duke of Rutland had slept willingly with a Yankee, rebel, pirate and traitor!

A shriek of anguish fell from her lips. She threw off the sheltering arm with a snarl, and, struck Thorne in the shoulder. The impact rolled him onto his back.

Thorne snored, out cold and into a heavy slumber that she had worked so hard to launch from the beginning. She rolled away, unsteadily planted her feet upon the floor and glared through brimming tears to where he lay sprawled naked on the bed. Weeping bitterly, she witnessed the evidence of her destruction. Blood! Her blood! Smeared dark red blood contrasted on the white muslin. She spun and tripped on her coat, the very article of clothing that caused her ruin.

"I hate you—I hate you," she cried between sobs while shoving on her clothing. What man would want her, now that she was no longer a virgin? Many, surely, she reflected inconsolably, but none for his wife unless he was some ancient and impoverished lord who paid a handsome price. And even if she succeeded escaping the infamous Captain Thorne, her purity could never be recovered.

Even far worse raised the sudden realization and more humiliating by far, was her reaction to Jacob Thorne's caresses. She had given herself to him as entirely and fervently as he had taken her. The magnificent memory of his male hardness, deep and powerful inside her, was now a memory of shame, causing heat to flow to her cheeks, not this time from passion, but from the most degrading humiliation. Added to this shame—a new and potent fear. More than ever, she feared Jacob Thorne, the one man who could stir her passions to new heights and whose power could create a pulsing, throbbing need. Better to play the role as filthy cabin boy than to succumb to the charm of Thorne's seduction. She lifted her chin. As the ragamuffin lad, she remained safe and safe she would stay.

"Lucette!" Thorne dreamily smiled.

Abby put her fist in her mouth. She had given him her greatest treasure and he thought he had made love with the harlot. Damn him! Damn him to eternity! She gathered her pallet, slammed the door and sought the security of her room in the bow. On stiff rope coils, she burrowed deep beneath her quilt, curled into a tight ball, jamming a pillow tightly over her head. There, in total exhaustion, she sobbed out her misfortunes, allowing the sweet peace of slumber to overtake her.

Chapter 12

Thorne gripped the rail of the foredeck, surveying his crew as they labored in the hot tropical sun to make ready for sail. His head throbbed like a poleaxed bull and his temper grew short at the time it took to unload cargo and load fresh supplies to ready his ship for the journey to Boston. At the last minute, William Bingham had ordered him to take an additional consignment of desperately needed military munitions, an overload that would encumber the *Vengeance*'s swift speed through hostile waters.

A gust of wind shook the ship. "Sou'easter blowing up," Lawton reminded him. Again.

Against his lieutenant's warnings of a gale brewing, he hastened his crew, determined to depart Martinique. He had delayed enough. To free his cousin from British hands was critical. The threat of Ethan hanged on a mad King's whim menaced with each passing day. A nice fat British Colonel cooled his heels in a Boston jail, guaranteeing an exchange. He had to get to Boston as soon as possible before General Washington decided to exchange that officer for another American prisoner.

He rolled up his sleeves and grimaced. Why had he wasted valuable time on a prostitute when he should have initiated departure?

If only he had tamped down his base needs. Yet warm rum, long incarceration at sea and Lucky Lucette had provided a heady challenge. Her ripe curves had rubbed up against him in Demanjer Tavern and her willingness to remedy the itch that settled in his groin demonstrated too potent of an antidote to resist.

Yet his licentious behavior stood inexcusable. Hadn't that flaw spelled disaster for his family—a flaw that had yielded the death of his younger cousin, Thomas, and near defilement of Rachel? For those sins, he would be damned.

Adding to his sins was the image this morn of a red blood stain on his sheets. Thorne raked his fingers through his hair. He did not take virgins. His moral code and upbringing remained adamantly opposed to the debauchery of innocent women. Yet there remained little recollection of Lucette and his trip to the *Vengeance*. Vague remembrances of the night in his cabin haunted him. Perhaps the oddest remembrances were the deceiving shadows of the night and the blurring disparities of those apparitions. In his mind's eye, Lucette boasted a larger anatomy and certainly her behavior at the tavern spoke of seasoned experience. Thorne's brows drew together. The woman he held in his arms, was slim, her hair silky and shorter. Thorne shook his head, his thoughts muddled. He had learned Pascale had rowed her to shore. Jacob sent Enos to find Lucette, to leave her gold and where to contact him in the eventuality of a child. He would not leave a bastard behind nor would he allow his child to suffer the rejection he had borne.

Abe walked across the deck, his gait peculiar as if he rode a horse for three days. Jacob's jaw clenched. Abe had put him in a delicate position with the American representative, William

Bingham. What had gotten into the boy's head to spy on him? Bingham assured him affairs would be fine if Jacob kept a stern eye on the boy until they reached Boston.

Jacob scrubbed his hand across the back of his neck. Hadn't he locked the lad in his cabin? No doubt the boy had witnessed part or all his degenerate behavior with Lucette. Abe had packed up his pallet and disappeared sometime during the night. "Abe, get over here."

Abe hooked his slim thumbs in his rope belt and looked him up and down. "What?"

Defiant. Always. "About last evening—" He cleared his throat, worked to form an apology. "So you were—"

Abe nodded jerkily and wiped his nose, scratching an ear with the other hand. "You looked pretty stupid."

Thorne chafed. He deserved Abe's rebuke, but he didn't have to like it. The censure coming from his cabin boy soured his stomach. "Have you finished your chores?"

Beneath red-rimmed eyes, Abe drummed his fingers against his hips. "No, and if you don't mind I'd like to get back to work. All that wailing and yowling, drowning my ears kept me up half the night."

"That's enough," Thorne snapped. Had his harshness with the boy the night before cause the lad to vent tears? Like his cousin, Thomas, the boy had a sensitive nature hidden behind his bluster.

The nose met the sleeve again. "Don't worry, Captain. Your secret is safe with me. I slept in the bow."

Thorne glared. "Don't you ever stop talking?"

His rebuff brought a cackle of glee from Abe, "Touchy. Did Lucette bless you with some wee beasties? Or did you lose a sea urchin in your breeches?"

Before Jacob could get in a word the lad turned his back. An ocean-sized chip rested on Abe's slender shoulders as he slowly shuffled to the foredeck. Jacob restrained himself from falling on the boy and beating him for his insolence.

A net of casks broke from the winches. Abe stood beneath the descending barrels. Men shouted. Thorne froze. Casks crashed on the deck. The boy darted sideways, twisting, leaping over rolling barrels that thundered across the deck. And errant barrel smashed into the bulwarks. Two sailors wrested it from farther travel. Abe stood gasping, his hand placed over his heart. Thorne frowned. The movement held a girlish grace. His jaw clenched. The crew's inattentiveness was too close a call, a carelessness that could have spelled death for thc boy.

"Dammit! Can't you men have better control of the winches?"

Abe's hat fell off, revealing thick blonde curls tied back in a thong. Thorne shook his head. Wasn't the boy's hair black? No doubt from the grime the lad was acclimated to. Perhaps Abe had finally taken a bath. The boy hugged that hat to his head like a hatch cover strapped to a cargo hold then looked around to see if anyone noticed. How peculiar.

With scornful eyes, Simeon glared at Jacob from the galley door, muttering something about cooking up a meal of mandrake. What in Hades was wrong with his cook? Pascale stopped and folded his massive arms and glared at him. Enos came aboard, glanced to him then spit a neat stream of spittle over the side. Thorne scowled. Was his whole crew ready to lynch him?

"Here's your gold back, Captain. Couldn't find Lucette." Enos tossed the bag to him.

Abner Bosworth appeared with a steaming mug of coffee. "The hairs are up on my neck with that gale brewing, Captain."

There it was again, a reprimand about leaving port too early. Why did everyone question his command? If they left Martinique now, they'd bypass the storm. Of course, the men were in short temper, rounded up prematurely from shore leave. "Don't you have enough work?"

"Aye, Captain." Abner scuttled away like a crab. Now Thorne had completely alienated all his crew.

What nagged at him from the hazy fog of his mind was Lucette with her dark hair flowing about her shoulders. If only he could get out of this infernal dark pit. Phantoms crisscrossed. Jacob rubbed his aching head. There had been a woman in the dark. A willing body beneath his, fulfilling his desire with a potency that had brought him burning, extraordinary pleasure. Why couldn't he connect the woman with Lucette? With cruel spurs of will, Thorne troweled his memory. He could put no face or name to the woman. He must have had a total blackout.

Despite his throbbing head, and the fuzziness in his brain, Jacob managed to supervise the rest of the cargo loading and endured the rasp of anchor chains as they were weighed. A fresh wind blew out of the southeast, kicking up chop along the Lesser Antilles. White water cascaded from the top of gray seas, and bursts of cooler air swept through. Rain in the distance promised to soak anyone unfortunate enough to be standing on deck. The sails billowed out and soon Martinique grew nonexistent on the horizon as the *Vengeance* glided past the Windward Islands toward home. Thorne sighed. If only he could eradicate the intoxicating creature that muddled his mind from the night with such ease.

Chapter 13

There had been no time for rest. Abby worked hard to support the hurried departure, immersing herself in the heavy labor to numb her mind from the remembrances of the night before. Hours had passed since morning when she had dragged herself from bed to conquer the laborious and time-consuming chore of winding the bindings around her breasts. The task had grown increasingly difficult to hide the unboy-like bounce of her bosom. Then the pain between her legs had been excruciating, but she'd been determined to stay on top of it. The soreness had faded with the day's activities along with certain memories that fell short in forcing them to the hollows of her mind.

The day grew rough and gloomy as the trade winds blew up a gale. She entered the galley, her bosom sufficiently subdued and heavy boots scuffling on the wood floor. Simeon wiped flour from his hands and picked up a steaming kettle of water. She sank upon a bench and rested her head in her arms on the table. Glad to be alone with Simeon, Abby strained the sorry condition of her hat, twisting the wool threads in her hands against the need to cry out. The awful realization of all that passed between her and Thorne came flooding back to her and with it a feeling of loneliness so acute she could scarcely bear it. Losing her maidenhood to Thorne thrashed her insides like the waves smashing against the ship. The worst part—the part that haunted her—was that she had found something forbidden and dangerous to her, a feeling that shouldn't, *couldn't* exist. Even worse was that Abby had freely shared the most cherished part of her. What she had kept for her husband she had given to a pirate.

She glared at the hat her hands. Thorne was a fool. He had even sent Enos to give gold to Lucette, the same woman who tried to rob and carve him with her knife.

Simeon placed a plate of warm biscuits and stewed chicken next to her. "Here milady, eat. You must keep up your strength. 'Tis a long voyage to Boston."

When they were alone, Simeon deferred to her rank. Abby raised her head and gave him a rueful smile. She was far from the titled lady. The meager comfort Simeon offered did not lighten the load that settled in her chest, nor did she have the appetite to eat. Outside Thorne roared out orders with the severity of a fire-breathing dragon. From all the rum he had consumed, she wished him the worst of headaches. And now they were on their way to Boston, some primitive frontier where she would be farther and farther away from her cherished England. Farther away from helping her father and brothers. Had they survived? Her throat went dry. Of course they survived. No, she would not give in to despair. She picked at a biscuit, normally flaky and buttery, now rolled like sawdust over her tongue.

Simeon sat down next to her. "Lady Abigail, I cleaned the captain's quarters for you this morning."

Abby could not go back to Thorne's cabin. Too many emotions tore at her. Simeon hesitated overlong and she blinked. "What?"

Simeon grimaced. "I changed the sheets. And don't tell me the blood was Lucette's."

Abby paled. What could she say? Lie that the blood was Lucette's or that she had cut herself in the struggle with the prostitute? The reality was that the sophisticated Lady Abigail Rutland, distinguished in artful refinement, cultivated with thorough respectability, bred on the highest of decorum, had lost her virtue. That she could have wings and fly. Now she faced her friend's condemnation.

Simeon dug two spoons of sugar into her tea and stirred. The metal clanked against the sides so hard she thought the mug would break. "The captain should be hanged for his crimes. Defiling a gently bred lady? He is an animal. I've half a mind to brew him Hemlock tea. 'Tis no less than he deserves."

Abby pulled the mug away, the scalding tea cupped in her hands. What she had done with Thorne, she had done willingly. "No, Simeon. It is just as much my fault as was his."

"He didn't force himself on you?"

Abby pressed her palms to the rough-hewned table. The miserable lantern light swung with the ship, alternating light into the gloom and back again. Words clogged in her throat and she stood up, woefully inadequate to articulate what happened when she could not explain to herself what had transpired. Driven by licking flames of desire, Abby had lost her innocence. A real lady would never have entered such a shameful charade. On top of that, Thorne's inability to distinguish between the two women savaged her pride and fed her anger. Abby turned over her hands, acknowledged her dirty fingernails, and tattered boyish garb, and in it, she saw the incongruous vision of Abe. If only, to crush it all beneath her feet.

"No. He did not force himself on me and he was too drunk to know who it was." She stood, her deepest secret revealed. She could not look Simeon in the eye no more than she could let Thorne take the entire blame, and with that admission, tears sprung into her eyes.

Men hailed Simeon and crowded into the galley with hearty greetings and hefty appetite. Abby yanked her hat down low and passed the ranks of seamen that hauled to the benches to get their dinner first. Not desiring any questions, she climbed the stairs to the deck, intent to get to the bow before she broke down.

Numb to the storm that had blossomed into a full-blown gale, she fought for footing. Rain slashed at different angles from the wind changing direction and blinded her. The deck raised slippery beneath her feet. She stretched out her arms for a handhold and grabbed air. Someone shouted a warning. The ship heaved. Abby fell, hurled on her back. Her fingers clawed a rope coil. She looked up. A giant wall of water crashed over her, possessing an otherworldly, wicked force. Its curved hollow felt like the inside of a clenching fist as it hurled her across the deck and slammed her into the bulwarks. She clung to the railing with one hand. The upside-down contortion of her body left her free hand flailing. Her fingers entwined in a halyard. The ship heaved again. The upsurge broke over her like a ton of bricks, breaking her free and sweeping her up and over then drawing her down into the gray depths and holding her there.

The sea tumbled her round and round in a rolling motion. She had no idea what was up or what was down. Perhaps the oddest awareness was that she would drown and no one would be aware or care. The universe sucked the world out and in a chest-squeezing panic, a sense arose that the ocean held all the power. Shadows blanketed and fogged at the edges, in time with the sea that undulated and yawed. She lost all sense of where or who she was.

She heard Jacob's voice. It was as if he were calling from the top of a well. Did he have a rope to pull her out? Fleeting thoughts swirled and echoed then dispersed to nothing. What was he saying? If only she had the strength to fight, the urge to go on, but she couldn't. She was so weak against the merciless sea, her coat heavy and pulling her down. Fatigue settled in, and with it, she allowed the monster to swallow her up. She just wanted to let go, let go…

Thorne cut through the devouring swells with long sure strokes. If only he could get to Abe in time. *Thomas. He had not been there for Thomas.* No way would he repeat the mistake with Abe. He had to save the boy. A wave rolled over him carrying him down, down, down. He fought for the top, took a breath of air before another surge slapped seawater into his gullet. He choked on the salty brine. The rough hemp rope tied around his midsection tangled in his legs. He kicked it loose, always keeping sight of Abe's head. He fought the water. Abe's head disappeared. Jacob dove. He shot through the murky depths. His lungs collapsed for lack of air. He reached out. His hand settled on hair. He seized the seaweed mass and kicked to the surface. His lungs burst for air. He waved. Men hailed from the ship and the rope about his waist tightened as they pulled him back to safety.

He held Abe as his men lifted him, the wailing sea screamed below denied of its meal. He allowed Enos to take the boy only for a second. Jacob climbed over the rail and took the boy back in his arms and headed down the companionway away from nature's wrath. In his cabin, he laid Abe on the bed.

Pascale hovered in the doorway.

Simeon stood next to him. "Is he alive?"

Dim and low beneath his finger, Thorne felt a pulse. "Aye. He's full of seawater." Thorne worried if the boy would wake. He had seen similar men who had been submerged who never woke. He turned the lad over and pounded his back. The boy wretched out half the sea. That was a good sign, wasn't it? Abe was so pale and cold. Didn't his aunt have the same pale look about her before she had died of pneumonia?

"I have to get the lad's clothes off before he catches a chill," said Thorne.

"I insist on doing it," Simeon offered. "There is hot tea for you, Captain in the galley."

Was his cook trying to get rid of him? Thorne did not miss the warning glances exchanged between Simeon and Pascale. "I can manage," he waved them away, struck odd by their sudden solicitude.

"Whatever you do, you will not be angry with the boy, will you, Captain?" said Simeon.

Thorne stopped. What an odd remark. Hadn't he been responsible for the boy's welfare? Hadn't he risked his own life to save him? Thorne lifted Abe's head. How different the boy's face looked swept clean of grime. *How soft and vulnerable.* His fingers threaded the bedraggled mop of wet hair, blond hair. Like the wind buffeting the *Vengeance*, why were all his senses screaming? Suspicion brought him to his knees.

Thorne's hands shook as he gripped the lapels of Abe's huge sodden overcoat, a boat anchor around the boy that could have dragged him to the bottom of the sea.

Simeon grabbed the coat from Thorne's hands and closed the flaps over the boy's chest. "I'll take over from here, Captain."

Did his cook dare to command him? Thorne narrowed his eyes on Simeon. The old man drew back, his throat fluttering like a crow's wings.

"You won't take anything out on Abe?"

Simeon's accusation chilled Jacob's blood. Did Simeon think he'd harm the boy? "Move aside. I'm not in the mood for any games." Thorne had enough of his cook's insubordination.

Thorne ripped the garment open. The buttons flew across the bed. He tore off the coat and tossed it at Simeon then took off one of *his* silk shirts the boy had snatched from his chest. "What the hell!" Bindings constricted the boy's chest. *Boy?* In that abbreviated second, Thorne was certain on one thing. His cabin boy was *not* male.

Memories sifted, the soft bottom of the boy beneath his palm when he pushed him up the mast, the girlish movement to jump the errant barrel, the feminine press of his hand to his heart—all were female gestures, taunting him. A dread like a spider crept across Jacob's chest.

"I have been conned." Thorne glared at Simeon. Of course, the old man had been with the boy aboard the *Civis*. No wonder Simeon had rejected the idea of Abe sleeping in his cabin. The idea that Abe was a girl was incomprehensible. Thorne shook his head unable to grasp the notion. Thorne who prided himself on knowing every detail of his crew had been victimized by his own gullibility. To pull off a monstrous deception such as this was monumental.

He glanced over his shoulder to where Pascale hovered in the doorway ready to put a dagger in his heart if he harmed the girl. Like a ship without a rudder, and the sport of every wind, he'd been a fool. To think he was the laughingstock of his crew

His fingers probed the bindings, wrapped too secure for him to unwind, a wonder Abe could breathe. "Give me a knife."

Simeon hesitated.

"Now." Simeon tentatively placed the hilt on his palm. Thorne sawed the wraps. Soft rounded breasts popped and puckered. Perfect breasts. He flung the sodden material at Simeon then covered Abe with a sheet to conceal *her* from Simeon's and Pascale's view. What a successful disguise.

He had believed in Abe. In a level of his subconscious, Abe had been Thomas's inadvertent replacement. Had he wanted to believe in Abe so badly that he allowed himself to be taken advantage of?

Abe's blustering had been a clever device to hide her sex. Thorne had mistaken the ranting to hide an insecure boy. *A simple lad?* No way. The girl used smarts to survive. His insides grated with her intellect. His pride lay shredded to pieces. Thorne surrendered reason. What was left to guard against the absurdities of deception?

A reluctant smile curved his lips with her cunning. He'd never admit it, of course, and would never find occasion to, but he admired her spirit. Instead of getting all womanish and hysterical when met with terrifying odds, she resorted to subterfuge—cleverer than most men.

A thousand questions plowed his mind. Never would he get the truth from Simeon. No. The old man would never give him a straight answer. How did she win the favor of the huge black? No one had been able to communicate with him. Or did she have the capability?

How old was she? Twenty? Beneath the omnipresent greasy hair, besmudged face and bulky garb was the mature form of a young woman. Definitely perfect breasts. Thorne raked his fingers through his hair. "Out," he commanded, Simeon and Pascale, "before I have you keelhauled." The door banged.

Thorne grimaced. Abe was not a suitable name for a woman. He brushed the sheet aside and removed her sodden breeches. Her femininity disclosed Thorne covered her again. How had he missed the subtle curve of her hips? Jacob swore. Of course, the huge coat the lad wore, refusing to take it off, buttoned to her chin on the hottest of days.

He lit a candle and probed the shadows for her features. Thorne was drawn to the fine lashes that swept down over sculpted cheekbones, giving way to a straight nose and full sensual lips. At the bottom of the sea lay her tattered woolen cap that had been pulled low to cover the arch of gold winged brows. Her tangle of damp hair untethered from its tie, and cut short, curled disobediently at the ends. She shifted like a cat, moving her head upon his pillow and groaned. He ran a hand behind his neck, kneading the tense muscles there. Why had he never seen the female?

It was the sea she heard, the guttural deep-toned call of wind and waves. It was a good, strong sound to her ears, never ceasing, never dying, the wind and waves booming as loud and rhythmic as a heartbeat. She stretched and nestled in her pillow. Sweet wonderful sleep. Why was her bed rocking? Abby drifted through a patch of darkness, a sense of nothingness. Her maid would come in soon with her hot chocolate. Her maid would explain. But she did not live near the sea.

"Who is Abe?" His voice was like honey rolled over thunder.

Abe? Her eyes flew open and the blood ran from her face. Reality cut like a cleaver. No she was not home in her bed. She was in the middle of the Caribbean with a ruthless privateer.

He knew!

"I want answers. Now!"

Abby scrambled to the edge of the bed, grabbing the quilt around her and planting her feet firmly on the floor. Black spots clouded her vision followed by a wave of dizziness. She had to get out. She had to get away from Thorne. Her knees buckled.

Thorne swept her up and deposited her on the bed. Abby tried to slip away. He grabbed her wrists and she fought him, wildly twisting and writhing to gain her freedom.

"Be still!" he commanded. Breaking her hand free, she landed a punch in his chest. He planted her wrists in one hand. She cried out from the pain. He straddled her and the implications of his heavy weight covering her came to bear. "No." She fought wildly.

Thorne dropped his head next to her face. "I take no pleasure in battling you, Abe or whoever you are. If you stop struggling, I will free you. Besides, where would you run to?"

Reason won out over hysterics. Abby forced herself to lay still and prayed he keep his word. Thorne shifted and moved from the bed. What would he do with her? He sat in the chair next to the bed his elbows rested easily on his knees, far from the ease he portrayed. Deep inside Abby knew Thorne would not harm her—or would he? Hadn't he befriended a cabin boy?

"I want the truth."

Abby remained mute. A multitude of possible things he'd do to her crossed her mind. How to handle Captain Thorne? The storm railed outside. This was his ship and she was alone with him, exposed to his whims.

He angled his head. "I assume Abe is not your real name?"

Abby sat up, the quilt held tight to her neck. Aware of her state of undress, heat rose from her toes to the roots of her hair. Under the persona of Abe, she was protected, however this was unmapped territory. Her old tools of cajolery and flattery that she used in England were also useless to a man like Thorne. He wanted answers and he wanted the truth. Anything less, he'd see through it, especially since she had fooled him for so long.

"Abby," she exhaled.

He snorted. "Of course. How appropriate. Your last name?"

Abby swallowed. Never could she tell him her real name especially after his vocal hated of England's aristocracy. In addition, the war in the American Colonies was predicated on freedom and equality, a far cry from the legally, social, privileged classes in England. The powerful Rutland family defined the aristocracy American colonists targeted their hatred. Her father was twice removed inheritor to the Crown. To tell the truth of her identity to a man like Captain Thorne after what happened to his family at British hands would be suicide.

In a shaky voice, Abby compromised on a half-truth. "Abigail Marie Hansford." There she said it, saying part of her name and leaving off the Rutland surname and keeping her mother's maiden name. If only he'd show her the same mercy he had with his cabin boy.

Thorne tensed. "I don't think so."

Did he recognize her from the ball? She had worn a mask and a considerable wig. Her fingers grappled the covers. She repeated her name. "Abigail Marie Hansford."

"Are you sure?"

Abby lifted her chin. Of course, he didn't trust her. "I am quite sure."

He nodded his expression tight, not fully committed. "Why were you aboard the *Civis*? The truth this time."

How to convince Thorne? Abby bit her lip and strategized. To share the bare minimum was the only way to maneuver him. "As Simeon told you before, our circumstances were dire," she began, comfortable in speaking in her own natural tones. "I had to be disguised as a boy."

"Who would want to murder your family? Or was that a lie?"

Abby open and closed her mouth. He referenced what Simeon had told Thorne during the capture of the *Civis*. "Do you know how many times I've asked that question?" Abby looked away, the pain and sorrow and uncertainty of her family was destroying her in pieces. On the wall, the flickering candlelight built crude outlines of them. Thorne's shadow engulfed hers, a grim reminder of her vulnerability. She returned her gaze to him. "I must get to England. I must see if anyone survived and to find my family's enemies. I cannot go to Boston."

"Impossible."

Abby wrung her hands. "Would you not do the same for your family?"

"I am fighting a war, in case you have forgotten, against *your* country."

"It is not my war. I understand your bid for freedom, but I don't wish to be any part."

"Then we are at an impasse. My cousin, Ethan rots in a British prison and hangs between life and death. I must get to Boston. There I will intercept a British Colonel to secure a prisoner exchange." Then in a more soothing tone, he added, "You are a young female. Whoever went to the trouble to put you on board the *Civis*, wanted you dead too."

Thorne was right. But her father had powerful friends who would come to her assistance. Uncle Cornelius for one. If only she could get to him. Uncle Cornelius would use his power and influence to find out who had done this to her family. He would also protect her. "Couldn't you at least drop me off at a British port?"

Thorne's lips pressed into a tight line. "I have a price on my head. Do you think I relish the idea of swinging from a gallows tree?"

Under Thorne's cool regard, a cold knot formed her stomach. What shrewdness ruled behind those cobalt eyes? Did he see the fear she worked to hide? She balled her hands to calm her trembling fingers. "I can imagine you have a fond attachment to your neck."

"You are short on your history. You don't fit the image of a gutter waif or farmer's daughter. From your refined accent, I'd hazard to guess, you are straight from English nobility."

Abby swallowed. When she dropped the husky tones of Abe, she had forgotten to speak like one of her father's crofters. He had guessed her ancestral roots?

She winced. One lie bridged to another. She was never good at lying and the idea filled her with self-loathing. Ever since the lie she told about her engagement to the time she had been kidnapped, and assumed a different identity for survival, she had lived a lie. What was one more falsehood? In the middle of the ocean, who was going to argue points of deception? Thorne drummed his fingers on the arm of his chair. Abby labored to grasp a plausible story, a past Thorne would find believable.

His face hardened. "I sense you are highborn. Are you going to share with me who you are or do I have to toss you back into the ocean to get a straight answer?"

She dropped her quilt in the wake of his threat and flashed him a cold smile. "Of course, Captain Thorne, you would bully me. I am a daughter of a goldsmith. My father married the fourth daughter of an impoverished earl. Are you going to punish me for my humble roots?"

He weighed her words. The goldsmith idea came as a lark. She had procured a set of gold candlesticks for her parents in London and had spent hours with the talented merchant in detailing the design. In that time, she had learned from the cheerful merchant of his trade and his family. A wealthy goldsmith would attract the daughter of an earl who had inadequate funds. "My father is very good at his trade and has provided well for his family."

His sensuous mouth thinned into a hard-grim line. "What kind of enemies does a goldsmith have?"

Abby shrugged. "I don't know. There was a nobleman who was delinquent in his payments and my father took to court. The nobleman later married a rich wife. Perhaps he held a vendetta against my father?" The truth remained, she had no idea who would want to destroy her family. Only the thin reedy voice of her kidnapper preoccupied her. Never would she forget his voice.

Thorne was not convinced. She slanted him a sideways glance, but he was consumed, his eyes lowered to where the quilt had slipped away. In the guttering light, the peaks of her breasts were silhouetted beneath the sheet. Abby felt the blood leave her face.

Then the captain's hard dark eyes moved over her body. He was appraising every inch of her, and what remained hidden below. Of course, he had undressed her and seen everything. Abby seized the quilt up to her neck and schooled her features into a mask of calm. As Abigail Marie Hansford, could she draw out Thorne's gallant side? "I will need to have something to wear." She raised her brow pointedly.

One corner of his wicked mouth turned up. He opened a drawer then tossed her a key and angled his head to the foot of the bed. "Avail your needs from the trunk. Before I leave, do you have any other requirements?"

His voice oozed like vinegar. He was adjusting to his cabin boy as a woman. She placed her hand over her mouth and yawned, nearly drowned, the shock of her discovery and dealing with Thorne had drained all her energy.

He leaned forward in a sort of grudging bow. Interesting to note that he had a small, miserly store of manners.

"I'm terribly sleepy from the ordeal," Abby said in her most proper drawing-room English.

"I look forward to our continued discussion, Miss Hansford," He stalked from the room, but Abby was already half-asleep.

Chapter 14

The next morning dawned bright and powerful. Thorne had removed himself from the cabin, and had slept elsewhere, affording her complete privacy. The prospect of wearing a gown tingled up her spine. She grabbed the key he had given her the night before and leaped from the bed. Unlocking the trunk, she rummaged through a colorful array of brocades, jaconets, bombazines, velvets, silks and satins that he'd been saving for his cousin. The sapphire she had tried on the night before was too fine and she placed it aside, instead choosing, a green muslin day dress trimmed with lace.

She shook out the dress and hung it over a chair. She pulled out a fine lawn chemise, a pair of white silk stockings, two dainty satin garters and put them on. At the bottom of the trunk lay a bunch of ribbons banded together. She tugged a green satin ribbon, and smiled, the same hue as her dress. She took a silver hair brush and swept her short hair back, weaving the satin ribbon into a neat chignon, and hummed a favorite tune, *All in a Garden Green.*

Jacob blew in with a bracing wind. Abby whirled, her tune cut-off midstream. She yanked the dress from the chair to cover her but not before Thorne had a full view. "Don't you think to knock?"

"It's my cabin. We've shared it before."

Could he scowl anymore? "I was your cabin boy then."

"Pardon me if I'm adapting to the remarkable turnaround. How could I have missed such a pleasurable sight beneath my nose?"

He walked by her. Abby backed up two steps, hiding her backside from his view. He unbuttoned his shirt and took it off. She stood startled. Her heart shuddered, stopping for a moment, and then began beating anew at a frantic pace. To watch him dress as Abe had been one thing, but quite another when she was an unattached female. This was a new intimacy, seeing him without his shirt, his shoulders a yard wide and molded bronze, and the muscles that rippled on his abdomen. His shadowed jaw made him look even more disreputable, so he looked more of a demon than a privateer plying his crimes upon the open seas. She swallowed. Images of their night together blended in sensuous shadows. How she had touched every one of those bunched muscles, her fingers falling over every plain.

She averted her eyes and he laughed. "Where did the maidenly modesty come from? Didn't you scrub my back and swear like a fishmonger?"

"Do you think I enjoyed my charade as your cabin boy? Do you think I like to live in fear of what will happen to me? What are you going to do with me?"

He snatched a new shirt from his armoire and jerked it on. "You are a guest on my ship and will come under my protection. But there are strings."

"Of course, there would be strings." She lifted her chin, his innuendo clear.

She was ready to tell him otherwise but held back her retort, and said, "In addition to Lucky Lucette, I'm sure you've seen a goodly number of ladies, but I am not one of them—nor do I wish to be."

Thorne sneered. "You are mistaken, Miss Hansford. I do not touch young innocents." He strode past her, halting at the door. "When you are finished dressing, you may join me on deck."

His directive was a command not a request. "Wait," said Abigail. "What are the strings?"

"From now on, the truth. Only the truth. You cannot fathom what I will do to you if I have been lied to. Make a fool of me once, I allow. But twice, my wrath will fall on your head."

Jacob watched the girl climb the stairs, her posture correct, her movements graceful, and, except for an occasional tendency to swagger, her carriage as refined as any gently reared lady he had ever known.

She was like a fair flower tousled in the wind. Her dress was simple of green muslin, the bodice shaped close to her slender figure and accented her tiny waist. From her shiny blonde hair, pulled back in at fashionable arrangement was a green silk ribbon, flowing in the breeze. With avid curiosity, he saw a spark in her eyes and flushing of her cheeks, a delightful shade of rose. She was a vision to bedazzle the most hardened of men. The sailors, busy with their chores, could hardly keep their eyes off her. And neither could Jacob.

She climbed to stand next to him. From the corner of his eye, she bit her lip to keep it from trembling and to stay as inconspicuous as possible. The devil in him, refused to speak to her. He'd teach her a lesson and let her cool her heels. He'd let her suffer the reaction of his men in silence.

From his questioning of Simeon and Pascale, none of the crew knew the truth about his cabin boy, *yet*. He'd make the announcement and through his control as commander would make sure no ill will by the crew came to Miss Hansford because of her deception. He was confident in his authority that the crew would adjust to her exposed secret, probably shocked at first, as he was, and he anticipated a certain amount of anger, as he had. He prepared himself for the questions that would result from the revelation. He would allow a few inquiries, thank them for their input then set guidelines to fend off remaining hostility. He concluded once an open discussion was made available, and complaint aired, the sooner normal shipboard life would resume.

Already her appearance had caused quite a stir. On the lower decks, several of his men quit their chatter and worked silently. Of course, a woman appearing on ship from out of nowhere would earn inspection. Their ears were cocked and their furtive glances, telling. Sailors scrambled down from the yardarms, busy or pretending to be with securing the lower sails that were already tightened. Thorne smirked, all of them nosier than a bunch of old peahens at a noonday tea.

Enos darted from sailor to sailor, taking in and dispensing coins. Some laughed, and others were disconcerted that Enos mollified with a slap on the back. After every transaction, each sailor peered up at Thorne and smiled, in fact smiling more when they looked at Abby. From the shared winking and uncontrolled whimpers of mirth, Thorne's fingers curled around the railing. What was his ship's carpenter up to?

"Enos!"

Enos walked mid-ship, just beneath Thorne. "Yes, Captain."

"What is the exchange of coin for?"

Enos worried his hat between his fingers. "A friendly wager, Captain, between me, and the men."

"Care to enlighten me?"

Enos dipped his chin. "We made bets to when you'd guess Abe was a female."

When Abby gasped, Thorne tightened his grip on the rail. "And how *long* have you and the men known?"

"Pardon me, Miss," Enos said, placing his attention on Thorne's ex-cabin boy. "Abe was so nice taking care of Ben and me when we almost died with the fever. When Abe started singing lullabies and wiping our brows, crooning to us like our sainted mothers, I pretty much figured Abe was not a boy."

Thorne exhaled, ready to pluck out the main mast and throw it into the horizon. "So how many of the crew had been aware of Abe's gender?" He reeled with the knowledge that everyone knew except *him*—Abe who had shared close quarters for two weeks without a hint of Thorne's knowledge. He scowled at his crew. The men on the lower masts worked their way up to the top. The men below tripped over casks and rope coils to find new tasks on the foredeck. Enos remained to bear the brunt of their captain's wrath.

"Captain Thorne, you can't be angry over a small oversight."

"Small?" He turned and glared at the object of his idiocy and she paled. In his cabin moments before, he could barely keep his hands off her. What a stimulating sight that was. She had stood scantily clad in garters, stockings and a chemise, her pert breasts thrusting out at him. He imagined letting his fingers draw across the delicate lace, over her sweetly curved bosom, rising and falling with each marvelous breath. How easy to cup each mound and…? He gritted his teeth at the decay of his thoughts then shifted, the hardening in his loins, a reaction to the memory scorched on his brain. Cabin boy? Woman? Thorne raked his fingers through his hair. For the millionth time, how could a charade such as that have gone on? If it weren't so vexing, he might have laughed. How could he not have seen the face, fine-boned and lovely as hers nor the beautiful clear blue eyes and thick black lashes?

Abby shuddered. Jacob's face might have been carved by marble, so expressionless did he hold himself. To be humiliated in front of his men was unforgiving.

Enos cleared his throat. "Go easy on the girl. She's a sweet young thing. I don't blame her and neither should you. She had to do what she had to do."

"Since when do I need your lecturing? How about the cat o' nines to your back? Would that evoke the same sympathy?"

"You'll be giving me the cat o' nines when hens grow teeth. I knew once you figured Abe out, you'd be like a roaring lion with an arrow lodged in its haunches. Boy or girl, what's the difference? Abe is still with us."

Abby's heart went out to the grizzled old seaman, her lone champion. Of course, it was a shock to learn the crew knew of her sex, and she could fall on her knees thanking them for their generous acceptance of her fate. If only Captain Thorne could be so sympathetic.

Thorne grunted. "It's hard to tell who has your back, from who has it long enough to stab you in it."

Enos wagged a finger at the captain. "Settle your pride in your nappies. If the crew is forgiving then so should you. Look at the humor in it and let it be done."

"You stretch our friendship, Enos."

"That I do. I was part of your raising and brought you up to be a just man. When you see the irony of the situation, you will be laughing too."

"I find humor in docking your wages."

Abby could no longer stand aside and let Enos suffer Thorne's wrath. "Captain, your quarrel is with me." Hadn't Abby suffered a long line of stubborn, prideful Rutland men? Was Captain Thorne any different? She summoned her resolve. As Abby, she could give him options.

Like corking an exploding volcano.

She dared to place her fingers on his arm.

He stared at where her hand lay.

She remained steadfast and suffered under the glare of those incredible cobalt eyes. "You are not betrayed. I can offer two suggestions," she smiled shakily. "You could throw me overboard and end all of your troubles. Or..." In the awkward silence, she began more forcefully than she intended. “You could drop your incivility and make me laugh. I much prefer the latter.”

Through her fingers, she felt the tension leave him, saw the severity in his implacable expression soften, and the corners of his lips turn up in the slightest hint of a smile. Out of the corner of her eye, Enos backed away, rubbing his hands in glee.

Jacob grunted. “Miss Hansford, are you always so bold?”

“Only when I wish to torment an overbearing personality.”

“Overbearing? What else am I?”

She tilted her head. “Do you want Abe’s opinion or Abby’s?”

“God forbid, Abe should come back and torture me.” He laughed, and his laughter boomed across the ship, so infectious, she found herself laughing too.

Chapter 15

With a good strong wind of twelve and twenty knots, and the seas nothing more than a moderate swell, Thorne estimated they would arrive in Boston in a few weeks. They had passed the Turks and Caicos, and he almost regretted the speed with which carried them home, enjoying his voyage with the lovely and enigmatic Miss Hansford. He stood on the foredeck when she materialized at his side. He didn't have to look to know she was there, like the caress of the wind an innate quality stirred with her nearness. In an alluring pink dress, she exuded classic beauty, and her diminutive grace made him feel so large and manly.

Where are we today?" she asked, although transparent. Each day that went by, she grew more anxious.

"At the southern end of the Bahamas."

"The seas are more turquoise."

Her voice faltered for a second, too complicated to assign to a single emotion. She was afraid to go to Boston. She wanted to go home. He didn't blame her. He wanted the familiarity of home. The topic of going to England lay just below the surface. Best to keep it buried. It was too dangerous for her alone in England with the prevailing circumstances, regarding her family. Boston was the safest place for her. She had to be reasonable, he was only thinking of her welfare. "The seas are shallower," he said at last.

She left his side and crossed to the point of the bow, her skirts flowing behind her. Why did he follow in her wake? He thirsted for the warm glow that flowed from her. He needed it like a parched desert needing rain.

Dolphins. It started with just four, speeding through the *Vengeance's* bow wave, left, right, crossing each other, doing little hops out of the water. Joy bubbled in her laugh and shone in her eyes. But it was that smile, wicked in its genuine, magnificent beauty that keeled him over like a nor'easter.

She pointed starboard off the bow. "What are they?"

"Dolphins." Within minutes there were six of them and more of them in the distance coming toward the ship, jumping high out of the water in graceful arcs, playing with each other. Fifteen of them frolicked around the ship, vying with each other for the coveted spot around the bow. White bellies up in the water, looking to see if Abby and he were watching. For two hours, Abby stood next to him, her exclamations, her upturned face, blissfully alive. She shouted to the dolphins and clapped with delight when they twirled and dipped with her laughter. The trappings of the past dimmed, allowing in rays of sunshine on his long forgotten soul. For the first time in a long time, he truly smiled, finding happiness in her joy.

Thorne had to be careful. Miss Hanford was weaving chains around his heart.

But things didn't add up. He wondered about her past, wondered who in the devil she was. She reminded him of Lady Abigail Rutland. That girl far from his reaches. No way would Lady Rutland have been set out to sea with an ex-slaver resolute on her demise. No one would dare go up against her father, one of the most powerful dukes in England, the Duke of Rutland. No. This girl had to have a different history.

He watched her steel herself, saw the way her eyes had turned a deeper shade of blue. He was about to speak when she interrupted him.

"The men say there is much discouragement in America. It has been a bad year."

Jacob frowned slightly. From reports by Bingham, she spoke the truth. He'd be damned before he'd acknowledge failure.

She waved a hand. "The harsh winter at Valley Forge, men defecting and starving. The defeat of Lafayette at Barren Hill… these occurrences dampen the spirits. You are not discouraged?"

Thorne folded his arms in front of him. "Sometimes setbacks occur. But setbacks always yield a return to a better position. The men at Valley Forge worked harder, trained harder. The harshness made them strong and more committed. At Barren Hill, Lafayette escaped unscathed and the Continental troops that have grown in numbers have chased the Redcoats from Philadelphia to New York. And then there is the alliance with the French," he reminded her. "These are times that try a man's soul. Americans perceive the persecution and tyranny of a cruel ministry and will not tamely submit—appealing to Heaven for just cause in a determination to die or be free."

"Shall we promenade?" he offered her his arm. Something about her taunted him, challenged him, made him desire to strip away that veneer and see what was underneath. He told himself he shouldn't want to know her. "Then there are appearances that are deceiving." He let that thought drift over, to strangle her, an attempt to remind her of her deception as a cabin boy. He replayed her discovery. Pink-tipped peaks of perfectly formed feminine breasts. Clever. Bound and hidden. He perused her slender figure, a build concealed beneath an over-sized coat that fooled him into believing she was lad.

"Of course. The charming part of Captain Thorne?"

Her smile skewered him again, warm shafts of sunlight melting frozen flesh until it ached. "I believe, Miss Hansford, I shall revel in the unexpected when it comes to you."

"You are flattering me, Captain Thorne."

"It was not meant to flatter."

Abigail lowered her head and a smile came fleetingly to her lips. "Now you are being provocative, Captain." Like a dog with a bone, he clung to his damaged ego.

How life had changed. Just days ago, she had been so assured and confident. The cabin boy scampering unnoticed about the ship, included in male camaraderie. She had laughed with them and shared their chores. But now, the deference and bowing and scraping, chafed her nerves. She often winced when they passed a group of the sailors, and felt their discerning winks to one another. They knew that she slept in the captain's cabin and the captain slept elsewhere.

"I see Enos is busy carving something but he won't tell me what it is for. He cut himself the other day and I bandaged his wound," said Abby.

"No doubt he will suffer many cuts so you can administer his injuries." Thorne muttered under his breath.

Abby burst into laughter. The captain was so vexed she couldn't help herself. "It is interesting to note that the entire crew has had a sudden list of injuries and complaints. After I bandage or give them special concoctions that Simeon brews, their recovery is rapid."

"Of course, to have a female administer their complaints has added to their unexpected infirmity."

Abby pasted on an innocent expression and looked him in the eye. "I am resigned to make the best of the situation." Was the proud Captain Thorne, jealous?

"I've noted the hive of activity, surrounding you. I'm sure the crew is happy as oysters. My fervent prayer is that my crew does not become so ill that there will remain but one soul to lift a sail."

A block and tackle swung loose. Abby ducked. Thorne caught the heavy block and cursed. "My point exactly."

She helped him secure rigging, tying a neat bowline as Abe had learned to do. "I hope you aren't going to harangue me with some superstitious repartee about women on board being bad luck. I'm trying to earn my keep and be helpful." The man really needed to enjoy life. She'd seen a glimmer when he watched the dolphins with her and again when he mused about his ailing sailors. But she had looked at him too long. The image of his perfect naked form was stamped on her mind, the times she seen him undress in the cabin when he thought she was a boy. She lowered her eyes, remembering it—all of it, and what had come after it. Her heart sank. He did not recognize the virgin he had slept with was her.

She walked over to a rope coil and nudged it with the toe of her slipper. He was suddenly standing there next to her, but just to pick up his telescope to consider the horizon. Yet he didn't walk away after he set it down.

She kept her eyes off him, but could feel his on her. Was he always going to make her this nervous? Abe would have offered a firm retort. But she was not Abe anymore. What was this unsettledness that he made her feel? Whatever it was, it was disturbing. She started walking, anything to take her mind off the image of his perfect dark hair, chest damp, long legs and that other naked, perfectly aroused part.

"Captain, when I ponder events…that even the strangest of circumstances, the most troubling episodes of one's life, the greatest divides from home and familiarity, there have been times like these of indisputable joy."

He stopped and stared at her, his eyes turning darker cobalt. "Then there are circumstances that are beyond my control—like discovering a mysterious female beneath my nose."

She stepped back, her heart pounding with alarm, the double entendre at once, suspicious and sensual. "Some circumstantial evidence is very strong, like when you find a grouper in the milk. You take him out and heave him overboard."

She saw a glint of humor then the amused twitch of his lips followed by a deep resounding sound that came from his sensual mouth. Her heart turned over. Thorne had laughed at her witticism. If only his mood weren't so fickle. He had the predisposition to find humor in the things she said and then study her with distrust. They stopped portside. A cloud mass had leadened the skies.

Even the waves curled and foamed in grey. "You remind me of an acquaintance. Lady Abigail Rutland."

Abby held her breath. The wind made a dreadful roar, pinging the shrouds against the mast. Did he suspect? She had been so caught up in their jovialness that she forgot Thorne might have intended to trap her. To be demure as a nun might serve her. "I-I have heard of her, but never have I been compared to her. I understand she is beautiful and accomplished, everything I am not."

Thorne balanced himself with the roll of the ship, caught and righted her as well. His touch burned where his hands lay on her arms. He removed them. "You are more beautiful."

Abby expelled a sigh of relief, at the same time flattered with his compliment. "Thank you." At least he didn't suspect her yet the insatiable, curious part of her thirsted for his reaction to Lady Abigail Rutland. "You mentioned Lady Rutland was an acquaintance. But how?"

"You mean, someone of my lineage rubbing shoulders with her pedigree?"

Abby snorted. "I mean nothing of the sort. I-I cannot imagine you, an American privateer, having any association with the lady unless she is an undeclared pirate."

Thorne chuckled. "Ask away. I shall be open to your feminine interest."

Abby rolled her eyes, but refrained from rubbing her hands in glee. She had endured kisses from English lords who paid her court, yet nothing, nothing near what had transpired in the garden with Jacob. And nothing like the soul-shattering lovemaking she had permitted in his cabin. On top of that, she was still reeling from the fact that he had called her beautiful. "How did you meet and what did you think of her?"

Thorne stroked his chin in thoughtful reflection. "You must know about her that badly?"

Abby tapped her foot, her mirth barely concealed. "You promised to tell me. I expect you to keep your word."

"I had business with a relative and was invited to her engagement ball."

"A relative in England?" If only she could find out his relationship to Humphrey.

"She descended the stairs like a queen, holding court over so many admirers. It was all I could do not to fight them all off and carry her away."

"Captain Thorne, you are teasing me." Drat. He was not going to tell her who his relative was. If she probed on that subject anymore, he'd get suspicious.

"What did she look like?"

"She wore a mask and a wig. I could not see her face or her hair. It was a frivolous masked ball. From what I recall, she had your shape and build."

Abby bit her lip. "Did you talk to her?"

Thorne put his hands up. "Did I find her witty, clever, charming and intelligent? Now who is being provocative, Miss Hansford?"

"We are discussing *your* romantic designs. Besides, I am helping you relieve shipboard boredom. The least you can do is supply me with details." And because she couldn't stand the wait any longer, she blurted, "Did you kiss her?"

"I never kiss and tell."

"You did!" Abby clapped. "How did it make you feel?"

His face darkened and he stalked her. Abby retreated until she was backed up against the foremast. The man was like a powerful natural force, like the shifting seas, a force so intense that nothing surrounding him could turn away or remain unaffected—least of all her. He leaned his head forward.

And then Thorne did the unthinkable. He kissed her.

"Like this…" Thorne brushed his mouth down on hers again. "And like this." He wanted to teach the lovely Miss Hansford a lesson for being so stirringly provoking. Inside he knew he couldn't… wouldn't…do any more than kiss her. But the minute his lips touched hers, his calm was shattered and his senses fled him.

He hadn't foreseen the reaction to this kiss, especially when Abby curved into him, holding onto him for support, her soft full breasts flattening against his chest. He yielded his own expertise, tempting, gradually persuading, enticing her lips to open, and when they did, he swooped in and commanded her sweetness. He reached down and pulled her rigid against him. Her tension lessened, and she melted into him. He drove his tongue deeper, to exploit her passion. Jacob took full dominance. He breathed her, tasted her, and savored her. His mouth brutal on hers, twisting, bruising, rousing, his tongue thrusting through her like a brand, searing her, having her.

A part of him wondered what had come over him. He only meant to challenge her. But another part of him understood his motives well. He wanted total possession. He stood on the precipice of desire.

Any longer and they'd both be lost.

Abby felt nothing but shock in those first few seconds, then panic. She was terrified that her feet weren't touching the deck; with her hair grasped back in a brutal clasp so she couldn't escape the insatiable onslaught of his mouth, her body behaved shamelessly, crushed to his. She gave up resisting.

She liked what he was doing to her, but his kiss overwhelmed and confused her. The arm holding her up was going to fracture her ribs. Her own resistance did not slacken the tiniest bit. Breathing was unattainable and she felt she would perish from suffocation.

Her hands groped to his chest, firm healthy male flesh tingled beneath her fingertips. Her mind desired to touch him everywhere, to explore every part of him like she had that night in his cabin. She brushed her fingers over muscle, heat, moisture then slid her arms around his neck, sighing.

With every touch, he made her realize how very female she was. A wild sensuality stirred to life inside of her, and she recognized it for the dangerous sensation it was. No. She could not tamp down the wealth of hidden feelings that leaped from her, blossoming, exploding, no more than she could have stopped him when she had given herself to him. She had had a taste of him and desired more, and she acknowledged it for the perilous sensation it was. His lips left hers. She seemed to float until her feet met the deck, her arms fastened to his neck to support her.

He drew away. The gap between them gave way to chill. Abigail managed to gulp in sweet air, her bosom still heaving.

Jacob leaned back to study her. "Does that answer your question?"

He was just as rattled as she. Mutely, Abby nodded, clinging to his arms for support. "More that adequately."

A round of cheers hailed from the ship. Abby clapped her hands over her mouth. The crew watched with blatant stares expectant of the silent tableau between her and their captain.

"Enos!" Thorne shouted.

But Enos was too busy with the crew exchanging coins *again*. Simeon and Pascale stood first in line with their palms up. Sweet Judas!

"Enos tipped his hat to her. Just a friendly wager when the captain would first kiss you. No offense, Miss Hansford. The bet relieves shipboard boredom."

Chapter 16

Thorne found Abby hours later closeted in his cabin, sitting on the long, cushioned bench beneath the transom windows with her legs tucked under her. "I suppose we should have seen that coming." He attempted to mollify her mortification but rather liked the blush that rose to her cheeks. She was affected by the kiss as much as he and there was a certain male satisfaction to that revelation. He intended to pursue the sweetly intoxicating, Miss Hansford.

"Easy for you to make a humorous gesture from it instead of the terrible scene that it was. I must appear a wanton woman to every member of the crew."

Thorne chuckled. "From Enos's first bet, we have drawn even."

"I didn't realize there was a competition."

She was getting her hackles up. He hid a smile. The temper of Abe had not disappeared. "A wise woman cautioned me at one time, to abandon my incivility and laugh."

She dropped her sewing to her lap. "Leave it to you, Captain Thorne to have me choke on my own words. It is my reputation that is ruined."

"You are assuredly an uncommon young lady. You have strength, and courage. You are a survivor. Most women could not have endured what you have gone through."

"Thank you," she snapped and returned to her work. He could see his words somewhat assuaged the feelings of remorse about their kiss. Thorne shrugged. There was nothing he could do about her status and distracted himself with the delicate tendrils of her golden hair that curled around her face as she bent over her work. She repaired his shirt with fine even stitches, the same stitches, *Abe* used when carefully repairing the sails. He shook his head with the amazing transformation then took in the long, lean curve of her arm, the straight line of her back and the way her every movement was graceful.

He could not envision a more domestic scene and assumed, like all young women, she spent hours, embroidering. Under his intense stare, she smoothed her hair back then put her work down. Did she tremble? She stood and walked around the table, the farthest she could to get away from him and turned her back. She set to arrange the already organized charts.

He grinned and moved to her side. How dear she looked in her appealing pink dress, a slender pink satin ribbon edged on the bodice and bared the tops smooth white bosom. She spun around. An avalanche of charts rattled to the floor and their gazes collided.

The chaos vanished, the clatter silenced and time froze. In the stillness, he saw her unguarded, her feelings exposed. A lasso of emotion slammed around him and anchored his heart to hers. For one perfect moment, they were bound and tied together in an immeasurable way, and he could see something he hadn't before.

Her heart. Tenderness washed over him and he struggled with the unpredictable magnitude of such consequence.

She cleared her throat and bent to retrieve the maps. "I'm clumsy."

"Allow me." He stuffed the charts into a cabinet.

She retreated again. Predictable. What she did next, he did not like. She retrieved one of two books that she had left spread-eagled on the bed, wriggled backward on the settle and commenced to read.

An Essay Concerning Human Understanding?

Even he, a self-made scholar had difficulty with Locke's philosophical treatise.

His illiterate cabin boy, the same one, he had spent hours tutoring, could read?

"I gather you found our reading lessons, amusing?"

She winced and plumped the pillows behind her then turned to him, those large blue eyes, regarding him with frank appeal. "I found the exercise selfless and admirable, that you would take the time to teach a poor cabin boy."

"Am I correct to surmise you own a familiarity on different subjects?" Jacob slid into a chair, rewarded with a broad smile as she warmed to the topic.

"Mathematics, with a good grasp of calculus, literature, chemistry, and elementary physics." She shrugged her dainty shoulders as if it were a minor accomplishment.

Thorne lifted a single eyebrow. "Unusual. A woman to be so—sophisticated?"

She cleared her throat. "My father provided generously for his family, insisting on a tutor, a scholarly old Jesuit to educate my older brothers. When I was three, the tutor discovered I could read and convinced my father to include me in the education of his children. The priest, a strict taskmaster, sharpened our debate skills on all matters of learning, employing a healthy competition between us. And I might say—we did not disappoint."

Her voice cracked, and she spoke too quickly, her response half-apologetic. Jacob picked-up the book she left on the bed and thumbed through the pages of *The Dialogue Concerning the Two Chief World Systems* by Galileo Galilei. He had read the book twice fascinated with the Italian scientist's theories and was impressed even if she had a minimal of understanding. Even more thought provoking was the fact that *his* copy was in *Italian.* "You are aware of Galileo's objections and rebuttals to the traditional philosophers, Ptolemy?" He dared to test her and a thoughtful smile curved her mouth.

"I first read the translation in Latin but found your original Italian version, not my strong suit, yet doable nonetheless," she sighed, a most provocative sigh.

Thorne grunted. "In what other languages are you proficient?"

One beautiful hand fiddled with her skirts. "I demonstrate a proficiency in Latin, a dash of Greek, but very strong in French."

"Your camaraderie with Pascale?" he said, his gaze fixed on her. She bit her lip, the same luscious lip he wanted to taste and draw out with his teeth.

"Poor Pascale. No one aboard can speak French and everyone thought he spoke only Creole. His master was French thus he had learned the language. Pascale had no one to speak to. I felt sorry for him. He has a dreadful past."

Thorne raked his fingers through his hair, mystified with the many sides of his cabin boy…and the ever-emerging, Miss Hansford. "Of course, he knew of your gender?"

"About Galileo. He was quite contentious for a man his age, don't you think?"

Had she not changed the subject? How diverting. Thorne folded his arms in front of him ready to debate. "From what I recall, Galileo argued that the earth was always in motion, but philosophers at that time considered his thinking heresy."

"You of all people, Captain Thorne, should relate to his prescription of the earth in motion. Wasn't his study of the ebb and flow of tides, regarding the earth's motion— stimulating?"

Thorne found *her* very stimulating. "Written in the language of mathematics, and with the main characters as triangles, circles, and other geometric figures…without these, one wanders about in a dark and obscure labyrinth. Of course, one who has a firm grasp on such subjects, might reflect?"

She clapped her hands. "I thank you for the compliment."

"It wasn't meant to compliment. Your pretense was like having a stone in my shoe."

Abigail burst out laughing.

And, alas, his lovely cabin boy had the most bewitching laughter, an alluring melody that stole up his spine.

Simeon knocked, and Thorne bade him to enter. The cook set a tray of fresh baked scones with butter and guava jelly on the table. "I hope you find this to your liking, Captain."

Thorne frowned. Ever since Abigail's secret had been revealed, his cook had attempted to make amends for concealing that fact by enticing him with added fare. With a certainty, the old man deemed himself her chaperone. Of course, to Simeon's estimation, Thorne had spent too much alone time with Miss Hansford in the intimacy of his cabin. After Simeon rearranged the silverware five times, Thorne had enough. He rose out of his chair and towered over the old man. "You may return to the kitchen."

His cook scurried to the door. He had the audacity to hesitate at the threshold. "I-I'll return in fifteen minutes to retrieve the tray, Captain."

Thorne slammed the door in his face.

Abigail bit her lip to hide a smile. "He is protecting me."

"I gathered as much, but I don't have to like it."

Simeon's mother hen antics irked Jacob, but the real reason for his displeasure was learning his cabin boy could read and expound on several subjects. "How is it you have such a good education?" she asked him, fingering the spine of her book.

He scorched her with a black look. "For a cloddish colonial?"

Abby giggled. "You did suffer Abe. I'm curious Captain Thorne," she said unable to stop her impulsive questions in spite of herself. "How is it you are so informed on many subjects?"

He lathered two scones with butter, lopped a teaspoon of sweet guava jelly on top and handed one to her. "My uncle insisted on my education, setting a straight course, barring no deviation and demanding I receive the best education. With the family struggling financially, I objected the expense. Where he obtained the money to hire a scholar from Oxford remains a mystery."

Abby nibbled on her scone then tilted her head to the side, the guava, an intriguing taste in her mouth. “A scholar from Oxford in the Colonies? Very unusual.” She wanted to ask him so many things...what he had left behind in his past that she sensed remained buried, what he expected of his future, but she held her tongue. The lessons of the past few months had taught her caution.

She sat in silence, considering this side of Jacob Thorne. In her young life, she had been courted by many swains, and seeing men from different angles, yet she regarded him as unique and unnervingly interesting.

He leaned over and wiped a crumb from her chin. The movement was only for a second, but it seemed a lifetime, and so incongruous with the roguish adventurer. Abby stopped breathing.

“So,” he said, his grin slightly off center. “The seed of discovering had been planted by my instructor then cultivated with questions and reasoning until my appetite for learning became voracious. I read everything I could get my hands on. To the surprise of my tutor, I had eclipsed him in a few years.”

“Your uncle was quite a man. Your mother and father must be proud?” He had said nothing of his parents and had earlier disclosed he had relatives in England. The man was a closed door.

He thought for a moment, obviously weighing what he would reveal to her, but it was the gruffness of his voice that caught her and added to his mystery. “My mother had traveled from England and we lived with her sister, Ester and her husband, Hugh Thorne. I never knew my father. My mother died when I was ten summers. My aunt and uncle adopted me, a natural and logical inclination since I had lived with them from the time I was born. They extended their love and extended their acknowledgement of me as a child of their own, nullifying my bastardy. I owe them a great debt."

Abby swallowed. It took a lot for the proud Captain Thorne to acknowledge the facts of his lineage. He bore with a heavy mantle, the shame of his illegitimacy. Did he know who his father was?

Thorne was looking inward, his expression shuttered. She grasped the moment to consider him, and let her senses inform her mind of all they could identify.

What she saw made her shiver. He was not the man she believed him to be and his tortured secrets he kept hidden beneath his arrogant façade. To keep her distance would be wise. When so moved, she could be very, very wise.

Chapter 17

Star shine glowed along the deck when she climbed through the hatch. Abby had been restless in her cabin and sought the solace of the deck. She realized she was becoming accustomed to the sounds of the sea—the wind as it whistled through the rigging, the waves as they lapped and crashed against hull and bow. And as she closed her eyes to savor the gentle sounds of night, she recognized, unhappily, that she was also becoming accustomed to Jacob Thorne.

Overhead, intermittent clouds floated and in the dark velvet, stars glittered like millions of diamonds scattered carelessly across the sky. She breathed in, the warm air a balm to her lungs, and the awe of creation leaving her to wonder, to speculate over the events of the past weeks and how her life had changed far from her beloved England.

Thorne had ordered her cabin boy duties retired and divided between Simeon and Pascale. Gone was the Yankee captain's hostility replaced by an over solicitousness of her welfare. Every comfort had been afforded. Was Thorne courting her? Abby smiled. She rather liked this genteel side of Thorne.

Their life aboard ship had acquired a certain routine. More often than not, they shared their meals. And every night he escorted her around the deck and to his cabin. And every night she longed for him to join her in his bed, waited to feel his heat, longing to curl against his powerful masculine strength, to touch him, to be held. It was torment to know that she must escape him—when she could not, inside herself, disavow his desirability, when she could not pretend that his arms were not those of a solid and captivating man, that he was not fascinating, that his eyes did not touch her all the way to her soul. And so she lay awake, sometimes barely breathing, sometimes yearning that he would shift and slip his arm around her, stroke her hair, edge closer to her—and then praying fervently that he would not.

If only she could renounce the idea that she was falling beneath his spell. Possibly, falling a little bit in love. Sometimes, she allowed herself to dream. To envision that he might marry her, love her, and treasure her.

It was a sweet fantasy, a bitter dream. Yet it never-ended. Could he love her?

If he loved her, would he marry her?

It was a dangerous fantasy. Very dangerous. Jacob Thorne was a Patriot, and a man as fiercely independent as she longed to be. She drove herself to move away from menacing dreams and fantasies, to remind herself of the impulses of infatuation and to firmly remember she must maintain her detachment from him—and escape as soon as possible. Before she lost more of herself to him than she already had.

You must be practical, Abigail Marie Hansford Rutland. Do not lose your heart.

Even under the best of circumstances, a match would be forbidden. She was a Rutland, born to a different life far from the man whose existence was privateering. Didn't the lines of nobility prevail? She smoothed back a loose tendril, mulling over the divinely sanctioned division of society in England opposed to the fervent, raw freedom Jacob fought for. Didn't she see equality among the crew? Weren't they happier? This she had to admit was true and with that evidence, she determined that what the Americans were fighting for was the greater good. Yet she had made a pact with the Almighty that if her father and brothers were somehow alive, then she would be the compliant, obedient daughter and marry whoever her father decreed.

In the event her family did not survive, Abby prayed the letter she penned to Uncle Cornelius sent through Yvette would reach him. As her father's best friend, the Duke of Westbrook would use all his resources to find who murdered her family. She would do anything to get back to England.

Violin music started from the far end of the ship, and she wrapped her arms around herself retreating inward with the nostalgic strain. Her heart seized on Joshua, her brother who had disappeared in the American wilderness. Joshua, who had secretly taught her how to throw a knife. She half-smiled from the memory. Swearing her to secrecy, her brother had taken her to a secluded meadow in the woods where he had placed a target on a tree. Repeatedly, he instructed her, encouraging her until she at last, became proficient. He was alive. He had to be. By now, he'd be in touch with their Uncle Thomas Hansford who lived in Boston? No doubt, he had finished dinner with her uncle, and was ensconced comfortably before a fire.

In Boston, she'd seek Uncle Thomas's aid and breathed a sigh of relief, a comfort to have family in the Colonies where hostility to her presence would be strong. Abby had not told Thorne of this relation. No. It would serve no purpose. He was unreadable where her future was concerned. At least she would have a place to go and perhaps a way to secure passage to England.

"Abby," Thorne's voice broke out of the dark, startling her. She slipped, but his hand caught her elbow. A southern zephyr had kicked up by the time they reached mid-ship and she shivered. He took off his coat and placed it over her, an affectionate, considerate act. Abby brushed her lips over the collar, inhaling Jacob's comforting scent. Side by side they stood in companionable silence, peace descending with only the creak of wood where full-masted sails strained, fortified by the wind.

"Captain, how is it you know so much about the sea and ships?"

He bowed his head, the action contrasting with his unshaven face, for a day's beard was visible. "My uncle, Hugh was a brilliant sea-captain. Early on I was exposed to life on the water. He grew too old for the sea and retired. With the help of an investor, we began a shipbuilding yard in Boston. I showed an aptitude for the trade, drawing and designing, improving the speed and gainliness of the ships we built."

Thorne stopped and tightened rigging on a halyard then motioned for her to walk with him again. "I spent a few years dabbling with the business but my restless spirit had me yearning for the sea. My uncle finally relented and I sailed out to test one of our ships, proving the vessel faster and sleeker than any on the seas. Of course, history changed the course of events. The British took control of Boston. When my uncle was cut down at Breeds Hill…" his fists tightened. "As he lay dying in my arms, he made me promise to care for the family."

"I see," she whispered, but she wondered what other layers he hid beneath.

He stopped. "No. You don't see. I did a rotten job of keeping my promise. I drowned my sorrows in whiskey, sleeping in my ship tied in the harbor and never going home. Aunt Ester died of pneumonia, probably more from a broken heart. I sank further into drink. The Quartering Act was passed. Without my knowledge, British soldiers bordered in my uncle's home and preyed upon my eighteen year old cousin, Rachel. She had pleaded with me to come home. By that time, I was so in my cups that I was not aware she existed. Then Thomas died…"

"You were going through mourning," Abby explained away his guilt. Didn't her brother, Nicholas react the same way when their mother had died? Didn't she in her own way act out in rebellion?

We both have our scars. We work so very hard to bury them.

A wave of sorrow swept over her as he relived his past, his voice devoid of all emotion. Her own heart fluttered with the loss of her own family. "Losing someone you love affects you so deeply that it remains buried inside of you and becomes this big, bottomless hole of ache that never goes away." She could feel the tug of his gaze, the rugged insistence of his presence, and she wanted to look at him. But she was afraid of coming to care too much.

His revenge against the people who had done this to his family stood atoned in his careless behavior and shown in contempt for England and everything British, so great, he raided their very shores. But Jacob, she sensed, had other demons.

His hand curled in the ratline. She hesitated, studying that hand. The long, strong fingers, hands of a man of the sea, calloused by hard work and hard weather—a pirate's hand, one that had held a sword and pistols, and killed men. How could it be the same hand that had plucked a drowning cabin boy from the sea?

Through sheltering clouds, the light of a half-moon kicked up on languid waves. Then a low lifeless pitch of self-loathing resonated in his tone. "The fact remains, I wasn't there when my family needed me. If I could reverse everything—"

Aching for him, a deep understanding of him roused inside of her. This confident, strong-willed, sometimes harsh man, she could picture, overcome with grief and unable to protect the ones he loved. The unspoken, suppressed guilt he shouldered increased the gravest of his flaws, making him more reckless, impatient and demanding.

Don't fall in love with him, Abigail. Be completely unaffected by him.

Abby looked down at her open palms, conflicted with her own swirling emotions. Who was she to give comfort? As Abe she could not. As Lady Abigail Rutland she could not. But as commonplace Abby Hansford, she could. Denying the wisdom of it, she took his hand in hers. This was madness, pure madness, and yet she could no more resist it—or him—than she could resist the wind upon her face. If only she could will his festering wound into her body—and release him from this agony.

Jacob had measured the risk, wondering what it would cost him to tell this compassionate, perceptive woman something about himself. He had grown so used to holding back the truth by not verbalizing it, that once he overcame the difficulty of saying the words aloud, he was unable to hold back. Like an undertow pulling him, his past flowed.

"You have bared yourself to me, Captain Thorne. I hold no censure, no reproach and no blame upon your head. Life deals us unfair justice and tragedy. No matter what our difficulties, to lose hope would be the real disaster. Real strength is when we pick ourselves up and move forward."

He wanted to savor the honey sweetness of her voice and all the less condemning ways she made him feel. Suddenly the night seemed like a thousand burning suns. He wanted her. He wanted to see her face in the morning, and then at night and a million times in between. He wanted to hear her laugh, to hear her sigh and all the mundane things linking them together. He wanted to grow old with her, bounce their children from his knee and witness all the best there was to be. He wanted to marry her.

His fingers folded down to lace with hers. He knew pushing her hard, too fast would be a big mistake on his part, so he held back. The wind blew tendrils of her hair around him, wrapping him in an enchanting snare. She leaned into him and he pressed his lips against her forehead in a kiss. Her heart beat fast against his chest. He dared not kiss her on the lips, to take her mouth's nectar, to bury his nose in the valley between her breasts. A jolt of heat pulsed in his groin. He'd never be able to stop.

When she shivered, his arms went automatically around her. She wanted him as much as he desired her, he knew it in his bones, knew it in the way her body melted into his. She had unnamed needs and he could easily cultivate those needs. She was an innocent and untouched and he'd do his damnedest to keep it that way.

A feeling he did not wish to name stirred behind his breastbone. She was truth, beauty and goodness personified. She'd be a fool to have him. A privateer, a wanted man, a man with a price on his head. He could not love her, for if he loved her, he could not leave her alone in Boston while he went on with the war.

And yet putting her aside he must. He could not make promises. No. He could not allow her to fall in love with him. Straining against all desire, he pushed her away from him.

"Jacob?"

Her voice broke and the stricken look on her face tore his heart from him. So be it. He had to separate for her own good. Why did his decision howl through his veins?

Chapter 18

The estrangement between her and Thorne over the past few days weighed heavy on Abby's heart. How convenient he'd be working on the opposite side of the deck or go beneath when she was about. Thorne and his dreadful history crossed her mind more than once.

Never again would she offer comfort and chastised herself for the prior evening's weakness. Abby shrugged, unable to sort out the reasons of men. Best to keep things the way they were. She sighed. How to isolate the loneliness?

Twelfth Night had arrived and everyone wanted to erase the unstated melancholy of not being home to share the occasion with their families. For Abby, it was especially hard not knowing if there would be any of her family to go back to. In his cabin, she had finished bathing and selected the violet gown. The décolletage was scandalously low but she didn't care. She ran her hands down the skirts, the satin folds smooth to her fingers and gazed into the mirror, surprised her hair had grown past her shoulders. She swept it up in a stylish fashion, allowing little ringlets to dangle free. A growing confidence met the woman reflected in the mirror, yielding femininity and power. This was *Lady Abigail Rutland.* This was the young woman bred of conviction and prominence.

Simeon had worked all day in the galley and promised a grand surprise so she had taken extra care to set the table. Beeswax candles dripped down silver candelabras, thieved no doubt from raided ships, and illuminated the captain's cabin in a warm festive light. The silverware was polished to an extra luster and the crystal possessed an additional sparkle. The glitter did nothing to assuage her melancholy.

The temperatures had dipped so she draped a shawl around her shoulders just as Lieutenant Lawton, Enos, and Benjamin Lee filed in, dressed as impeccably as they could manage. Everyone was there to celebrate, bestowing happy felicitations, everyone except Thorne. He had left orders for them to celebrate without him. If he wanted to wallow in misery, then so be it.

"Simeon, you have outdone yourself," toasted Lieutenant Lawton. Simeon had butchered one of the geese earlier in the day and roasted the bird to tangy crisp perfection. Bread pudding followed with potatoes, fish with a lemony cream sauce, and oranges from Martinique, everything to tempt the palate. Everyone was buoyed with high-spirits. Everyone except Abby, who pasted on her most brilliant smile, saying little, pushing the food around her plate, and unable to eat. If the crew were aware of any distancing among the Captain and her, they did not comment.

Midway through the meal, Enos stood up. "I'd like to make an announcement. The crew and I would like to make a special presentation to you, Miss Hansford. For taking care of our wounds and ailments especially what you did when Ben and I were sick."

She took the crudely wrapped package from Enos. "I am touched." Her voice wavered. She pulled away the linen to reveal a beautiful carving of the *Vengeance*, fully-masted with sails, detailed rigging, whittled right down to the rudder. "I don't know what to say, except thank you. Thank you all."

"Our names are carved in the bottom, Miss Hansford."

She turned the piece over, struck between wonderment and awe. They were her family. Before she could say anything, warm air rushed into the cabin. She didn't even have to look. Thorne. Abby frowned. Rum. Thorne had been drinking.

He slid into the empty chair beside her, the tension palpable between them. When she looked up, she swallowed down a wave of panic. She hadn't quite prepared herself for... And it definitely took some preparation. Refined in his dress, he lounged far from the rough privateer. His white shirt tucked into unfashionably tight fawn-colored trousers, clung to powerful thighs, the corded muscles rippling beneath, in what could be barely considered decent.

It pleased her to look at him.

More than it should have.

He held his freshly shaven chin between his forefinger and thumb in thoughtful reflection then waved his hand. "We shall have a festive celebration this night. I command it."

Of course, he would command it.

He motioned for Simeon to fill his glass then refill Abby's. He forked some meat into his mouth. "Excellent," he said to the beaming Simeon then tapped the table for his cook to leave the bottle.

Why was she so relieved to see him? Why her burgeoning nervousness? Because he was looking at her even while he was talking to Simeon. She blushed. When she grasped her fork to quell her shaky fingers, her shawl slipped from her shoulders to the floor. She bent to retrieve it, but Thorne had procured the garment for her. In lazy regard, his gaze paused at her décolletage then slowly moved up to her face.

A crackle of energy passed between them. Abby breathed in the heady scents of allspice, rum, and—the scent of him, felt the heat from his knee pressed to hers. Every breath wove into her brain and spiraled there. When she straightened four pairs of eyes stared at her. If only she could slide down her chair and hide beneath the table. In London, her gown would have been exceptional. On the *Vengeance*, it created a sensation and perhaps one she was not prepared for.

"Captain, so glad you could make it," Enos broke the silence. "I was about to raise a toast to our beautiful Miss Hansford

"Aye," Joseph Lawton seconded, "To have a fair flower aboard the *Vengeance*."

Benjamin Lee raised his glass. "Even my love, my dearest Sally…" he referred to the ship's figurehead. "…cannot compare to our Miss Hansford."

Thorne, too, lifted his glass, his eyes never leaving hers, his lips pressed in a cynical line. "A toast to our admirable, Miss Hansford, so chameleon-like—from cabin boy to seducer of the world."

Did he dare to call her a seductress in front of his men? How she itched to rake her nails across his face. To think he was jealous. Oh, to teach him a lesson. Risky.

Like confronting a jackal in its own den?

"Lieutenant Lawton," Abby began, "Did I tell you how handsome you look this evening? And Enos, how divine you appear. Benjamin, did I remark how dashing you have been?" How long did she go on, charming them with platitudes, making it a point to ignore Thorne? Over the rim of his wine glass, he watched her with hooded eyes. Despite his calm manner, he did not fool her. At any moment, the stem of his wineglass might snap in two. Good.

You are walking on dangerous ground, Abigail Rutland.

Thorne tilted back in his chair. "I see you are making an effort to charm me."

"I wasn't about to beguile," she snapped.

Thorne's fork clattered to his plate. She could see him glowering at her, clearly disliking her answer.

"What, no wagers this evening, Enos?" Thorne rolled up his sleeves.

Enos put his glass down. "It's Christmas, Captain. A sacred day. Wouldn't be proper."

"I can well imagine what wagers are spinning through your mind. Like when I will bed our cabin boy."

Abigail gasped. Enos choked. Benjamin Lee's jaw dropped.

At that moment, she wished Thorne to perdition, fully aware she should withdraw from the darkness that surrounded him. If only she could resist diving into it, to succumb to the lure of his menace. She finished her wine. "Captain Thorne chooses to embrace self-pity. He wraps it around him like a rope on a winch."

Lieutenant Lawton tapped his finger on the table. "Captain Thorne, you're out of bounds. The crew and I will excuse your behavior due to the spirits imbibed this eve, but Miss Hansford has done nothing to deserve your callous treatment. You owe her an apology."

She had definitely confronted the jackal in his own den.

Abby smiled inwardly. Now she was backed by his crew. She held out her glass for Thorne to refill. "Captain?" she challenged.

His face went through a host of changes. The hostility was gone. In its place was something else, something more calculated and measured. Was she treading in shark infested waters?

"You're right, Joseph. I do owe, Miss Hansford an apology. I was completely out of line." He refilled her cup and his own. "Miss Hansford, you have provided me a liberating moment. Like Lieutenant Lawton has suggested, the rum, the wine has done the talking and blinded me in many ways. I pray you do not think the worst of me."

Abby's hand flew to her chest. He had humbled himself to her in front of his men. Or was it a ruse? The man was maddening, always ensuring her turmoil. He looked at her for a long time, but she saw no arrogance in his gaze now, no insolence. Only acute interest—and gentleness that made her hurt for what she had said to him. "I accept your apology, if you accept mine for the harsh words I have spoken, Captain Thorne."

"Jacob," he demanded.

"Jacob," she whispered. Despite the melody of the waves and wind against the ship, she could hear his heartbeats, feel his pulse pounding along her nerves. It was as if everyone else, and the walls and the world all-around had faded away, leaving only her and Jacob. Too see his soul naked, to know it mirrored hers, reduced from complicated epiphanies, balancing all the pain, loss, awkwardness, idiocy, compromise, and clumsiness that threaded life. The neediness and loneliness reflected made her acknowledge that together they had the power to banish that sense of isolation. They were two woven threads. She could not deny their connection any more than she could forego breathing.

Enos cleared his throat, hurtling her back to earth. Abby took a deep sip of wine. To have something else, anything else to focus on she took the carving of the ship Enos had carved on behalf of the crew. "Again, I thank all of you for this treasured gift."

The first time Jacob became aware of Abby as a woman, he could barely get over her beauty. But this—this was beyond perfection. She was bewitching and enchanting. Her grace spurned mere earthly mortals. The suggestion of defiance in her unwavering eyes only made her that much more captivating. Yet he was unable to keep his eyes off her. Everything about Abby shimmered as if her gown had been woven by ethereal beings out of sapphire starlight.

The sight of her seized him as well as every robust man in the room. Jealousy churned in his stomach, for every one of his crew gawked like fish caught in a net. Hadn't Enos leaned over a little too close to whisper some witticism in her ear? Sitting opposite of her, Lawton had bowed—a little too far, informing her of how she rivaled all women of his acquaintance—as if the Bible-thumper had any women of acquaintance. And Benjamin Lee, how he wanted to punch that school boy obsession right off the old salt's face. Thorne poured more wine in her glass.

"Captain, I will drown." She waved him off but he filled it none the same.

"If we did not have the winter, Miss Hansford, we'd never appreciate the spring," Enos said. "Having you as our cabin boy was one thing but to have you as you are now is like having a blossoming rose."

Enos's sentiments scorched Thorne's ears. A genuine smile built up and lit her face. He should be the recipient of that smile, not Enos. Jacob viewed the scene through a red haze, and watched as she turned her attentions from one male to another, always smiling, nodding and gazing into his face.

On two accounts, the intrepid Miss Hansford had thrown down a challenge. First was her method to make him jealous. His stomach hardened. She was succeeding at that. Secondly, he couldn't get her words out of his mind. "*...I hold no censure, no reproach and no blame upon your head. Life deals us unfair justice and tragedy. No matter what our difficulties, to lose hope would be the real disaster...*" Damn her. Damn her to hell.

He had been an ass where she was concerned. He had strung out her future not giving her any hint of what was to become of her. Part because he had not figured it all out and part because he didn't want to let her go. No doubt, after he rescued his cousin, he'd be ordered out to England again to raid the coasts. There was no security in his future. But the gods were clearly not inclined to leave him be, leaving the golden-haired enchantress to weave her spell.

When he made his apology and saw her heart soften, saw her eyes search his, he was lost. In that one look, a most intimate message was made, and everything else ceased to exist—to understand that they were broken, magnificently imperfect and tangibly connected. There was no denying it. She had stolen into his heart. A part of her would always be there.

She deserved better.

From his pocket, he pulled a package and placed it in front of her. He liked her quick intake of breath, the way her lips parted. "For you, Miss Hansford."

"I am overwhelmed, but I do not have anything to give you, Captain." Her fingers trembled as she gingerly opened the lace cloth to reveal a pearl encrusted comb.

"It is beautiful." In the radiant candlelight, she bestowed a smile on him like a princess would her knight in shining armor. How he'd like to freeze that look of wonder—forever.

How many times had he made the trip to his cabin door at night, raising his hand to knock but then turning away? Damn his moral code.

"I have another gift for you."

When she tilted her head in question, Thorne put up his hand. "I have given considerable thought about your future once we arrive in Boston."

He watched her breath hitch, the way the light flickered in the hollow of her throat. "I plan to set you up as a companion to a wealthy widow. Mrs. Smith is a trusted friend of the family and would find it incumbent to help a young lady. Her discretion is complete. I would set you up with a plausible story, saying your father had expired and left you stranded in Martinique. I gallantly obliged your circumstance and gave you passage home to America. The crew will swear to your story."

The men nodded in agreement. Thorne had it all figured out. He would be worry free. A privateer's life was rife with risk and high rate of mortality. He would not burden Abby with that risk nor have her worrying about him—or leave a child behind with a widowed mother.

Yet he wanted her in every way a man wanted a woman, possessing her until she depended on him for the very air she breathed. His expression carefully neutral, he continued. "Your reputation will be salvaged with no hint of your misfortunes. You will find a comfortable environment in Boston—safe."

"Thank you. You don't know how much this means to me."

But Thorne saw her hesitate…then lift her lips into a smile. Odd? He assumed she would be delighted. Was she not happy with this arrangement? His decision was made.

Lieutenant Lawton interrupted. "Miss Hansford will be the toast of Boston."

Jacob gritted his teeth, contempt of that prospect filled him with disgust. No doubt every proper eligible male would court her like dogs after a butcher's cart.

"You will love Boston," said Enos. "You will find it much different than England. Vast wilderness, Indians, half-savage whites, wild beasts."

"Don't let Enos fool you. He comes from Nantucket, a long line of whalers and a long line of story," said Jacob. "Boston is civilized and quite progressive."

"The cradle of civilization…" Enos winked, "Bostonians built a church that cost fifty pounds and a tavern that cost five hundred pounds."

"The city has its own excitement," added Lieutenant Lawton. There's delight and joy."

"Of course, he finds Boston exciting. He has a sweetheart to get back to." Enos elbowed Benjamin. "But first he has some making up to do."

Abby looked at the blushing Lieutenant Lawton over the rim of her glass, considering him. "En amour on pardonne mais on n'oublie jamais...in love, we forgive but we never forget."

Thorne raised an eyebrow. He did not know French, but the flawless accented language was nagging and familiar. Lucette?

Lawton looked at her expectantly. I know Latin and the language is close to French. "I hope Helena forgives me for leaving, but at times, I consider that absolution an illusion."

"Si l'amour n'est qu'une illusion alors qu'est-ee que la re'alite'?" she smiled. "If love is nothing but an illusion, then what is real?"

There were those same husky tones again.

From the realms of darkness and confusion, the soft purr of a courtesan formed bright in Jacob's mind. Pieces and parts of that half-dream were flooding back to him. There remained no orderly sequence, and he could find no reasonable explanation for what he recalled. He scowled darkly, finding no balm for his troubled thoughts and irritated with his own inability to remember that night clearly. That voice. Was it possible?

She turned in her chair. Thorne had a clear view of full breasts that rose and fell with her breathing. It was a scattered set of impressions he dealt with. His fingers flexed on the arms of his chair. He cupped his hands as if to weigh the creamy mounds in his hands.

Images blended. An elusive familiarity surrounded his cabin boy, alias Miss Hansford. Lucky Lucette had massive dark ponderous breasts. The woman he made love to had just the right size. A sharp vision sizzled through his mind. The woman he made love to was light to Lucette's dark. Another flash seared his brain, so strong that for a fractured second, it hurt to think. The woman he made love to was slim and small not large and brawny like Lucette. Hadn't he locked Abe in the cabin?

Enos threw down his napkin. "If I had a gold piece for every time Lieutenant Lawton told me he missed Helena, this ship would sink."

Abby laughed and with a wistful expression said, "Ma générosité est aussi illimitée que la mer, Mon amour est profond: plus je te donne…My bounty is as boundless as the sea. My love is deep, the more I give to thee."

Thorne jerked his head up. His mind broke through the chatter. Weren't those same words whispered to him that night? No way in hell would a French courtesan know Shakespeare. But the educated daughter of a gold merchant would *know.*

Thorne dropped his chair to four legs in a loud bang. *Damn.* The undeniable truth of having sex with his cabin boy hit him dead center. But Abe wasn't a boy. Blessedly that fact did nothing to assuage the disgust he held. The reality was—he had deflowered a virgin, and all the ramifications with it, slammed into to him like a tidal wave.

Abigail was so enjoying herself, she did not see Thorne's incline of head, barely aware of Simeon retrieving the dishes and scarcely conscious of the men departing. She turned in her chair. Enos bid his adieu and closed the door, the last to go. Over steepled fingers, Thorne glared at her, his face ominous. Abby blinked. For the life of her, she could not fathom his sudden change in behavior or his simmering animosity.

Her voice suffocated as that pair of piercing cobalt blue eyes bore into her like lightening searing through the sky...cold, probing, speculative eyes. Knowing eyes. She paled. Dear God.

He *knew.*

"You were the virgin in my bed."

Chapter 19

Get away. Abby stood and pivoted, took two steps. Her skirts hampered her speed. A chair crashed. An arm shot from behind. The bolt slammed into place. He caught her and swung her around, flat against the door. She fought him, tried to ply his hand from her arm. The night they had laid together remained far too vivid in her memory. Alone with Thorne, in his cabin, and with the door barred against entry from the rest of the crew, she was far too vulnerable. She wanted to be safe, to have Thorne on the other side, and the door barred between them. She thrust her palms up against his chest, anything to separate her from a hard rock wall of muscle and tendon. Blindly, she shoved, dislodging him. He fell into the table. A wine bottle plunged to the floor.

"Stop it." He took her hands then held her against the door. "We will have this out."

Abby stilled her frantic thrashing. Thorne's discovery hung over her like a shroud. Indecision raged at her, and tears she refused to shed, ached in her eyes. No way would she let him intimidate her. Squaring her shoulders, she reminded herself of her resolution to be wise.

"So, you figured it all out," she said. *But how?* In the waning silence, her blood pounded wildly in her ears.

His thighs crushed her quaking limbs. He tilted her head back and she considered his unyielding face, consciously aware of the weight of his body, conscious of her breasts pressed to his chest, and too aware of his increasing arousal pressed rock hard alongside her abdomen. Abby moaned. Moisture popped from his pores and the scent of sweet wine and male filled her nostrils. She stopped struggling. No. She would not misjudge his strength or his ardor.

"Let me go," she ordered, her voice far from the bravado of that command.

His breathing uneven, he took a step back, his hands slowly moved down her arms. Thorne refused to let go. "We have matters to discuss."

"I will not disappear." She studied his hands on her arms afraid if he let go she would collapse to the floor. He yanked her to a chair.

"Sit," he barked out in that implacable authority she loathed.

The room spun. If only she hadn't drunk so much wine. Abby grudgingly complied. With the revelation of what had happened in his bed was the small satisfaction that he was rattled as much as she. Thorne kicked up his overturned chair, propped his foot upon it. Like a specimen beneath a magnifying glass, he scrutinized her.

"That's better now."

Her voice cracked. "What do you want?"

"I intend to find out what the hell is going on," he said darkly.

She lifted her chin. "If you already know, then what is there to tell?"

"I already know the truth. Now I want to know how it happened." He leaned toward her, brushed her arm and for one second, thought he'd do violence. He retrieved the wine bottle and slapped it on the table.

"I don't owe you any explanations." She looked away, pointedly ignoring him. Out the transom windows a storm boiled to the south. The air was like soup. Clouds covered the moon and the last of moonlight dancing on the water diminished as dark as pitch.

He cupped her chin in his hand and lowered his face, inches from hers. "You do owe me an explanation. This is my ship. I am the captain."

Abby licked her lips. "Of course, only a boorish Colonial would resort to threaten a woman. What next? Keelhauling?"

He gripped her. "Damn. You will tell me and tell me quickly." He drew her face closer to the wavering light. Thorne loomed larger than ever, his face demonic, his winter cold, blue eyes skewering her. With his other hand he touched her hair, examining it as if it weren't real. Illusions shattered. He then drew a calloused finger down her cheek and over the curve of her lips. She inhaled. A low rumbling chuckle emanated from deep in his chest. Had he gone insane?

"How do you know the crew will not return?" she challenged.

"I commanded it."

"I did not hear it."

"They know when I'm not to be disturbed."

Her hands balled into fists and she darted a glance at the door, weighing the time it would take for her to reach it, throw the bolt and dash up to the deck. But where would she go?

"Don't even try it," he warned. "I should have bathed you the day I captured the *Civis*." He straightened but not for one second did he relax. He dropped his hands as if she were not worth his contempt. It was that sweeping gesture that angered Abby.

"You think I will plead for my deliverance from you? Do you think I will beg for absolution for what happened? Or bend to some misplaced pride and honor you carry around like a shield? I do not hold you accountable for events nor do I expect anything from you."

She choked. "Just leave me alone." Through a blur of tears, she did not see the myriad of changes mirrored on Thorne's face, numb to the workings of his mind. She cried for her parents, for her brothers and all the injustices she had gone through and now this. Gruffly, she heard him speak and when he lifted her face up to his, the anger in his tone had softened.

"Abby, I just want to know, why?"

"Why?" She cried more. How did she explain when she didn't even know herself? Her senses were so dulled by the wine. She couldn't even think and started blubbering about the events that led up to them ending up in his bed. She described how Lucette, the prostitute had attempted to rob him and carve his face. How she had awakened from her pallet and fought with the prostitute to save him. How she had ordered Lucette to be thrown overboard but by Pascale's good graces, the black had rowed her to shore. Thorne produced a handkerchief and she blew her nose.

"Abby, you still haven't told me why." His tone brooked no argument.

Abby truly wished he'd go away, his presence wreaking havoc on the peace she so desperately needed. Rain smacked against the windows, drops as big as herrings.

"My coat."

When he frowned, she nodded to him, affirming the truth. "It was my coat. When you locked me in the cabin for spying on you, I figured you wouldn't be back for the night. In my anger, I threw my clothes about the room and took a bath. I went to sleep without putting my clothes back on." Heat rose to her cheeks with that part of the confession. "You were drunk and asleep and I couldn't get my coat from beneath you. I had to retrieve my coat before you discovered me in the morning. I tugged and pulled. You awoke… thought I was Lucette. I played along, hoping you would fall back asleep. So you see…" she sniffed, "…it was all for a coat."

Thorne rubbed the back of his neck. He was getting a clear picture of the events of that night. Damn. He had taken her maidenhead. He had forced himself on an innocent girl who only sought to survive, a helpless girl in his care. It slammed into his gut with such a force he could barely breathe.

But there was more to the story. He wanted answers and neither would he settle for the coat as an alibi. "You still haven't told me *why*, Abby."

She pulled her arm across her eyes like Abe would do, momentarily forgetting the unladylike gesture. "Go on." He wanted to hear it. He wanted all her explanation.

On a ragged breath, she peered up at him. Her clear blue eyes brimmed with tears. Like a wounded animal, she beseeched him.

"From the time you took us aboard from the *Civis*, you showed mercy to a boy and an old man. You gave the boy a job, defended him against torment by the crew, took the time to teach him to read, and despite his fear of heights, made him climb to the top of the mast to see a beautiful world he would never have the chance to see otherwise. You put up with a boy's sarcasm, seeing through his bluster as fear. You showed benevolence inherent in your nature."

Thorne sighed. "That's not all of the story—" He wanted to hear her say it. To atone him for his sin and that he wouldn't be damned in the eyes of God. He hated the fact that he insisted on her honesty and that because he had come to care for her more than he should have that she might loathe him for what had transpired. "There's more isn't there? I forced you against your will?"

Her voice dropped to a whisper. "No." She shook her head, filled with shame and helplessness, and a million other feelings Thorne could not recognize.

"No?" he repeated. A potent feeling of relief surged through him. "Where am I wrong?" he asked, his voice low, but insistent. "Tell me, where my reasoning is flawed."

It was a truth Abby could not name, so intangible, and so significant. He did not thunder out a command like he did with his crew. No. He asked her gently, less incriminatingly, almost pleading for her honesty. Memories flooded of his incredible, powerful lovemaking. How he made her feel like a woman. How he made her feel with his whispered words of praise, his heady fervor, his kisses, his touch, his hands on her neck, her breasts, everywhere to make her keen with desire. It was the most wonderful experience in the world. And part of her wanted to make him hurt for what he had done, to extract a promise from him to take her to England. But that would not be the truth. To add this lie to the many other lies she had told would damn her forever. “Once I was in your bed, I did not want to leave,” she answered in a muffled whisper. Mortified she covered her face with her hands, to shut out the intensity of his gaze, and to hide her inner soul.

Abby did not see the tenderness in his slow smile, or sense the rawness that burst in his chest. “Take your hands away, Abby and look at me,” he commanded.

Slowly she pulled her hands away. He extended his hand to her. “Come, Abby.”

On shaky limbs, Abby stood up and walked over to him, her sense of right and wrong lurched with the magnitude of what was to unfold. He was supposed to be her enemy. He was a privateer fighting against her country. If he knew she was Lady Abigail Hansford Rutland he would hate her, and hate her for deceiving him, a sin, a man like Thorne would never forgive. Hesitantly, she placed her hand in his warm palm, watching as his long, tanned fingers closed around hers. The compelling look in his eyes, the extraordinary reassurance in the warmth of his grip all but made her knees buckle beneath her.

And when his arms encircled her, drawing her against his hard, muscular length, and his parted lips touched hers, robbing her of speech and breath, her sense of right and wrong blurred, and she surrendered to his complete and total possession.

“I am sorry, Abby. Can you forgive me?”

Jacob had taken her innocence without knowing it, and imagined the violence of what a drunken rum-soaked fool had done. Yet this sweet vulnerable woman, who he was completely accountable for, absolved his guilt by her admission.

Once I was in your bed, I did not want to leave.

The soft magic of her lips heated and tormented Jacob, rousing a fever so empowering, he could not get enough of her. She had confessed her desire and it slammed into him with the intensity of fire melting metal. He knew well enough where it would end and the raw, primal hunger feeding him smacked with a wall of restraint.

"You showed benevolence inherent in your nature."

He was going to make love to her again, but this time he would feed her fires slowly, to teach her what lovemaking was really meant to be. He slid his tongue across her lips, urging them to part, persisting, and the instant they did, he dove into her mouth. Impatiently, he slipped his hands up and down her arms, her breasts, sliding possessively across her spine and pressing her tightly to his hardened thighs. With a moan of surrender, she wound her arms around his neck, stroking his skin there, and a violent hunger struck him. He struggled to squash that need down. His hands froze on her hips. Reluctantly, he dragged his mouth from hers. "Are you sure?" he asked quietly.

She exhaled. "Yes."

"I promise you this time will so much better." He took her mouth again and delved his tongue into the deeper recesses of her mouth. His hands trembled undoing her buttons, the rich silk, gliding to the floor. Clad in her chemise, he could not envision anything more erotic. He removed the lacy camisole off her ivory shoulders and full, rosy-tipped breasts gleamed in the candlelight.

"Now take the pins from your hair," he commanded. She did and shook her hair free. Thorne groaned. "You tempt a man to his soul." He could barely breathe, and felt her body quiver from his stare.

With a look of uncertainty, she did something he did not expect. She undid the buttons of his shirt then pressed her palms against his bare chest, stood on her toes and kissed him.

Shocked and aroused by her boldness, Thorne willed himself to remain motionless yet blood surged through his veins like quicksilver. Her mouth explored him, her lips hot against his, her sweet tongue, stroking him, fanning fires in his loins. She pulled his shirt off, slowly down his arms then tentatively reached for the laces on his breeches now painfully swollen with his erection. Thorne threw back his head. Her sweet uncertain touch would be his undoing.

"Not now," he warned, pulling her hands away and glimpsed the hurt in her eyes. "You'd scorch me with your touch. I need to keep my promise to you." He tossed back the covers and on a surge of pure lust, he took her dewy lips in a long, sweet kiss, and then swept her up into his arms, laying her gently on the cool soft sheets of his bed.

She bit her lip, her head turned away, and Thorne saw the lovely flush that swept up her shapely legs, her slender curves, staining the glowing ivory skin across her breasts. Despite her embarrassment, he could not extinguish the candles no more than he could banish this glorious sight. He removed his boots and breeches, then stretched out alongside her, pulling her into his arms and turning her face to him. Abby became rigid. Thorne cursed himself.

He ran a forefinger over her lovely cheek. "Again, I apologize for my brutish behavior. What is about to take place is between a man and a woman, a sharing of intimacy born of my desire for you, a need to be close to you, to become a part of you."

Abby mutely nodded her head.

"And it will not end here, Abby. When we get to Boston, we will be married."

Thorne inhaled. He had told her they would marry and as odd as the oath fell from his lips, it set easily in his mind. He was just as surprised as she. They would marry and he'd do his damnedest to make her happy. She was his.

Abby pressed a finger to his lips and shook her head. "But I-I cannot..."

"...Burden me? Is that what you think, Abby. You are a burden? Only once in a million lifetimes, you find someone who can completely turn your world around. Someone you can tell things that you've never shared with another soul and they absorb everything you say and want to hear more. Someone you share hopes for the future, dreams and any disappointments life has thrown at you. When something wonderful happens, you can't wait to tell her about it, knowing she will share in your excitement. She makes you laugh. She builds you up and shows you things about yourself that make you better. Most importantly, she weaves faith and confidence around your heart. All these qualities I find in you. I want you, Abby. I will protect you and cherish you until the end of my days. I will give you a dozen children and we will raise them together in bliss. You are mine, Abigail Marie Hansford and always will be."

He ran his hand soothingly over her naked back, touching briefly her thighs. In the next few moments her breathing quickened, and he seized her sweet mouth in a kiss. He bent his head down and suckled her breast. He let her nipple slide out of his mouth. She pushed him back, but he was more riveted in running his gaze over the sheen of dampness on her breast, dampness he had caused. A surge of possessiveness seized inside his chest. Yes, she was definitely his.

Abby opened her mouth to protest, to tell him the truth of why she could not marry him. All her could-haves and the not-haves a reality, she resented. Oh, those sweet words, to protect and cherish...and the brush of his warm mouth against her swollen breast, spiraled a longing she could never stop even if she wanted too. His kiss was fierce, wild, almost violent, making her heart rip. Hadn't she lain awake at night, consumed with thoughts of him, wanting the gnawing hunger he had created to be appeased? If only she could tell him who she really was. No-no-no. Raw potent fear drove her, fear she would not experience his arms around her, fear he'd believe her actions wanton and shameful, fear he'd send her away or worse.

"Jacob, I must tell you..."

"Hush, dear Abby. Everything will be fine."

Abby spiraled from sensual onslaught, whirling with desire and helplessly, she wound her arms around his neck. Thorne increased his ardor, his nose nuzzled the sensitive skin behind her ear, arms like bands of iron twisted around her, rippling arm, shoulder and thigh muscles gleamed in the candlelight, his manhood magnificent, probed her side. His hand moved from her breast, down her waist, his fingers lightly circled her thighs and to the spot in between, caressing the hairs of her mons.

"I will pleasure you, Abby." The deep timbre of his voice and his eyes so dark now took on the hue of indigo. He sank his fingers into her depths, circling inside her then drawing out. Abby gasped and tilted her pelvis upward, unsure and unable to get more from him. She closed her eyes, waited, as he slid his hand then withdrew in rhythmic timing. Wherever he touched her, his hands were magical, awakening her body to his power. She could scarcely breathe, swamped with the growing slickness between her legs and the stroking that raised her to a pinnacle she could not reach.

He lifted his head, the sight of his dark, disheveled hair, eyes glinting with longing in the lamp light, the gorgeous spread of his shoulders, tapering down to his narrow hips, made her womb ache. When he rose-up on his arms and straddled her, cool air touched her skin except where his manhood laid hot, heavy, throbbing across her abdomen. Gazing into his scorching eyes now, she surely thought she would melt from the tenderness she saw there and all the wonderful things he said to her. *"Only once in your life, I truly believe, you find someone who can completely turn your world around."* She lifted her fingers and traced his cheek and his lips, while inside her, an emotion sweetly unfurled, so appealing, so overpowering that it made her tremble.

"Kiss me, Abby."

"Someone you can tell things that you've never shared with another soul and they absorb everything you say and actually want to hear more."

With unshed tears, his words evoked heartbreaking tenderness like a warm soft blanket of down, softly covering and gently capturing her soul, and to know that this strong, vital man treasured her. And Abby did. She offered him her parting lips, moving them against his, kissing him as deeply as he was kissing her. Abby's fingers slid up the bunched muscles of his chest and shoulders, then glided her hands round his hips, pulling him toward her, anything, anything to abate the growing need. And when she ran her fingers down his arousal, he reared back, separated her slick folds, withdrew his hand and eased into her.

"Abby," he whispered, kissing her forehead, cheeks, lips and neck. "Abby..." he whispered again and again.

A shudder shook him. He withdrew by inches, and shifted forward again, and then withdrew and plunged again and again. She wrapped her arms around him, protectively and her hips rose to receive him. Her hands ran, through his hair, down his back, and her nails raked his hips.

"Please," she begged him in a whisper.

Abby reached the top of wave after wave, yet that elusive pinnacle she could not reach. Her skin grew damp but what was happening inside her, the emptiness filled with him, an ache that grew stronger with each stroke, a need so desperate, like clawing air. She wrapped her legs around his hips. "Now Jacob!" she screamed. With her last breath, she found herself hovering on some sharp and shimmering precipice. She bit her lip, held her breath, arching her hips to his rapid thrusts, forcing her closer to the brink. The fire inside her blazed white-hot. The delight stunned her; frightened her and she could not help to cry out. "Jacob..."

In answer, he grabbed her hips and gave one last thrust deep into her womb and shuddered. Ecstasy seared through her, molten and exquisite, almost terrifying in its intensity, bombarded by sensation after sensation.

He rolled to the side and gathered her in his arms, his body still intimately joined with hers. In sweat-soaked sheets, a musky scent rose—their scent. He kissed her, wiped her damp curls from her eyes and held her close. *Cherished.* She traced her fingers along the damp sheen of his nipple and nuzzled him there, then rested her head upon his chest, his heartbeat strong and steady in her ear.

He stroked her back and Abby lay there saturated in joyous contentment, a languorous peace, unlike anything she had ever known.

He tilted her head up to meet his eyes. "Are you happy, Abby?"

She smiled at him. "There are no words that describe the beauty humming in my heart." She stretched, her leg over Thorne's, reveling in the moment, refusing to acknowledge the past or the future, allowing her eyes to close.

"I imagine come morn, the crew will know of our night together."

She cuddled up to him to get his warmth, and he pulled a sheet over them. "Um-hm. No doubt Enos will be collecting wagers, creating enormous wealth to retire on Nantucket."

"No doubt," Thorne whispered. She could feel him grinning in the dark.

"Like children, they will be told of our impending nuptials and Abby, I'll do my best to find what happened to your family. I have powerful contacts in England."

That brought her wide awake. This could never *ever* happen again. Thorne wanted to marry her. Now he was going to find out what happened to her family. And she repaid him with her deception. She was going to have to lie to him, a lot. She'd have to tell him that what had happened was a mistake. A second mistake? She'd break out every excuse she could think of not to commit to Jacob. Abby swallowed. By the time they arrived in Boston, she'd disappear. He would forget her completely. Why did she feel like crying?

He nuzzled her hair. "You'll be the most beautiful bride Boston has ever seen."

Tears filled her eyes. He was so happy. Dear God, what had she done, giving herself to this perfect, extraordinary man she couldn't have? Abby's breath hitched. He wanted to marry a woman who didn't exist. Jacob could never find out who she really was.

He was worthy of the best of women, one who had integrity and honesty. Her life lay along a different path, one of title, rank and what was browbeaten into her head from birth, *duty*. How she loathed that responsibility.

If there were some way she could stay in Boston, to live with Jacob as his wife, to be treasured and protected. To have all the possibilities of a life she desired without the burdens of her class.

You've gone crazy, Abby. He deserves better than you.

Here amongst the privateers, she was at home. They were her family. She was plain Abigail Marie Hansford, an orphan…and they had adopted her with all their heart.

Then why do you wish to go home, Abby?

Was it a demon's voice inside her head? No. Clearly, it was her revelation. Sweet temptation crept from the corners of her mind where it had been lurking and reared its alluring, enticing head—to see a lifetime that lay within her grasp—a wonderful husband with long nights of lovemaking and a baby to hold. Yes. A handsome son like Thorne with bright blue eyes so like his father.

Abby smiled and closed her eyes, holding that vision in her mind, and felt something break inside her heart, pain so earth-shattering it forced the breath from her lungs. She could no more betray her family than she could betray Jacob. She opened her eyes, the vision slowly fading, leaving emptiness inside her.

For just this once, she capitulated to her needs. She held Jacob closer. *Just promise me, you'll always have understanding for me.* While Jacob slept, she pressed a kiss to his heart. Just a few weeks she promised. Just a few more. She caressed his hair, face and arms, loving everything about him.

Loving him.

Chapter 20

Abby picked up her skirts and walked backward. "The clouds are exceptionally beautiful today," she said breathlessly.

Thorne stalked her. I'm not looking at the clouds."

"You're not?"

"No. I'm looking at you."

Jacob's hand settled against her jaw, the warmth of his palm and the slight abrasion of his calloused fingers felt dearer than anything she'd ever known. All her willpower was not enough to keep her from pressing into his touch.

"I could drag you down to the cabin—" he threatened.

She looked him up and down. Memories stirred of long lusty insatiable nights of lovemaking. Warmth flooded her cheeks. "And then what would you do?"

Thorne laughed, then whispered huskily into her ear. "Images of you draped naked across me, your hair tousled, arouses many wicked thoughts on what I'd like to do to you. *Now.*"

He picked her up and swung her around.

"Put me down, Captain. The crew. What will they think?"

With Thorne colors seemed brighter and more brilliant. The sea glittered blindingly over endless hues of blue and turquoise, sunrises ascended with scorching yellows, oranges and pinks, ablaze with the brilliance that aroused passion and the dawning hope of a new day.

She slanted a sideways glance below. "Enos is stuffing his pockets with bets again. The man is incorrigible."

"Enos!" Thorne called over his shoulder. "What is the wager now?"

"That you'll be marrying our cabin boy and soon," he winked.

"You old seadog, you'll have enough profit to buy all of Nantucket and at my expense. Make sure, men, when we arrive in Boston, keep room for our wedding day," Thorne shouted.

Deafening cheers from the crew reached to where the earth and sea met the sky. Jacob kissed Abby. She blushed from her toes to the roots of her hair. To stop him from kissing her in front of the crew was impossible. Not that she wanted him to stop. Of course, the accompanying smiles with the knowledge that their captain slept with her made the heat rise to her cheeks even more.

They had been inseparable the last two days, living in bliss… *living a lie.*

Yet to yearn to dream of the 'what ifs' despite the terrible sham she played, deluding herself that their fairy tale relationship was real, and to warn him that she was about to repay his compassion, trust and affection with deceit.

How would the crew react to her deception? How would Jacob react? Of course, the crew would despise her. And Jacob… she shuddered. No longer could she allow the charade to go on. She opened her mouth to tell him the truth. Words clogged in her throat.

"Good day to you, Miss Hansford. It's a beaut, isn't it?" Abner Bosworth yelled from up in the nest.

"Good day to you, Abner." Abby waved to him, envying his position on top of the world.

How wonderful Abner had been to her, surprising her with his skill, the little carved toys he had made for his two small children and sharing besotted stories of his wife. Abner was fortunate, his wife lucky. She swallowed down a bitter agony that welled up inside. To have the power of marrying the one you loved, the one of your own choosing, to be cherished and adored, not imprisoned by duty and rank.

"Captain, due South, a ship!" Abner pointed.

Abby followed Thorne to the stern and watched as he swung his scope across the horizon. "Ship?" That sounded serious. "Is it a worry?"

"We're taking precautions is all." His baritone was tender.

"Who is it?" In these waters, the King's ships could be anywhere. He took her hand and placed it in the crook of his arm. It felt awkward, standing like this, the merriment sobered into crushing reality. Now this.

"It's a British Man O' War. He's been trailing us for some time. I don't relish a fight, but a fight we will give them."

"We've sailed close to shore as possible, believing the British warship unlikely to follow in charted shallow water flats. My intention is for them to run aground." When he saw the worried expression on her face, he collapsed his scope. "Put your mind at ease. *The Vengeance* is built sleek and swift. I'm confident we will outrun them."

What if Jacob was caught and thrown into a prison or worse hanged for his crimes? She could not bear it No. Never could she endure Jacob to suffer such a fate.

Abby, I'll do my best to keep you safe."

And she knew he would. *But who will keep you safe, Jacob?*

And in that vein, the fear Jacob felt wasn't for him. All his fear was for Abby.

He jumped up on an arms chest to see unencumbered. There she was, all right. She was no mirage, a British thirty-two gun warship bearing down on them fast. Three great masts upward, courses, tops, royals unfurled, barreling down on them, making a picture against the blue skies. His muscles tightened. *The Vengeance* was deeply laden with captured military stores and dense sea growth. Damn Bingham for expecting him to carry so much from Martinique. Turning the scope in his hands over and over, he couldn't say why he felt so strongly, but the premonition of danger, of impending threat, was impossible to deny. He smelled Captain Rowland Davenport. Thorne had humiliated him, raiding the coasts of England then disappearing like a ghost. Especially when Jacob had the arrogance to post a proclamation in Lloyds Coffee House in London, proclaiming he would sink, burn, destroy and capture British merchantmen in their own territorial waters, and striking terror in the hearts of British citizenry. And he had done it repeatedly, sneaking across the Channel and hiding in obliging French harbors to sell his prizes, always to return to pluck another fat trophy. Jacob liked a challenge. A challenge he would give Davenport.

He leaped down and patted Abby's hand, his dear sweet Abigail, white as a ghost. This time he had her welfare to consider. To put her in the midst of a sea battle? He and his men would fight to the death. His jaw clenched, Abigail his Achilles heel. If only he could outrun the bastard. "I'm not a man to be frightened off by a few cannons. I've crossed many such battles and survived to tell the day." He crossed to the bulwarks. "Benjamin, Enos, run out the guns! Man the tops'l sheets and halyards! Sheet home! Hoist away the topsails."

Months ago, at the Duke of Rutland's party in England, disguised as a vicar…Thorne shook his head…the arrogant British commander didn't even know he was sipping champagne with his archenemy. Thorne grinned. To give Davenport the pleasure of his company again?

Memories lingered of that crisp and clear night in the garden of the Rutland's estate, a stolen kiss from Lady Rutland, a harmless flirtation. He looked down at his Abby so like the highborn lady, but so much more passionate. Lady Rutland, the spoiled wealthy progeny of aristocratic breeding, part of a class system, so familiar and despised. His blood boiled. He tamped down that part of his past, but the less forgiving part of his nature remained focused on the pampered, shallow offspring of the Duke of Rutland—Lady Rutland whose ascendency had been predetermined at birth. He compared her to *his Abby*, the endearing beauty that curved her slim legs around him and kept giving and giving as if each night were her last.

With incredible speed, the gaskets were off and sails fluttered from the yards. When the sails hoisted and trimmed, the *Vengeance* trembled with the eagerness of a stabled stallion released to run.

With Abby, laughter was a part of daily life, where before it was infrequent or didn't exist at all. In her presence, there was no need for continuous conversation. He was just content in her being nearby. Things that never interested him before became fascinating because he knew they were special to her. He thought of her in everything he did. Simple things brought her to mind, the afterglow of twilight, the song of the wind, or even a storm cloud on the horizon. Determined not to give away his fears, he met her worried eyes. "When the cannons fire, you go below."

The sun reached its zenith and he labored with his men to ready for battle. Jacob climbed the ratlines and peered through his glass. Damn! *Solebay* fast approached. As predicted, Davenport. "Ben, fire an occasional shot from the stern to keep them at a respectable distance."

Jacob jumped down, to address his grim Lieutenant. "If we tack farther to the east, we'd find open seas. *Solebay* will also tack on the same southern breeze." He turned to the bow and shook his head. "We will have to risk threading a needle."

"Impossible! We will wreck upon the shoals. The scheme is madness," said Lawton.

"I will not play by Davenport's rules and go out to sea and engage. The venture is suicide. *Solebay* will be breathing on our gunnels in a blink of an eye. Be good enough to command the deck." Jacob swung up into the shrouds, climbing to the cross-trees where he commanded an excellent—if discouraging view of the situation. To starboard lay a string of islets like a pearl necklace, yawning with sharp teeth. To port was the island of Abaco, a hundred-mile spit of land, shores wreathed with shallows and treacherous reefs.

In between lay a narrow stretch of water for Jacob to negotiate the *Vengeance.*

Like Theseus wandering the labyrinth with the Minotaur stalking him.

Almost twice the size of the *Vengeance,* the *Solebay* approached rapidly astern. Her men ran out her larboard guns and tacked starboard to give them a broadside. Jacob grinned. Blinded by the *Vengeance* to their front, the arrogant Davenport missed the narrow channel Jacob had invited him to trail. "Lawton, run in close to that islet."

His Lieutenant's crisp commands echoed up to him. "Ready about! Ease down the helm and rise tacks and sheets. Haul taut."

Drowned in a squeal of blocks the *Vengeance* danced on a new tack. With the wind on her beam, she tore straight for the monstrous islet as if to ram it, then veered up to clear the hawse. The maneuver put them in narrower waters. Jacob stared aft.

The *Solebay* learned too late. The forbidding islet they were led to rang a death knell. Her helmsman turned sharp. The crunch of her sides scraped the razor-sharp bluffs of the islet. British sailors stared in terror. The maneuver barely freed them of significant damage. Davenport urged them on.

Jacob frowned through his glass. Up ahead there was scant space for steering through the islets. With the wind so flighty and the tide barely turned, his present course proved fatal. "Lieutenant Lawton, stand to wear ship! Put her before the wind!"

Enos's upturned face bloated like a puffer fish. Abner Bosworth's jaw worked up and down like a fireplace bellows.

Lawton's astonishment mirrored his horror. "An evolution we dare not attempt at such close quarters, Captain."

"Dammit. Go through those islets. Now," Jacob roared. He shielded his eyes from the sun and speculated their chances. If only they could run through the gauntlet of islands. The odds were against success. He had designed and built the *Vengeance* for sleekness and maneuverability. To have any less faith in her performance was to see them all imprisoned. He was not going to give up without a fight. Jacob hung hard to the mast. He knew what was coming. Far below he heard the calls. "Haul taut. Up helm…clear away the bowlines." Under a gust of wind, the *Vengeance* heeled sharply and leaned horizontal to port. The sea blurred past. Salt spray coated his face and stung his eyes. Would he fall into the sea? "Brace in the after yards!"

The gap woefully small, the *Vengeance* rose to an even keel and charged into the opening between the islets. "Steady as she goes," ordered Jacob. Glancing astern, the uncertainty of the *Solebay* registered in her actions and unwilling to be caught in a trap, she hauled wind, costing her valuable time. Too busy to concern himself with Davenport's idiocy, Jacob stared at the looming island angled straight for their larboard beam.

Below, Lieutenant Lawton stood solidly at the helm waiting for his command. He grimaced at the worried expression on Abby's face, wishing he did not have to put her through this ordeal. If only he could take her in his arms and reassure her. How hopeless it must appear from the deck. From the cross-trees, his sight lay more confident. The *Vengeance* traveled at unparalleled speed. He waited until the last possible moment. "Hard port!"

Lawton put down the helm. The *Vengeance* reeled around with the wind. The island fled by with less than a fathom to spare. Like a hound too big to follow the rabbit that cut a hole in a fence, the *Solebay* hauled up sails and threw out an anchor to stop their progress. A cannon was brought up to the bow and fired. The shot fell short in a spray of water. Unable to follow, Davenport cursed his men. Jacob smirked. The British frigate would have to double back.

For the next half hour, they zigzagged a serpentine course. At the first opportunity, Jacob ordered starboard for a clear run into open seas. How long had he held his breath? The men cheered. Abby stared at the fore-topgallants, a palm pressed to her heart.

"What do you think, Miss Hansford?" He climbed down and jumped to the deck in front of her. He wanted to hear from her what she thought of his seamanship.

She planted her hands on her hips. "Foolhardy, risky and dangerous."

"Is that all?"

"Brilliant...breathtaking." She laughed and he hauled her into his arms and planted a kiss on her lips. The roar of elation died when two British frigates rounded ahead of them from the northern tip of the island. The cannon fire from their encounter with *Solebay* had brought them to heel. A white mushroom of smoke blossomed from the muzzle of a nine-pounder. He released Abby. A heavy feeling churned his gut. All their sail was sheeted home with no more speed to add. The two frigates breathed on their bow, dividing to entrap them.

Abby came up behind him, the swish of her skirts flowed into his legs. "Jacob?"

"They'll sink us, Captain," wailed Abner Bosworth.

"I'd soon as drown as get caught by them Brits," spat Enos. "We'll be put into that devil's hole of a bulk off Long Island to perish."

"It's not my intention to do either, men. Enos, Ben, Lawton. Make a dash for the sea." Even as he spoke the words, hairs went up on the back of his neck. He sprinted to the stern and swept a hand across his forehead to get rid of sweat. The *Solebay* sped towards them. Damn Davenport. Jacob had underestimated him.

"Abby, go below," he ordered.

"No. Jacob there is something I must tell you..."

Jacob jerked his head around. He prodded her to the companionway. "Later, Abby. On the chance we are taken, tell them you are a British subject and were taken from a merchantman. You had your own cabin and were treated with respect. My men will vouch for your treatment. I want you protected at all costs."

A cannon blast came short, swished a torrent of seawater over the sides, soaking them. The fool woman dug in her heels. He turned her toward him and kissed her long and hard. She was scared. That was it. She was concerned for his welfare.

She laid her hand against his cheek. The warmness of her palm was so tempting. "You must forgive me. You must believe in me."

Jacob didn't have time to entertain her puzzling remarks. Despite the crew's remaining efforts, they earned only a half-knot of speed. The three British frigates closed in on them. A lucky shot from the *Solebay* struck the fore-topgallant mast. Jacob thrust Abby to the bulwarks. The mast crashed to the deck. His men scrambled like rats before a flood. Jacob cursed. The wreckage missed them by inches. He dragged the wild-eyed Abby across the deck and shoved her down the companionway. "Simeon, take her below and keep her there. Elijah—take a gang aloft and clear the wreckage."

"Ben, fire into that nest of adders," he ordered. The *Vengeance* shook with deafening thunder. The smoke cleared. The British frigate closest to them crippled with two holes below the waterline and bilging fast.

A dark cloud blotted out the sun and with it any chance for escape. From the opposite direction, the *Solebay* roared off a broadside. More shots splintered the spars, damaged rigging, breached the hull and mortally wounded Abner Bosworth. The *Vengeance,* hit at the waterline syphoned water and pitched the ship like the heaving heart of a man struck with a fatal arrow. Coldness passed right through him, a matter of time before they'd sink. His men looked to him with increasing doubt. To go on was futile.

Captain Davenport rubbed his hands together barking out commands from the deck of the *Solebay.* The raising of the three gold lions on the mizzenmast roared Davenport's conceit. There was nothing more Thorne could do. The tinny taste of dread filled his mouth, and he wiped his hand across his eyes, sticky from the blood that poured from his head wound.

They were beaten. When you played at games of war, you lived or died. He and his crew knew that fact. If Abby were not aboard he would have fought to the end. Trapped he could not risk further battle. To hazard sending her to a watery grave was not an option. "Enos, man the pumps to keep us afloat. Lawton, send up the white flag. Surrender."

After Captain Rowland Davenport ordered his ship's carpenters to keep the *Vengeance* from sinking, he changed into a new uniform, one he had been saving for this occasion. The golden epaulets gleamed in the sun and mimed his mood to intimidate this specific Colonial. To catch an American prize such as the *Vengeance* was monumental. More satisfying was the fact he had captured the most infamous of the Colonial privateers, Captain Jacob Thorne. To come face to face with his adversary after so many months of chasing him brought undue pleasure.

Secured with grappling hooks, and balled rope fenders dropped in between to protect the sides from chinking with the waves, Davenport crossed the plank between the two ships. Several of his armed men waited with poised bayonets, swords and loaded muskets. The procedure was overkill. The prisoners were heavily chained to the point they could barely stand. He strutted to mid-deck and dusted a speck off his immaculate blue frock coat. So many humiliations he had suffered from Thorne's machinations that left him ridiculed by his peers, scorned by his superiors, and mocked by the English society he craved. How his fingers tingled with the prospect of making the Yankee Captain pay for those humiliations.

He scanned the motley group and wrinkled his nose with the offense of smoke, grease and sweat from the filthy savages. Clasping his hands behind his back, he swaggered up and down the line. He did not know his adversary's countenance. Their engagements had been swift, rendering him impotent to glean a closer look. This sordid bunch had the audacity to glare at him. He'd teach them a thing or two about defeat. One man stood solidly above the fray. Davenport halted in front of him.

"Have we met?" The prisoner remained mute. It was a ludicrous question. Of course, he had never met the scoundrel. Beneath the grime nagged a familiarity. The prisoner stared boldly back at him. Did the Colonial dare to smirk? *The Vicar.*

"Pray tell me, your occupation has changed much from holy man. Am I right…Captain Thorne?" The prisoner raised an infuriating brow. In the afternoon light, even the Colonial's shadow dared to spread over him.

"You are quite astute," he mocked.

Davenport regarded the menace and object of his hatred. "You and your men are in a precarious position. The King has a price on your head for your capture."

"I'm sure it's a goodly sum."

Davenport's fists balled. The innuendo of his incompetence rang clear. "Guards, tie this man to the mast. He needs to learn who his betters are."

It gave him gratification the fight the Colonial gave, his chains weighing him down. The guards gave him appropriate strikes with their clubs, the thuds on flesh, charming to Davenport's ears. Normally such blows would cripple a man or at the least, leave him weeping. Too bad the Colonial did not beg. Impressive.

Once the chains were undone, it took eight of his men to wrestle Thorne to the mast. Four of his men suffered cracked ribs, black eyes and one broken arm.

Impatient Davenport waited until Thorne was secured. "I'll perform the deed myself. I have great enthusiasm for novelty." He held his hand out, palm up. His fingers clasped around the handle of the cat, an occupation he relished. He raised his arm. One. Two.

Three. He snapped the whip on the Yank's back. The Colonial's body jerked with each lash. His shirt shredded. Dark red blood oozed down his back. If only he would whimper…a matter of time. Davenport smiled with his handiwork and swaggered to an inch from Thorne's face. "Do you know how long I have dreamed of this? I'm a terrible insomniac. Do you know how many lashes I counted until sleep came to me?"

Thorne sneered. "The greatest fools think themselves cleverer than the men who laugh at them. Do your worst. You'll get no satisfaction from me."

"I have experience in breaking men," Davenport gloated.

"To dream of confronting the jackal while he still lived…what if you find yourself trapped by the jackal?" Thorne snarled.

"A pathetic threat." Davenport raised the whip again.

"Stop!" A female voice commanded…a very cultured female voice.

Davenport pivoted. He could not believe his eyes. "Lady Rutland?"

Abby stepped from the companionway. Hot bile rose in her throat. To see Jacob tied to the mast and beaten like an animal and at the mercy of a man like Davenport. Pascale, Enos, Lieutenant Lawton, Ben all of them battered and in chains. Men who had showed her nothing but kindness, humiliated and defeated. Like rubbish, Abner Bosworth's body was heaved overboard. No canvas to shroud him, no proper burial, nothing to bless him to the next life. Abby said a silent prayer for Abner, a quiet man who had a family who depended on him, a man who had been considerate of her welfare. Her nails curled into her palms at the appalling lack of decency and respect, and the vile treatment by her countrymen.

The *Vengeance* leaked fast. The rasp and whoosh of hand pumps were worked by men to keep her afloat. Carpenters hammered away on lowered scaffolds thrown over the side of the ship. Of course, Davenport would want to keep his prize.

She had taken precious time dressing in the violet silk before she made her presence known. Her old tools brought an intake of breath about the ship.

"Lady Abigail Rutland? Is it truly you?" Davenport didn't quit staring.

Neither did his men. Numerous British sailors, her countrymen, held bayonets pointed at her *countrymen?* Yet they were Colonials. How could they be *her* countrymen? She didn't have time to consider the paradox. A plan. She required a plan to get Thorne and the crew out of this disaster. Risky. To help them spelled treason.

She dared a glance to Jacob and paled from the ferocity of his glare.

"Lady Abigail Hansford Rutland." Jacob enunciated each name. "Of course."

Now *he knew* the truth and the hellish lie she told. She stopped thinking...but she needed to think. If only she could move. She stared at Jacob, feeling his vulnerability, feeling every sting of the lashes he received, feeling all his hatred. If only, to go back in time and change everything.

Move. *Now.* Abby straightened her spine and sailed forward, using her bearing of the high-born, she hoped to manipulate the British naval captain.

Davenport turned on the Colonial captain. "You did not know the precious cargo you had on board? This is rich. Lady Rutland, however did you pull it off?"

"Captain Davenport. It is good to make your acquaintance again." She fought not to look at Thorne, keeping her eyes on the British captain. How Thorne suffered because of her. He had surrendered to save her, knew it in her bones. Her heart twisted with the condemnation she must give Jacob, to let him think the worst of her. How he would hate her for what would seem like her betrayal.

Davenport narrowed his eyes. "How awful to be in the company of these savages."

"Savages?" she trilled, stopped before Davenport, and gave an appropriate curtsy, the low bodice of the lavender gown doing the trick, his gaze arrested on her bosom. "Captain, it has been a terrible ordeal and a long story. I am so happy it is you who has saved me from these dreadful Colonials." Was that her embracing English snobbery? She shuddered.

"Captain Thorne, you had the impudence to kidnap one of His Majesty's peers?"

Jacob's voice hardened. "She was disguised as a boy on board a captured merchantman. Did you think I'd abandon my mission because some damned English bitch happened to be on board the ship I seized?"

She stiffened. *Stay the course, Abby.* She looped her arm in Davenport's and shifted him away from Thorne, anything to spare Jacob another lash. Her stomach reeled with the bloody whip in Davenport's hand, gelled with Jacob's blood. "Please escort me from this horrid scene." She begged prettily, guiding him to the *Solebay* and pressed a hand to her throat, the shocked faces of the *Vengeances'* crew, damning her.

Why was Simeon bound in chains? "Captain Davenport. There is a mistake. This man is a loyal subject and was kidnapped with me aboard the *Civis*. He has saved my life, acted as my chaperone, and has no more loyalty to these cloddish Colonials than I do. You must free him at once." At the nod of Davenport's head, Abby let out a sigh of relief, Simeon's chains dropped in a clunk to the deck, the old man's eyes tearing up in gratitude. To have Simeon's help in whatever scheme she devised to liberate the Colonials was paramount.

"You deceitful bitch," Jacob sneered.

Davenport let go of her arm and swung to Thorne. "I cannot allow any more insults to Lady Rutland." Glittering hatred fired between the two men.

Jacob snorted.

"Arrogant dog! Enough of this insolence!" Davenport angled his head. The guards on each side of Thorne closed in with short, hard jabs to the stomach and ribs. Jacob crumpled, held upright by his bonds. Davenport smirked.

Abby resisted the urge to run to Jacob and release him. No. She had a part to play.

While the guards stood over him, ready to strike again, Thorne's breath came in short, painful gasps. Her eyes locked on his in shock and horror.

"Lady Rutland. You have nothing to fear from this barbarian anymore." Davenport sought to reassure her. "This lawless villain will never have the opportunity to harm you. My men have him well under control."

For how long had she held her breath? Despite his beating, Thorne looked dangerous.

"My dear. There is no reason to be afraid. To face your enemy," Davenport continued, with a hint of irritation seeping through his tone. "He's a rebel who will pay for his crimes. Lieutenant Smith, take Lady Rutland to my quarters and see that all of her needs are met."

She clutched Davenport's sleeve. "I cannot be thrust in the company of strangers again. Please, I am frightened. These long months at sea…tell me what has happened to my father and brothers. Are they all…dead?" She sobbed. "I must know."

Impatient with a weeping woman on his hands, Davenport half relented. "Your father and brothers are alive, Lady Rutland."

"Alive? I saw an explosion…"

"Your father and brothers were spared. They had grown impatient in the laboratory and went looking for you."

Abby pressed fingers to her trembling lips. The Rutland men and their blessed impatience had saved them. "Who would do this to my family?"

Davenport lifted his heels, rising to emphasize his knowledge. "The Duke of Westbrook was highly involved in helping your father to find the culprit and speculated on a past revenge. He found a note in the library to the heinous crime committed against your family, signed and detailing what the perpetrator Percy Devol, had done. In the letter, Devol outlined how he ended your father and brothers' lives, how he was going to make the Rutland's pay further through you and your eldest brother, Nicholas with a slow death. Percy had an ax to grind with your grandfather, the Duke of Rutland and desired to wipe-out the family line."

Her mind spun. Her father and brothers were alive! Joy filled her soul. "Did they catch Percy Devol, and why did he have such hatred?"

"Many years ago, Devol's mother was the vicar's daughter on the Rutland estate. A bit unhinged, she held a fascination for the duke, your grandfather. In fact, she was a nuisance. But when she had a child out of wedlock and bandied about the village that the duke had molested her and the child was his, the situation became a matter to be addressed. Due to the great friendship the duke enjoyed with the vicar, her father sent her away. She beat the boy, Percy and told him he wasn't any good and would never measure up to the duke. Percy Devol grew up deranged, hating the Rutland's and feeling he was the rightful heir. He has escaped England but your father has a host of investigators on the case."

"Nicholas? What has happened to my brother?"

"Your father ordered the world turned upside down to find the both of you. With his connections to the crown, a flotilla of His Majesty's ships has been dispatched to comb the Caribbean. Nicholas had been traced to a Portuguese slaver bound for Brazil. For an exchange of coin, it was discovered you had been taken aboard the *Civis*. I volunteered my services for immediate departure. We came upon the floating wreck of the merchantman, the *Civis* and learned from two seamen who had hidden in the hold that they had been attacked by the pirate, Jacob Thorne."

He is not a pirate.

Davenport flicked his eyes to Jacob. "We did not know if you survived the ordeal on the *Civis,* but followed near to Martinique, a Colonial favorite. I sent for a rendezvous with a British spy from the island who had confirmed observations on the activities of the *Vengeance*. He had not seen you. He interviewed a French woman, Lucette who said she had seen a female aboard, answering to your description. On assumption it was you, we followed through the Windward Islands, assuming the traitor would be running supplies back to the rebels in the Colonies. My assumptions were correct, Lady Rutland," he boasted, his icy grey eyes looked to the other two awaiting warships where the red cross of the Union Jack waved in the breeze and roared the power of England.

Or luck, Abby concluded. Of course, the puffed-up peacock would take full credit for her rescue, to endear him to the Duke of Rutland and commend him to the Crown. With certainty, to capture Captain Jacob Thorne would add to his promotion and prominence, labeling him a hero.

Davenport toyed with the whip in his hand and Abby blanched.

"We will resupply and arrange matters in Nassau before taking you home."

"Home?" To go home. Tears formed. Isn't this what she wanted? To see her family again? All her prayers were answered. The commitment she had vowed, to return to her father and do what he decreed reared its ugly head. Her eyes roved over Enos and Benjamin and all the crew of the *Vengeance*. Weren't they her family too? Longingly she looked to Thorne. Her breath hitched. The wicked nights of lovemaking, all the things she loved about this man.

Loved? She loved him.

And with that admission, her heart tore with the pact she had made with God if he spared her father and brothers. Joy rolled to ashes in her mouth, to leave her Colonial friends, to leave Jacob, to leave them thinking that she had duped them?

She didn't know how she would pull it off to help them. Stealth, wits and persistence. Davenport must never suspect. Pride was his weakness. She lifted her chin—to play on his vanity.

It was apparent the strain of maintaining schooled interest waxed a heavy toll on Davenport's patience. It distracted him. Exactly what Abby intended. "All the horrors I have gone through... Captain Davenport, I cannot do without your company." She dared to lean her bosom into his arm.

Jacob raised his head with an effort, saw how she had pressed into Davenport then scorched her up and down. "Did Lady Rutland tell you how *comfortable* she made my voyage?"

If only she could collapse to the deck and hide in a ball, the insinuation read clearly on Davenport's face. The damage Thorne created. Now everyone would suspect she had slept with the Colonial captain. How could she repair her reputation? The fool. Didn't he realize she was trying to help him?

Davenport stiffened. "In Nassau, Captain Thorne, you will go before the governor. You will be inquired of, tried, heard, determined and adjudged under his full power and authority. I am told he does not hold a particular affection for pirates and has a fondness for the gallows."

Abby dropped his arm. "Are you implying hanging? He has letters of marque."

"Not anymore." Davenport held up the notes and let the breezes blow the documents out over the ocean. "He is pirate and will be hanged accordingly. He also kidnapped you. These are treasonous crimes. The king will look the other way. Of this I am sure."

Abigail stood stunned. "This cannot be true."

Davenport looked at her sharply. "You have affection for the Colonial pirate?"

"Jacob…I mean, Captain Thorne…" her whisper was barely audible to her ears. "You see, I was—I was rather…" She stared at Jacob.

"You're nothing but a spoiled aristocratic bitch." He turned his head away but in that split second she saw the torment that covered his countenance, bringing a deep cutting pain to her chest.

"Go on." Davenport encouraged her as if anything more from her would make any difference. Suspicion flickered across his face.

Her fingers spread out in a fan against her breastbone, the predetermined revelation of his sentencing unquestionable. *Keep up the charade, Abby.* "Despite him treating me well during my imprisonment, I'm afraid I must confess that I took a severe dislike to Captain Thorne. He did treat me with proper decorum for a lady but I found him to be a bit supercilious for one of his station." Abby fluttered her hand, the gesture, a queenly dismissal, one a highborn peer of the realm would have discussing the inadequacies of a contrary servant. She appeared to forget Jacob's presence, settled between the two husky guards, not more than four feet from her.

She continued silkily, beguiling Davenport with her smile, anything to quell his doubtful assessment of her.

She walked away as if strolling through a garden. How could she plead to the governor in their defense? How could she stop their execution? In this uncivilized part of the world, she was unsure of her family's influence. Abby inhaled, far from England, a woman wielding the power of the Rutland's was like nailing water to a tree. Inches from Pascale, she dropped her handkerchief and bent to pick it up. His heavy chains clinked. Pascale procured the handkerchief, met her eyes halfway. She whispered rapidly in French. "I will find a way to help you escape."

Pascale grunted.

She turned back to Davenport and pouted. "You must understand that to continue in the company of a man I've held in strict contempt from the start is a torment I no longer wish to endure. You do understand, Captain Davenport, don't you?"

"Of course." Captain Davenport flicked scornful eyes to his nemesis then offered Abby his arm. "Guards throw this scum in the bowels of the ship with the other rats and let them rot for all I care." The guards obediently hustled the prisoners below. Abby bit her lip and looked away.

Before the guards could drag him from the deck, Jacob shook them off with sudden, furious strength, and whirled to face her, his eyes glared his unconcealed hatred. "Abby or *Lady Rutland* or whoever you are, if it is the last breath I breathe, I will have my revenge on you for your lies."

Chapter 21

Nassau, Bahamas, December 1777

"Your voyage must have been dreadful," said Denise Gambier Cornish, widowed sister of Governor, John Gambier of Fort Nassau.

Abby perched on the brocade settee in the parlor of Governors House and reached for the teacup the black servant girl offered. "Thank you, Louise" she smiled. It was the day after her arrival in New Providence, the colony brimming with excitement from the capture of the *Vengeance* and the consequent rescue of Lady Rutland.

She had been appointed a room with a spare dressing room, surprised with the comfortable accommodations for a remote outpost of England's realm. After a hot bath, Abby had slept for over a day, the battle, journey to Nassau, an exhausting blur that had played havoc on her nerves. An assortment of gowns had been laid out for her to choose, left from the governor's four daughters who had married and moved to England. Not the latest style, the gowns had been taken in to accommodate her small waist. She smoothed her hands over the fine fabric grateful to have something clean and serviceable in the tropics until new gowns were made for her. She sipped her tea and sighed deeply, luxuriating in civilization. If only the nosy widow wasn't so provoking.

"What was it like aboard the *Vengeance?*" Denise asked for the twelfth time.

Did the crew have horns and cloven feet? Did they make ritual sacrifices? Abby flinched every time Denise opened her mouth, prying for every detail of her journey. Women like the governor's sister were malicious gossips bent on ruining a girl's reputation.

Aboard the *Solebay,* it had been a dance of words to protect her reputation courtesy of Jacob's insinuations. Like a rat terrier on the hunt, Captain Davenport burrowed right in with his questioning. Putting on airs that she had been too stressed to continue, Abby had demanded her privacy, anything to delay his inquiry until she had time to develop a logical account. No doubt deeper inquiry would arise. She gritted her teeth. To whitewash Jacob's innuendoes would be a miracle. Now that investigation became a matter of time, necessitating caution in her approach. Abby exhaled, smiled at the widow, giving as little information as possible.

Next to the door, stood Simeon, ramrod straight. The only inclination to Mrs. Cornish's prying was the rolling of his eyes. Abby placed her cup in the saucer. "I suppose one could consider them barbaric."

Mrs. Cornish leaned forward all agog. She splattered tea in her cup followed by a splash of milk. "Barbaric? Whatever do you mean?"

Predictable. A little excitement was needed for the old scandalmonger bored with island tedium. Abigail leaned over to speak low and confidingly. Were Mrs. Cornish's eyes popping out of her head? "The Americans are barbarous in nature. They had no clotted cream to put on my scone. They held out their pinkie when drinking their tea. The worst of their crudeness was that they added their milk *after* they poured their tea."

"I can't imagine." Mrs. Cornish sat back in her chair not even realizing she had placed her milk in *after* her tea.

Simeon's lips twitched and Abigail nodded her head in the affirmative, closed her eyes and let out an appropriate groan.

"The horrors you suffered. What of the captain? I understand he is ruthless. Did he—" Denise cleared her throat. "—did he?"

Ravish me? He did more than ravish me. For a fractured second, the way he made love to her, the way her body responded and all the intimacies they shared, flashed in her mind, so strong, it felt almost real. Abigail opened her eyes. "You have been so kind to me, like a mother, and I do need someone to desperately confide in," Abby dabbed her handkerchief to her eye.

Was Mrs. Cornish about to bust out of her corset? Denise waved Simeon from the room. The door closed and her bosom heaved like a full-masted ship, trembling in the wind. Abby shook her head. "Captain Thorne is a monster. Once he lent me his handkerchief and there was a stain on the corner. Can you imagine my vexation? Then the man had an unnatural profundity to find fault in me. I wanted to stay on deck, but he insisted I go below. I would not pretend to diminish that a squall brewed and that he had the right to insist since it was his ship."

"What else?" Mrs. Cornish pursed her lips, breathless with glee.

Abigail placed the back of her wrist on her forehead and affected a brilliant pose of woe. "Did I tell you he has a monstrous passion?"

"Passion?" Denise squawked.

Mrs. Cornish was ready to swoon. Abigail suppressed her laughter. The woman was a purple, bobbing fishing cork on a surging wave. "On two accounts." Abby held up two fingers. "He has an oafish predilection for pickled herring. Eats them by the barrels." Abby paused sufficiently before firing her next salvo. "But his most avid passion is poetry. He recites sonnets and poems the whole live long day. He even sings them while he steers the ship. In fact, he makes all of his crew sing sonnets with him."

The widow fanned herself, no doubt, bursting to share this news with the whole island. Abigail stood and walked to the window, her back to Mrs. Cornish. Out in the hall, Simeon had a coughing spasm. Abby smirked. How long would it take for the news to reach England? America? Captain Jacob Thorne regaled as the most terrifying American privateer, the scourge of England reduced to a bard singing pirate? The pleasure was all Abby's. Served him right for the insinuations he had hurled to sully her character especially after he had told her he would do everything to protect her reputation.

She fingered the satiny fringe on the heavy drapes. Her fingers went cold, her triumph short lived when she thought about Jacob and the crew. Were they still imprisoned in the hold of the ship? Had they been given food and water? Treatment for Jacob's wounds? Despite the hateful way Jacob had spoken to her, she could not bear to think of his suffering. How could she blame him for the way he had acted? Beaten and degraded, to learn of her identity while she beguiled the commander who had taken his ship. To have behaved like the aristocrat he despised? No, she could not blame him. But there had been no alternative. If there were any way possible to help him, she must maintain a loyal appearance to the Crown.

Why had she never told him the truth? A hundred times the rant lashed through her head.

Abby tapped her finger on her lips, thinking about the harrowing sea battle. A man that can do the things Jacob did earned his rank as master seaman. To thrust the *Vengeance* deliberately through a maze of shallows and ragged-sharp islands and turn the tables on Davenport was as admirable as it was foolhardy. It had proved Thorne a natural leader: courageous, inventive, and a little mad. He lived up to his reputation, his revolutionary seamanship to be respected. His brilliance for naval tactics rose legendary and had created a sensation in Europe, not to mention, hatred by the King of the most proficient sea-power in the world. He had become the symbol of adoration in the eyes of the Colonists. As a result, he had been targeted in a massive manhunt and captured.

Abby sighed. Government House stood high on a cliff, commanding a beautiful view of the sea and the town that surrounded Fort Nassau, a formidable monolithic four-pointed star built of stone with two high-walled ends, projecting northward into the harbor, and guarding the west end of the port. If Jacob and his crew were held in the dungeons there would be no way to help them escape. Her hope lay in her pleas to the Governor.

"Fort Nassau has sixty-four cannon and twenty-six brass mortars," Denise bragged. "My brother has refortified this fort and its sister, Fort Montagu in the north since the American attack two years ago. No one can breach either fort's defenses."

Abigail pivoted. "Mrs. Cornish, when does your brother return?"

"Denise. Please call me Denise. He is visiting Eleuthera and is expected in a week. During that time, I have taken the liberty of arranging a few parties for you."

"I could not impose, Denise. You have done enough in providing me with comforts."

Denise snorted like a hog in heat, a rather annoying habit; her rolls of fat sweated and strained her laces beneath layers of black wool that asserted her ten-year stake of widowhood. "We rarely get visitors of your prestige and I will not let it be heralded around England that New Providence is in anyway deficient. The ladies of the town are dying to meet you. Teas, parties and a dance have been scheduled."

Abigail took Mrs. Cornish's hands in her own. "I cannot wait. When is the first social?" Of course, Abby would do her best to capitalize on her status in hopes of influencing the Governor, anything to avert his strong appetite for executions. Her insides twisted. Why did she feel that no matter what she did, it wouldn't make any difference?

Two weeks had passed with a whirlwind of parties and teas arranged by the governor's sister. Lady Abigail Rutland had been an instant success, the island agog with the Duke of Rutland's daughter. To host her in their homes spoke volumes of their own preening importance. Never one to disappoint, Abby bestowed her most gracious manners with appropriate gratitude.

The carriage wheels ground over hard limestone rock and Abby shielded her eyes from the brightness of the Bahamian sun. When Mrs. Cornish had suggested a tour of New Providence, Abby had been elated until she discovered they were to be accompanied by none other than Captain Davenport. Abby sat in a snug leather seat, gripped her parasol handle and twisted it like a lamb roast rotating on a spit over a fire. Recalling what he had ordered for Jacob and done to the maids in his employ, Abby refused to be alone with the lecher. Per her insistence, Simeon rode next to the driver and Mrs. Cornish faced across from her to act as proper escort. The captain flicked his gaze to the firmament not at all pleased with the chaperons.

She had not seen Jacob or anyone from the *Vengeance*. The wait for the Governor wore on her nerves. What else could she do to stop the execution? She squeezed her fingers together as if to plumb the answer out of her hands. The Colonials had been put to work to pay for their reprisal against England until they were tried. The loathing of the Colonials and their probable execution met with approval by the islanders. For Captain Jacob Thorne, the consequence of such disadvantaged fame fashioned him the symbol of the depredations of American privateers they desired to eradicate.

Davenport's eyes roved over her and she prickled in the heat. "Captain Davenport, could you explain that particular flora?" Abby persisted in the mundane, asking Davenport ceaseless questions on everything. "How many coconuts does a tree produce? Why is that palm tree angled like that? What do fishermen eat? I see you rubbing your head, Captain. Do you have a headache?"

Dressed in his buttoned tight, embroidered blue coat, bleached white breeches and stockings, he flicked an imaginary speck off his golden epaulet, no doubt to lionize his rank. He could have been handsome except for his longer nose, crooked like it had been broken before. She had experience with broken noses. Her brother, Nicholas was a pugilist. A very good one. He had broken many of his opponent's noses.

Davenport narrowed his eyes. "Fascinating, *your* interest in everything Bahamian." He swatted at a horsefly and missed. The insect bit his cheek and he swore under his breath.

Mrs. Cornish clucked.

Abby smiled. Davenport was no fool and again his eyes roved over her body. "This is new to me. Why wouldn't I find it fascinating?" How long to break his tolerance?

He tapped his foot in staccato. Distrust and lust.

Through the narrow streets of New Providence they traveled, the town quaint amidst a collection of coral pink, mint green, and cornflower blue painted clapboard houses with white picket fences, gingerbread-latticework and balconies. Stores flouted supplies of tobacco, sugar, barrels of molasses, rice, salt, rum, fabrics and lumber. Slaves sold rainbow-colored parrotfish, strawberry snapper, sea turtles as big as footstools and scorching pink conch shells.

Despite the dreaded company, Abigail reveled in the vivid magentas, purples, and salmon bougainvillea draped over fences and porticos. The horses clopped beneath a canopy of Royal Poinciana, igniting the skies with flames of red, then turned the corner of Bay Street. Abigail gasped. A lone figure stood chained so tight to a palmetto that there remained no room for movement. Pascale? He had a large swollen eye, bloodied lip and his arms were stretched so high over his head that his toes barely brushed the ground. Disconnect from life shown in his face. Simeon turned to her.

"Stop the carriage at once," she commanded.

Mrs. Cornish pursed her lips.

Captain Davenport raised a brow. "What is it?"

"That man. Why is he imprisoned like that?"

As if humoring a young child, Davenport exhaled. "A French planter from Haiti recognized the huge black as an escaped slave from his plantation. He set a tidy sum that I approved. Some old feud he has with the slave, has ordered no food or drink. Taunts the giant black every day and keeps the key to his chains in his pocket. Who am I to question when there is profit for the Crown?"

No doubt, Davenport pocketed the proceeds. Pascale moaned. How she wished to alleviate his misery. Aboard the *Vengeance,* he had been a free man and remembered his story of the French planter who had lived to taunt and beat him. Abby shuddered with the cruelty Pascale faced. "Simeon, give the man water."

Mrs. Cornish gasped. "You cannot possibly give sustenance to another man's property. Monsieur Joubert is an important man. If he wishes to discipline his slave then he has the right to do so. Last week, I had to put Florence, one of our maids in the hotbox to teach her a lesson." In which case, Abby would happily hang Denise to relieve the human race. "Why should we care what a Frenchman orders? Has not France declared war on England?"

Abby thrust a jug of water into Simeon's hand. "Do as I say." How could she free Pascale? Even if she could release Pascale where would she hide him? Pascale drank, the awkward position causing water to dribble down his chin.

"Indulge Lady Rutland's amusement." Davenport smiled his benevolence. "His master is leaving in a few days. Claims he can't wait to get his slave back to Haiti."

In a few days? Oh, to be like Nicholas, her brother, and have his pugilist ability to relieve the sudden itch to plant her fist in the British captain's face. *Monsieur Joubert keeps the key in his pocket.* Ideas spun. Abby tucked away that bit information.

They skirted newly dug broad embankments and entered through the opened gates of Fort Nassau. Soldiers drilled in the yards and above, guards walked the parapets. Simeon offered his hand and Abby alighted from the carriage. Shoulders back, radiating superiority, Captain Davenport escorted them about the fortress, showing the barracks, munitions storage, bake house, officers' quarters. Where was Thorne kept?

"The dungeons are down there," Davenport said, his gaze glued to Abby...apparently gauging her reaction.

She kept her expression blank. *Stay alert.* Locked door, steps leading below into a darkened cavity. Was Jacob imprisoned in a dank, stinking hellhole?

"Is that where the rebels are being kept?" Denise squealed.

Not the sharpest knife in the drawer.

Davenport didn't say anything, pointed with his chin to the office door. They entered and Abby waited until her eyes adjusted to the dark. On the walls were guns, swords, England's flag and a tortoiseshell. Davenport motioned for a soldier to seat the ladies. A well-dressed gentleman, a bewigged male version of Mrs. Cornish sat behind a desk. *The Governor.*

This was what the excursion was about. Denise nodded. *She knew.*

"Lady Rutland," began Governor Gambier, "I arrived this morning and have been told of your lovely presence in Nassau as heralded by the towns' people and my sister. I've never met the Duke of Rutland, your father but his reputation, I hold in much-admired esteem."

Abigail curtseyed. "Thank you, Governor." Good. He understood her status, a thin, tenuous thread to play upon to influence him.

He studied Abby over steepled fingers. "I have heard of the successful capture of the *Vengeance* and am prepared to hear your account. Captain Davenport will lead the discussion."

Of course, Davenport would control the cross-examination. Simeon warned her with his eyes. This was her chance—her one hope to save her reputation, her future, and to wipe away Jacob's double entendre. Her heart beat faster. No thinking time. Slow down the interrogation. Pause sufficiently. Davenport stared. Denise rubbernecked. A soldier standing guard next to the door tried to be invisible. Rain started to fall. It hammered on the roofs and drummed down the rainspouts.

Abby took a deep breath and plunged in with her story, glossing over many details. What struck her odd was that the British captain never once inquired of her ordeal aboard the *Civis*. Instead he focused on the American privateer. Davenport's face was of such virulence, such naked spite and tangible hate that she stood rooted while recounting inane offenses of Captain Thorne, from the poor food and absence of entertainments. She left out the part of the bard-singing privateer—that Davenport nor would the governor swallow. "Simeon acted as my chaperone, and had taken the greatest care to see that I had all the comforts there were available," she lied blithely.

Davenport interrupted, to stop her rhythm. "There are two rules."

Try me. I can count that high.

"Answer the questions. Tell the entire story."

To retrieve a bayonet off the wall and skewer Davenport had merit. "The only good remark I have for Captain Thorne was that he proved a gentleman and insisted I take his cabin. Thank goodness, for I don't think I could have tolerated the stuffier lieutenant's cabin." Abby invented further tales of an uneventful voyage lackluster with the deprivations of her station.

"And that is all…Lady Rutland?" He crossed his arms in front of him with exaggerated casualness.

Abby lowered her eyes. She had a sudden startling vision of Jacob Thorne standing at the bow of his ship, hands on hips, his hot cobalt eyes raking her slowly with inviting promises. *Stay focused, Abby.* She saw the gleam of Davenport eyes. With certainty, he expected a ribald tale of ravishment. She stood then paced, her skirts shifting with her movement, a calculated performance to draw attention. In the width of Governor Gambier's smile, his generous chin tripled altogether. Denise snored in her chair, an attack of narcolepsy. The guard stood at attention and behind him hung numerous labelled keys—office, armory, munition and dungeons. *Noteworthy.*

She stopped in front of the desk, and saw the governor exchange glances with Davenport. "Forgive me, if I'm boring you, for there isn't much to tell other than I found the company aboard the *Vengeance* humdrum and uninspiring." The last time Abby had seen Jacob, he had been in chains. With a horrid wrenching of the heart she had watched him, his face hard and grim as granite one moment, then unconscious, thrown roughly into the hold. Pascale, Ben, Joseph, Enos and the rest of the crewmen locked in behind him. That last heart-shaking vision had not faded from her tormented mind. She was free to go home. Her ordeal was over. Jacob's fate gnawed at her insides.

Davenport narrowed his eyes. "If you say so, Lady Rutland."

Abby snapped back to attention. "I can't wait to get home. I miss my maids, the balls, soirees and shopping. You cannot imagine how horrible it is to be without my personal seamstresses and milliners. I haven't had a new gown or hat in I do not know how long." She passed Davenport, ignoring him and stopped in front of the governor. "My father will be quite pleased when I return from this adventure whole, safe and sound."

"Captain Davenport has volunteered to take you to England. After your ordeal with the Colonials, it is my hope you find respite in Nassau. My sister has seen to your comforts?"

"She has been wonderful." Abby cleared her throat. "About the crew of the *Vengeance?*"

The governor's expression showed a flash of annoyance. "Captain Davenport has informed me of your regard for the

Colonials. In Nassau, we operate according to the laws of England. In high treason, and offenses such as this, the laws of England preside. The writ of habeas corpus denied."

"But they had letters of marque."

"You are excited, Lady Rutland and have gone through a torment," Gambier placated.

"My father has influence..." She let that knowledge drift over to strangle him.

"There are no letters of marque. On top of that, Captain Jacob Thorne has caused significant damage to England's economic and commercial prospects as testified by Captain Davenport. In his Majesty's islands, we are vested in full power and authority to perform all things necessary for the effectual suppression and final determination of piracy."

The governor snapped open a drawer and laid a document in her hands. "This came from King George, verifying the Piracy Act of 1698 to be applied in determination of cases to rid ourselves of the pestilence that surrounds us."

"Are you saying there will be no trial?"

"Lady Rutland, the pirate, Captain Thorne, is as slippery as a cobra, just as venomous and with enough gall to reach the gates of hell. He will get his due."

"And the crew?"

"Accessory to piracy, criminalized under the same statute."

"They will be sent to England as prisoners?" The air rose dank, heavy, suffocating.

"No, they will not. They will be hanged as soon as they finish repairs to the *Vengeance*."

The blood drained from her face, any trial a farce. Davenport smirked. He won. Nothing she could say or do would stop the wheels in motion, nothing to spare Jacob or the crew.

Once inside the carriage, Abby reeled with the governor's decision. The door of the dungeon loomed to her left. Locked. No guard. Thirty steps from the office door. If only she could get the key. To break them out under cover of darkness. How to get into the fort?

Davenport sat next to her. "Lady Rutland, I believe there are more—events that you have forgotten. I have planned a special tour of the harbor that will be of interest to you—perhaps jog your memory."

Was she playing a game of chess? Abby held the piece, weighing her next move. What was he up to? Surf thrashed against the shore and the carriage wheels flogged through hard sand. Captain Davenport snaked his arm around her shoulders. How dare he take such liberties? She stiffened, and he laughed. The old harridan said nothing of the captain's familiarity. *Speak-up, Mrs. Cornish and act like a chaperone—like teaching German to a poodle.*

Barrels and wooden crates were stacked high on the beach. When Davenport saw the direction of her gaze, he said, "Munition stores and gunpowder, generously supplied by your Captain Thorne and quite a plunder to supply Fort Nassau. I can imagine General Washington's frustration…as if the rebels would even have a chance against their English masters."

Gunpowder. No guards. Your negligence, Captain Davenport will be your undoing.

Abby collapsed her parasol with a snap and stuck it between them. "Indeed." Below a dock stretched into the bay, dinghies tied securely to the side. The *Solebay* lay anchored with six smaller ships. Further down the beach, another ship was pulled up on rollers, rested on its flank and staked with heavy ropes. Half-naked men toiled in the hot sun, scraping barnacles and seaweed off her bottom. Others carried buckets of hot tar to smooth over the cleaned portion. Carpenters hammered and sawed, patching and repairing the damage. In heavy chains, men labored, shuffling in the sand. Their carriage came to a halt. The prisoners stopped and stared.

"I am preparing my prize for the trip home to England. Can you imagine the fanfare?" Davenport plucked a piece of lint from his spotless blue coat.

"Ooh to see the *Vengeance!*" crowed Mrs. Cornish. "What savages." Her neck craned to get a closer look, as if she were viewing a sideshow of unnatural oddities.

Now Abby understood. The figures became clearer. Davenport jumped from the carriage and offered his hand. Abby sat paralyzed. Enos struggled under a heavy load. Benjamin staggered in the sand with tar buckets. Lawton scraped the hull balanced on shaky scaffolding. A score or more of men she didn't know also labored. All Colonial prisoners?

Her heart pounded, eyes scanning. Where was Thorne? Turning, she saw him just as he raised a beam to men perched on deck above him. His hard, muscled body was bare to the waist, and sunburned, and his raven-black hair matted to his forehead. When his gaze fell on the visitors, he froze mid-motion. Cobalt eyes seared her. Davenport nodded to his officer. A whip cracked.

Jacob tossed the beam aside and started toward the guard who had struck him. A red stain oozed across his bare back.

"You appear troubled, Lady Rutland?" Davenport baited her.

There were no words. In sickened silence, she watched as Jacob was struck down by two guards and commanded back to work. Davenport grabbed her about the waist and brought her to the ground...like quicksand under her feet...swallowing her. Her heart wrenched. She couldn't do this. Couldn't bear it. Had to get away.

Davenport paraded her forward, lowered his head to nuzzle her ear. "My dear, you cannot possibly hold any affection for these brigands."

She stumbled. Davenport righted her, his palm on her ribcage and his thumb scraped over her breast. Her nostrils flared. She pushed him away, her mind scrambling on how to protect Jacob and the crew of the *Vengeance, and* in what manner to protect herself, and keep up a pretense without giving herself away. "You forget yourself, Captain Davenport."

"Do I? Your reaction to Captain Thorne? Unusual. Your memory appears to be jogged. I'd like to hear more of your travels with the Yankee traitor."

Abby swallowed.

"Captain Thorne," he shouted, his dry voice, deliberate and thoughtful. "Do you know any reason why Lady Rutland should respond so dramatically to your presence? After all, she claims she was treated kindly under your command even given your cabin. Her reaction suggests otherwise, does it not?

"Why don't you ask Lady Rutland that question, Davenport? I am not the least qualified to explain her behavior. Nor is it of any concern to me."

"Jacob...Captain Thorne..." She pleaded with her eyes, her whisper barely audible.

Thorne cut her off sharply. "You are an overindulged aristocratic witch. If I were ever to get my hands on you, I'd make you pay, by God."

"Make her pay for what, Captain Thorne?"

Thorne remained mute, his glinting eyes burrowed into hers unmercifully.

"Now put your hand on my arm." Davenport ordered her. When she refused, he put his arm tightly about her waist and led her forward, away from the carriage.

"What game do you play?" she hissed through her teeth. He was obsessed with Thorne.

He dared to touch his head to hers again, to imply an intimacy then threw back his head and laughed loudly, "Games? I love the *games* you play, Lady Rutland." She raised her hand, stopped halfway when she saw that all activity about them had stopped. Of course, Davenport had orchestrated this drama, for all the men, including the guards. Ben, Joseph, Samuel, Enos, what they must think of her.

And Jacob. He stood like fire transformed to ice, glaring his unconcealed hatred.

Blood pounded in her ears. She longed to kick sand in Davenport's face, to bloody his shins with her toes. Too late, this game of chess, just as she had taken her finger off the piece, she panicked with the mistake she had made underestimating Davenport. Her hands grew clammy. What disaster had she left herself open to?

Simeon thrust her parasol between them. Bless Simeon. "Lady Rutland need not get any more sun." He scowled at Captain Davenport.

"Come, my dear," Davenport purred. "These men do not need any distraction. They have work to do." Abby refused his arm and he laughed as if they were playing some lover's game.

"Guards, take this scum away. Make sure he works double the others."

The flushed, sweating guards grabbed Jacob again and thrust him roughly to the ship. Except for the muffled scuffling sounds through sand and harsh cries of gulls that screamed overhead, there was silence.

Abby bit her lip and looked away. "You must give them proper sustenance."

"I'm not in the mood for favors." A smile played about his lips. "However, I might reconsider if one…was more obliging."

Abby ignored him. She would inform the governor of Davenport's behavior.

When they reached the carriage, the British Captain addressed Mrs. Cornish. "Brilliant, don't you think, the crew of the *Vengeance*, repairing their own ship? Why use slave labor when I have rebel resources at my disposal? Normally it takes a month to careen a ship for repairs, but these Colonials with a whip to their backs have been persuaded to speed their efforts. I assure you Lady Rutland; we'll be able to set sail in two weeks."

Two weeks to go home. Two weeks until their execution.

"They are receiving what they deserve," Mrs. Cornish carped like a fishwife. Abby fumed with the condescension of her countrymen. She took Simeon's hand to assist her into the carriage, a slight to Davenport.

"Are you sure your man, Simeon isn't loyal to the Colonials?" Davenport climbed in the carriage next to her.

Wind whipped through the coconut palms. With her handkerchief, Abby dabbed the perspiration on her upper lip, the suggestion of Simeon's imprisonment and Davenport's power over her. She was a Rutland. Never would she be beaten. Unflinchingly, she stared into his cold grey eyes but spoke to the governor's sister. "Mrs. Cornish, did you know my father is a cousin to King George, a very close cousin."

"The King? I had no idea," Mrs. Cornish squealed. She had been asleep during the interview. Davenport blinked and drew away from her. He was not as confident as he portrayed. Good. Right where she wanted him.

Jacob's gaze slid unwillingly to that golden witch—her slim, lovely body, her blue eyes flashing into his. Dammit! Women that beautiful ought to be thrown to the sharks. The force of it slammed into Jacob. The sting of her lies, the love of his life brought a deep cutting misery in his chest. She was an aristocrat to the highest degree. Why did he expect anything less?

To think he was in love with her. To believe she felt something for him—that heartless lying bitch. Time he faced facts: like better men before him, he could not change the heart of a soulless highborn creature that she was destined to be. He lowered his head against the rough planking of the ship, letting it scrape against his forehead, realizing he let the sun burn his back and the wind beat against his face. He had dared to foolishly dream, to have a wife and a child. To think he gave up his ship, his men and his life to protect her. The gallows awaited him.

His hands curled into fists. Visions of her kept him alive, yielding to haunting dreams that staved off the hopelessness and despair of endless backbreaking work. He developed a talent to discover the joy in pain. Long into the night, wrapped in chains, he fought off the insects the hunger and the despair. He thought of her, longed for her, that glorious ghost of the past that haunted him. Did the pain she cause outweigh the tender moments? Could the pain make him stop loving her?

It was as if the curtain fell. All emotion passed from his mind.

"Don't let Davenport get to you. She isn't worth it, said Enos.

Jacob snorted. "I wasn't thinking of her at all."

"Sure you were. That mind of yours is working overtime on her."

"Worse than death is betrayal. I can conceive death, but not betrayal, Enos."

"Get rid of those thoughts and concentrate on escape."

Jacob laughed and Enos looked sharply to him, considering his sanity. They were trapped on this hellhole and there was no way to escape.

"We have much work to do tonight so keep your wits sharp about you," Abigail whispered to Simeon, procured a glass of wine from his tray with one hand, while she worked her Chinese silk fan with the other. She smiled and nodded to guests at a late evening dinner social, held in her honor by a wealthy merchant and where everyone of significance in town had been invited. With a tray of crystal glasses, Simeon, graciously on loan for the night, served the elite of Nassau and moved into the crowd.

A thin gentleman, well-dressed in a white frockcoat, breeches and powdered wig approached. "Lady Rutland," he murmured in perfect French. "I am Monsieur Joubert; your compassion for my slave speaks volumes of your character."

"Honored, Monsieur Joubert." His words articulated the opposite of his intention. Abby had requested her host, Mrs. Swain to put the Frenchman on the guest list.

"Philippe. I insist. And the honor is mine."

"Philippe," He kissed her hand. She shuddered. "What brings you to the Bahamas?"

"Business. The uniqueness of which would confuse your ladyship. I own a plantation on Haiti; perhaps you could one day afford a visit to my island. I'd be happy to show you my home." His dark eyes darted over her.

She gritted her teeth at the Frenchman's insult, his manner no different than Davenport's. Of course, she had gone to the governor about the English captain's behavior which precipitated orders for him to patrol the Bahamas while the *Vengeance* was repaired.

Simeon approached and she savored her wine. She stumbled then. Her red wine spilled onto the Frenchman. "How clumsy of me, Philippe. Your beautiful white coat. Simeon, please take Monsieur Joubert's coat for the maids to clean."

His dark eyes flashing, the Frenchman ripped off his coat and threw it. With garment in hand, Simeon reached into the pocket, smiled, flashed a thumbs-up, and then vanished out the rear door. Abby exhaled. He had the key. If the key were not in Joubert's pocket, Simeon would have had to search his hotel room. If only the rest of the evening could pass as smoothly.

"I do hope you can put it in your heart to forgive me, Monsieur Joubert. Perhaps you can be my dinner companion this evening. Later I will be playing the pianoforte for everyone's amusement. I'm sure you will enjoy the entertainment," Abby demurred.

Some of the air was taken out of the Frenchman, mollified to be seated next to the guest of honor. Putting up with Phillippe's intolerable arrogance for the evening was a trial, made worse when she moved to play the pianoforte and he pushed the host aside to stand over Abby. Across the keys, strains of Bach and Mozart flowed from her fingers. Her gaze flitted around the room, her mind racing along another track. The heat was punitive. The humidity made it even more difficult to bear. Even her light silk dress was soaked through with perspiration and clung uncomfortably to her damp petticoats. Where was Simeon?

With a strained smile pasted on her lips, she charmed the Frenchman and those gathered around her. People were fatigued from her playing but too politic to complain. Mr. Swain, the host looked to his wife who nodded admirably because Lady Rutland chose to spend the most time in their home, precipitating a rise in their status. The clock in the hall chimed eleven bells. Her fingers ached. How much longer could she play? Why was Simeon taking so long? Something must have happened. Would soldiers burst onto the assembly and arrest her?

Simeon rushed in, a bit disheveled, the Frenchman's coat grappled in his hands, murmuring apologies for the time it took to clean the garment. He winked at Abby and slid the garment onto the Frenchman's shoulders. She bowed her head, finished the melody. Applause rent the room. She stood on wobbly legs, inattentive to the congratulatory remarks and praises and begged departure due to exhaustion.

At Governor's House, all were settled in for the night. A soft tap sounded on her door. She yanked Simeon into her room. Pascale followed. "What happened?"

"I unlocked Pascale and we headed to the beach. There were two guards posted on the munitions from the *Vengeance* and that presented a bit of a problem. Pascale took care of them quietly. They will have a monster of a headache coming morning. We loaded a cask of gunpowder into a dingy then rowed half mile north, came ashore buried the cask like you told me. We capsized the dingy, shoved it onto the outgoing tide and walked back circling the town."

Abby wanted to fall to her knees and thank the heavens. "I can't imagine what tomorrow will bring but we'll deal with the ramifications as they come. It was good the guards saw him. With the dingy missing they will presume he escaped and if the boat is discovered washed-up on shore, everyone will assume he has drowned.

Monsieur Joubert will be in a terrible temper. Regardless, he will have the island turned upside down to hunt for Pascale."

"He will be upset but he will not be able to venture out of his hotel room."

Abby narrowed her eyes. "Why are you grinning?"

"From the locals, I discovered a noxious tree on the island called, "Poison Wood". With great care, I collected the oil from this tree and lathered it on the inside of the Frenchman's coat. He will suffer a burning rash in the days ahead and will be unable to leave his bed."

Abby laughed. "You didn't."

"I'm sure he is scratching up a storm. But we have one problem. Where to hide Pascale?"

"In my wardrobe room, it will be the last place anyone will look. I'll keep the door locked. For now, go into the kitchens and get Pascale food and drink. He needs it."

Simeon left and she translated everything in French to Pascale.

"Merci, my lady. You take great risk," he bowed. "I do not know how to repay you."

Abby waved a dismissive hand. "You have done much for me. Now I return the favor. In two weeks, the *Vengeance* will be ready to sail. At the right time, I'll need your help to free Captain Thorne and his men. You can sail to the Colonies a free man."

Simeon reentered with a tray of sweat breads, sausages, fried chicken and papaya. Pascale attacked the food like a starved man was meant to do. Abby locked the door.

"Now for the rest of my plan."

Abby ran her finger across several dusty bottles on the shelf of the apothecary. "I need a sleeping draught. I have trouble sleeping and a great fear of the sea. With my impending departure, I'd like to obtain enough of a supply for my long voyage." Abby said to the pharmacist. Inadvertently she bumped into an older man. "My apologies, sir." He didn't look at her and ran from the shop.

The pharmacist smiled. "Lady Rutland, don't mind Albury. He's a recluse but one of the three best pilots on the island. Lives by himself in a small cottage near the docks."

"Pilot?"

"Ships can't get out of the harbor without a pilot to guide 'em. Albury knows the shoals, reefs, tides like the back of his hand. Deadly without him aboard. Once the ship is safely out to sea, they drop Albury down in a dinghy and he returns to shore."

Abby gasped. She had never considered the dangers of the harbor.

"Forget about your fear of the sea. Don't worry. With Albury aboard you'll be safe. He handed her a weighty package. "I put enough draught to put ten elephants to sleep."

Once outside, Abby stood beneath the shade of a frangipani, heavy with luminous white blossoms and intoxicating fragrance, waiting for Simeon's return to share this new revelation. To get Jacob free was one thing, yet the dangers of the harbor created another prison.

Again, Jacob's thin, ashen face emerged, the ugly bruise on his cheek, and the men standing over him with raised fists. She cringed at the memory. Ever since she had returned from the beach with Captain Davenport two weeks before, the all too grim picture of Jacob at his captors' hands had flashed before her eyes repeatedly, until she wanted to scream as if someone had cut her heart open with a dull knife.

From the sawmill, a rider galloped up the road, the horse's hooves kicking up puffs of dust. He stopped in front of her and dismounted. "*Lady Rutland*."

"Captain Davenport, your company of late has been in short supply. What do I owe this honor?" His manner was circumspect—enough to freeze the tropics. Governor Gambier must have given him a severe tongue lashing. Abby smiled.

"I've been patrolling the Caribbean." His eyes were stony. "The Colonials have finished cleaning, caulking and overhauling of the *Vengeance,* and along with the *Solebay,* resupplied. As a formality, I'm to inform you of our departure in two days."

"I'll be ready." From her exploration, she already knew the rebel vessel was rolled off the beach and anchored in the bay.

Keep your friends near, keep your enemies nearer.

"Captain Davenport, I'd like to make a peace offering. Since we will be traveling together...I think we should call a truce."

He choked. "I am at your disposal."

That bit of humility cost him. "There is one last party tomorrow night and it is my hope you would attend." To gain his trust was important.

He narrowed his eyes. "Are you sure the governor would approve?"

"I don't see why not." She took his arm in hers and promenaded a few steps.

He withdrew his arm. "What do you want, Lady Rutland?"

I want you to stop the hangings. “A dance.” He stood there staring at her. Too quiet. Was he mentally running through every suspicion in his head? Her hands grew clammy.

His tone of voice fell flat. “A dance it will be. Did I mention a witness has put your servant, Simeon at the same locale and time of Monsieur Joubert’s escaped slave, an offense that carries harsh punishment?”

Abby forced a smile. He was bluffing. “A mistaken identity. My servant was on loan at a soiree that evening. Mr. and Mrs. Swain, the hosts would have recollection and numerous townspeople could affirm. Of course, you were at sea, so how could you know?”

“Have you seen the gallows?”

Touché. Abby did not change her expression. She had seen the gallows. She raged and trembled with the construction. “I’ve reconciled with the governor’s judgment.”

“Why the sudden change?”

“Everyone makes life choices and those choices are sometimes punitive. Unfortunate for the Colonials…they are to suffer the penalty of their bad decisions.” Did his shoulders drop?

“Your servant, Lady Rutland.” He swaggered to his horse. “Until tomorrow evening.”

She patted the parcel from the apothecary in her hands. “Until tomorrow evening, Captain.”

Chapter 22

"Are you going to the lynching, tomorrow?" Mrs. Sawyer said, her fingers groped primly in front of her in a fat, meaty ball of flesh then fluttered upward, signaling the orchestra to begin.

Abby's stomach clenched, the grisly scene of Jacob swinging from the gallows appeared before her eyes. No. The execution had to be stopped. She fixed a smile on the old harridan. Mrs. Sawyer beamed, determined to make her send-off for Lady Rutland, Nassau's event of the year.

The emerald-colored watered silk, Abby wore, cut in the latest French court style, molded snugly to her narrow waist and pushed her breasts high enough to mound impressively over the bodice. The sleeves were tapered to the elbow and from there flared to allow the falling cuffs of her chemise to spill forth in a fine profusion of creamy lace. She smoothed her hands over the straight shimmering folds, her fingers gliding over a vial concealed in a pocket. Soldiers and officers from the fort, the governor in his ceremonial dress, ladies garbed in their finest gowns; seemingly the entire town was in attendance.

"I'll be busy preparing for my journey," Abby said.

"Have you heard of the strange malady affecting Monsieur Joubert? The hotel owner wants him gone. No one will stay there. Too bad his slave escaped and drowned."

Abby nodded, the mundane chatter making her head pound. Courtesy of the Governor's sister, Denise, a medicinal cream had been sent to the Frenchman to cure his inflammation. Of course, Abby had Simeon deliver the restorative after mixing in poison wood oil. To add to the Frenchman's problems, Abby confided to Denise that the Frenchman had procured an incurable disease that swept across Haiti. The rumor spread like fire through a cane break.

"Too bad about the slave," Abby concurred. "To be eaten by sharks. What a horrible fate." Abby fueled the dire consequences of the slave's escape. As predicted, the capsized dinghy had been found washed-up on the beach. Wouldn't they be scandalized to learn he dwelled in her wardrobe room, eating his fill of the governor's largesse? Wouldn't they be shocked to know he was helping her with an escape that would rock the island?

Everything hinged on this night. Abby had introduced a secret campaign, implementing the tactical intelligence of a military commander. Over the past weeks, Simeon and she had done reconnaissance. Dressed as Abe and under cloak of night, they had counted the number of guards at the fort, shift changes, when the gates were locked then timed the villagers' movements and when they went to sleep.

"May I beg this waltz?" Governor Gambier bowed.

"I'd love to." Abby curtseyed. The governor moved with the grace of a gorilla.

Abby danced with an endless stream of partners. Her feet ached where the governor had stepped on them. Minutes ticked by. Hours. Perspiration beaded on her upper lip. Where was Davenport? Simeon angled his head to the clock. She clutched the vial in her pocket. Was Pascale caught? *Stay calm.* She fought to feign interest in her host.

"You trade in sugar?" Abby said.

"You seem distracted, Lady Rutland. I've mentioned several times, molasses."

"Of course, Mr. Sawyer. Molasses. My apologies. I'm thinking about going home." *I'm thinking that Jacob will die tomorrow and I cannot do anything to stop the execution.*

Servants rushed to open the door. Simeon straightened. Captain Davenport had arrived. He came straight toward her. She turned to her side, pretending she had not seen him. Abby took a deep breath and slowly exhaled—to get him alone.

"Lady Rutland," Davenport droned.

She whirled from a deep conversation on the price of molasses. "Why Captain Davenport, I'm surprised to see you."

"What else did you expect?"

His answer was too clipped. Her throat grew dry. "I'm so glad you came. I did promise you a dance but to tell you the truth, I need some fresh air. Care to escort me to the gardens?"

"Your servant," he bowed.

"Would you like refreshment? The host's wine stores are excellent." She motioned for a servant and ordered wine to be brought to the terrace.

When the servant deposited two glasses on the table and left, Abby turned to Davenport. "I can't wait to see my father and brothers." Lanterns dangled and blinked like fireflies.

"What are you really about, Lady Rutland?"

How to get his attention diverted from the wine? "With our journey ahead, I'm offering friendship. If you don't care to be in my company then I shall leave." She started toward the house. He grabbed her arm.

"Not just yet."

She stared at where his hand lay. He dropped her arm.

"Forgiven," she said not waiting for his apology then turned away to allow him to see her profile. A crescent moon rose in the western sky, enough to provide some light on a dark night, enough to hide in the shadows what needed to remain hidden. "I will miss the Bahamas. The turquoise waters and bright sunshine by day, giving way to dark velvet sky at night, a myriad of stars like so many diamonds, so unlike anything I've ever known." Three steps to the wineglass. Three seconds to pour in the sleeping draught.

He said nothing. What was he up to? A woman cried out and a rush of murmurs originated from the house. Davenport darted inside. Abby plucked the vial from her pocket and deposited the entire contents in a glass. Half as much she had planned to give him. Had she been too careless, dosing him with too much of the drug? No. He had arrived too late. When he returned, she held the drugged glass of wine out to him and tilted her head questioningly.

"Mrs. Sawyer swooned. If she leaned against the *Solebay* it would bend."

Abby laughed. "A sense of humor?" *Hurry.* She had sent each of the guards at the fort a basket that included a piece of cake, and a portion of punch with a generous dose of laudanum. Included was a note from Mrs. Sawyer explaining she was sorry they could not attend but could share refreshment. The soldiers should be sleeping.

His eyebrows furrowed then released. He accepted the glass of wine and slid his fingers over hers. Abby gasped and he smiled. "Did I offend you?"

"Not really." *Drink it. All of it.* The effect of the drug took thirty minutes. Valuable minutes. She had to get inside the fort. *Now.*

"Why this sudden interest in me?" He drank the wine.

A servant came upon the terrace and offered more refreshment. Abby declined anything to get rid of the servant. She turned back to Captain Davenport. He had finished his wine.

Abby exhaled. "You are provocative, Captain Davenport." She ran a finger around her neckline where it chafed. Davenport ogled the movement, his eyes glowed.

"You are an enticing woman. The stars, do they seem brighter?"

Good. The opium in the laudanum aroused euphoria. *Faster.* By now, Pascale should have the guards on the beach incapacitated, Albury, the pilot kidnapped from his bed, tied and bound in one of the dinghies ready to board the *Vengeance.*

"You have breasts." He weaved.

Altered mood. Inability to concentrate. Good. The laudanum was taking affect. "Captain, you've had too much to drink."

He raised his finger at her accusingly. He stumbled. Simeon put Davenport's arm around his shoulder.

"The carriage. We need to help Captain Davenport to Fort Nassau," she said. The drug worked quicker than she estimated. Would he collapse before they arrived? Abby supported Davenport on the other side. The carriage bobbed with his weight. Abby scrambled into the back seat and straightened the captain. Simeon climbed onto the driver's seat and tapped the whip on the horse's flank. In minutes, they arrived at the fort entrance.

"Who goes there?" The sentry came to her side. Drat. He had not drunk his punch.

"Captain Davenport is not feeling well," Abby explained. "If you would open the doors."

The sentry held up a lantern, gauged the state of Captain Davenport's illness, assumed intoxication. With raised eyebrows, he opened the gate. She heard a thud and looked behind. Pascale dragged the unconscious guard away then sprinted toward the harbor. Abby sagged against the carriage seat.

No sound in the fort. Good. The guards on the parapet were asleep. How perfect her plan worked. Odd? Not even the hum of a cricket—an unnatural quiet. Abby shivered.

A furtive search of the grounds revealed the high walls of the fort, a flag hanging limply, an empty forge and the locked door of the dungeon. A tranquil garrison: nothing to fear.

The carriage stopped in front of the office. They tugged Davenport from his seat. His body shifted. His weight crushed on top of her. Abby splayed to the ground. Simeon yanked him off. Rising, Abby nudged Davenport's shoulder with her satin slipper. Out cold. Too heavy to drag him into the office. "We'll leave him here. Simeon, hurry north and light the gunpowder. The explosion will draw the attention away from the harbor, enough so Jacob and his men will have time to escape. I'll drive the carriage to Sawyer's before anyone knows I am missing."

Simeon disappeared through the gates like a phantom.

Heart pounding, she picked up her skirts and hurried into the office. She snatched the key from the highest hook, the key to the dungeon. In two steps, Abby was grabbed by the neck. The back of her head cracked against the wall.

"Captain Davenport!" She bit off the urge to scream. To think he had faked his stupor. "Let me go!"

"I think not. I'll have a warrant out to arrest your servant, Simeon. Taking gunpowder, helping a slave escape and whatever else I can think of. He will be hanged with the rest."

"All suppositions." Sweat slicked her body. His strength for the high dose she had given him, unbelievable. When would the drug kick in?

"I heard everything. And to think you could drug me? I did not drink the wine. I tasted the laudanum, knew what you were up to and dumped the contents. The rest was an act."

But she had seen him drink…no…of course, the servant had distracted her. How stupid she had been.

He twisted her hand, lifting the key to her face. "Your arrest looms, Lady Rutland. Treason in assisting enemies of the Crown to escape does not bode well…unless…you yield a concession."

"You wouldn't dare." An edge of hysteria rose in her voice.

"I have the power."

"This is blackmail."

"I know. A wonderful institution. I will have unfettered promotion."

"Through me. Through the power of the Rutland family." The greedy, vulgar weasel of a man would use a woman to gain wealth and privilege.

"You're a smart girl. The choice is yours." He smiled indulgently.

She raised her chin. "Simeon must be released at once. The crew of the *Vengeance* will not be hanged and sent to England as prisoners of war."

Davenport licked the corner of his mouth. "Regardless we marry tomorrow. With discretion, we will say you were victimized during your captivity and as a gentleman I am preserving your honor and reputation by marrying you in a precipitous way."

"There will be no nuptials unless the crew's status is changed. This I guarantee."

"The latter, I'll consider. You don't have room for negotiation." He picked up a stray curl and ran his finger down her breast. She slapped his crude hand away. "I expect a good wedding night. The same you gave that traitorous Colonial."

She sucked air in her lungs. "A man like you would only earn his stripes this way."

"It is the way of the world. Why not start now?" He slipped his hand into her bodice and pinched her nipple. He covered her mouth, wet and nauseating.

A sick knot twisted in the pit of her stomach, the reality of a life time commitment to this lecher. He forced her fingers to let go of the key and moved her hand to massage the bulging organ beneath his breeches.

"No!" She pushed him away. Davenport shoved her onto the desk in the office. Grunting brutally, he heaved her onto her back and climbed on top of her, his eyes lit wildly. Saliva dribbled from the corner of his mouth. She pounded his chest.

"So you like it rough?" He was upon her in a tangle of arms and legs. She thrashed and sobbed beneath him. His thick lips sucked at the flesh of her throat while his hands squeezed her breasts with awful ruthlessness. He panted obscenities in her ear, his heavy breathing, hot on her neck, while she struggled frantically to free herself. He reached beneath her skirts and groped between her legs, the pain agonizing.

An explosion splintered the air.

Davenport jerked his head. Simeon had lit the cask of gunpowder. Now the town's people would run north to the other fort to see what had transpired. She had failed to free Thorne. Several more explosions tore through the air. Where did Simeon get the extra gunpowder? No time to ponder that fact. She brought her knee up against Davenport. Crack. Like wood hitting bone? Davenport's weight collapsed upon her. She pushed him off and he thumped to the floor. Abby scrambled off the desk and to her feet, adjusting her skirts.

A lantern was lit. Two cobalt eyes scorched her. "Jacob?"

"In the flesh, *Lady Rutland*."

Abby blinked, her mind reeling with his sudden appearance. She didn't care. She was so happy he was free and had come to save her. But the edge of his voice held a chilling menace that limped up her spine and entered her skin with pinprick accuracy, congealing her blood to ice. "How did you—" Men crowded. Blackened faces gawked. Enos, Ben, Lawton with ugly twists to their mouths.

Jacob waved a hand to his companions. "How fortunate, Captain John Trevett and his Colonial Marines chose to make a precipitous landing this evening. We control the fort. You and your lover are my prisoner."

"Prisoner?" Abby's jaw dropped. She stepped over Davenport and moved to Jacob but something in his implacable expression stopped her. She glanced to a blue-eyed man in a naval uniform, obviously, Captain Trevett. "He is *not* my lover."

Jacob snorted. "Enough of your lies, your insatiable lust with Davenport is evident to every man present."

Of course, her charade with Davenport, playing the spoiled aristocrat then Jacob mistaking her presence in the fort…seeing Davenport's near rape and how he had assumed a carnal assignation. "I was attempting to help you escape."

Jacob smirked. "On your back with Davenport, rutting between your legs? The disadvantage of having your tryst tonight is a trip to Boston."

"I was attacked. Davenport nearly–" A dry sob burned in her throat. "I have to go—go home to my family." Abby appealed to Captain Trevett with her eyes. *Do something, save me.* Uncertainty shadowed his face.

Captain Trevett cleared his throat. "You will take the woman?" He sounded as though he didn't want to know the answer.

Jacob pointed his sword right at her heart. "She is the Duke of Rutland's daughter. I'm sure the Duke will do anything to get his daughter back, ensuring, my cousin, Ethan to be freed. I picked her up during my capture of the *Civis* and she will remain under my authority."

"Jacob, please listen to me—"

"You would do anything to get home, Lady Rutland. We've heard the sob story about your family while we waited for our death on the gallows." Jacob planted his sword next to Davenport's head. How he wanted to kill him for touching Abby. To think she was the prey of such a monster. Jacob fought the urge to take Abby in his arms; to reassure her but the rage screaming in him from being duped was branded on his brain. *Abby. Lady Rutland.* His vision clouded unable to separate the two. No doubt she spoke the truth but the bastard inside him wanted vengeance. She was a member of the aristocracy he disdained and he could not forgive her for that sin.

"In terms of her lover, Captain Davenport, he surpasses the vilest work of God's creation. A wonder we survived his brutality. I'll take pleasure in running the bastard through."

Captain Trevett interjected. "I will take the British captain. Washington needs a trade. For now, Captain Thorne we need to secure the fort. I have only twenty-six marines and twenty-four freed privateers up against a town of one thousand loyalists. So far we have exercised fait accompli without firing a shot."

"There are significant stores of gunpowder and small arms. Getting past the colony's militia to load the cargo aboard the ships will be another matter. Five ships are anchored in the harbor, one is the *Vengeance* and the other is the *Solebay*. They are mine," Jacob said in a carefully controlled tone, his eyes never leaving Davenport's body. *Keep your head, Jacob.* How he'd like to flay every inch of the British captain's skin from his body and hang him from a mast for the crows to feast.

"Men get a move on and take what you can, including the British captain," ordered Trevett who must have read the violence on Jacob's mind. They lifted Davenport from the room.

Abby sprang past him. He snapped his hand out, grabbed her and spun her around.

"I will not be your prisoner." With the fury of a lioness she lashed out, struggling to break free of him. One fist found its mark. "Get away from me! Don't touch me!"

He grabbed her wrists to hold her writhing body still. "What's the matter, Abby? Angry because I interrupted your rendezvous?"

"I have done everything in my power to help you escape. Committing treason and…near defilement. Ask Simeon. Ask Pascale, they will tell you. And you, Captain Thorne are the most loathsome creature of them all."

"Enos, Lawton," Jacob stopped their departure. "Get rope. Lady Rutland will be our guest on the *Vengeance*."

Enos hesitated. "Perhaps we should hear the lass out."

"Do you dare to defy my orders?" Jacob snapped and the flat of her hand hit the side of his face. "Rip your shirt if you can't find any rope, or would you prefer I hit her with the hilt of my sword as I did to Davenport?"

"But, Captain, do we need to take her along?"

"I gave you a command, Enos and I'm not about to repeat it. Unless you want to be left behind and swing from the gallows, move. Now!"

Enos looked away, shrugged out of his ragged, grimy shirt and tore off wide strips, handed them to Jacob, and then left with Lawton in silence.

"You will regret this, Jacob," Abby bit out.

"I've had enough regrets to last a thousand lifetimes, Lady Rutland. From the bowels of a filthy dungeon, my men have been chained, starved, beaten and worked beyond human endurance. Suffocated by the heat, many suffered wounds, undressed and festering, caused by continuous floggings and savage insects while you cavorted as the fine Lady Rutland." He shook his head, glaring at his fingers, now turning white from his grip on the bindings as he wound tighter and tighter the bonds about her ankles and hands. To trust her was like putting a knife in Delilah's hands.

Her eyes glistened, and he hesitated. Yet an unfamiliar, twisted weed of jealousy leapt in his heart, towering over all other emotions and stinging like nettles. "No amount of tears will affect me. You made a fool of me in front of my men. To contemplate your laughter when I asked you to marry me. The devil I'd be anywhere the sight of you exists." Surely her soul was blacker than a witch's bottom.

"I need to consult with you, Captain Thorne," said Captain Trevett. "I have sent three marines to Fort Montagu at the other end of the island, claiming I have two hundred and thirty marines at my disposal. A bluff that I hope will work. We approached Nassau, our ship, the *Providence* disguised as a trading sloop and anchored in another cove offshore in darkness. We traveled overland, slipped over the walls and knocked out the guards. I'm having the *Providence* come around Hog Island and into the harbor. It will be midday before all this comes about."

Time. Getting into the fort was one concern, getting out was another matter. "I assume you are short of provisions."

"That would be correct," said Trevett.

"Captain Thorne, a man is at the gate. He says his name is Simeon and demands to see you. But there is a mob coming up the road right behind him," said a marine.

"Let him in," ordered Jacob. He looked at Abby. She would have nothing to do with him.

When Simeon arrived, his eyes grew as big as shillings. "Why is Lady Rutland tied like this?" He knelt by Abby and glared at Thorne. "She has done everything to free you. How dare you treat her like a criminal? Lady Rutland and I worked tirelessly at night, watching the fort, planning and scheming, she drugged Davenport's drink, helped free Pascale..." On and on he went, casting her just short of sainthood. Enos and Lawton grunted her praises.

For Thorne, what she had accomplished smarted like lemon juice on an open cut. Jacob rolled his shoulders in a defensive gesture, produced a knife and cut her bonds. He held his hand out. A protracted silence fell between them. She refused and allowed Simeon to help her stand.

Jacob rubbed his chin, his whiskers rasping under his fingers. "I owe you an apology, Lady Rutland."

She massaged her wrists. Chin held high, she swept past, disregarding him as a flea stamped under an elephant's foot. "Captain Trevett, I will help you with your departure, but in return I need a favor. You must keep Captain Davenport as long as possible, at least until I can make it back to England and my father can ward off any damage he might create for me. Captain Thorne has another individual he can trade for his cousin. I must travel to England. I ask that you release me when this is over."

"Done."

"No," said Jacob.

Trevett held up his hand. "I'm in command here. Let the lady speak. Why would you help the Americans?"

In her mind, Abby replayed Jacob's accusation. All she had risked for him. Of course, he apologized. *To err is human, to forgive, divine?* She was not divine. Spine straight as sugarcane, she stared into Captain Trevett's face. "This is not my war. My war is a private war with the enemies of my family. I need to assist my father and make these faceless cowards pay for their crimes. The Americans aboard the *Vengeance* treated me well and rescued me from certain death. I cannot forget that fact. Their judgement and punishment was wrong. I could not allow it."

"I appreciate your sincerity. We have done a disservice to you," said Captain Trevett.

Abby tapped a finger on her lips. "With certainty, the militia will storm the gates."

"No doubt," said Trevett.

"You may use me, Captain Trevett as a hostage to negotiate terms and use Davenport. I believe the governor can be persuaded."

Captain Trevett nodded his head thoughtfully.

"You need provisions. Send a note to the governor to have provisions and conveyances made available. With the number of ships you are taking, you will require additional pilots to negotiate the harbor. The shoals and reefs make it impossible to depart without guidance. Simeon, did Pascale get Albury, the pilot?"

"And none too happily," said Simeon. "Pascale disabled the guards on the *Vengeance* like you ordered and put Albury aboard. When I heard the added explosions, I ran back to the fort to see if you were all right."

"As you can see I am quite fine." She brushed the dirt off her silk gown, keeping her back to Jacob. He deserved it. He'd been a buffoon where she was concerned. "I know the identities of the two other pilots. Make this in your demands to the governor as well," she said to Captain Trevett.

Their little group made their way up the ramparts overlooking five hundred angry loyalists that had gathered. Captain Trevett made his demands. Abby put on a desperate face in hopes the people she had cultivated friendships would force the governor's hand.

"The bastards have Lady Rutland," said one of the loyalists.

"What is that flag? We've never seen it," shouted another.

Abby turned. A stars and bars flag flew over the fort, replacing the flag of England.

"It is the flag of the American Colonies, get used to seeing it," warned Captain Trevett.

"There is that dam butcherer come again that carried away Governor Browne," shouted another.

Trevett blew air from his teeth and glanced to Thorne. "They remember my raid two years ago."

Abby's breath hitched from Trevett's gall, to believe that the townspeople or governor would surrender twice? No way. She placed a shaky hand on her chest, if the Americans should lose? The terrifying likelihood of a forced marriage to Davenport loomed. To win the battle was to convince the crowd. She cried out, "Please do as he says. Save me."

Tall and formidable, Thorne moved in between her and Trevett and shielded her from the mob in case an errant musket went off. His dark hair a mass of damp, tousled curls, and his eyes gleaming dangerously, he was not the same flawless figure who had taught a poor cabin boy to read. Yet even clothed in grimy rags, full beard, and with his sunburnt skin filthy from dust and sweat, he was alarmingly forbidding. *Zeus exploding with violence.* "They will need more convincing. Redirect the cannons onto the town. Show them we mean business."

Captain Trevett ordered his men to haul the fort's cannon about. He addressed the crowd. "I will blow your town off the map if necessary."

Mouths slackened, several backed off. A few leaders remained.

"Hurry and be about. You have three hours. If my demands are not met then I will start blasting," said Trevett.

Jacob turned and commandeered her arm before Trevett did. "Let them stew for a while. Shall we, *Lady Rutland*."

The careful mask was back in place. He had apologized for his treatment of her when he had wronged her, but had not forgiven her deception. Forced to navigate the narrow steps first, she listed the reasons why she hated Jacob Thorne. She had sacrificed her reputation, her country and her life for him. The ungrateful wretch, there were not even enough steps to enumerate the grievances she held against him. And if he sneered, *Lady Rutland* one more time.

By noon the American commander met with a small contingency of his men in the fort's office for a report. There had been no news from the governor and they could not be barricaded in the fort forever without provisions.

"They surrendered at Fort Montagu, Captain Trevett. My men spiked their cannons and poured their gunpowder into the sea," said a marine.

Another American, a naval man, Captain Rathburn took off his hat and mopped his brow. "The *Providence* was brought around. We sent boarding parties to the other ships in the harbor and convinced them to leave. A British privateer, the *Gayton* has moved in front of the harbor ready to attack. We are trapped."

"The townspeople have caught onto us faking our superior numbers. There is a mob outside the fort, still undecided, yet I fear their militia may initiate an attack. We need to depart as soon as possible."

"Grim. Very Grim." Captain Trevett pivoted to Thorne. "What about your crew? In their current state, can they be split to sail two ships?"

Jacob ran his hands through his hair. "My men are tired, some sick, but they will meet the challenge. Anything to get out of this purgatory. All's they need is some nutrition."

At the mention of food, a pulsing beat of urgency sprang from the front gates. "Captain Trevett, wagons and foodstuffs have been delivered."

Jacob smiled. "Looks like the governor agreed to our requests. Let's hope he keeps his word on allowing us to leave without mishap."

For the next two hours, the men ate heartily of a dinner of turtle meat from china plates furnished by Nassau's wealthy harridans, their desire to see the Yankees leave post haste. Men filled the supply wagons with sixteen hundred pounds of gunpowder and several lots of firearms. Unheeded they filled the ships.

Beneath the flagstaff where Trevett had nailed a flag that symbolized a fight to the death, Jacob collapsed his telescope and smiled. "Captain Trevett, the *Gayton* in its haste to attack your ship has run upon the shoals. We need not worry any trouble from her cannons. Where are the two pilots promised us?"

Trevett gritted his teeth. "The damn swine have fled to the hills."

Jacob raised a brow. "Have they? Lady Rutland, could you show us where they live?"

While the ships were finishing loading, Jacob took her with him. In front of the townspeople, she was properly incensed; her manner was not an act. With Simeon and a group of large marines they surprised the errant pilots in their homesteads and at point of muskets convinced them that to see the end of the day was to assist them.

On the docks, Jacob was the last to depart. Other than the squawks of pelicans diving for fish and the marines rowing the pilots over breakers to the awaiting ships, they were alone.

Abby drew herself up and squared her shoulders. “I bid you farewell, Captain Thorne.”

“Farewell?” he laughed. “I never agreed to a farewell.”

Chapter 23

Jacob put down the sextant, watching Lady Rutland's progress across the deck. Not one word had been spoken between them since he kidnapped her off the dock in Nassau hours before. If he fell overboard into the jaws of the sea…she'd feel not one shred of pity.

Thorne considered their escape. A wonder he had the strength to move the munitions and stores out onto the ships, and the strength to divide up the freed men to crew to best advantage the great number of ships they had taken.

Odd, how the need to breathe the air of liberty gave energy to a man who had been chained for so long. The power and vigor renewed when one had the chance of freedom, to escape from being treated like a dog, and to be master and commander of his ship again. The nightmare of that blighted island wiped away by the glory of the open sea.

The hardships of imprisonment had left their mark on him; he ached from the blows and beatings, and the endless days in the merciless sun, toiling beneath the whip. The meagre food and close, suffocating damp atmosphere of the dungeon further weakened him. It had been a month since he bathed or felt anything softer beneath his back than the hard dirt floor, and his hands were rough and bleeding from the beams he lifted and carried all day. The grueling labors had turned him to iron. If only he and his exhausted men could muster their strength long enough for the sail home.

Home. What would he find when he arrived home? Had Boston been retaken? Bingham said it was in the hands of the patriots. Although in times of war, lines became blurred. Perhaps the conflict was over. So much had occurred in America since he had left two years ago. Communications ran unhurried across the ocean. Trevett had been grim. News of victory or defeat? He shook his head. More likely the battle still raged, savaging the land with blood and violence. Rachel? Ethan? What news of them? A yearning scraped his insides to know how they were. Soon.

His gaze slid unwillingly to Abby. Why had he taken her? There was certainty in a trade for Ethan, her father desperate to get his daughter back.

The curve of her breast spilled from a dark green silk gown. His eyes followed the line of her long, elegant neck to a stubborn chin. Memories of long, lush nights, the sweet, salt taste, the feel of her mouth on his, her tender moans and soft breasts—certainly it had meant more? The simple evidence, so very clear at this moment, suddenly burst the fires of hell in his mind and body. Fiercely, he wanted to damn his desire and end the fascination that had so rapidly carried him to such flaming heights of wanting. He fought the wild longing to seize her then and there, fought the furious destinies that had brought him to her.

A demented laugh sprang from his throat.

"You're worse than a rutting stag. No good will come of it, Captain."

Enos. A spark of anger flared inside Jacob. "Since when did you become my conscience?"

"Leave her unharmed," warned Enos. "Make the trade for your cousin. War or no war her father's tentacles reach far. He won't take kindly to having his daughter misused."

"She lied to me."

"Your pride's as big as a mountain. Don't blame the girl."

Middeck, Abby lifted her face into the wind. Gone was Abe' short mane. Her hair tumbled in golden waves around her shoulders. More vexing still, she was running her hands through the gleaming tresses, letting the silken strands spill from her fingers like pure molten gold.

Unaware of her audience, she attempted to knot the hair with a slowness meant to seduce. Jacob gritted his teeth, the performance well done.

Enos stood next to him, his clothes flapping against him in the strong wind. "The fine honorable Captain Thorne above mere mortals cannot talk to a girl?"

"I'm warning you—" Thorne directed his gaze on the white-crested waves. He refused to look at her. The conjured image of Davenport between her naked thighs cracked him with the force of a blacksmith's hammer on an anvil. Why had he not taken her into his arms and comforted her? Now she wouldn't even look at him. "You press your argument too far."

"She's scrambled your brains."

"No, she's laid a scythe to them."

"Have you noticed the newer wet-behind-the-ears members to our crew? Do they not appreciate the sights as well?"

Jacob folded his arms in front of him. Several of the men stood slack-jawed, negligent of their duties. "It matters not a whit to me how many green lads fawn over her."

"You're jealous."

"I have the sudden urge to heave you overboard."

Descending to middeck, Enos arched a mocking brow. "When frogs grow hair."

She swiped the back of her wrist across her eyes. Tears? A knot tightened in Jacob's chest. He swore beneath his breath. "Back to work, men."

Abby curled her hand around a ratline looking out over endless ocean. Long ago, there had been something elating, intoxicating almost, about the smell of water and grease and jute and holystone and lingering salt that went with the aura of the *Vengeance*. Now with her hair blowing about her shoulders and face, tears fell softly on the back of her hands. She wiped them away. She would not give Jacob Thorne the satisfaction of seeing her reduced to tears.

A splash hit the other side of the ship and she jerked her head around. Sailors shouted. "Good bye, Albury."

The pilot. Of course, Jacob had used the pilot's unwilling services to navigate Nassau's harbor. Rude fanfare was bestowed upon the released pilot. He rowed toward the island of Abaco then shaking his fist, swore perdition on bard singing pirates. If only Abby weren't so miserable, to have laughed at the pilot's recriminations born of her rumors. She turned her head east again. How long had she stared where a flotilla ran abreast? No British Man o' War would dare challenge the heavily armed Americans.

Abby breathed a heavy sigh thinking about the wild, tumultuous events in Nassau. An air of unreality choked her. The nightmare blurred. The consequences were enormous and life altering, casting in her in a direction she feared—irrevocably to America.

"Captain Thorne wants to see you in his cabin," said Lawton.

The question remained. What about her made Jacob so angry that he felt compelled to kidnap her? Abby knocked. He bade her to enter and she blinked, stunned by his transformation. Dressed and shaved, he was her dear familiar Jacob, seated at his desk, measuring his charts. She stiffened and awaited the conversation between them that was long overdue.

"You may use my cabin as your private quarters. I will need to use my charts and maps at times."

"I see." Her breath halted. The hunger and naked longing swimming in the depths of his brilliant blue eyes was a window into his soul. The lines in his face hardened and, without warning, he reached out to touch her cheek. Abby recoiled but his hand did not retract. Instead it lingered to lightly trace the line of her jaw.

"I'm not going to cry. I'm not going to lose my temper or beg. I demand you take me back to Nassau. That was the agreement."

"That was Trevett's arrangement, not mine."

"You know who I am. My father will pay you handsomely. Return me to Nassau."

He stood, towered over her with enough unleashed anger to blow a storm. "You delude yourself, Lady Rutland. Do you have any idea how vulnerable your position is?" He spoke in an even monotone, his mood unreadable. "Like the wing of a butterfly, fragile and trembling on the point of extermination at a touch." The door slammed and reverberated on its hinges. How little she knew him hit her square between the eyes.

He was a man of deep secrets. None of her affair.

Enos brought in a tub and filled it with water.

"You needn't do this. You are undermanned as it is."

"As I am grateful to you Abby, I mean Lady Rutland for all you have done. We were all stupid in not seeing your selfless act to help us," he offered apologetically.

When he left, Abby sank into the tub. Her body was numb; even her mind seemed static. The imprint of Jacob's fingers-tips burned raw on her cheek. An instinct stirred in some far-away recess of her brain, ominous and gathering strength. She knew that with that touch, Jacob was affected as much as she. That deep down he still loved her. But something stopped him. It wasn't her. It had nothing to do with the war. Something insidious brewed deep inside him, some hurt that he projected on the rest of the world and now focused on her.

She picked up the sponge and squeezed the water onto her neck. Oh yes, Jacob Thorne was in layers, had built an impenetrable fortress. Given a chance, she would pull off those layers stone by stone.

He was changed. Ever since he had learned she was Lady Rutland. But why? Because she was an aristocrat? It didn't matter. She could help him. Just as he had spared her from death aboard the *Civis,* saved her from drowning in the angry seas, she knew she must draw him into her light and free the man behind the glacial cobalt eyes.

She dropped the sponge in a splash. Loud alarm bells rang around her, warning her of the danger, like a deadly undercurrent in the ocean, it threatened to drag her down into depths she would not know how to navigate. Despite the frightening awareness, the awful warnings and however loud the alarm bells rang around her, she would not adhere to them.

She wrapped her arms around her knees and sighed.

It was already too late for that. Despite all that had happened to make her hate him, she was still in love with Jacob Thorne.

For three days, he ignored her. Every evening he bathed, calculated his charts then without a word, left to sleep elsewhere. For all intents and purposes, he seemed unaware of her presence, his sullen taciturn silence and refusal to engage yielded a painful keening in her chest. How she missed his arms around her. But in the dark entrails of despair there still glimmered flashes of hope in the remembrance of what had been left unsaid between them, of distant echoes of emotion, of silent flashes in those tormented eyes, and that thin, tenuous filament between them that could not be denied.

A heavy squall brewed outside, keeping her inside. Bored she set about straightening the cabin. She rerolled the charts and tied them securely. Drawings of ships, Jacob's designs drew her attention, his detail, mastery and creativity she could not help but admire. She put a finger to her lip, something vague and familiar about the drawings haunted her. She gave it up, stood on a chair and restacked them neatly in overhead cupboards. The last cupboard refused to close. Abby peered inside and frowned. A velvet bag lay in the corner. Of course, the contents of the bag were important to Thorne. That he kept it hidden. Abby looked toward the door. Wouldn't she hear his booted footsteps before he entered the cabin?

She withdrew the bag and extracted two items each wrapped securely with tissue paper that had yellowed with age. By the number of wrinkles in the tissue paper, the items had been opened and reopened again and again. Beneath the folds of the first item lay a painted miniature of a beautiful woman with remarkable cobalt eyes, Jacob's eyes. His mother? Whoever the woman was, she was important to him. A burning sensation rose in her chest. The chestnut-haired woman stared back at her. With reverence Abby placed the miniature on the desk and opened the second item.

Her eyes widened. A heavy gold ring. Not just any ring. Embedded with a glittering ruby, her fingers trailed over the fine engravings. Shadows fell into the deep grooves. Her father had a similar ring. *A duke's ring?* She held the ring near the lantern, running her finger over the grooves where light fell into the deep veins and noted the familiarity of the crest—a crowned lion's head. Where had she seen the emblem before?

She sat down, scanned the inside of the ring and surveyed an inscription. *Duke of Banfield.* How did Thorne come into possession of the duke's ring? A hundred questions mushroomed and remained unanswered. Why was Thorne with Humphrey at her party? Why was Thorne so closed-mouthed about his relatives in England? Was he related to the duke? Was not the physical similarity remarkable? Or had he simply stolen the ring from Humphrey's father?

Boiling with suspicions, her mind bubbled like a cauldron about to overflow. Loose ends dangled, puzzles cried out to be solved, inconsistencies abounded.

She gazed with focus out the transom windows. The rain had stopped but the wind and cloud cover remained. Yet far over the horizon, an aperture opened, and rays of sunlight poured down from the sky. The ring was a breach into Thorne's background. *The key.*

Wind roared in her ears.

It wasn't about her imagined betrayal. No. Not about her at all. The real reason Jacob projected his anger toward her was that he was a bastard, the bastard born son of the Duke of Banfield and Humphrey's older half-brother. This was the demon that possessed him. Envisioning the events of Thorne's history, she put herself in his shoes. Thought about what it would be like to have that stigma. She placed the ring on the table. When he came to do his charts, he would see.

She would confront him.

Thorne was her mission now.

Jacob had a smile on his face. Nothing could put him in a bad mood. The squall had not pushed them off course. In fact, it had blown them toward home and with that the happy prospect of cutting their journey, short of two days. Already Captain Trevett had split off with most of the squadron, sailing toward Rhode Island, leaving the *Solebay* as their sailing companion. Jacob descended the companionway and whistled a familiar tune thinking of Abby. She had never complained or cried or threw tantrums like a wealthy spoiled daughter of an aristocrat would do. No. She held her head up with grace and dignity, and even helped in the galley since they were sailing with half a crew and needed every man on deck in shifts.

His whistling tune trailed off in a rapid decrescendo. That was not the real reason for the twinge of guilt that caused his chest to tighten, and that fact bothered him. She'd be leaving him soon. She'd be gone as soon as they made port. He'd secure her a place at Widow Smith's until the trade was secured.

This was exactly what he had planned. He should be grateful. The whole ordeal would soon be over. He'd have Ethan back. He'd have his life back. Just the way he wanted it.

Except he wasn't sure he wanted it anymore.

He opened the door, expectant of Abby's presence. In a thin linen shift with a wool shawl draped across her shoulders, she sat on the settle, her feet tucked under her, sewing. A subtle tantalizing hint of lavender mixed with *her* scent assailed him, yet her unnatural silence troubled him. He threw his tricorn on a hook, turned and froze. *The ring.* "You dare to search through my things?"

"I dare."

She shoved her sewing aside and had the audacity to stand up to him, defiance thundering in every bone of her body. He thrust the ring and the miniature into the bag. "I've killed men for less."

"I know who you are, Jacob. I understand your anger."

"Shut-up, Abigail. Not one more word." He advanced on her, staring down at her beautiful frightened face. He wanted to put his hands around her slender white throat and strangle her. "You have no business."

"You told me once, camouflage is a game we undertake, but our secrets are surely revealed by what we want to seem to be as what we want to conceal. You are the Duke of Banfield's eldest son. From the first time I laid eyes on you I saw the resemblance. The woman in the miniature is your mother. Tell me it is not true."

His hands convulsed into fists. "Not one more word, I'm warning you."

"There is a canker in your soul, Jacob."

"I'm a bastard, born out of sin."

"Bastards are born out of women, just like everybody else. Men make the stamp of illegitimacy, not God."

Something shattered inside of Thorne, splintering his emotions from all rational control. A blind rage like fire swept over him. "A bastard whose father never wanted him, whose mother left England in shame, cast off by the same aristocrat who used her. As a young child, I watched helplessly, seeing her stare off to some other time and place, so sad and distant. A void I could not understand nor fill."

Abby saw how terribly he suffered, a deadly quiver, nothing more. She needed to goad him, to let him cleanse the infection, the canker that imprisoned his soul, bracing herself and listening.

"She died of a fever when I was nine. And it was I who closed her eyes then stood watching as her casket was lowered into a cold grave." His handsome jaw was taut, his mouth, drawn into a ruthless, forbidding line.

"Do you know how that feels?" His eyes clouded, grappling with a myriad of emotions—anger, hate, bitterness, heaving resentments, bewilderment—all emotional famines.

Pin-points of heat seared her inner eyelids. "I cannot imagine."

"Your concern is touching," he said with biting sarcasm. "Born on the right side of the blanket, coddled and cosseted, you'd have no idea." He turned away, as if he couldn't stomach the sight of her.

"After my mother's death, I searched through her things, anything to be close to her. I found a box. Simple in its outward ornamentation, but the complexities inside held the underpinnings that formed the rest of my life. The ring. Written in her Bible was *his* name. The mother who I cherished and honored had kept him a secret all those years? How many times had I asked her who he was and she said nothing. Why?

"I had always wanted to know who my father was. Other boys had fathers. I wished and dreamed of mine even fancied him to be someone famous. That day I learned my father was the Duke of Banfield. I also learned what it was to be a bastard."

He stared into the dark vacancy of the night. "As a boy, when I was alone, when I was lost and confused and searching for my identity—I wondered to myself what it might be like to hear a man such as Lord Banfield call me 'son'. That my mother cherished and treasured him...so I excelled at my studies, promising myself, I'd be a better man than the father who abandoned me. The war came and all its miseries. I took to the seas, picked up privateering. I cruised the coasts of England and decided to visit my father. You can imagine his shock, seeing his illegitimate offspring.

"The only thing I asked him was to use his power to free my cousin. The only thing I had asked him for my whole life he refused. Do you know what he said to me? He offered me lands and a title. I never took him seriously. No doubt, he must be senile. Can you imagine, a son that he abandoned? I threw it back in his face. Humphrey entered then and we silenced our altercation."

Jacob laughed. "First time I even knew I had a half-brother. My father suggested I get to know Humphrey and look around before I made any decision. On a lark, I showed up at your home curious to see Humphrey's intended, to see what wealth and privilege bought. My early departure was precipitated by Captain Davenport's presence."

"Does Humphrey know you are his brother?"

He shrugged. "Best to keep him in happy ignorance."

At the mention of Humphrey, memories swirled like a dense fog, mocking and dancing. She must tell Thorne. "Growing up on neighboring estates and the same age, Humphrey and I became great friends. As youngsters, we played hide and seek. My favorite place was the cupboard in the Duke of Banfield's library. One day, the duke entered. No way could I reveal my untoward presence. The door was slightly opened and of curious nature, I studied him in repose. Out of a locked drawer, he withdrew several sketches. I did not know at the time but now realize they were architectural drawings of ships, ones that you drew. Other sketches were younger versions of you. He also had the same painted miniature of your mother. He must have had an investigator following you and giving him regular reports."

Abby trembled. If only to meet his anger with love, to break open his heart. She pulled her wrap tighter and braced herself. "I know your father loves you."

He swept his arm across his desk. Charts scattered to the floor. "I don't want to hear it."

Abby stepped toward him. "Once I had heard gossip that the Duke of Banfield almost gave up his title over a serving girl. I believe that girl was your mother. Not wanting him to lose his heritage, I believe she did what she felt was noble, moved to Boston with no trace of her footsteps. People make choices."

"Shut-up, Abby."

"No. You will listen to me, Jacob. My guess is the Duke of Banfield searched everywhere for her but to no avail, and eventually married." Jacob glared at her as if she were some strange animal, a curiosity, deformed and loathsome to his sight.

Could she reach him? Could she release the demons he locked inside? Abby searched his face, terrified of the growing aggression in him, a volcano ready to erupt. "Knowing the Duke of Banfield the way I do, and in that unguarded moment, the way he caressed the picture of your mother, the way he touched your ship sketches with such tenderness, the way he had that distant dreamy look that carried a love so great that he was lost, I know he loved her and loved her deeply."

"Say his name one more time..." Thorne lashed out, "...and I'll kill you, so help me God!"

"Your Oxford tutor? A shipyard? How could your uncle afford the expense? I'm guessing the duke found your mother. But she made him promise not to reveal the truth to you. That she didn't want your world rocked."

In two steps, Thorne's hand shot out, her wrap fell to the floor. He twisted the thin fabric of her shift at the neckline, drawing it taut. Her chest rising and falling in rapid, harsh breaths, she stared down at the strong, roughened hand at her breasts, the same hand that had once caressed her with gentle passion. Abruptly the hand tightened and with one quick jerk he plucked the thin garment over her head, flinging it away from her body. He picked her up and threw her on the bed.

In a blur of unreality, she saw Jacob strip off his shirt, and she stared blindly at the rippling muscles of his powerful shoulders and arm. When his hands went to the waistband of his pants, she took a burning ember and blew it into a raging fire. "You put up walls of hate, afraid to let your heart feel, to believe what I'm telling you is true. Your mother didn't want to entrap him with a child and by going away she made the ultimate sacrifice. Did you ever think it might have been your mother who was responsible? The one who kept secrets? Yet her sacrifice became the duke's agony, and her agony, and *your* agony."

The bed shifted beneath his weight as he stretched out on top of her naked body, his heavy weight covering her. Pain slashed across his features.

Panic tickled through her veins in icy little dribbles. The storm she had cultivated was now a reality—a grim, living reality. In a shivering trance of fear, Abby refused to give up. "Jacob, you need to see through all of this." She stared at his cynical, ruthless face while her tortured mind superimposed other, gentle memories of him. She saw him pointing out letters in the alphabet, his face full of compassion. She saw him sharing the glory of the crow's nest, she saw him bending over her the day he rescued her from the sea, his face white with alarm. She saw him gazing tenderly into her eyes when he made love to her. She remembered him just a month ago, the way he stood on deck and proudly announced their wedding date.

She was right. Jacob did love her. She did not delude herself that she had a choice to tell him of his history, however painful it was. She loved him. Love, hate—both were competent puppet masters, pulling the strings to command the movements of their lives. No. Beneath his feelings of abandonment and his bastardy, Jacob maintained his scorn. That he was punishing her for being an aristocrat was certain. He shifted between her legs, and Abby's fear gave way to a deep, shattering sorrow. Her eyes ached with unshed tears for the boy who had lost so much. She looked in his eyes and hesitantly laid her trembling fingers against his rigid jaw. "I—I'm sorry," she whispered, her throat clogging. "I'm so sorry."

"I don't want your apologies and I don't need your pity."

His mouth came down on hers with savage brutality. He wedged his knee between her legs, grasped her hips, lifting them. Her eyes flew open. His harsh, bitter expression reeled above her just as he drew back and then rammed himself full length into her tight passage. A dry sob burned her throat as she offered her body as a vessel for his anguish. She wrapped her arms around his shoulders, taking it all in, anything to release him from the torment and anger of a lifetime.

With a violence bred of rage, he stamped out his rejection and hurt and pain into Abby. Rock hard and fully aroused, he drove into her, again and again, desire pulsing through his swollen rigid flesh, his gut ablaze with a need for her so ferocious he could not stop the impulse if he wanted to. His head dipped toward her honeyed breast and he suckled until she cried out, her breath hot upon his neck. He stroked, caressed, fanned the flames he'd created, anything to punish her for the past she threw in his face. He wanted to bury himself inside her as deeply as he could and not come out until he got his fill. His fingers stroked her in time with his thrusts, his hand swept down her body, slicked across the small, sensitive piece of flesh at the core of her, rewarded when she raised her hips to him and whimpered. He'd make her pay.

Except when her fingers raked through his hair, her tender touch inflamed him. The sweet offering of her body, the submission to his rage, her head thrown back, the adoration in her eyes, completely exposed in her trust of him. He plumbed the hot fire in her loins, a heat he never imagined, her body arched to meet his deep plunging thrusts.

"I love you, Jacob," she gave way in a half-whisper, a half-cry, and it unraveled the last thread holding him together. Instantly Jacob covered her mouth with his, taking all that she was giving and reacted to the spasmodic tightening of her muscles, pouring his seed into her womb.

Afraid that his weight would crush her, Jacob gathered her to him and rolled onto his side, taking her with him. Lying there, with Abby cradled in his arms, his body still intimately joined to hers, he experienced a peace, unlike any he'd known in years. The blackness in his soul faded. He could feel it like the sun burning away the shadows, bringing light and warmth to a place that had known only darkness and ice for years. To see himself in his own reflection. He brushed back a wayward silky tress and cupped her chin in his hand until her blue eyes met his.

"Thank you, Abby."

She curled her finger through his hair and kissed him gently before laying her cheek upon his chest. There he held her close, reveling in the feel of her as he cradled her with his body, her heart beating next to his.

"I am so sorry for not trusting you, Abby, for every failure and every wrong and for the heartache and sorrow."

"There is nothing to forgive. You needed to figure things out. I pointed the way."

"You really believe my father—"

"Without a doubt. My instincts tell me you must have surprised your father when you showed up on his doorstep. He was probably nervous, excited and joyful. He offered you lands and a title. If he didn't care about you, he would have had you thrown out."

"I never gave him a chance—"

"No you didn't. He even insisted on you staying. He wanted you, loved you. I'm sure he knew of your privateering activities and was secretly proud. Jacob, you have so much love, find somewhere in your heart to love your father."

"I have a lot of making up to do," Jacob sighed. "Now tell me from the start how a duke's daughter was on the merchantman, *Civis*?" He listened asking questions, going back to where they had left off that night in the garden. He listened to her talk about her home, her brothers, her mother's death and more. The floodgates opened.

"You see, Humphrey had agreed to the ruse of our engagement to put off my father's insistence I marry. My last argument with my father…"

"Guilt. That's the real reason why you are driven to get back home, Abby. Not so much for revenge as it is to seek forgiveness from your father."

"How clear you make that revelation."

They talked about her capture aboard the *Civis* up until Jacob rescued her, life in Nassau, Joubert, the French planter and her subsequent saving of Pascale, her attempt to get Jacob and the crew released. They talked about Percy Devol.

Jacob frowned. "You realize that Percy did not act alone. More are involved. They may hide for the time being, lick their wounds because your family survived but they will strike again. Of this, I am certain."

On into the hours of darkness they talked of a myriad of topics. She drew circles on his chest and he was already hard for wanting her again. With a growl, he rolled her on her back and made delicious sweet love to her. Time passed slowly, for he made love to her again and again, and then held her while she slept. Jacob exhaled and glanced at the sky framed through the transom windows. Night still loitered in the west, holding fast to a dark amethyst ribbon studded with stars, but eastward the upper crown of the sun stole over the horizon. He was overwhelmed by what had happened and never had he felt so content. That this beautiful woman had risked much, to taunt him, to suffer his wrath and to relieve him of his torments was more than he deserved. Without fear, she reached into his soul and ripped out years of latent festering wounds, the liberation like a meteor exploding through the sky. That she did so proved without a doubt that she was far braver and wiser than any woman he had ever known.

That she loved him slammed into his chest.

That he had to give her up destroyed him.

Jacob let out a long breath he didn't know he had been holding.

He asked himself—did it hurt more to love someone, or to force himself not to love her?

But love her he did.

The ramifications of letting her go? He knew the answers. A family, a home of his dreams, a place he belonged. Her. Those many answers burned his tongue. It was a profoundly alluring fantasy, though—fulfilling the primal desire to find his perfect mate, finding the one woman who filled his needs, who belonged with him and to him, who completed him.

She was well-bred, natural for position and privilege. Regardless of the title and lands his father could give him, he was an American and his life was set on a different path. No bargaining with his maker could change that fact. The idea was ludicrous. With the entire British Navy looking for him? An enemy of the crown? The king would have him swinging from the gallows in a heartbeat. He could not offer her the life she deserved, her rightful place in society. Holding onto him was not an option. He had to let her go, had to protect her foolish heart. Was there anything in the world more painful than hurting Abby?

Of course, marrying Humphrey was the right course. No doubt his half-brother was a decent man. No doubt he would cherish and honor her. Love her? The muscle's in Thorne' neck corded. No. The thought of any man touching her…even Humphrey, made him want to bloody his half-brother to a pulp.

Without a doubt, he was an American, born and bred and his loyalty lay there. Blood and sweat were forging new ideas, concepts less tangible but nonetheless, promised glimmerings of freedom far from the chokehold of aristocracy. No. Jacob was not of the world of entitlement.

His half-brother, Humphrey was reared for his role as the Duke of Banfield.

He would give Humphrey the most precious love of his life.

He eased himself from the bed and stood barefoot gazing out the transom windows. He watched the pale surf appear in an endless roll and crash. When he returned to the bedside, Jacob's breath caught, air hooking painfully into his chest. He lingered a few moments longer. The room lightened with a golden dawn. He told himself he should leave, ordered it, but still waited, caught up in horrific fascination. The delicate beauty was blatant, taunting. A test—to see if he was strong enough to resist an angel's face? She shifted and he observed the way she rested across the bed in comfortable abandonment, one of the quilts had fallen in a heap on the floor. He picked it up and covered her then soothed back her hair as she slept and knew if he were God he would have made the world just so and no different.

She awoke, sensing his hesitation. "What's wrong?"

Unbearable pain hammered into him, shattering through his ribcage like a mortal blow. "You will go home and marry Humphrey."

Abby burst into mad laughter. "Humphrey? Humphrey is like my brother, my best friend. I could never—"

His hand reached up to stroke her cheek. "You will wed Humphrey. You will become the Duchess of Banfield…have children—"

"No I will not."

His hand suddenly fell away. "We are not fated to be together. You are meant to live the life you are meant to live."

So the mask was back. Abby gripped her hands together to keep them from shaking as the hope for a life together which had so suddenly risen, hung in the air. *What was wrong?* His implacable expression did not falter. Was she losing him? *You want me. Admit it.* Alarm bells clanged. "In my family's gardens, I told you I wanted adventure."

"And I told you adventure is just a romantic name for trouble. It sounds exciting when you think about it, but to set your life on the cast of dice is hazardous."

He remembered what he had told her and her heart soared. "I told you that the purpose of life was to live it, to taste, to experience, to reach out without fear for newer and richer experiences. It's not adventure I want," she said with complete honesty. "Only love would ever induce me to marry. Jacob, I know you feel the same way."

He shook his head. "That's where you are wrong. I don't love you, Abby."

Blood drained from her face. The door closed. She could not save him. He would destroy himself no matter how much she tried.

He held the scarred bitterness in his soul like a drowning sailor grasping at flotsam in a turbulent sea. With a small cry, she buried her face in her hands, recognizing once again where she was—once again at a crossroads. It was dark and she could not see her way. A dense fog ascended, shrouding her, blinding her. She could not fight it. Where was the resourceful Abby? Where was that infallible sense of logic, that strength on which she prided herself? She searched frantically, despairingly; she could not locate either of them.

She hadn't moved from her spot at the edge of the stern. Her gaze turned out to sea, her thoughts a stark statement of everything wrong between them. Love was not an emotion which Jacob could find again. His heart was closed. No matter what she did, there was no unlocking it.

Thorne had not spoken to her again. Enos remained his messenger. She tossed back her head with her face into the sea breeze, the wind shearing cold from the north. That poisoned darkness inside him rang with undeniable truth. She had opened her heart to experience a love and joy she never dreamed possible and to know it had been shoved away like so much refuse.

She had cast the die and lost.

For three mornings, she had awakened and purged her insides into a bucket. Now she knew. In her womb, she carried Jacob Thorne's child and with it, the horrors of what that meant for her future.

The crew roared with excitement as they neared home, passing an American Naval flotilla. Along the shore of the Charles River, the Americans had made their defenses. Men rowed out to guide the *Vengeance* and *Solebay*. Local militias had set up channel obstructions near the city, making navigation hazardous for British vessels. Unwary ships might become impaled or receive a heavy dose of American hospitality from the entrenched shore batteries.

Captain Jacob Thorne was a returning hero. His harassment of British Naval vessels around England had reached the ears of Boston. There would be celebration tonight.

The wind streamed through his hair and caught at his shirt, plastering the fabric to his chest and causing the sleeves to billow around his shoulders. She could imagine the joy on his face of finally being home. He glanced to her as if he knew she was looking at him. Regret? She swiped slim fingers against the sides of her skirts. For a moment, she felt quite breathless as if he was drawing the soul from her body. A cannon blast saluted them from shore and his attention was diverted. She forced herself to look away.

His denial scourged her like a knotted whip. Tears stung her eyes, but she refused to shed them, refused to let Jacob have the satisfaction of his denial of her.

As the *Vengeance* neared Boston, they passed a massive shipyard. Steeples of the city's churches rose above a tight cluster of wood frame houses wrapped in a blanket of snow. Cheers and shouts ascended from the docks, and ashore there were crowds amassed to celebrate the return of their loved ones and heroes.

From now on, she would control her own destiny. No one noticed her disappearing into the cabin below. No one noticed the slim lad in the oversize coat emerge onto the deck. And no one noted the boy moving across the gangplank and disappearing into the busy Boston streets.

Chapter 24

Abby had spent hours wandering the streets of Boston, asking residents if they knew of Thomas Hansford's residence. A merchant knew her uncle and travelling to that end of town offered the lad a ride. In her Uncle Thomas Hanford's parlor, she recanted the truth of her journey and how she showed up on his doorstep far from home. He listened with gravity. Against her ribs, Abby's heart thudded and the sweat on her clasped palms felt cold.

"I am pregnant."

He did not judge her. She thanked providence, finding relief in confessing her difficulty. When he hugged her like her papa and told her not to worry, everything went from a blur to a full-blown weeping.

"I am a powerful and wealthy merchant in Boston. You tell me the man's name, and—"

"No." She swallowed hard with the shame she must further admit to her mother's sweet brother. "It is as much as my fault as it is his. Besides, he does not love me and I refused to be tethered to a man who does not. You must promise on your honor not to pursue this any further."

"Does not love you? Impossible? Have you thought of the child?" He let go of her, frowned beneath a perfectly coifed white periwig, his shrewd brain churning away like flood waters over river rock. No doubt the questions being tossed about in the whirlpools would be reexamined in the future. He dropped the subject.

"You can't go back to England. There is the issue of your confinement. It will be too dangerous for you to travel further on the seas in your condition. I forbade it."

Her child would be the bastard of a bastard. "I cannot allow my child to be subjected to the brutal rages of social vultures ready to pick at any flesh that will provide an entertainment for gossip. No doubt they will pick clean whatever remains on my bones. I must marry and soon."

He shifted to the fireplace and studied the flames as if conjuring some magical solution to an irresolvable crisis. "I will need help to pull you out of this predicament. I have a widow friend who is very discreet." He glanced at her questioningly.

Abby nodded. "I put my complete trust in you."

He waved her off. "I'm a lonely old man and excited at the prospect of having a grandniece or nephew to spoil. That said; the easiest solution to the situation is to launch you into Boston society, in style and let you pick, hurriedly, of course, an acceptable suitor. You may marry and go back to England after the baby is born and time is appropriate. Or...you may be so entranced with Boston, you may wish to remain. This old and lonely bachelor's heart would be filled with joy if you chose to do so."

"It would have to be someone I respect."

"I expect nothing less. I have received missives from your father via a mutual friend, in New York regarding what happened to your family. It is the only way to get family messages through in these times. The spineless acts against your family are mindboggling. I will pen him a letter immediately to let him know you are safe with me in Boston and that you are here for an extended stay."

Abby nodded. "Did my father's letters contain any idea who was responsible? There is more than one man. The whole crime was well planned and could not be acted on alone. Captain Davenport told me his name was Percy Devol and he had a vendetta against my grandfather. He also told me that my father had said that Percy had fled England. Simeon, the man traveling with me said he heard a cultured gentleman in the room next to mine before I was taken aboard the *Civis*. He was making the directives. I cannot imagine who would hate our family enough to destroy us. I will also pen a letter to my father if you would be so kind to include it in your dispatch. These men are dangerous and must be stopped. If only I could travel to England to help and…have you any word of Joshua?"

He shook his head sadly. "I'm sorry. The frontier is as uncertain as it is dangerous during these times. I fear for his survival despite his expert skills in those conditions. You are aware he works for General Washington?"

Abby widened her eyes. Her brother a patriot?

"As ardent as I am. We have something special going on here in the Colonies. Our bid for freedom has blown into a full raging fire, a contagion that you may even come to appreciate." He coughed and eyed her attire. "Tomorrow after you've rested we will see about your wardrobe. There will be no catching any suitable husband in that garb. You need rest." He rang the bell. A maid entered and her eyebrows rose with the boy-woman sitting across from her employer.

"Bridget. This is my niece, Abigail. Show her to the pink suite, a bath, something to eat, make her as comfortable as possible. She is to have the best of care."

Abby melted. How she loved this man for taking control of her life.

Very late on the fifth night after the *Vengeance's* arrival, as he stood staring out the window of his dining room overlooking a fog-shrouded harbor, Jacob thought he had died a hundred deaths. Where in the hell was she? Discreetly, he had commandeered his search. With patriotism running high, any person related to the King would be at risk. If she fell into the wrong hands...Jacob shook his head. He didn't even want to contemplate what could happen to her. He checked the White Horse, Cole's, the Green Dragon, every inn, tavern and coffee house. All fourteen churches had been searched. The docks had been scoured and witnesses questioned.

Nothing.

When he had first discovered her disappearance, he was in a mood for murder, figuring she had holed up somewhere and would reveal her location after being frightened in a foreign city. When she had not been found after the first night, he lost his anger and his thoughts gave way to guilt. He had broken her spirit and defeated her and she had reacted to that hurt.

Thorne paced. So much damned spirit. No one had seen a woman. He let out a maniacal bark of laughter. But had anyone seen a boy? He stumbled into a chair and kicked it—of course, the ever-resourceful Abby.

When she had not returned by the third night he was in a frenzied state of alarm. Did some drunk get her? Was she lying hurt and cold off some roadway? She had to come back. After all, who would shelter her, an enemy of the colonies? Except she wasn't an enemy. Yet her distinctive cultured voice could get her in trouble. It would lead to questions.

"If you don't get any sleep cousin, you'll be good to no one and least of all, finding her," Ethan said from the doorway. He moved into the room, put a log on the grate, and pushed the coals around until a fire brewed. "Thought I'd never see this room again. The simple things you take for granted." He righted the chair Thorne had kicked over and sat, hooking his leg over the arm while Thorne paced.

Thorne cursed. "So you know."

Ethan leaned back on his chair. "With Enos, Ben and you running around Boston at all hours? Did you really think you could keep her a secret?"

"I was going to trade her for you. Once I arrived in Boston, I had decided to send her back without the trade and substitute someone else."

"A trade? Had to be someone important. Who is she?" Ethan gave him a lopsided grin.

Ethan's cheerful demeanor wore on Jacob's ragged nerves. "Lady Abigail Rutland. The Duke of Rutland's daughter, neighbor to my father and Humphrey's fiancée."

Ethan let out a shrill whistle. "No wonder you're in a lather. I learned she had been kidnapped while hiding at your father's estate after he arranged my escape. Dastardly thing what happened to her family. How did she end up with you?"

"It's difficult and boring."

"No doubt. But I'm in the mood to be difficult and nothing about you is boring."

"Rachel must not hear of a word of it."

Ethan clapped his hands together in prayerful repose and pointed to the heavens. "May I suffer eternal fires, not a word from my lips."

Thorne directed a look of such rigid warning that Ethan's smile froze. Keeping out certain particulars, Jacob plunged into his story. When he was done, Ethan dropped his chair to all fours.

"You have it bad. You're in love, admit it." He whooped.

"I'm not of that world."

"No, you are not," Ethan nodded slowly. "Ever think she might be part of your world?"

Thorne glared at his cousin.

"This is my night to be annoying and you have put me off long enough. When your father helped me escape from Old Mill Prison in Southern England, and believe me it was a bold plan, he secreted me to his estate north of London. There I witnessed a starved man who could not stop talking about his son. Can you imagine my surprise to learn of your heritage, that your father is a duke?"

Thorne grunted.

"I learned things about you that I didn't even know. Did you really steal Mrs. Crowder's chickens? Did you really nail the parson's boots to the floor? And then the fact that you took the silversmith's white dog and dyed it red. I got the whipping for that."

"The duke knew all that?"

"And more. He had you trailed from the time he discovered you on your ninth summer, reports given all the time, drawings made of everything you did. His way of protecting and learning about you. Apparently, he was all set to marry your mother but she left England, left him heartbroken. He knew why she left, that she didn't want him to lose his title, went crazy looking for her and didn't find her for many years until she was dying. She made him promise never to reveal himself to you, thought it would upset your life too much. He honored her wishes, killing him to know he had a son and could not be close to you. Since he couldn't be your father physically, he insisted on being there other ways."

Like Abby had guessed. It had been his mother who had kept confidences.

"I never saw a man prouder of a son. The buttons were popping off his chest. He showed me drawings of you, climbing trees, reports from your tutor, and your ship designs. It hurt my ears to hear so much praise."

"I'm sure it did," Thorne said grudgingly. His father had kept accounts of him?

"He told me how he worried when he heard you had been arrested two years ago in Boston. Was going to come to here and use his influence to stop the hanging. He regaled me with your escape from Boston Harbor and never ceased on how proud he was of your privateering. Can you imagine a peer of the crown proud of an enemy of his country? He went on and on about your seafaring exploits, telling every detail with excitement and with tears in his eyes.

"Never was there a prouder father. Then he plied me. I had to answer all kinds of questions. He locked me up in the library with him night and day, bellowing whenever a servant entered. He gave me the finest food, clothes, every comfort as long as I kept talking about *you*. Even delayed my departure by another week, claiming I needed to recuperate more and some nonsense about the Channel too stormy to cross. When it was time for me to set out, he was reluctant to let me go, hugged me for the longest time as if it were *you* he was hugging. He gave me money, took me to the smugglers himself, arranging my safe passage to France where I picked up a ship home. Without his help, I would have died in that prison."

With a virulence that nearly strangled his breathing, Jacob wished he could turn back the clock. He had been unfair, too prideful and had prejudiced his father wrongly.

Abby's needling shot through him. *The tutor? The shipyard? His mother's secret.*

His hands fell to his side. He had missed an opportunity to get to know his father.

People make choices…

Jacob stood stock still filled with self-loathing. The years of hatred and contempt he held for his father vanished bombarding him with regret and shame. His father had *wanted* him. Had been a part of his life. Had honored his mother's wishes and under those cursed boundaries realized his role as a father the best way he could.

Your father loves you.

Swearing savagely, he surged to his feet. His sweet wise wonderful Abby had made it all plain to him. “I have to find her.”

“Without a doubt.”

“Remember not a word to Rachel. I don’t want her to know what a rogue I’ve been.”

After Thorne closed the door, Ethan sat, contemplating the flames. “You can come out, now, Rachel. I’m sure you heard everything.”

“How did you know?”

“I know you, sister. Our cousin needs our help.”

“Yes, he does,” said Rachel pulling a chair up in front of the fire. “Jacob’s flaws are his pride and arrogance. He has always felt less no matter how much mother and father adored him. Most importantly, he needs to forgive himself.”

“You have a depth, sister, that understands people.” Ethan sighed and stood up. “I hate going out in the cold.”

Abby stretched beneath the layers of woolen quilts piled high to keep her warm. Her hand moved automatically to her abdomen, nothing evident to mark a baby’s development other than the ruthless urges to empty her stomach. The night wore on refusing to give to daylight and with it the leadened clouds heaved another snowstorm. A beeswax candle burned low on her nightstand, and around it, bent on apparent self-destruction, fluttered a large fawn-colored moth, a survivor from the earlier summer. With fool-hardiness it swooped about the flame, its wings shredding with fire then dropped in a smoldering ruin and died.

Jacob.

The night wore on. The clock in the hall ticked away sullen moments. Only the footsteps of the staff removing sleepily from their quarters on the third floor, down the back stairway to the kitchens below demonstrated any kinds of life. The wind whooshed up a blanket of snow against the windowpanes. The candle starved of wax, sputtered and fizzled out. Abby didn't perceive the swollen darkness. Rambling fragments coasted across her mind, hauling impressions and imaginings, reveries and dissolutions—as if she was observing the fleeting marches of another life. Strange to her, they leapt off her numb mind like snow off polished ice. Only the persistent beats of her heart, constant and never-ending, told her that she was still alive. All else lingered as an illusion of shadow and silences and the smell of impending uncertainty.

Jacob...

Benevolent mists of sleep offered sporadic oblivion. But when sleep frittered away, graver unrealities, greater confusion left her hovering between dream-worlds that gave her no clue as to where she was, who she was, why she was at all.

The night gave way and then as if ordered by some divine command the light poured through the parted curtains. The greetings of merchants and workers hurrying through the streets rang from below. Abby rose, reached for the chamber pot and heaved. In bitingly cold water, she rinsed her mouth and washed her face, then collapsed on the bed.

Another dawn, another day.

"My niece is not doing well. I worry about her," said Thomas Hansford taking a sip of his coffee over breakfast.

He held Agnes Quick, a widow, in high regard and had recruited her to take Abby under her wing. The handsome woman, her hair elaborately done and not tucked under a cap like most of the ladies of Boston, breakfasted across from him, boyishly beautiful in her silk. She had married young with her husband dying twenty years into their marriage. From their shared enthusiasm of the rebellion, a friendship had sparked. Both were not ready to marry, and although Thomas had suggested the franchise at one interval, Widow Quick made it known she wanted to remain untied. Thomas respected her wishes and did not push the subject any more, feeling she would warm to the arrangement in due time.

Agnes was haloed by the glorious sunlight that filtered into his dining room. "The storm has stopped. After her fittings today, I suggest a ride about the city to show her Boston so she can get an idea of her new home. We are not all wigwams and savages. I can introduce her to a neighbor of mine, about her age who is a wonderful girl and can offer Abby companionship. Sometimes shared confidences with someone her own age can lift the spirits."

"Brilliant suggestion. The fresh air will do her good. The girl has closeted herself in her room for the entire two weeks since she arrived." Thomas helped himself to another sweet roll, slathering on a generous dollop of strawberry jam.

Agnes dipped her spoon in sugar and stirred it into her tea. "Has she told you who the young man was?"

"That's a dead issue. Spirited like her mother, she may never tell me." He looked over his buffet table filled with breads, poached eggs, and sausages. "Too bad my cook is leaving, married a farmer and is moving to the country. Will be difficult to replace someone of her talents." He motioned to the servant to bring him sampling of each. "Have you considered the likely candidates?" He referred to Abby's prospects.

"I have three in mind, of exceptional means—one in publishing, one in old money, and the third in shipbuilding. The latter we must cross off the list because he will be out of town for a length of time. Too late for our Abby."

Abby woke with a start, realizing she had fallen asleep again. She dressed with Brigid's help then hurried downstairs and into the dining room, making appropriate apologies to her uncle and Mrs. Quick for her tardiness. A servant pulled out her chair. "I'll have the pancakes and maple syrup." She sampled a warm buttered cake and savored the sweet syrup that rolled over her tongue. She swallowed. So far so good, her stomach did not rebel. She had developed a special fondness for the sweet syrup and maple sugar cakes that her uncle had regarded as an expression of protest against the British Parliament to tax the American colonies.

"We shall go to the seamstresses today and finish the final alterations. You can select the trimmings and we'll have a quick tour of Boston. After that, I have arranged a tea with a neighbor of mine. She's a lovely girl about your age," said the indomitable Mrs. Quick.

Her uncle shook out his newspaper to read. "With the new treaty with France, I don't think there has ever been so much excitement for our cause. It will mean supplies, arms and ammunition, uniforms, and, most importantly, troops and naval support to our beleaguered Continental Army."

A bubble of laughter rose in Abby's throat. Undeniably, she had learned all this spying on Jacob outside William Bingham's window in Martinique.

"I see they are still giving Captain Jacob Thorne a fair amount of press. The Continental Congress has proclaimed that he gave the United States a sorely needed act of heroism in which to display military pride."

"Captain Thorne?" Frustration slashed a deep, agonizing wound of what could be, and what could never be, and it spiraled uncontrollably, yielding quickly to resentment. Resentment with the way things were, anger for the differences dividing them, and rage against the prospects of no future.

Like a diurnal bird of prey, Mrs. Quick rounded her gaze on Abby. "He owns the shipyard. You must have seen it on your arrival. It is massive and growing in leaps in bounds with the war and all."

Her uncle continued reading from behind the paper. "'His great experience and abilities in naval matters is of much service to our cause. Mark his majestic fabric; he's a sacred temple, built by hands divine.' My word they have elevated him to a god."

To fear an encounter with Jacob? Not anymore. Not on her life. Abby sliced her pancakes with solid even strokes. Protected by her uncle, a man of great influence, Jacob would not dare to touch her. "Why doesn't everyone in the colonies break out in song and croon his praises? Such adulation no doubt fans his vanity and the leaping hearts of women."

Agnes Quick halted her teacup halfway to her mouth. Her uncle lowered his newspaper.

Had she slithered that snake of suspicion into their heads? Abby's perpetual smile ran stakes through her jaws, her throat surged with her rising nausea and her eyes glassed over with the shine forced into them, but not for one instant did she dare let her façade slip. "I believe an outing is long overdue."

After her indiscretion at breakfast, Abby appreciated that no one pried into her past.

"The red velvet, matches your coloring wonderfully," said Mrs. Quick, holding up the fabric against Abby's cheek in the dressmaker's shop. "Add this to our order," she commanded the seamstress.

Abby liked the way Mrs. Quick took control. She also delighted in the grand assortment that had just arrived from Paris and surprised that the colonies were on top of the latest fashions. In a blur of dressmakers, measurements, adjustments and selections of fine fabrics and trimmings, her day sped by. Her dear uncle spared no expense.

The excitement of having new gowns lifted Abby's spirits, even more so when the widow ordered her driver to give them a tour of the city, passing the King's Chapel, the Old North Church, a bookstore, the South Meeting House, and beautiful Georgian homes. Even the stinging cold was pleasurable and she marveled at the avid commerce, bustle and animation of Boston, a city far from the raw wilderness her brother, Joshua had shared. A pang came to her stomach. Was Joshua alive?

"We have to cut our tour of the harbor as we have to meet for tea with my neighbor," reminded Mrs. Quick.

Spared a possible encounter with Jacob, Abby sagged against the seat. They passed the Old West Church and stopped in front of a three-story stately mansion with large bay windows that projected outward, a graceful entrance and above that a fine Palladian window. The widow's neighbor was of obvious importance.

Hustled into the entry way, Abby admired the magnificent curved stairway with artfully carved moldings of grapes, pears and other fruit. A servant ushered them into a beautiful parlor and gave Mrs. Quick an envelope. Abby warmed her hands by the fireplace, noting the high style furnishings, plush carpeting, and brightly colored wallpaper. A tapestry of griffins, unicorns, castles and other fanciful embroidery covered the wall. The home rivaled her uncle's.

"I am so pleased to meet Thomas's niece."

Abby twirled to meet her hostess, a stunning young woman with reddish brown hair, the deep russet of chestnut, soft blue eyes fringed with long curving lashes, and a smile that had a hint of mischief.

"Oh dear," said Mrs. Quick. "I cannot stay, I have and emergency at home. I'll beg my farewell and leave you two young ladies to chat and to get to know each other. When you are done, my driver will take you home, Abby," said Mrs. Quick. "I almost forgot to make introductions. Abby and this is Rachel." She rushed out the door.

After her coat was taken, Abby clasped her hands together in unnatural stillness. Why was she so nervous? Was it because she had been so long without the companionship of a female her own age?

"Please, let's sit in front of the fire," smiled Rachel, her every movement graceful without even realizing it. "These late winter storms chill the house. How long are you staying in Boston?"

Abby smiled. "For the indefinite future. Mrs. Quick told me you have some unusual hobbies."

Rachel gave her a sidelong glance. "Most would look down their noses that a woman would have an interest in inventing."

Abby widened her eyes. "Absolutely not. Please tell."

"I have made a bathing creation by warming water over a fire in the kitchens and using a bilge pump from a ship, to carry the water to the upper floor and into a tub. I even made a drain system. The invention saves hauling endless buckets of water for the servants."

Abby sat back awed and immediately taken with the girl's brilliance. "You are like my brother, Anthony. He is always tinkering and discovering things."

"Please tell me about what he has discovered."

Rachel's enthusiasm was so contagious that for the first time in a long time, Abby relaxed. Hours sped by, tea was served and both girls never ran out of things to say, always finding something to laugh and joke about. Abby sighed. If she were to have a sister she would want one just like Rachel.

"When did you arrive in our fair city?"

"Two weeks ago." Abby had counted every day, every minute. Never did she stop thinking of Jacob. If time softened feeling then it also unknotted memory, distinguishing the sharp vivid detail of some moments while others faded into nonexistence. With tenderness, she remembered his smile, when he threw back his head and boomed with laughter, the sparkle of his blue eyes, and the furrow in his forehead when he frowned in concentration.

Why was Rachel studying her so oddly?

"My cousin, Jacob had to sail out on an errand for General Washington."

Did Abby hear her right? "Jacob? Captain Jacob Thorne?" She had been so nervous when Mrs. Quick made introductions. Had she even said Rachel's last name?

"Do you know him?"

Know him? Heat rose to her cheeks. To know the nights they spent together in his cabin. His hands, his lips, his mouth, his hot kisses, and smolderingly, strong embrace. To know the sense and power of what it was like to feel like a woman. She had played over those scenes in her head countless times. The time apart had not dimmed.

"There has been fanfare in the newspapers," she prevaricated.

"How did you arrive here?"

Abby had the distinct feeling Rachel was not a simple colonial. "By ship from the south."

"With the British blockade, I pray your voyage was uneventful."

Abby cleared her throat. "To say the least."

Abby's frown faded replaced by a sad introspection. She wandered listlessly to the window and stood gazing out. "So, this is Captain Thorne's home?"

Rachel rose and stood beside her, studying her. "Yes. There were only two ships that arrived two weeks ago. One from the north and the other was Jacob's ship from the south. May I address you as Lady Abigail Rutland?"

Rachel was Jacob's cousin. A dry heave choked her followed by another. If only, to force down her traitorous stomach. Why now? Abby clamped a handkerchief to her mouth. The room spun.

Rachel guided her to a chair and made her sit.

"How did you know?"

"I'm a terrible eavesdropper. Naturally my curiosity was aroused when my normally composed cousin, Jacob began turning the city upside down, not sleeping or eating. Even now, he has Ethan and the crew combing the city for his Abby."

"Ethan? I thought he was in an English prison."

"Ethan is in Boston. The Duke of Banfield helped him escape. You can imagine my surprise to learn someone of that great importance was Jacob's father and that he helped Ethan escape. So many surprises." She looked meaningfully to Abby and smiled. "I want you to know you can count me as your friend."

Tears swelled in Abby's eyes. Lonely and far from home she had found someone she could trust. "My reputation is in shambles. I cannot go back to England. But I'll never force Jacob to marry me. It would be for the wrong reasons."

"You love Jacob?"

"Yes. But I can't compete with that stubborn righteous mindset."

Rachel laughed. "Jacob needs a lesson. You put everything in my hands. In four weeks when my irascible cousin returns he will be beside himself. He'll be chomping at the bit to get back to Boston and set it ablaze to find you. During that time, you'll be made into the toast of Boston society. Jealousy can be a strong motivator."

"And how will that occur in such a short time?"

"Leave that to me. Teas, socials, dances. Word spreads fast. You will be the most ravishing creature of all. The icing on the cake is the ball your uncle is giving in your honor—precisely the time when Jacob returns." Rachel giggled. "I can't wait to see his expression when he clasps eyes on you."

Abby gave a tremulous smile.

"I know he loves you. He needs a good woman but most importantly, he needs to make things up to you." Rachel leaned closer. "Answer me one question, Abby."

Abby paused to wipe her tears.

"Does Jacob know he is going to be a father?"

As Rachel predicted, Abby was a resounding success. Invitations poured in like a flood drenched river with two or three events to attend inside a day. Rachel along with Mrs. Quick delighted in guiding and accompanying her. The sickness wore off and she felt stronger than ever with the advent of the spring of 1778.

At a dance, she whirled with countless partners in tempo with the waltz. Where was Jacob? The British controlled New York and Philadelphia. What if Jacob were caught and rotted on one of those horrid hulks in Wallabout Bay where thousands of men died and without regard their corpses thrown overboard? Abby shuddered. She had been so deep in thought she was barely aware of a man that had cut in.

"May I have this dance?"

He had light hair and was dressed in breeches and frockcoat that complimented his wide shoulders. She should have taken exception to his boldness, but the twinkle in his eyes made her lift her hand in acceptance. The orchestra started a minuet and she followed his lead.

"Most accounts of feminine beauty and charm are gross exaggerations. However, I can see that accounts of yours are not."

"Let it be a lesson not to follow idle gossip."

"The accounts I received came from Captain Thorne."

Abby missed a step but the muscular colonial held her tight so no flaw was apparent to their audience. "You know Captain Thorne?"

"We were in plenty of scrapes when we were younger, had our disagreements lent more to that obstinacy of his, but living under the same roof—"

"Ethan?"

"He was going to make a trade of you for me but decided to send you back without the trade. Now that I've met you, my cousin must have been out of his mind. Then there is the point I've suffered night and day of harsh New England cold looking for you."

"I apologize for the inconvenience."

Rachel smiled and waved from the side of the room. Of course, Abby had been set-up and she immediately fell in love with the sibling camaraderie, Jacob's cousins imparted. "I hope we can be friends."

"On one condition. You don't put yourself in front of oncoming carriages to save young boys. Jacob would have my neck if anything happened to you."

Abby winced. Two days before she had seen the runaway carriage and the young boy beside her. Without thinking of her own peril, she had picked up the boy and rolled out of the way, a hair's breadth from being crushed beneath the wheels.

"You heard about that?"

"All of Boston heard about it. That the Duke of Rutland's daughter saved an important patriot's son? Are you kidding me? You are the heroine of Boston. You could have been killed."

A gentleman tapped Ethan's shoulder to cut in. Ethan gave him a look that could set fire to the arctic. "Not to mention the darling of every available male craving the ground you walk on. I can well imagine the raging volcano Jacob will be when he returns. If I know my sister, she is orchestrating this whole affair. How she loves to pile tinder on a fire."

The evening concluded and Abby, Mrs. Quick and Uncle Thomas waited outside for the carriage. Abby stepped away to allow them some private time and to savor the lovely night, the peace she and Jacob had shared when the darkness fell from the firmament leaving the starlight to wander on the sea's dark smooth tide. How she missed Jacob.

Percy Devol had been watching her, followed her every movement for two weeks. Waiting for this moment when she had moved from her uncle and the old widow. He could not believe she was still alive. The night he captured her outside her home in England, letting her see her family explode in flames. To think she survived the slaver captain aboard the *Civis*? What had happened? Her slow death had been guaranteed.

How he hated the Rutland's and their progeny. He should have been the heir. His mother had told him so. That he was the bastard son of the Duke William Rutland, Lady Rutland's grandfather. How he hated his mother, her endless beatings and telling him he was never good enough. How he had loved sliding his hands around her throat, squeezing, her eyes bulging from her head until the life drained from her.

After kidnapping Lady Rutland, he left England and had set sail for Boston via a French packet. That English dandy had planned the affair, didn't want the crime to follow them, had paid him handsomely although he'd have done it for nothing. How powerful he had felt. Now that power was reduced to ashes. The Rutland's survived the fiery blast and on the heels of this news was the survival of Lady Abigail. How close he'd come to crushing her beneath the carriage wheels the other day. He looked forward to making her suffer. His prey moved to the end of the block, and into the shadows, far from the lantern light and unaware of his presence.

Percy caught her around the neck and covered her mouth with his hand. "We meet again, Lady Rutland except this time fortune will not shine in your favor. How you escaped the *Civis*, I do not know," he rasped. She tore her nails down the side of his face. The bitch. She kicked back at him then dragged her feet, dead weight. Her teeth clamped on his hand.

"Bitch!" he howled and dropped her. Her screams tore into the night. He didn't look back. Footsteps crashed behind him. He kept on running.

Abby scrambled to her feet. Ethan came beside her and she pointed to where her assailant disappeared down a dark alley. She fell into her uncle's arms. "That voice. High and reedy, uneducated. I'll never forget. Percy Devol is here in Boston."

"He escaped," said Ethan returning from his chase. "Disappeared."

"To go against the Duke of Rutland would take money, influence and a certain amount of lunacy. To send Abby and her brother off on separate ships? To rig an explosion. No. Not one man could have done this. Think Abby. Who would hate your father enough to perform this cowardly scheme?"

Abby's shoulders slumped. "How many times have I asked that question?"

Ethan leaned in. "Never was able to get a glimpse of her assailant. He obviously planned his escape well. The runaway carriage incident? That was not random. It was an attempt on Abby's life. Whoever the perpetrators are, they will not stop. Abby will need to be protected around the clock. I'll post guards around the house. When Jacob gets back, he can decide what to do from there."

"I can take care of my niece," Thomas Hansford pulled himself up with indignance. "What does Captain Thorne have to do with this?"

Abby pleaded to Ethan with her eyes to remain silent.

"To do with this? Since Rachel and Abby are such good friends, I know my cousin would *insist* on this. On top of that Jacob will owe me a big favor."

The *Vengeance* had made port. Ethan had worried his cousin would be delayed by weather, but now breathed a sigh of relief and waited with a spare horse. As predicted, Jacob ran down the gangplank. "You look tired, cousin."

"Cut the excessive concern. Have you found her?"

"Searched all the outer towns like you told me. Nothing of her there." Of course, she wasn't outside Boston. She was *in* the city. Ethan deleted that detail. To see his cousin's frenzy was pure enjoyment. Served him right for being so bullheaded.

"If you find her, what makes you think she'll have you? Maybe she caught up with some loyalists and sailed home, maybe she's infatuated with a fancy English lord by now."

"I'll sail to England and kidnap her."

"With the British fleet on your heels?" Ethan grinned inwardly, the devil in him primed.

To protect Abby, Ethan had posted men around Thomas Hansford's home night and day. Jacob would never have forgiven him if he had done anything less. He placed Pascale out front. No one would think to go past the giant Haitian. His inside man was Simeon. Of course, Thomas Hansford was in raptures with his new cook's genius.

Never had Ethan seen so much hugging, crying and carrying on when Abby reunited with Simeon and Pascale. Her uncle's heart had been so warmed he obtained freedman papers for Pascale. Who was Ethan to comment on the legality of those documents?

Jacob looped his leg over his horse. "Where are we going first?"

Everything Ethan and Rachel had planned was in place. To convince Jacob was another matter.

Ethan fired his next salvo.

"We're going home to clean you up. We're invited to a ball, a friend of Rachel's, supposed to be a beauty."

"No doubt some hag to marry off. I'm going out on my own."

"I've exhausted everything and this social is the one last place we have a chance of finding anything about your Abby. Half the city is invited. Some lingering loyalists presumably turned patriot will be there. To investigate a collection of stalwarts might be a good idea. Care to join me?"

His cousin grumbled.

To hide a grin, Ethan clicked his heels into his horse's flanks, leaving his cousin in a cloud of snow. Ethan was getting payback for the whipping he got for Jacob dying the parson's dog.

Jacob had never been so miserable or fraught with worry in his life. He stood tall above the crowd in the massive three story home of well-to-do merchant, Thomas Hansford, a rabid behind the scenes patriot. Jacob was aware of Thomas's marked camaraderie with the Sons of Liberty. Where had Ethan disappeared to?

What if Abby slipped back to England through the assistance of a loyalist? A waltz started and a crush of dancers twirled in satins and silks. Several unmarried ladies tittered, their eye on Jacob. He paid no heed to them.

If you find her, what makes you think she'll have you?

Damn Ethan for putting that thought into his head.

"Good to see you, Jacob."

Jacob turned and shook his friend's hand, Samuel Adams. His gaze turned to Benjamin Elias, publisher of the Boston Gazette, Dr. Warren, and then James Otis, a prominent lawyer and all members of the Sons of Liberty. Jacob had not been part of the dissidents group during the British occupation, too lost in his drunken guilt. But he knew the clandestine group played a part in his escape from the Boston prison when he was framed for Thomas's murder. The Sons of Liberty also kept a fortified barrier against the departing British, keeping his shipyard from being burnt down.

"It's been a long time," said Samuel Adams.

"Too long," Jacob replied, and he meant that. "And too long for my gratitude."

Samuel waved him aside. "We are in *your* debt, Captain Thorne."

"Captain Thorne!" His name echoed throughout the hall. A subdued commotion erupted among the sidelines as wandering guests galvanized into action, rushing toward him. Greeted by a tsunami of well-wishers, Jacob tolerated the hand shakings, backslapping and ingratiating remarks of a conquering hero. He did not want the trumpet blast—hated it. He wanted anonymity.

Jacob shouldered through the crowd to a group of former loyalists, a stamp man, custom official and assorted gentry.

"You've had quite an adventure," said John Stanford.

The custom official had wreaked havoc on Thorne's shipping enterprises during the British occupation. Did he have the gall to smile? Jacob wanted to smash his fist into the swine's face.

"Have you seen a young woman, new to these parts about six weeks ago, helped her in any way?" Thorne remained cryptic, gauging the loyalist's response.

"Who would this woman be?"

Equally cryptic. Thorne's muscles tightened. How long would it take to drag him outside and pull off limb by limb to get the answers he wanted. "You would know her."

The man put up his hands. "I'm a patriot now."

"You're whatever way the wind blows. I don't like playing games."

"What kind of games?"

"The kind of games where I count to three, and if I don't get the answers I want, it gets interesting."

"What do you mean interesting?"

"The kind where I drag your carcass down to the *Vengeance*, and strap you to the muzzle of a cannon with a short fuse."

"Now see here—" His larger friend, a member of the gentry and dressed in a scarlet brocade frockcoat poked his finger on Jacob's chest.

Jacob looked down at the man's bejeweled finger. "What I see is that if you don't remove your hand, I'll be obliged to remove it from your wrist."

The stamp man snorted. "Why don't all five of us meet with you outside, Captain Thorne?"

"Just five?" Too much drink had emboldened their tongues. Jacob could smell the fumes. Ale for breakfast followed by chasers of rum. If not for the marble column to support the stamp man, he'd be languishing on the floor. Three, he counted would be slow to respond. The dandy next to him would get confused in his froth of lace. No big problem. The tall guy's palms sweated, had never seen a callous, a leftover spoiled aristocrat with a new periwig. No major threat. The other dandy to his left was hefty, stood a head taller. Jacob was right-handed. One passionate swing and all sorts of things would go slack. Was he volunteering?

Just the kind of situation Jacob had a hankering for.

The hefty guy to his left, a little brighter than his friends, cleared his throat, trying to be casual about it, trying to salvage some dignity. "We are not here to fight you, Captain Thorne. If you would give a description of the lady—"

"Blond, blue eyes, slim build, about this tall." He raised his hand to his chin to demonstrate Abby's height.

The aristocrat cleared his throat again, a particularly annoying habit.

"That's a quarter of the women in Boston."

"You'd know her when you saw her. She's incomparable."

"There is a young lady who is to be present tonight, a guest of her uncle, Thomas Hansford. I have been in her attendance since she arrived. I am afraid she is spoken for as I plan to ask her uncle for her hand tonight."

Ethan sidled up to him and thrust a cup of punch into his hands.

Rachel flanked him on the other side, linking her arm with his. "Charming everyone with your company?"

The music from the orchestra stopped. The dancers were at a standstill. Throngs of people crowded the dance floor. A hushed murmur rose, growing into a cacophony. Why were Rachel and Ethan staring at him? Something was wrong. He did not like it, not one bit. He focused his attention on the crowd. The loyalists were in raptures. Everyone had lifted their gazes. Thorne had enough. He downed his drink and turned to leave. Rachel held fast, smiling up to him. He remembered that smile. From the time she was a child that smile meant trouble.

Maybe she is in England and infatuated with an English Lord.

Thorne growled. Had she gotten back to England? Married Humphrey?

His attention was focused on what the dandy was saying to him. Jacob glanced left. Ethan had the same sappy rapture as the loyalists. Turning his head, he looked for the source of his cousin's interest, looked higher, toward the staircase….and he froze. Jacob stared at the woman on the staircase. The woman he'd been searching for.

Lady Abigail Marie Hansford Rutland stood at the top and descended like an immortal goddess, granting divinity to measly mortals. She was wearing a gown of red velvet, her breasts fuller and rising with every breath she took. Her blond hair was caught up in an elegant coiffure, entwined with tiny diamonds; Abigail was a breathtaking vision of beauty and breeding. In the weeks since he'd been gone, her figure had ripened, and her delicately boned face had acquired a radiance that was spellbinding. Jacob's shock vanished as quickly as it hit him.

She was on the arm of an older gentleman. He patted her hand and said something to her. She laughed. She was having the time of her life while he had not slept in weeks.

Jacob shirked off Rachel's arm. He smelled his cousins' hands in this business. He'd deal with them later. Now his sole goal was to get to Abby and wring her neck. No. To drag her out of here. To lock her in his cabin aboard the *Vengeance*. To never let her go.

The aristocrat clenched his arm. Did he dare to detain him? Jacob glared. The fool quivered in his breeches, unable to contain his idiotic grin.

"She is the girl I'm going to marry. Thomas Hansford's niece."

Thomas Hansford...Abigail Marie Hansford...Rutland.

He never saw it coming.

"Like hell." Jacob launched into the crowd.

With practiced grace, she began her descent and confidently glided to the bottom to greet the rush of young suitors vying to take her hand for the next dance.

Jacob's eyes fastened on his quarry.

"Abigail? Is it really you?" A male voice boomed above the din from the entrance hall.

Jacob paid no mind to the desperate greeting. But he saw Abby's beautiful blue eyes widen in joy, her hands clapped to her cheeks as she hurled herself through the crowd, and then leaped into the arms of a man dressed in buckskins and leggings. The frontiersman picked her up, hugging and kissing her, swinging her around. Tears streamed down her face.

Blood pounded in his ears. Bitter bile clogged his throat. Like a fire, it burned and raged. Jacob barreled through the throng. He tore the woodsman from Abby and threw a punch. His hand connected with his jaw. It felt good.

The frontiersman swung his left fist from left to right. Jacob dodged, but the next blow came from his foe's right and knocked Jacob to the floor. Jacob scrambled to his feet and planted his fist into the frontiersman's midsection; the momentum knocked him to the floor. Wiry bastard. Agile, the frontiersman rolled and came to his feet.

"Jacob! Stop!" Abby tugged his arm. He turned. "Please, Jacob," she pleaded.

The frontiersman landed another punch on the side of his head. Jacob shook it off. He deserved that for getting distracted. He lunged again, but Ethan, Samuel Adams, and Dr. Warren grabbed him from behind. Other men pulled back the fuming frontiersman. Abby planted herself between them, her arms outstretched, shaking her head.

"You are acting like children."

The older gentleman who had escorted Abby down the stairs was a bit too casual.

"I don't think we've had this much excitement in a long time. Gentlemen, we have a war to fight. Not each other. I think we need to straighten out this matter in my library." He looked meaningfully to Jacob. "I need to introduce myself. I'm Thomas Hansford, Abby's uncle."

Jacob grudgingly extended his hand, keeping a baleful eye on the frontiersman.

"And this gentleman that you decided to fight in my home is Abigail's brother, Joshua."

Her brother. Jacob winced. The brother who had been missing on the frontier.

They all herded into the library. Ethan held up the mantle behind him. Rachel worried her hands in the corner. Abby gave him a faint inclination of her head then fretted over her brother who reclined on a settee and stared daggers at Thorne. Mrs. Quick, a widow, appraised him with the speculation of a hawk. Thomas Hansford glared at him like a tutor ready to whip him.

What a way to win favor with her family.

"Captain Thorne, you upset an important party to launch my niece to be married. Can you explain your actions?"

Ethan waded into the deafening silence. "My cousin is the soul of diplomacy. He believes in using his fists to ingratiate himself with the family."

"I'm not laughing, Ethan and I want Captain Thorne's answer," Thomas Hansford snapped.

Ethan blithely ignored the swirling emotional tensions and moved across the room. "Anyone want a drink? All this excitement has made me thirsty," he said cheerfully.

In a state of misery, Abby patted her brother's head with a cool damp cloth. "Joshua, you have no idea what has happened to our family. I must tell—"

"I received communications from Uncle Thomas and came as soon as I was able. The whole despicable act is beyond comprehension."

"Percy Devol, the one who kidnapped me…is here in Boston," Abby said and filled him in about the explosion and Nicolas's disappearance.

"And he has made two attempts on her life," Thomas confirmed. "I have investigators combing Boston. The house is guarded.

"Two attempts on your life?" Jacob exploded.

Abby wanted to go to Jacob, but he looked so forbidding and so ruthlessly cold that she sank back into the cushions. Her nerves had been fraught for weeks. Worried that he might be killed or maimed, then not knowing if Jacob would come for her, and now that he had… Well, she didn't know what to think. He was angry for sure and had searched all over for her. But was he angry that she had duped him and left the ship without a word, or because of Percy Devol?

And she was angry too. Angry for the way he had treated her during those last days on the *Vengeance* and furious for the way he brawled this evening.

But seeing him here, seated across from her, his polished booted foot resting casually atop the opposite knee, his long legs encased in breeches and white hose, like he was master of this home instead of his ship and overall he surveyed... Never had he looked more handsome—or more impossible.

Ethan seated himself on the other side of Abby. "Did I ever tell you about the time my cousin bloodied the smithy's boy for calling Rachel a name? Twice the size of Jacob. No way did that deter my cousin. In one punch, the smithy's boy fell like a hammer on an anvil. That was when Jacob was five. Been scrapping ever since. Ask the British. Ask the Royal Navy. It's his winning ways, he is ever so popular."

"I fail to see your point," Jacob snapped and threw Ethan a look of unwavering disgust.

"Exactly." Ethan grinned. "It has to do with getting even. You see, I took the whipping for you dying the parson's dog. Couldn't sit for a week."

Thomas Hansford drummed his fingers on his desk. "I find this discussion lacking."

Ethan put his drink down. "My dear cousin always uses unparalleled strategy when he wants something and wants it bad."

He had come for her.

Abby had no idea what game Ethan played. She looked at Jacob's unyielding expression and all she wanted to do was throw herself into his arms and be comforted. To tell him how sorry she was for leaving him the way she did, but then he had to apologize first for his behavior.

"Shut-up, Ethan, I'm warning you."

Ethan gave a sharp bark of laughter. "And let all these fine people see another exhibition of your savoir-faire? Jacob tends to grab the moon in the water but you must admit he does it with enthusiasm. Would someone hand me that decanter of whiskey?"

"Get it yourself," Thorne growled. "I'm certain, Ethan, that included in your other talents is an ability to get your own whiskey."

Rachel handed Ethan the decanter and he poured a generous glass. "Listen to that strain of poeticism as soft and lyrical as a stallion kicking down the stall door to get to the mare."

Mrs. Quick gasped.

Her uncle harrumphed.

Abby curled into a tight ball of anguish and withered from the blast of those cobalt eyes. Silently she counted the minutes wishing this fiasco would end. She was pregnant and her emotions were running away from her. If she had wings, she'd fly. Ethan slid his arm about her shoulders and the veins on Jacob's neck popped out.

She had clung to the hope that Jacob wanted her but as time wore on and Jacob clutched his hostility like a jackal denied its prey, Abby grew resentful. A little niggling voice wormed its way into her brain. No. She was the injured party. Jacob needed to make reparation to her.

The silence of an ancient tomb settled over the room. Her stomach flip-flopped with the familiar queasiness that had escaped weeks before. She tamped it down. Never would she allow Jacob Thorne to intimidate her again. If he thought he could come into her home and bully her again he had a lesson to learn. She raised her chin, bolstered by the confidence that she sat safely under the protection of her uncle and brother. "I don't think we need to continue this discussion."

Jacob clenched and unclenched the wood handle on the arm of the settee as if willing it to snap… and, she was certain he wished it was her neck, not the arm of the chair in his grip.

"We do need to continue this conversation. *Now.*"

Abby bristled when he used that tone of voice. "I am sure Captain Thorne you have your crew to browbeat. As for me—"

"If you had just followed orders, there wouldn't have been all this trouble, turning Boston upside down to find you. Do you know how worried I've been?" Thorne bellowed.

"Not that she ever did follow orders," muttered Joshua.

Abby glared at her brother, not liking his amused expression one bit.

She turned her full wrath on Jacob. "I will not follow any *command* you give me, ever. You gorbellied, dog-hearted barnacle." How easily she swore like a sailor.

"The beast!" Ethan said gleefully, helping himself to another glass of whiskey. "I suggest a proposition. Since half of Abby's suitors have left for the evening and the other half are listening at the door—"

Abby's gaze swung to the door. Ten? Twenty? Listening? She would become the flagship of gossip to be touted this night.

Ethan raised his glass in a toast. "To save the Thorne name from Jacob's skillful lack of tact this evening, I am throwing in my honorable character to court Abby. We will be married and soon. What do you think about the proposition, Mr. Hansford?"

Jacob surged to his feet, a muscle leaping furiously along the taut line of his jaw. "Like hell she will. Abby, I demand a word in private."

Her uncle slapped his hand on the desk. "Now see here, Captain Thorne."

"I'm not going anywhere with you." Sick with embarrassment, Abby dug her nails in the flesh of her palms. Now her uncle knew who she had run from.

Her brother stood beside her. "You heard her. She's not going anywhere."

"I do not want another brawl," Jacob cautioned. He pulled Abby up. "We are getting married and that's it."

"No." She jerked her hands from him and ran, out the French doors and let the darkness of the gardens envelope her, anywhere to be away from him—from everyone.

Ethan hooted.

Jacob bolted for the door.

Rachel straightened. "Well, that was well done, Jacob. Why not hit her over the head and drag her to the nearest hollow?"

Clouds scuttled in front of a half-moon that illuminated the garden, dead from a long winter. "Abby?"

He heard a muffled sound…a whimper. Hair lifted on his neck. A knot grew in his belly. In the corner, next to a high wall. Thorne moved.

"He has a gun," Abby shouted.

Cold white fear climbed up his spine.

The cloud cover disappeared. A pockmarked man, his pig-like eyes open, shabbily dressed, and even at this distance smelled of rum and moldy cheese. He gripped Abby, his arm around her throat. The other hand pointed a pistol at him. His gut clenched.

"That's far enough, Captain Thorne."

Jacob gritted his teeth. That thin reedy voice—the voice Abby had told him about. "What do you want?"

Thorne took a step closer. Devol's sallow face expressed benevolent malice. Thorne needed to keep him talking, as long as he pointed the gun at Jacob and not at Abby. He took a step toward him. "You have one shot. What if you miss?"

"You think I'm that stupid."

"Yes, I do."

"Why the Rutlands?" Pascale moved behind Devol. The giant Haitian blended with the shadows. But Jacob didn't want him dead...he needed information first.

"I hate them. I should have all the power and money they have. I'll be the duke." Glazed eyes, the deranged man waved his gun.

Thorne took another step. Logic never made a difference to a madman. "What do you expect to get from eliminating the Rutland's?" Joshua moved from the right. Thorne warned him with his eyes. *He's mine.*

Devol leveled the gun to Jacob's chest. "Title, wealth, privilege, respect."

How did you do the deed against the Rutland's? How did you pull everything off? Must have had help?"

"Lots of help. Influential. Powerful," Percy bragged. "Things went bad. The duke and Anthony left the laboratory too early. We did get Nicholas on a slave packet to Brazil, Abby on board the *Civis* where she was supposed to die. Then she showed up here in

Boston. How'd that happen? She'll die before the night is out. We will get the rest of the Rutland's. We won't fail."

"We?" Thorne's hand flexed into a fist.

Devol scoffed, gave a maniacal laugh. "There are four of us."

"You mean three," Jacob said.

"No four," Percy's voice shrilled.

"Not after I kill you."

Everything happened all at once. Abby brought her heel down on Devol's foot and pushed the gun away. Jacob leaped forward, hurled himself between Abby and the crazed man. His teeth jarred as they hit the ground with a thud. He twisted the gun, wrenching it from Devol's hand, then pulled back and smashed a fist into the ugly man's face, feeling the satisfying crack of his knuckles on bone. He lurched to the side, dodging another swing, before Devol's fist slammed into his eye.

Devol's madness made him stronger, more dangerous. He fought like a demon. Eyes, slits of rage, the man snarled, returning ham-sized fists into Jacob's gut, head, and neck. Jacob had enough. With one deep blow beneath the chin, he shattered Percy's jaw, and he dropped to the ground like and anvil, out cold.

Joshua extended his hand and yanked Jacob to his feet. Abby stood next to her brother. *Safe. Thank God.* Jacob released a long breath.

Then from the corner of his eye, Jacob saw the downed man's hand move toward the gun and in the blink of the eye, Devol grabbed the handle and cocked the hammer...

Click.

In that same moment, Abby gasped, grabbed the knife from her brother's boot and threw. The wink of metal flashed, end over end it flew to its mark—buried deep in Devol's chest just as his gun went off. Another gun fired from behind them.

Sulfur curled in the air.

Jacob crashed like a boulder. Blood poured from his head.

Abby dropped to her knees beside him, raised a corner of her dress to Jacob's head to staunch the bleeding, then held his hand to her lips. "Jacob, darling. Please tell me you're alive. I'll do anything—" On and on she went begging bargains with her Maker.

Jacob's eyes opened. He would use her pleas to his advantage. "Will you marry me?"

He saw her blink back a rush of emotion. "You have the most dreadful way of proposing. Of course, I'll marry you."

Simeon served refreshments in the library. Jacob's flesh-wound had been attended to and Abby was seated next to him, her head tucked beneath his chin, his arm tightly around her shoulder. He was not letting go. Ever.

Thomas Hansford revealed what he knew of Devol's history as told to him by Abby's father in a letter. As Devol admitted in England, he had teamed up with three other men."

Abby shuddered and Jacob pulled her tighter and she was comforted by his embrace. "We are still in grave danger," she said.

"I will pen a letter tonight to warn your father. We must be vigilant at all times until this is resolved and the perpetrators captured," Thomas Hansford said. "It was a gunshot that killed Devol not your knife, Abigail. Pascale and the other guards are in pursuit but I have a feeling we will never find the assailant."

Thomas took a deep breath. "I have other business to discuss. More immediate business. I had inklings of you, Captain Thorne and your connection to my niece's sudden appearance. She refused to tell me. When you took a swing at Joshua, my suspicions were cemented. When will the nuptials be, Captain Thorne?"

"I was thinking of a Christmas wedding," Jacob said.

Thomas cleared his throat loudly. "With the current state of affairs the wedding will take place before next month."

Thorne leaned back, scrutinizing her. She felt the heat rise to her face. Everyone stared. Her eyes filled with tears, and there was a short silence, enough to fill a heartbeat.

"When were you going to tell me?" In the flickering firelight, Jacob gazed down tenderly on her. "I love you." He gently lowered his mouth to hers and kissed her soundly, possessively.

She never wanted him to stop.

Ethan whooped. "You can name him after me."

Epilogue

Six months later

Six new ships were nearing completion and Jacob had several orders ahead of him. One ship showcased his latest, sleekest design. It was to be his pinnacle of success, and he called it, *The Abby*. He hummed a lullaby, then smiled, thinking how little inane things gave him happiness. He looked over the architectural drawings of the fine house he was building for his family overlooking Boston. Everything had Jacob smiling these days. With Abby, life was full of smiles, laughter and love. He shook his head. Married in three weeks and the rest of the months had been a blur. He had tendered his resignation with General Washington, who remained disappointed at losing his services, but the general understood, placated with the ships Jacob promised to build for his navy.

Communications flowed back and forth across the Atlantic. The Duke of Rutland, who Jacob had yet to meet, had sent a generous gift as congratulations, so happy his daughter was safe and loved. The duke also had Simeon vindicated through discussions with Lord Gratham about Lady Gratham's activities, yet Simeon had decided to stay in Boston.

Long overdue, exchanges were initiated by Jacob to his father, the Duke of Banfield. He thirsted to know his father, asked him for forgiveness, and to compensate for lost time. With Abby heavy with child, and the war going on, visiting England would be impossible and he regretted that unfortunate circumstance.

The only dark cloud that remained was that no trace of the Rutland enemies had been found. Abby's father had not given up and worked tirelessly with the Duke of Westbrook, realizing that the ones associated with Percy Devol were more likely licking their wounds and reorganizing for another day. Abby's brother, Nicholas had not been found, but they were still scouring Brazil where the slave packet was supposed to have delivered him. No one had given up hope of finding him. Joshua was residing with Thomas Hansford for two weeks until he returned to the wilderness for General Washington.

Out of breath, Enos burst into Jacob's office. "It's time, sir."

Jacob had prepared for this eventuality. Pascale stood ready with his horse. "Good luck, Captain," he said in broken English, grinning.

Jacob ran up the steps of his home. Normally it took him forty minutes to make it from the shipyard but today he made the journey in twenty minutes. Thomas Hansford paced a worn path in the parlor rug. Simeon worried wrinkles in his tricorn. Ethan held up the mantle. Widow Quick and Rachel were upstairs attending Abby with the doctor and midwives. They had informed him once the process started it would be several hours and emphasized for Jacob to wait downstairs. No matter what.

The door knocker banged. "Who in the world would be visiting now?" Jacob ripped open the door, ready to give what hawking vendor dared to come at this hour a send-off. Instead he gave a double shake of his head. His father, the Duke of Banfield, and Humphrey his half-brother stood on his doorstep.

"Well, aren't you going to invite us in? We've come a long way and it is too cold for these old bones."

"Come in," Jacob swung wide the door, his mind suddenly not working.

"Had to come and wish you belated felicitations on your nuptials. Humphrey and I had to secret in a port in Maine and get smuggled up to Boston with the war and all. Do you have any tea?"

Jacob opened his mouth to speak, but his words caught at his throat. He nodded to Simeon to take their coats and hats then ushered his father and brother into the parlor, managing finally to make introductions. Jacob's heart pounded, his father was here and there would be a lot of talking and making up to do.

He was about to speak again when a huge shriek rattled the doors in the jams and with enough force to reach the docks. Jacob bolted up the stairs, only to be held off by Mrs. Quick's stern warning. Grumbling, Jacob returned downstairs, his body drenched in sweat.

"Good Heavens," said his father. "What do you have going on in the colonies?"

"You're about to be a grandfather." Jacob paced next to the steps.

"Did you hear that Humphrey, I'm about to be a grandfather and you're going to be an uncle."

Every minute that ticked by wore another year off Jacob's life. Sea battles, imprisonment—nothing compared to this purgatory. Another scream tore through the house, curdling Jacob's ears and enough to tear down the heavens. No way were those women going to stop him from seeing his wife. Jacob took the stairs two at a time. He burst into the room.

The doctor smiled and dried his hands on a towel. “Anxious, Captain Thorne?”

Jacob shouldered the clucking midwives aside. Rachel wrapped the infant in a soft quilt and handed the babe to him, pink and wet and wrinkled.

“You’re a father now,” said the doctor.

A father.

Rachel and Mrs. Quick beamed, shooing everyone from the room, leaving the parents with their new addition.

Jacob marveled at the tiny figure in his arms. Small. Wonderful. He could not get his fill of looking at the baby. He had no words. Perhaps because there were no words strong enough to name this moment. Emotion threatened to swamp him.

The baby puckered up a bright red mottled face and released an angry howl, tantamount to the roar of twenty cannons. “What do I do?”

Abby gazed up to him, her eyes glowing with love. Her husband, the scourge of England, fearless and reckless in the worst of battles stood helpless. “Bring him here, he’s hungry.”

“All that noise, and he’s just hungry.” Jacob hesitated. “He? A boy?”

Abby giggled and took her son. “Generally, “he’s” are boys.” Abby brought the baby to her breast where he suckled hungrily and greedily.

A commotion from down the stairs drew their attention. Hails and good cheer. Thorne strode to the doorway and threw it open. His father, and his half-brother, Humphrey, Simeon, Ethan…all smiled and stood expectantly. Enos, Joseph Lawton, Benjamin Lewis, Samuel, Edward Martin—his entire crew, and now his shipyard workers stood shoulder to shoulder. They all loved Abby.

Did he see Enos exchanging money? Even the duke and Humphrey were handing over money. "What bets now, Enos?"

"Well…what is it?" plied Enos. "Are you going to keep us in the dark?"

"A son." Thorne wanted to shout from the rooftops. After much felicitation, backslapping, and a disgruntled Enos, grumbling losses from his bets, Thorne closed the door. He sat next to Abby, putting his arm around her, watching his son suckle from her breast. "This adventure has probably been good for our son."

Abby snuggled closer against Jacob's chest and sighed. "Adventure is it? It's how you found me."

Jacob nuzzled her neck and he felt her shiver in delight. "If he's anything like his mother we'll have a whole lifetime of adventure ahead of us."

About the Author

Elizabeth St. Michel is the author of *The Winds of Fate*, which reached number one on the Amazon bestseller lists. Her second novel, *Surrender the Wind*, garnered several awards, including the National RONE Award in honor of literary excellence in romance writing.

St. Michel divides her time between New York and the Bahamas.

Author's Note

I have done my best to ensure the historical references that reflect the events in this book are as accurate as possible. My novel, *Sweet Vengeance* spans from the shores of England across the Atlantic to the Caribbean and on to Boston.

The lovely island of Martinique in the Caribbean was a French stronghold during the American Revolution and furnished a necessary port for American Privateers. William Bingham, an emissary for the colonial cause in Martinique, handled the unloading and resupplying of American ships, carrying munitions, guns, and other vital goods necessary for the fighting of the war. By the end of the American Revolution, Bingham was regarded as one of the richest men in America, with ownership of over two million acres. He later initiated the national Bank of North America, which has morphed into what we know today as the Wells Fargo Bank.

Part of my story takes place in the Bahamas, off the Southeastern coast of Florida, in an archipelago or collection of islands known as the West Indies. The island of New Providence in 1778 held a population of a thousand people. As a British Colony, it boasted a well-protected harbor that served as a convenient and favorite rendezvous place for British Naval vessels and functioning as the chief British Naval station on the American coast.

During the American Revolution, Fort Nassau was taken by a dashing and daring force led by Captain John Trevett of the Colonial Marines and Captain John Rathburn of the Colonial Navy. One can imagine the dismay of sleepy townspeople when they awoke in the morning to discover the scarlet flag of England replaced by the little-known stars and bars of the United States. For three days, the Americans held their positions, outnumbered ten to one. To reverse the intended assault of the local citizenry, Captain Rathburn trained the fort's cannons on the town. The English were relieved of their huge naval stores of ammunition, gunpowder and ships. Most remarkable, this engagement historically details the progenitors of the United States Navy and Marine Corps, initiating a tandem amphibious landing known as the Second Battle of Nassau.

Today the British Colonial Hilton Nassau Hotel sits atop the ruins of Fort Nassau. Hog Island is now known as the famed Paradise Island.

I always say that I'm a storyteller, not a historian, and as a storyteller, I'm more concerned with the what-ifs than the why-nots. I so enjoy taking a bit of license to bring you the most exciting, sensual, love story that my what-if imagination can create.

Acknowledgements

Most books wouldn't be written without the help of some special people. I would like to acknowledge Caroline Tolley my developmental editor and Linda Styles, my copy/line editor. Their insight and expertise were indispensable. Hugs also to my spouse, Edward, five children, eight grandchildren, Dr. Marcianna Dollard and posthumously, Loretta Bysiek—your love and comfort surround me.

Many words of appreciation to Andrew Albury, Gabrielle and Peter Lorenz of the Bahamas, who graciously added facts and information on elements of history of Nassau and sailing.

Many thanks to the gracious support of Nancy Crawford, Linda Bysiek, Brenda Kosinski, Paula Ursoy and Western New York Romance Writers Group.

Finally, a special note of gratitude to my readers. You will never know how much your enthusiasm and support enrich my work and my life. You are the best.

Dear Readers,

It has given me particular pleasure to write, *Sweet Vengeance* for you. There is no greater compliment to me as an author than for my readers to become so involved with the characters that you want me to write more. That said, I'm happily immersed in a series, with the powerful Duke of Rutland, a widower, and his four strong-willed offspring. As you know, my first installment detailed the journey of Abigail, his only daughter and the notorious privateer, Jacob Thorne during the American Revolution.

My second installment acquaints us with Abby's older brother, Anthony Rutland, a hopeless introvert, and brilliant scientist who wants nothing to do except work in his laboratory. Abigail sends Rachel Thorne, Jacob's cousin to her ancestral home in England to be introduced into society. How unfortunate, for Anthony to have his quiet world turned upside down by the spirited Rachel and even worse, with an intellect to match. But there are still enemies intent on destroying the Rutland family...

Although I can't tell you much more I can promise you this: like my last novel, it is written with one goal in mind—to make you experience the laughter, the love, and all the other myriad emotions of its characters. And when it's over to leave you smiling...

Warmly,
Elizabeth St. Michel

P.S. If you would like to receive an emailed newsletter from me, which will keep you informed about my books-in-progress as well as answer some of the questions I'm frequently asked about publishing, please contact me on Facebook or my webpage at elizabethstmichel.com. The greatest gift you can give an author is a review for her work on the website you have purchased the book. I would be thrilled to hear from you!

www.ingramcontent.com/pod-product-compliance
Lightning Source LLC
Chambersburg PA
CBHW050907250626
47155CB00001B/137

* 9 7 8 0 9 9 7 4 8 2 4 2 3 *